Stephanie Fisher

For my husband. I never thought I'd say this... but thanks for the puns.

CONTENTS

MAP

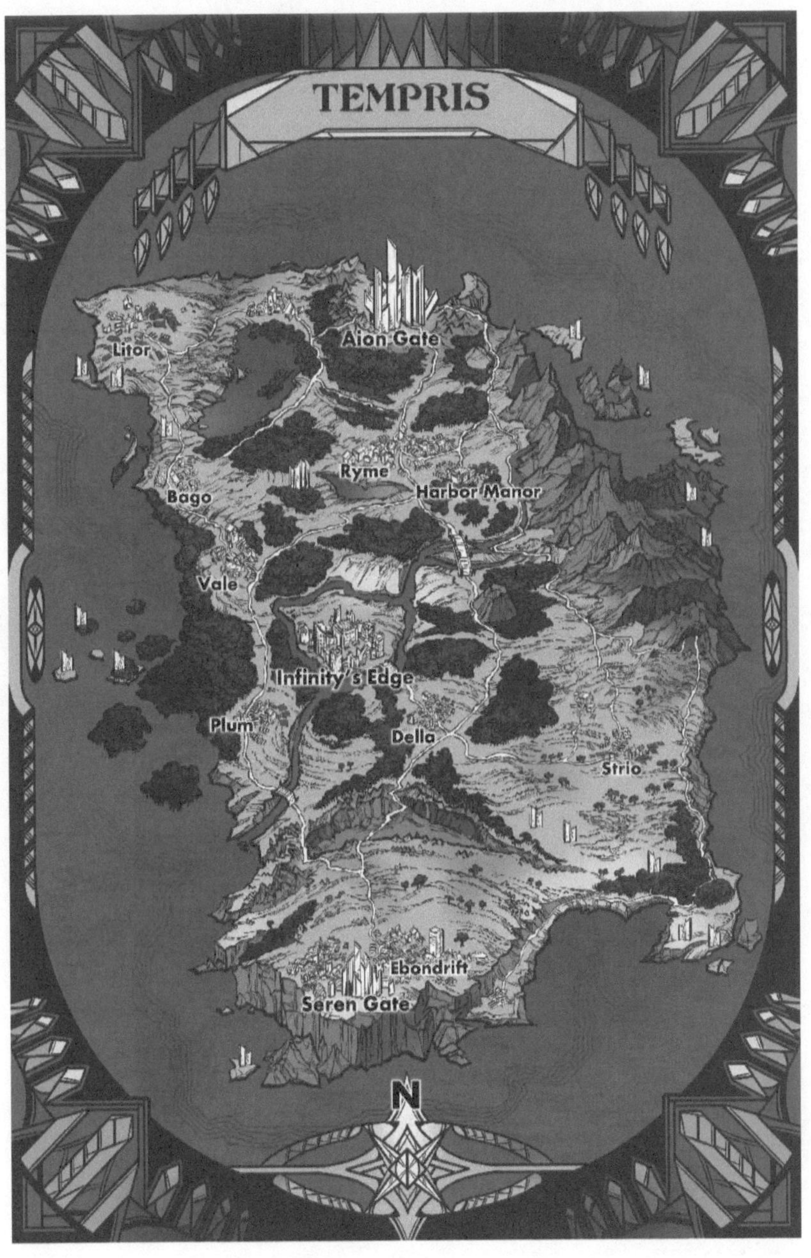

TEMPRIS
Aion Gate
Litor
Ryme
Harbor Manor
Bago
Vale
Infinity's Edge
Plum
Della
Strio
Ebondrift
Seren Gate
N

PROLOGUE

As Breena sat on the garden wall, sipping her tea and watching the colors of the new day ignite on the horizon, she had no way of knowing that this would be the day that she died.

It was a day just like any other day, following the same rhythms and patterns. Breakfast, then lunch; she cleaned the kitchen and swept the floors. And since she was as of yet completely unaware of her impending demise, when the sun began to set, marking the end of another ordinary day filled with ordinary tasks, she was content with its mediocrity and the safety that being average provided.

The sky had already turned dark when Breena finally set down her quill. She stood carefully, her bones cracking in protest. The aether was noticeably thinner on the island, and most days, it left her feeling tired.

Shaking out her braid, she took a moment to survey the meager cottage. The scuffed wood floors and whitewashed walls were a far cry from the luxury of her youth, but she had managed to make the space comfortable. The rugs may have been threadbare, but they warded off the chill of the morning, and the quilts on the beds, though secondhand, were soft from age.

The little garden beyond the open window was just beginning to bloom, and sprays of snowdrops and irises blanketed the ground outside. In this small, isolated town on the western coast of the island of Tempris, a cottage with its own garden was a rarity. Most of the villages in the region, though not lacking for space, were packed tightly together. The nights could be dangerous, especially when the gates were charging.

A peal of laughter rang out, and Breena smiled, stepping over to the window to observe the dynamic force of kinetic energy that was her daughter. A man with auburn hair and a plain canvas coat was trying to herd the rebellious child inside, but the little bundle of scraped knees and golden curls was having none of it. She kept darting in between his outstretched arms, disappearing and reappearing at will. First, in front of him, her tongue sticking out in a playful taunt, then behind him with a barely suppressed giggle.

Breena frowned. *Oh dear.*

It seemed Cori's magic was progressing more quickly than they expected—which meant that even more of the girl's aether would need to be locked away.

A familiar pang of guilt fluttered in her chest. Breena hated to do it, even if it was necessary. Until they could smuggle the girl through the Aion Gate and into the mortal cities, they needed to stay hidden, and taking away Cori's magic was a small price to pay.

The man still hadn't managed to capture the elusive child, so Breena called out in a forceful tone, "Corinna! It's time to come inside."

Her six-year-old daughter's silvery gray eyes searched for the source of the reproach, and a mournful pout blossomed across the girl's face when she saw her mother's stern expression. Surrendering, Cori allowed herself to be escorted inside the cottage. Breena was still amazed at how much her daughter was starting to resemble her. When the girl was older, they might very well be twins.

Breena took one last glance at her desk. Five wine-colored crystals sat inside a circle of faintly glowing runes, each one pulling in aether from the air and storing it away for a time when it might be needed. She knew she was being overly cautious, but she wanted her supply of shadow crystals fully charged just in case they needed to run.

She studied the various items scattered across the desk, plucking a half-empty inkwell from the clutter. Blood caked the sides and congealed at the bottom, turning black as it dried.

Holding her hand over the pot, she began to channel what was left of her magic, and slowly, the remaining fluid started to glow and roil before dissolving into the air.

A wispy, crackling haze of energy now hovered beneath her outstretched palm.

Breena took a moment to admire the apparition. Raw aether. As a shadow mage, her magical ability was tied to the manipulation of the very building blocks of magic. She waved her hand and felt the aether particles dance around her fingers, prickling her skin.

Placing the now empty inkwell into a small wooden chest, she waved the cloud over her other hand, where a large, half-healed gash traveled the length of her palm. The haze seemed to hang in the air around the cut before reabsorbing into her body, seeping into her veins and bolstering her depleted reserve of magic. She watched as her skin slowly knitted itself back together before kneading the unmarred flesh. Only a dull ache remained.

A thundering patter of footsteps echoed from downstairs, and Breena quickly put away the rest of her supplies—various quills, loose leaves of paper, and a small, ceremonial dagger her older brother had gifted her when they were children.

"Mommy! Mommy!" A small bundle hurdled its way up the stairs and into her arms. "Wanna see my new trick?" The little girl smiled, revealing a row of delicate baby teeth.

Breena couldn't help but smile back. While she knew she needed to teach her daughter to be more sensible with her magical abilities, she couldn't resist the contagious joy in the girl's expression. "I saw it already. But sweetie, I've told you before—you shouldn't use your magic outside the cottage. Your Uncle Esmund is going to stop taking you into the forest if you don't behave."

Cori, unfazed by her mother's gentle reproach, patted the older woman's cheek. "No. Not that one, silly. I learned a *new* trick." Jumping out of Breena's arms, she ran over to Esmund as he crested the stairs.

Though still quite young to be a Knight of the Crystal Guard, the faint weblike network of scars across the man's cheeks and brow made him seem older than his mere 3,200 years. Like most members of his order, he kept his reddish hair cropped close to his head and his beard neatly trimmed.

As he turned the corner of the stairs, Breena could see the subtle, pointed tips of his ears, an indisputable indicator of his fey parentage. He smiled indulgently at the small girl as she clung to his leg, handing her a glass jar. A single, blue butterfly flitted about inside.

"Watch, mommy." Chubby hands clumsily unscrewed the lid. As the butterfly rushed to escape the confines of its glass prison, the girl extended her arm, and a look of rapt concentration screwed up her delicate features.

After a few moments, the air began to crackle with energy, slow at first but building in strength and intensity. A golden fog formed around the child's outstretched palm as she summoned her aether, and the magic rippled through the air, weaving itself around the butterfly. Cori waggled her fingers, and the tiny insect abruptly froze mid-flight, entangled, suspended and motionless, in a web of flickering, gilded threads.

Cori giggled as she deftly twirled her arm, and the butterfly blinked out of existence. Breena followed her daughter's eyes to the far side of the room, where the butterfly now continued its frenzied dance, its movements speeding up and then slowing down like a dancer that couldn't quite find the tempo. Another wave of the child's hand and the butterfly could do nothing but obey, sluggishly retracing its path through the air until it settled back into the jar. The haze of sparkling aether dissipated as time once more found its correct rhythm.

Breena clapped excitedly as her daughter bounced at her mother's feet, thoroughly satisfied with her performance. "Fantastic! You'll be ready for your first crystals soon!" While the child was preoccupied with the quivering insect, Breena shared a worried glance with Esmund. Then, taking the jar, she stepped over to the open window to let the butterfly escape into the still night air, saying over her shoulder, "Alright, my dear. I think that's enough for today. Time for bed."

On cue, the small girl squealed theatrically. "No! No. I don't want to go to bed. I'm not..." A large yawn cut off the rest of the sentence, effectively silencing the child's desperate plea.

Breena leaned down to look her daughter in the eye. "Go peacefully, and you can take your bath tomorrow."

"Okay!" The young fey girl placed a sloppy kiss on her mother's cheek before lunging for the bed. She bounced once, then twice before throwing the faded quilt over her head.

"Eyes closed!" Breena said, watching the lump on the bed suspiciously. Almost immediately, the blankets started to rhythmically rise and fall.

Satisfied that her daughter was truly asleep, Breena dimmed the lamps and followed her brother down the stairs.

The main room of the cottage consisted of a sparsely furnished, open space with a blue door that led to the garden path outside. A ceramic sink with a rusted iron spigot occupied one corner of the room, and a plain, wooden table and three mismatched chairs had been carefully arranged in the center of the kitchen area.

Breena slumped into a chair, shaking her head when Esmund offered her a cup of wine from an unmarked bottle.

"Someone almost saw her today." The knight leaned against the sink, scowling into his own cup. "I thought you reinforced the spells."

"I did," Breena said with a tired sigh. "She burned through them again. Her magic is developing too quickly for me to keep up. Every time I try to lock it away, more bubbles to the surface."

Esmund watched her impassively. "We're only a few weeks out now. Once the Aion Gate opens—"

"I know. We'll be back in Faro. Cori will be safe."

"You don't sound convinced."

Breena sighed, picking at a crack in the table. "You were there that day. You saw the same thing I did, Essie."

"That was just a human walking in the woods."

"If you believe that, then you're a fool."

Esmund went quiet. Because he *had* been there that day. He had seen the afternoon light dissolve into shadows. And just like her, he had quietly been making his own preparations.

After several long moments, Esmund pushed himself off the sink and strode for the door. "It's time for my patrol."

"Essie," Breena called out, rising from the table.

Esmund paused, but didn't turn.

"Thank you," she said. "I've said it before, but… thank you."

"It was my duty to come."

"No, it was your duty to hand Cori over to the Crystal Guard." And that's exactly what he had tried to convince her to do—before she had shown him why that wasn't an option. "This went beyond duty. You didn't have to come, you didn't have to believe me, but you did. So... thank you."

Esmund jerked his chin. "You're my sister, and Atlas is my friend. There was never a decision to make."

Breena smiled sadly, sinking back down into her chair as she watched her brother retrieve his sword and slip out into the night.

The soft snick of the door felt strangely final.

The first thing that Breena noticed was the heat. It was still early spring, and the chill of winter lingered in the air. Most mornings, she would bury her nose further underneath the blanket at the first sign of wakefulness.

But the heat was oppressive. It demanded her attention. Even in her languid state, she could sense the sweat beading and rolling down her skin.

"Breena! Wake up!"

Someone was urgently shaking her now. Finally coming to, she opened her eyes to find a very distressed Esmund standing over her.

"Essie? Whatever is the matter?" she mumbled, rubbing the sleep from her eyes.

"The village is being attacked." He moved frantically about the room, a blue aura emanating from his form and filling the tiny space. He held a crystal in his hand, casting water dousing spells in each corner of the bedroom. The heat began to abate, bit by bit, as the harsh glow of the flames outside started to dim. "There was a commotion in the town square when I was doing my rounds. A mob—maybe 15 fire mages and a handful of water and shadow mages. They were asking about a girl. A time mage."

Dread coiled in her stomach as Breena spurred into action, rushing out of the bedroom and into the main room. She could sense water magic casing the walls, holding back the tendrils of flames that already lapped at the exterior of the little cottage. Water crystals had been placed at each corner of the room, anchoring the spells that had been haphazardly woven together into a protective web.

"Hurry," Breena mumbled, silently reprimanding herself. She didn't have time to dawdle. There was too much at stake.

The glass from the windows had already shattered, and it crunched beneath Breena's boots as she made her way over to the stairs. Thankfully, the original dousing spells Esmund had set when they first moved in were still intact on the upper level, effectively blocking the heat of the fires outside. Cori slept peacefully, unaware of the encroaching danger.

"Baby, wake up." Breena gently shook the slumbering girl.

Cori struggled to open her eyes, blearily gazing into the distraught face of her mother.

Breena said nothing as she picked up the child, and Cori's slight arms instinctually wrapped around her mother's neck. Balancing her daughter in one arm, Breena moved across the room to collect the small chest of enchanting supplies sitting on the desk. When her eyes flitted to the window, she could see a line of robed figures standing just outside the edge of the cottage property.

Her throat tightened. It had finally happened. The Sanctorum had finally found them.

An angry violet light saturated the air around the line of mages as they methodically dismantled the glamours and aether concealment spells she and Esmund had spent weeks cloaking beneath the stones of the garden wall.

Beyond the vanguard, the village was ablaze, and pillars of smoke blackened the night sky.

Muttering a silent prayer and wishing that she still believed in the Shards' mercy, Breena rushed down the stairs and followed her brother into the cellar.

"They're already outside," she snapped as she placed Cori on the mattress of a small bed stuffed into the corner of the dank room. She haphazardly dumped out her enchanting supplies, spreading them across a quilt that had long ago turned yellow with age.

"Something doesn't seem right." Esmund paused to pull out another glowing water crystal before continuing to cast a line of protective spells across the back wall. "I could see fires off in the distance. I think they may have hit Plum and Bago too."

Breena's mouth went dry. "You think they're burning the entire western coast just to find one little girl?"

"I don't know," Esmund admitted. "It doesn't make sense. None of this makes any sense. Even if they did discover us, to come into the Marquess Castaro's territory and start burning his villages… it's madness."

Breena forced herself to breathe as she began organizing her supplies. "We can figure that out later. What are our options *right now*?"

Esmund hesitated, still preoccupied with the various enchantments that now shrouded the room. The walls, the floor, the ceiling—every surface was awash with water magic. "If they've already made it as far north as Bago, that means the roads to Ryme won't be safe. Our best option is to defend ourselves here."

Right then.

Brandishing her dagger, Breena sliced open her palm and filled the small inkpot with a flood of fresh blood. Her heart pounded in her ears, her hands shook—but she paid her rising dread no mind. The stakes were too high to give in to panic.

Closing her eyes and taking a deep breath, she set to work, placing the shadow crystals she had charged earlier in a circle around the trembling fey child and sending out small wisps of her magic to each one.

The air started to feel richer as the crystals released their stored aether, and Breena breathed it in. Her shoulders straightened, and any lingering traces of fatigue melted away as she felt the aether saturate her blood. Grabbing Cori's arm, Breena waved her hand, methodically extracting the aether from the water glamour Esmund had cast to conceal the underlying web of spells. Braided lines of runes surfaced on the girl's pale skin, flickering to life and spiraling out from a crescent-shaped shadow crystal that had been embedded in the base of her palm.

The little girl had been uncharacteristically quiet, and she looked up at the older woman, fear clouding her expression. “Mommy, I don’t understand.”

Breena cupped her daughter’s cheek with her undamaged hand. “I know, baby. I know. But I need you to be very brave right now. Can you do that for Mommy?”

Cori nodded resolutely even as the tears overflowed and spilled down her reddened cheeks.

“Good girl. Now I need you to drink.” Breena held up her bleeding palm. When her daughter hesitated, she added, “Please. I know you don’t like it, but we don’t have time to argue right now. This is important.”

Cori nodded and took a tentative sip from the pool of blood welling around the cut, her face scrunching up at the taste.

Esmund paused, turning to face them. “What are you doing?”

“I need to seal away her magic—completely this time. She’s too vulnerable like this.”

Confusion clouded his eyes. Followed by stark realization. “That’s forbidden magic. And outside your specialization. How would you even know that spell?”

“You made your preparations,” Breena said, “and I made mine.”

Esmund stopped completely. “That spell requires a full contingent of mages. Where are you going to get the aether?”

Breena didn’t look up. “I’ve been charging crystals,” she said as she began to pen new runes across Cori’s skin.

“And you have enough in reserve?”

A pause. Barely a heartbeat of hesitation before she said, softly, “No. Not unless I give her my anima.”

Esmund crossed the short expanse of the room and stood over her, watching her work. "You'll die if you do that."

Breena stopped long enough to look up at the man who had given up his entire life to escape with her to this little island on the outer edge of nowhere. Over a year ago, he had left his own family behind to defend hers.

"Look around," she said tearfully. "Those monsters don't care who they kill. We're *all* going to die if we don't do something." Her face crumpled as she turned back, the crimson runes becoming sloppier and less evenly spaced as she failed to control the tremble in her hands. Cori's eyes started to droop as more and more of her aether—more of her essence—was sealed away inside the runes that now crawled up her arm like blood-drenched ivy.

Esmund stood by, silent, his arms hanging limply by his sides.

Breena worked quickly and quietly, pushing down the fear and doubt, and soon—too soon—the final enchantment was complete.

Placing her quill to the side, she laid both hands on the mattress and closed her eyes. Her breath came in gasped stutters, and her heart beat erratically in her chest. The color was already draining from her cheeks. She had completely depleted her anima casting this enchantment—tapped into the magic of her soul.

She didn't have very long left.

Esmund knelt beside her. Removing his final water crystal, he waved it over the complex mass of spells that were now etched into Cori's skin. The glamour slowly crept across the child's arm, hiding away the glowing crimson markings behind a wave of concealment magic.

"Are you sure you want to do this?" he asked. "It's not too late to undo the spells. Please, little sister, there are so many things that could go wrong."

"That was the Sanctorum outside," Breena said sadly. "Even if we survived the fire, they've already condemned the town. They plan to kill everyone. Including us."

Esmund hung his head, recognizing the truth in her words.

Shaking her daughter, Breena smiled sadly as Cori's eyes slowly fluttered open. She looked dazed, as if she was half-dreaming already. "Cori, you need to listen to me. Very soon, you're not going to remember this. You're going to go to sleep, and when you wake up, you'll have a new life."

Kneeling, Esmund gingerly handed his sister a polished mahogany box, steadying her hands as she felt for the clasp. The lid came away easily, revealing a small tear-shaped bauble resting upon a bed of crushed azure velvet. They both shared a look before Breena threaded the simple rose-colored crystal onto a piece of string and tied it around Cori's neck.

"The person who gave me this," Breena whispered, trailing her fingers across Cori's cheek, "said that as long as you have this with you, someone would always come to find you. Never take it off—understand?"

The girl nodded weakly, but her eyes were already drooping. She fought valiantly, her hand grasping at her mother's sleeve, but she couldn't overcome the fatigue that claimed her as the remaining aether in her blood burned away. Tears flowed freely from Breena's eyes as she looked at the face of her child for the last time. "I love you. One day, I hope you remember that."

Esmund tucked the blanket around the girl. "Have you given her a new name?"

"Yes," Breena said, refusing to look away from her daughter's face. She caressed the child's delicate features, committing them to memory. "Atlas should find it amusing."

Esmund watched the scene quietly, his face falling as Breena stroked the child's flaxen hair. Moving to stand, he said, "The dousing spells are strong enough to protect her from the fires, but I still need to fortify the concealment spell on the door from the outside. I'll come back if I can, but—"

"I know." The Sanctorum was already here, already beating down their door. They were working on borrowed time.

Breena could barely hold her head up as she tried to turn to face him. "Take me with you, Essie."

"Breena, that's not necessary. Stay here. Spend your last moments with your child."

"No. If you don't make it back, and I'm found down here with her, it will just raise suspicions. I won't take that risk."

Her entire body trembled as she struggled to rise, and when her legs gave way, Esmund caught her, slinging an arm underneath her knees as he lifted her. "Take me upstairs, brother. Let me face our attackers. Let them look me in the eye as they burn my bones. Let my spirit rise to the heavens on a cloud of smoke and ash. I can't think of a more fitting burial."

Her strength was fading, but instead of pain, she just felt a cold numbness creeping in as

Esmund carried her up the stairs.

The door to the cellar snicked shut, and she knew she wouldn't live to see it open.

"Do you think she'll remember me?" Breena asked as Esmund set her down at the same table and chairs where the three of them had eaten a peaceful dinner just hours before. If she concentrated, she could still smell the faint aroma of burned stew and fresh bread lingering on the air.

"I know the spell... but do you think it's possible?" Her body went limp, and her eyes were already starting to flutter closed as death drew nearer.

Esmund laid her head down gently upon the table, folding her hands underneath her cheek as if in sleep.

"Yes, little sister." He tried his best to smile reassuringly, despite the tears that rolled down his cheeks. "She'll remember. Every child dreams of their mother's face."

---

15 years later

CHAPTER I

-An excerpt from Practical Spellcasting for the Modern Mage

The study of magic inevitably begins with a single question: what is aether?

At its core, aether is a gaseous element, naturally occurring in breathable air. It is the building block of magic, the cornerstone of modern science, the foundation upon which the Fey Imperium resides.

In short, aether is everything, so ubiquitous within our society that even class divisions are defined by the genetic predisposition to absorb, refine, and transform this substance into various forms of magical output. The fey, as natural magic users, stratify themselves into sub-classes based upon birth and ability, whereas those that cannot wield aether to perform magic reside at the bottom of the social hierarchy and are given a single designation: shardless.

"Shit, shit, shit," Taly muttered between gasping breaths, her legs pumping frantically.

She could hear the wyvern behind her. Its claws scratched across the rocks that dotted the forested cliffside path overlooking Lake Reginea, and a feral yowl pierced the chill morning air. She spared a glance over her shoulder, and immediately regretted it.

The beast's body was a gangly, hulking mass, and the scales coating its skin looked like jewels—shards of ruby, agate, jasper, and emerald that glinted in the scant patches of light shining through the treetops. Great leathery wings protruded from its back, each one adorned with a long, bony hook that kept catching on the low-hanging tree branches as it barreled after her.

Taly veered off the overgrown hunting trail she had been following, sliding under a fallen tree and ripping the fabric of her trousers as she changed course. She could feel blood trickling down her leg, but she paid it no mind as she wove her way through the densely packed woods.

A series of snarls and growls trailed after her as the beast tried to press its way between the thickening tree cover. Twigs snapped and leaves crackled as they were shaken loose and thrown to the ground. The beast was frantic as it flung itself against the trees, splintering those plants whose trunks had yet to become gnarled and hardened with age. It had been slowed down, but so had she.

It was gaining.

Rays of morning sunlight peeked through the trees up ahead, and Taly was almost blinded when she finally emerged from the woods. The worn soles of her boots found little traction on the rocky outcrop, but she didn't slow down—not even when she approached the jagged edge of the cliff.

Saying a short prayer to the Shards, Taly jumped.

The sound of wind filled her ears as the world rushed by in a blur. Hugging her body, she braced herself for the cold shock of water as she dove feet-first into the placid waters of Lake Reginea almost 30 feet below.

Taly closed her eyes as she plunged deeper and deeper, and she jolted, biting her lip against the pain that rippled up her legs when her feet collided with the lake bottom. Golden tendrils of hair floated in front of her face as she peered up through the murky depths, and she hooked her foot beneath one of the various pieces of rusty scrap metal that littered the lakebed to keep from floating to the top. A dark, winged shadow passed overhead. It circled once, twice, its silhouette distorted by the rippling wall of water—like someone had swirled their fingers through a painting that wasn't quite dry.

Wyverns didn't usually venture this far south, so it had come as a complete surprise to Taly when she had accidentally stumbled upon a nest as she was walking through the woods that morning. Thank the Shards there had been a lake nearby. Wyverns hated water.

Her lungs began to burn, so Taly released her makeshift anchor and swam to the surface. Gasping for breath, she groped for a nearby piece of driftwood, her eyes scanning the trees. Although she could no longer see the wyvern, she could still hear a low growl coming from the forest's edge just beyond the scattered perimeter of junk and debris that decorated the shoreline.

The underbrush began to rustle, and a long, hooked beak poked between the trees. The strange bird-like jaws parted to reveal rows upon rows of jagged teeth as the wyvern stepped out of the shadows and took a long, languid sniff.

Shit. Why the hell wasn't this thing giving up?

Its eyes found hers, and it let loose a ferocious snarl as it pawed at the edge of the water with razor-sharp talons. Its massive club of a tail swung from side-to-side impatiently.

With a shake of its head, the wyvern's wings extended, and swirls of gravel and dust flew into the air as it began to lift itself off the ground. It flew higher and higher, and when it turned and began drifting over the treetops, Taly was sure that it had finally lost interest in her. Her stomach dropped when it did a surprisingly graceful somersault midair, coasting back over the forest canopy as it began circling the lake once more.

"Go away, you overgrown lizard!" she screamed, getting ready to dive again. Wyverns wouldn't usually risk flying over water, but on days like today, when the aether was so thin that even Taly, a mortal, could tell that something in the air felt off, the magical beasts could be unpredictable.

The creature arched its back, and its body dipped, but before it could attempt a dive, it gave an indignant squawk as a ribbon of water shot out of the trees and hit it square in the face. The beast shook itself, nearly falling out of the air as it struggled to recover from its surprise. Streams of water continued to lash at its body, and it eventually fell to the ground with a heavy thud that rippled the lake's surface.

"Go on! Get out of here!" A man that looked far too young for the gruff timbre of his voice stepped out of the trees. His skin was tanned from the sun, and the sandy mop of hair curling around his shoulders was windblown and swept to the side. He held a glowing blue crystal in one hand, and tendrils of water magic curled around his body. "Damn pest!" he barked. A wave of his hand sent out another lash of water magic.

The wyvern snapped its beak at the man but slowly backed away as the mage carefully picked his way through the scrap that littered the shore. The creature's beady eyes flicked back to Taly even as it retreated another step, its body already disappearing behind the tree line. A mortal wasn't a good enough meal to risk taking on a water mage.

With a final yowl, the creature disappeared into the forest, leaves rustling in the wake of its departure.

Approaching the edge of the lake, the man squinted. "Taly Caro?! I thought that looked like you falling from the sky. Shards bless… When I checked the forecast this morning, it didn't say anything about raining humans. The weather here on Tempris gets stranger every year."

Taly did her best to wave as she let go of the piece of driftwood and started to swim to shore. "Syn," she said when she was close enough for her toes to touch the bottom. The man laughed as he waded out to meet her. "You beautiful fey bastard. I owe you one." Slipping when her boot hit a particularly slick patch of rocks, she struggled to regain her footing as the water dragged at her sodden clothing. Her shoulder-length hair was tangled and matted as it clung to her neck.

"What the hell are you doing out here, girlie? Did that cheap bastard you call a landlord break your plumbing again with his so-called repairs? You know, if you'd wanted a bath so badly, I'd have given you a few coins for the bathhouse. All you needed to do was ask." Syn was still chuckling to himself as he wrapped an arm around her waist, practically lifting her off her feet as he helped her back to shore. Taly couldn't help but feel guilty about the line of water that now marked him from the waist down. Even though his worn leather boots were far from new, he'd likely be walking around with wet shoes for the rest of the day.

Taly gave him her best glare. "Despite Jay's continued failure to fix my shower, my hygiene is impeccable, thank you very much." Peeling off a dark canvas coat that was almost two sizes too large for her, she shivered when the chill air greeted her bare arms, making her pale skin prickle. Although it was still cold enough to be distinctly uncomfortable, maybe even dangerous for a human under the right circumstances, a wet coat wasn't doing her any favors.

Scowling, Taly kicked at a piece of junk that was half-buried in the mud. The object was rusty and jagged, and although she had no idea what it was supposed to be, she knew enough to see that it was worthless.

"No, I'm out in this hellhole this morning because I took some bad advice," she said, gazing out over the lake and letting her eyes trace the flat violet-and-gold crystal planes that loomed in the distance. The Ios Gate was just one of the many dimensional gates peppered across the island of Tempris. No longer functional, what had once been a shining edifice swirling with glistening eddies of aether was now nothing more than a dark wall of stone. "I heard that a new wave of scrap came through the Ios Gate last night, but, unfortunately for me, the site was already picked clean before I got here. I even searched the cliffs behind the gate since I've heard that stuff sometimes falls through in that area, but I didn't find anything good. Just a bunch of trash and a really cranky wyvern."

Syn clapped a hand to her shoulder, and she followed him as he began to push his way through the dense underbrush of the forest. Bright streaks of warm, buttery sunlight sliced through the trees, illuminating the overgrown forest path. Although it was almost spring, some of the winter frost still stubbornly clung to the ground.

It was a short walk back to the main road, and a skinny piebald mare hitched to a plain wooden wagon was waiting patiently on the recently repaired cobbled pavement. Syn drew back the tarp covering his wares and pulled out an old blanket.

"Well, I'm not surprised you didn't find anything," he said, taking her coat and then wrapping the blanket around her shoulders. Taly's teeth had started to chatter, and all she could do was nod in thanks. "The Fire Guild came out last night. Given how close it is to Ryme, they're always quick to jump on Ios. No salvager worth their salt ever bothers coming out to Lake Reginea."

"Yeah, I figured that out the hard way," Taly managed to say between shivers as she accepted a thermos of coffee that Syn had produced from beside the driver's seat. The brew tasted old and weak, but it was warm and made her almost feel alive again.

Syn smiled and shook his head. "Well, you'll know from now on. Sometimes I forget that you've only been at this a year. You learn a lot quicker than most salvagers I come across." Crouching down, he began dabbing at the scrape on her knee with a cloth soaked in blood wood, a plant native to Tempris that produced a small amount of earth aether in its sap. The salve burned, but the flesh was already starting to mend itself as the healing magic soaked into her skin.

"Thank you, Syn. I know blood wood's not easy to come by right now. I'll pay you for that as soon as I'm able."

Syn waved her off. "I don't want your coin, Taly. If you want to repay me, just tell me how you managed to get that wyvern so riled. They don't usually mess with humans—or anything without magic for that matter. What those beasts are after is aether. Any kind they can find." Giving her a wink, he added, "Except water aether, of course. Even though I have no doubt that wyvern would've loved to drain my blood, it would've had to get wet to do it."

Taly leaned against the cart, sipping at the thermos. "I wish I had a good story for you, but all I did was stumble into its nest."

"I've never heard of a wyvern nesting south of Litor." Syn rubbed at the stubble on his chin. "But then again, stranger things have happened when the Aion Gate was charging."

Taly nodded in agreement, pulling at the edges of the blanket. The Aion Gate was one of the only two remaining gates on the island that still functioned. In the wake of the Schism, the great disaster that had resulted in the closing of every gate on the island of Tempris, the Gate Watchers had been formed to repair and oversee the gates. However, with their limited resources, they could only focus on the two interdimensional bridges that had been deemed *essential*—the Seren Gate, which led to the fey mainland of Lycia, and the much larger, far more temperamental Aion Gate.

"I was reading that Aion's charging cycle is going to be pretty bad this time around," she said. "On the one hand, the Gate Watchers think that they'll be able to hold the connection to the mortal realm a little bit longer than in past cycles."

"That'll be good for trade," Syn remarked.

"True," Taly said with a sigh. "But that also means the aether is going to be fluctuating far more erratically than it usually does in the months leading up to the Aion Gate connection. The magical creatures will be even more rabid and difficult to contain than usual."

"I guess we know why the Marquess has been so keen on repairing the wards on the roads as of late." Syn glanced back at the nearly invisible veil of magic that shimmered just beyond the tree line. "Can't have the mainland travelers comin' face-to-face with any beasties, now can we? They might accidentally scuff their shoes."

Turning back to her, he added, "By the way, I'm headed to Ryme. It's not far, but you're welcome to ride with me."

Taly bobbed her head, still shivering underneath the blanket. "Thank you, Syn. I'd like that."

Syn gave her a kind smile as he pushed back his hair, revealing the pointed tips of his ears.

Even though he had too much human blood in his lineage to be considered anything more than a lowborn, he was still fey. His body could still absorb and refine aether, a trait that granted him both immortality and the ability to perform magic. From what Taly knew of him, he came from a fairly prominent family of blacksmiths back on the fey mainland, but he had never told her just how he had fallen into salvaging. And she had never asked. If he had given up a nice, stable life in favor of picking through junk and refuse on an impoverished little island on the outer edge of the Fey Imperium, then he probably wasn't too keen on rehashing whatever had driven him to leave all that behind.

To that point, she could relate. The set of circumstances that had led her to abandon her old life for one that left her scrambling for enough coin just to buy bread on any given day weren't pleasant.

"Boy!"

Taly jumped when Syn banged his hand against the side of the cart.

"Yes, uncle, I'm coming," came a surly reply. A lowborn man whose age she couldn't quite place emerged from the woods. Since most fey stopped aging after reaching 30, this "boy" could've been 30, 130, or even 1,030. His hair was dark and greasy, and his eyes were black, carrying only a trace of that strange, fey brightness that made the highborn nobility seem as though they were lit from within. Even though his face was impassive, his full lips turned down at the corners, giving him a permanent sneer. "What's with the shardless?" he groused.

Taly grimaced. *Shardless.* The word the fey

used to describe those without magic—those lower than the lowborn.

"Watch your language, Calo," Syn snapped. His expression hardened. "Your father didn't raise you to talk to people that way."

Assuming that the boy had been suitably chastened, Syn stepped off the road and began weaving through the trees as he made his way back into the forest. "I just need a few more minutes, and then we can get going," he called back. "Yoru said he dropped a crate of supplies somewhere around here—asked me to pick it up for him."

Calo studied Taly as she leaned against the cart, his fingers worrying a small red crystal that he passed from hand to hand.

A fire mage, she thought, refusing to look away when his eyes found hers. *Fantastic.*

"You're pretty… for a human." Calo tugged at the blanket still wrapped around her shoulders. Taly tightened her grip, but he held fast, managing to wrench the makeshift coat away from her.

His eyes slid up and down her body, and she had to resist the urge to cover her chest. Even though she wore a white camisole beneath her stained, sleeveless tunic, she was soaked to the bone, and her clothing clung to her body, leaving very little to the imagination. She had leaned out considerably over the past year, and the lines of her ribs were as visible as the peaks of her breasts beneath the wet fabric. Nevertheless, she supposed she could still be considered beautiful. Maybe even desirable. She had often been told that her features were almost fey-like in their delicacy, despite the human roundness of her ears.

"How much?" the sullen boy demanded.

"Not for sale," Taly bit out. Her shoulders shook as a violent shiver racked her slender frame.

Calo scoffed. "You should be honored I even offered to pay before bending you over, you little beast. How much?"

Taly met his eyes defiantly, and her hand moved to the pistol holstered at her waist. "Not. For. Sale."

Calo sneered, but before he could reach for her, he pitched forward.

"What the hell, boy?!" Syn cuffed the shorter man on the back of the head. The blow nearly sent the fire mage face-first into the dirt. Throwing the crate he'd retrieved into the back of the wagon, he said, "Shards, you've become a right prick since the last time I saw you. That's it—I'm fed up with your bullshit. You're walking the rest of the way."

Calo balked. "You're going to make me walk so you can ferry some shardless back into town? Just wait until I tell my father, old man."

A low, inhuman snarl ripped out of Syn's throat. "My brother will probably thank me for saving your sorry ass. How you treat people aside, do you have any idea what would happen to you if you hurt Marquess Castaro's ward? No? Well, let me tell you then. I'd give it an hour before you had two incensed shadow mages banging down your door. You'd be lucky if they left you alive and in one piece."

Calo visibly paled, and he turned to Taly, his eyes wide and fearful. *That* got his attention. Even though shadow mages couldn't cast spells in the traditional sense, their magic allowed them to control and manipulate aether. Everything in the fey world, even a mage's health and well-being, was connected to aether in some way. As a result, there was nothing more fearsome than an angry shadow mage.

Taly snatched the blanket off the ground and stalked over to the driver's seat. "I'm not the Marquess' ward anymore," she grumbled, taking Syn's proffered hand as he boosted her up. She saw Calo's head whip around at that, but his expression remained pale and frightened.

Syn laughed as he settled in beside her. "Keep telling yourself that." Tapping the reins, he called back, "And Calo, don't stray outside the wards on the road. There's a wyvern prowling around close by. I hear they love fire mages."

The young man was strangely silent as they began to pull away. Taly glanced back, and when she was sure they were out of earshot, she said, "That wasn't necessary, Syn."

"Sure it was," Syn replied, chuckling softly. "My brother sent me that boy 'cause he was afraid that all them highborn nobles on the mainland were rubbing off the wrong way. A walk back into town isn't going to hurt him one bit."

Taly shook her head but decided that she was too tired to argue. They both lapsed into silence as the mare trudged along at a pace that was barely better than walking.

Staring off into the trees, Taly let her thoughts wander as she gingerly fingered the pink quartz pendant that hung around her neck—the only evidence that she had lived a life prior to being found 15 years ago cowering in a pile of ash. She was only six years old when she lost her family, and despite the number of healers and menders that had looked at her over the years, no one knew why she couldn't remember anything from before the fire. Usually, that wouldn't bother her, but her birthday always had a way of making her feel strangely nostalgic.

They weren't far outside the city now, and Taly could already see the hedges that flanked the entrance to the private drive that led to Harbor Manor. Often referred to as the crown jewel of Ryme, Harbor Manor was a palatial estate that had belonged to Lord Ivain Castaro, the Marquess of Tempris, and his family for just over seven centuries now. It sat just south of town on a sprawling piece of land that took at least half a day to fully traverse from end-to-end on foot, and as the trees began to thin, Taly could just see the chimneys stretching towards the sky. By some stroke of luck, she had spent most of her life living at the manor, taken in after the Marquess' young apprentice dug her out of the rubble of what she could only assume used to be her childhood home. The fire that claimed her family and most of her village had left a wake of devastation that spanned the entire western coast.

"Well, what do we have here?" Syn chuckled when they rounded a bend in the road. He jerked his chin, a wide grin splitting his face. "Care to say hello?"

Taly followed his gaze, and her heart leapt into her throat when she saw two familiar figures emerge from the drive. The woman wore a long blue dress that perfectly complemented her fair skin and auburn hair, and Taly could tell that the man was lanky and fit even beneath the heavy fabric of his greatcoat.

"Shit," Taly cursed, pulling herself into the back of the cart and underneath the relative safety of the tarp. It was a tight fit between one of the crates and the outer wall, but she somehow managed. “Pretend that I’m not here, Syn!”

Syn glanced back at her, confusion evident in his expression. “Taly, that boy’s a shadow mage. He’s likely already scented you.”

“I don’t care,” she hissed in reply. “I don’t want to talk to him.”

“Shards,” the old salvager grumbled. “What kind of human nonsense is this?”

Taly held her breath as they passed. A thin sliver of light penetrated the darkness, and she caught a flash of a navy-and-gold sleeve as the man tapped the side of the wagon.

“Synna,” he greeted. Taly hadn’t heard his voice in such a long time, and it made her heart clench. Like hers, his accent was cool and cultured, not a trace of the relaxed islander drawl that she had become so accustomed to hearing over the past year. “What are you doing so far north?”

Syn laughed as he pulled on the reins. “Lord Emrys, Lady Castaro,” he greeted, bowing his head in deference to the two highborn nobles. “Funny you ask that. I’m transporting a load of scrap to trade at the Swap.” He glanced behind him. “And between you and me, I just picked up some very interesting cargo down at Lake Reginea.”

Taly clapped a hand over her mouth. Just what did that old salvager think he was doing?

“Of what nature?” Lady Castaro asked. Her voice was crisp and refined but somehow still laced with warmth. The Marquess’ younger sister, Sarina Castaro, was the heart and soul of Harbor Manor—and the only mother Taly had ever known.

“I’m afraid I can’t say,” Syn replied with a

shrug. "Very secret. Very precious."

"Is that so?" the man, Lord Emrys—Skye to those that knew him—replied dubiously. His hand grasped the side of the wagon, and his fingers curled underneath the tarp, blocking her view. "I must say, I'm curious now. What could you possibly have stashed away that you couldn't show us?"

"Now, Skye," Lady Castaro admonished, and Taly could perfectly envision the way she placed a motherly hand on his shoulder. Shards, how she missed Sarina. Even though the fey noblewoman made a point to keep tabs on Taly's whereabouts, they hadn't talked, *really* talked, since Taly left the manor. "Sorry, Synna. Skye's in a bit of a mood right now. He and Ivain had to meet with the Sanctorum this morning."

"I am not in a mood, Sarina. I'm being perfectly cordial." Skye's fingers drummed against the inside of the cart.

"I'd heard the Sanctorum was in town," Syn said carefully. "I hope there's not trouble. After the Marquess kicked those butchers off the island, I thought we'd finally seen the last of them. Do you think they've found another time mage?"

Taly tore her eyes away from the hand that was slowly creeping toward her. The Sanctorum was a special task force sanctioned by the Dawn Court. They had a single purpose: to hunt down and kill time mages and their sympathizers. If they were back, that didn't bode well for the little island.

"No," Sarina replied hastily. "Shards, no. They're just here to investigate a few rumors. Apparently, there's been talk that someone is trying to sell time crystals in the backrooms of the

Swap."

Syn shook his head. "Rumors are all they had last time, but that didn't stop them from burning our villages. It's a miracle your Taly managed to survive."

"We're keeping a very close eye on them," Skye said. "Ivain is even redirecting some of the Gate Watchers to oversee their visit. They'll be accompanied at all times."

"Yes," Sarina added. "And even if the rumors are true, there isn't anyone left that could use time crystals. All the time mages are dead, their High Lady is dead, and the Time Shard is gone. That means all of this fuss is over nothing more than a few pretty pieces of stone."

Skye's fingers faltered in their rhythm. "Are you sure we can't see inside your cart? It smells... interesting."

Taly's heart sank. As a shadow mage, Skye possessed the unique ability to enhance his physical form by channeling aether. While many shadow mages limited the use of this power to increasing their fighting prowess, Skye preferred to use his magic to sharpen his senses. When they were children, he was always listening for changes in her heart rate or breathing, sniffing her out when she was hiding. She could hardly ever get anything past him.

Which meant that Syn had been right. Skye already knew exactly what, or more precisely, *who* was hiding underneath the tarp. Depending on when he activated the aether augmentation spell, he could've known long before she and Syn had even rounded the bend.

"Skye, you're being rude," Sarina admonished.

Syn laughed. “Leave the boy be, Lady Castaro. I’d be offended if he weren’t a little curious.”

As Sarina began redirecting the conversation, Skye’s fingers continued drumming against the side of the cart, only inches away from her face. So far, all of his movements had seemed nonchalant and inadvertent, but Taly knew him well enough to see through the act. In his fidgeting, he had managed to move the edge of the tarp just enough that she had to press her back against a crate to avoid the beam of light that threatened to give her away. His head turned, and a set of eyes so green they almost seemed to glow peered into the shadows, searching. A second later, he had already turned away to nod at something Sarina had just said.

For a moment, she considered reaching out and twining her fingers with his. The temptation was so strong that before she knew what she had done, her hand was hovering next to his. She quickly pulled back.

Bad, she silently reprimanded herself. Even if she desperately missed the man that used to be her best friend, she shouldn’t do anything that might encourage him to seek her out. She had worked too hard to distance herself from her old life—from him.

Skye sighed as he pulled his hand away, smoothing out the tarp as he said, “Well, Synna—we won’t keep you. Make sure that *precious cargo* of yours gets to Ryme safe and sound.”

Syn tipped his head as he urged the mare forward, and Taly breathed a sigh of relief when she felt the cart begin to move. After a few moments of listening to the creak of the wheels and shying away from the edge of a crate that dug into her back as they lurched back and forth, she crawled to the back of the wagon and peeked through a hole in the tarp.

She barely managed to suppress her squeak of surprise when a pair of glowing green eyes immediately found hers. Even though they were far enough away that her human eyes could no longer pick out the details of his face, she knew that Skye could easily see her with his magically enhanced senses. He stuffed his hands into his pockets as he said something to Sarina, and Taly couldn't help but laugh when the noblewoman turned and whacked him on the back of the head. Gathering up her skirts, Sarina ran ahead, stopping to call back to him when he didn't increase his pace.

"You can come out now," Syn said when they passed another bend in the road. She could hear the smile in his voice. "Unless you plan to hide back there all day."

"Uh... yeah," she mumbled as she crawled back into the driver's seat beside Syn. It had been almost a year since she'd seen Skye in person, and it was by far the longest period of time they'd spent apart since she was six and he was ten. She had half-expected him to come running after them, but when she looked back, the road behind them was empty.

"Shards, girlie." Syn nudged her with his shoulder. "I've known you and that boy since you were younglings. Why don't you put everyone out of their misery and just talk to him? I don't know what's going on with you two, but surely it can't be all that bad."

"It's... complicated, Syn," Taly replied quietly.

That certainly wasn't a lie.

She slouched down in the seat and closed her eyes. On days like today, it was certainly tempting to give in to the ever-present urge to just go home—back to her old life at the manor.

But she couldn't.

She couldn't go back. She couldn't allow herself to get too close to the people who had shown her kindness in a world that had so little left to give.

The girl they knew was gone, and no matter what, she could never tell them why.

CHAPTER 2

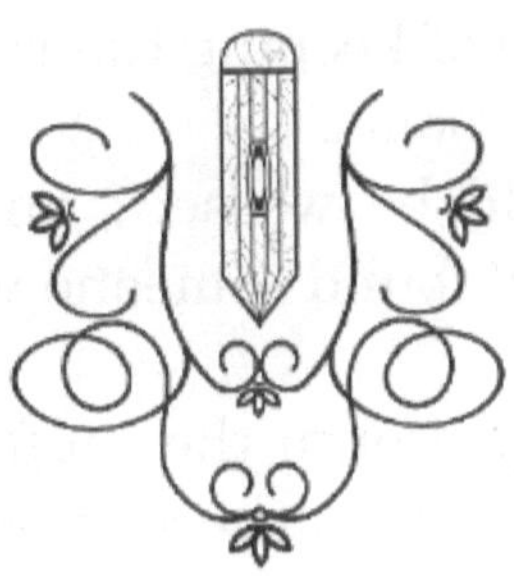

-An excerpt from Long May She Reign: The Rise and Fall of the Last Queen of Time

Once hailed as the greatest sovereign of the modern age, Queen Raine was a visionary and a philanthropist, a dedicated scholar. A remarkable woman whose final act nearly destroyed an empire.

No one can say why she chose to close the gates, but in the wake of the great disaster—the day many are now calling the Schism—the High Lord and Lady of Earth and Air consolidated their power under the name of the Dawn Court. They created the Sanctorum and declared war upon Queen Raine and her time mages, ushering in an era of fear and bloodshed that has never been rivaled.

With a sigh, Taly pushed open the door to the

drafty little room she now called home. It wasn't much—only a few flecks of paint still clung to the walls, the roof leaked, and stacks of old books she'd found around the gates took the place of furniture. Nevertheless, the rent was cheap, and the woman who managed the tavern downstairs generally did a pretty good job of keeping the riffraff away from the second-floor rooms.

Things could be worse... and certainly had been before she'd found someone willing to rent to a shardless.

Water dripped onto the scuffed wooden floor as Taly trudged across the tiny room, peeling off her wet clothes as she went. How she yearned for the days when she owned more than one set of clothing. When she had abruptly decided to leave the manor and her life as the Marquess' adopted ward, she hadn't thought to grab any extra clothes. That was a mistake in hindsight.

Straining her ears, she could already hear the telltale sounds of the tavern's kitchens opening down below, the staff likely getting ready for the lunch rush. Her stomach gurgled at the thought of food. It had been almost a week since she'd had the luxury of a full belly.

Looking at the bed stuffed into the corner, Taly debated just going back to sleep, but her stomach grumbled again, more insistently this time.

Okay. Shower first. Then food.

Except... Taly pushed aside the sheet that had been hung across the doorless entry to her washroom and turned the nozzle on the shower. Nothing came out. With a growl, she banged against the wall, rattling the fire and water crystals that had been embedded into a rusty metal panel on the side of the tub. The stones flickered, the tap dripped, but then… nothing.

Stepping up onto the lip of the shower, she peered over a small ledge near the ceiling. Two small violet gemstones—shadow crystals—were ensconced behind a jumble of dusty wiring. Unlike other types of crystals, shadow crystals could be used to store raw aether and then wired to power an array of different contraptions, including plumbing. The light shining from within the two crystals responsible for powering her shower was almost nonexistent, meaning that the crystals hadn't been able to collect enough aether from the tavern's primary aether grid to even allow her a cold rinse. This was not an uncommon occurrence. The last time she'd had enough water to take a full shower was almost three days ago.

"Happy birthday to me," she sang bitterly, wringing the water out of her clothes as best she could before dressing. At the very least, her unplanned dive into Lake Reginea had done a good job of washing away the dirt and grime.

Pulling on her soggy boots, she hesitated, studying the dark navy jacket she'd found at the Aion Gate several months ago. Although she considered herself quite lucky to have found a piece of clothing in such good condition, she didn't know how much good it did her soaking wet. Unfortunately, she didn't have a replacement. When she made her initial flight from the manor, she had been wearing a sturdy leather jacket inlaid with a series of very expensive protective wards, but she had traded it at the Swap last month when the salvage had been especially lean.

With a half-hearted shrug, Taly pulled on the damp coat and quickly appraised herself in the small, square mirror hanging by the door. Running a hand through her shoulder-length tresses, she scowled at the figure that stared back at her. Tufts of straw-colored hair stuck out at odd angles in a halo around her face—the tragic result of her first and only attempt at cutting her own hair.

The hairstyle wasn't pretty, but it was practical. Although she had loved her hair, after six months of trying to hold on, she had finally given up her long, gently curling waves. Vanity was a luxury she could no longer afford.

Grabbing her pack, knife, and pistol, Taly stepped out onto a small circular walkway that led around to the front of the two-story building. The sun was almost directly overhead now, and the sounds of the city filtered up from down below.

While Ryme was the second-largest township on the island of Tempris, that really wasn't saying much. Compared to the fey cities on the mainland, it was an unruly, chaotic mishmash of different styles and cultures situated at the northern end of the island of Tempris. Being so close to the Aion Gate, they were always far more susceptible to adopting mortal styles and customs than the rest of the fey world, and as a result, wooden and brick hovels sat sandwiched between newer structures that had been modeled after a strange collection of mortal architectural styles. There were also, of course, more traditional fey homes—sturdy stone great houses that were all windows and arched eaves—but most of those were situated outside the city walls on their own little parcels of land.

Some of the locals were already filtering into the main room of the tavern. Stepping inside, Taly retreated to the far end of the bar top and hopped up on an empty stool. She held up two fingers to signal the man behind the counter. At first, he pretended not to see her, but she knew it was just an act. With a tired sigh, she rested her chin on one hand, waiting patiently. Eventually, he ambled over and unceremoniously plopped down a bowl of something that may have been edible at one time in the distant past.

The very distant past.

A slimy sheen coated the surface of the porridge-like substance, and when she poked at the mush with her spoon, various chunks of unidentifiable vegetable matter floated to the top.

Taly leveled a glare at the man, who stood watching her expectantly. “What is this, Jay?”

“It’s leftovers,” the ruddy-faced man grunted. For as long as Taly had known him, the burly barkeeper had always made a point to maintain a neat, tidy appearance. This morning, however, food stains peppered the front of his white shirt, and she had seen him wipe his bulbous nose with the tail of his apron at least twice since she had walked in.

Taly grimaced. “Jay, you are many things, but you’re not a chef. Why does Laurel have you working the kitchens again? This is the fifth time this week.”

Jay’s scowl deepened, and he scratched the side of his head, moving aside the wispy strands of mousy brown hair to reveal the pointed tips of his ears. “She’s sick again. Pretty sure she gave that crud to me too this time.” Turning to the side, he began coughing into his sleeve. Even though he was only a few generations removed from his closest highborn relative, Jay was still considered a lowborn. In addition to breeding away most of the traditional highborn traits, like the bright eyes and arched brows, having mortal blood in his veins meant that he was more susceptible to human diseases.

"Well, I'm sorry to hear that," Taly said, refusing to back down, "but I don't want leftovers." She pushed the bowl away from her. "Especially cold leftovers."

"People who don't pay get leftovers." He picked up the bowl and held it in his hand, casting a simple warming spell before dropping it back down in front of her. A piece of something orange (a carrot maybe?) sloshed out of the bowl and onto the bar.

Great. Now it's warm garbage.

"For the last time, Jay. I don't have to pay. Meals are included in my rent. That was part of my agreement with Laurel." Taly frowned, flicking the questionable piece of vegetable matter at the disgruntled cook. "And also, my water's out again. Can I have the key to the shower down here?"

"No. People who don't pay, don't shower." He didn't wait for her reply as he trudged back through the open doorway that led to the kitchen.

Raising herself up slightly, Taly shouted at his retreating form, "It's called rent, you jackass! I pay you rent!"

Jay waved his hand dismissively, all the while grumbling something about shardless that didn't know their place.

Taly leaned back on the stool and studied the bowl in front of her. She hadn't eaten since yesterday afternoon when she had gotten lucky with some basilisk meat at the Swap. Needless to say, she was starting to get a little hungry.

Maybe it tasted better than it looked?

Crossing her arms and eyeing the bowl dubiously, she leaned forward and sniffed.

Nope. Rancid. It was like Jay was trying to give her food poisoning. Which, if she really thought about it, probably wasn't too far off from the truth.

It was clear by now that she would probably have better luck foraging the woods outside of town for her breakfast than she would trying to convince the surly cook to give her something decent to eat. With a sigh, she left the untouched bowl where it was and exited the bar to continue on about her day.

Most people she passed in the street tried to pretend they didn't see her, but every now and then, someone would smile in her direction—other shardless mostly, but some lowborn fey as well. Every time someone managed to catch her eye, she would give them a polite nod in reply.

Taly froze when she heard the faint clink of metal drawing closer, and she turned her head just in time to see a group of Sanctifiers rounding the corner. Ducking into a darkened alley, she pressed herself against the wall as she watched the group of soldiers pass by. Their shiny black chainmail glinted in the morning light, and each warrior had an enchanted ax strapped to his back. A retinue of Gate Watchers followed closely behind. Beneath the crimson cloaks draped across their shoulders, the unlucky few that had been assigned to babysit the group of mage hunters wore scaled leather armor. Each carried a rapier, the weapon that most shadow mages tended to favor.

A glimmer caught her eye in the alleyway behind her—a subtle twist in the way the morning light reflected off a stack of crates. That could only mean one thing.

Taly pulled her pistol and pointed it at the ripple of water magic. "I won't miss. So, I suggest you take that two-bit water glamour and go rob somebody else."

A low snigger echoed down the alley as the thief continued to creep towards her.

Taly fired off a shot at where she assumed the pickpocket's feet to be. The boy yelped loudly as he fell out of the unraveling water glamour, and the stack of nearby crates toppled over on top of him. Blood streaked the ground. She had managed to glance his ankle.

Taly's eyes flicked to the street and back. If this had been a normal pistol with a normal firing mechanism based solely on fire crystals, the shot would've been loud enough to draw the attention of the people passing by. But this wasn't a normal pistol. No—Skye had made her this pistol for her birthday last year, and that arrogant highborn had somehow figured out a way to incorporate an air crystal into the firing mechanism. The gun had almost zero kickback, and the sound barely carried over the sharp clang of metal against metal coming from the sparring ring just around the corner.

"That'll be your only warning shot," Taly said evenly. The boy's eyes widened as she leveled the barrel of her pistol at his face. He looked too clean to be a common Swap rat. That meant he was probably just some local lowborn kid out trying to cause trouble. The wound on his ankle was already healing—not as fast a highborn fey could mend himself, and certainly not as fast as a shadow mage, but the skin had already managed to repair itself so that only a small red welt remained. Taly cocked her pistol, readying her next shot. The boy started scrambling backward, wrapping his magic around him as he once again tried to blend into the shadows. While she couldn't easily kill him, she could still make him hurt. Taly smiled when she heard the sound of frantic footsteps careening down the alleyway in the opposite direction.

Re-holstering her pistol, she hid in the alley for a moment longer, breathing a sigh of relief when she saw that the Sanctifiers were nowhere in sight. To her knowledge, there were no more time mages left in any of the worlds; they had disappeared along with their High Lady. But that didn't stop the Sanctorum from finding *suspects.* Fortune-tellers whose predictions were just a little too accurate. The random lowborn that did just a little too well at a carnival shell game. The Sanctorum was always looking under rocks and listening for rumors, always guarding against the possibility that the long-dead scourge might somehow resurrect.

Taly often found herself wondering what would happen if they ever found an actual time mage, how much blood would be shed once those old fears were given new life.

Too many lives had already been sacrificed to that cause.

Counting to three, then checking to make sure that the street was still clear, Taly casually stepped out of the alley and continued down the street.

The Swap was just ahead now. The old great house that quartered the bustling marketplace had started out its life as a minor baron's mansion sometime before the Schism. In the aftermath of the great disaster, it had been used as a hospital and then as a halfway house before it was finally condemned almost a century later. Any hint of luxury or extravagance had already been stripped away and sold well before Sarina, the Marquess' younger sister, decided to refurbish the structure and turn it into a market. The roof still had a few gaping holes and children still dared each other to venture into sections of the upper floors that were "haunted," but somehow this decrepit monument had become the center of trade for their little community.

As she approached, a cacophony of voices echoed from beyond the gaping, door-less entry. Shardless, lowborn fey, and even a few highborn nobles all swarmed into the front hall of the crumbling estate.

Weaving in and out of the sea of bodies, Taly pushed her way to the back of the building. To her right, she could see that Yoru's new assistant had received a fresh batch of wands. Beneath the wooden exterior, each wand was inlaid with crystal circuitry and programmed to execute a simple enchantment. When the young shadow mage flicked a small switch located at the base of the handle, a gale of fire shot out of the tip of the poplar wand in his hand, singeing a few innocent passers-by and earning him some angry shouts.

Then to her left, an air mage had set up shop. The woman looked young, but most fey looked young regardless of their age. *Highborn,* Taly thought. If the arched brows and sharp cheekbones didn't give that away, the amount of magic she was throwing around certainly did. The mage levitated a few feet off the ground, and a group of people had gathered around her, applauding as she lifted several small children into the air.

Finally arriving at the back of the main room, Taly turned and made her way down a side hallway. It was still early in the day for most backroom vendors, but she knew Josiah had most likely set up shop hours ago. While he might not have been the most above-board contact, the old trader had a knack for finding things. Like shadow mages that adhered to more *flexible* crafting policies.

She found Josiah sitting alone in the back corner of the deserted hall, his small booth almost devoid of any mentionable wares. Random pieces of obscure mortal tech hung here and there, but, overall, the scattered array of worthless junk made the little booth easy to ignore. At least for those that didn't know to look closer. No, Josiah's choice stock was only available to those that knew to ask.

Sunken eyes peered out from a haggard, wrinkled face, and Josiah scowled when he saw Taly approach. Though he was technically fey, Josiah, like Taly, was shardless. He still had the characteristic pointed ears of the fey, but his body couldn't absorb enough aether to cast even the most basic of spells. Too many generations of breeding with humans had stripped away the two things the fey valued most—magic and immortality.

"Hey Josie," Taly said, sidling up to the trader.

Josiah's voice, graveled with age, carried a note of annoyance. "Taly. What do you want?"

"Good morning to you too," Taly remarked, unfazed by his surly attitude.

"Don't give me any of your lip, Caro," Josiah

growled. Lifting a splotched and wrinkled hand, he scratched at what was left of his hair. "Not after what I did for you."

Taly scoffed, burying her hands in her pockets as she leaned forward. "Don't act like you did me any favors, old man. I'm paying you far more than I need to."

"You're paying me because I'm discreet." The trader reached behind him and pulled out a small, nondescript parcel wrapped in brown paper. "What do you think the Marquess would say if he found out his precious little girl was messing around with hyaline?"

"He'd probably send me to my room," Taly replied with a confident smirk. While hyaline, or dead crystal as it was more commonly called, was highly regulated by an almost absurdly extensive set of laws, she hadn't *technically* broken any of them. "After all, there's nothing that says I can't take a bunch of crystals that are just lying on the ground. How was I even supposed to know what they were? Without the proper tools, hyaline is almost indistinguishable from quartz. If questioned, I could easily argue that I'm innocent—a victim of my own ignorance."

Taly batted her eyelashes, and her voice was all sweetness and light when she continued, "I can't say the same for you, though. I mean, you did test the crystals for purity before you agreed to smuggle them to Ebondrift. And you're also the one that paid the crafters, both for their services and their silence. Face it, Josie. You're as culpable in this little joint venture as I am at this point. Maybe more so. Your threats are empty."

Josiah's low chuckle sounded like sandpaper scraping against stone. "You've got teeth, kid." He handed her the parcel. “I knew there was a reason I liked you.”

Taly took the package and quickly stuffed it into her pack. “By the way,” she whispered, eyeing the door to the main room nervously, “I heard a rumor someone was trying to get rid of some time crystals.”

Josiah’s eyes widened in surprise. “And now you’ve gone and lost it... I didn’t take you for stupid.”

Taly shrugged. “Last I heard, the Genesis Lords in the mortal realm were trying to gather up the remaining time crystals. If there were someone with a stash, they’d stand to make some good coin when the Aion Gate opens.”

“If they managed to survive that long,” Josiah muttered. “Especially with the Sanctorum in town. Those butchers are edgy—you can tell just by lookin’ at ‘em. I swear to the Shards, if they break the treaty and try to hunt in the mortal realm, we’ll find ourselves in a full-scale war. The High Lord of Water is just lookin’ for a reason to break ties with the Genesis Lords in Arylaan.”

“Yeah, well... I think that scenario seems unlikely,” Taly replied, her lips a thin line. “Unless the Sanctorum finds something new to hunt. There aren’t any time mages left—even in the mortal realm.”

“Even so, I draw the line at peddling time crystals,” Josiah grunted. And with that, the surly trader turned back to his wares.

Taking that as her signal to leave, Taly started to walk away, back towards the crowd in the main room. “Hey Taly,” Josiah called, just loud enough for her to hear above the noise trickling in from the doorway.

Taly turned back to the old trader, noting the unusual expression on his face. He almost looked… concerned? She didn't know the old man was capable of something so sentimental.

"Don't go gettin' mixed up in that time crystal shit. Hyaline is one thing, but time crystals? You ask the wrong person the wrong question… that's how people disappear."

Taly nodded in reply, pulling her hood up to hide her hair and face as she re-entered the main room. She didn't want to draw any unwanted attention with such precious cargo on her person. As she headed back towards the light of the early morning flooding in from the entrance, she gingerly fingered the brown package. A slow smile curled her lips, revealing the dimples in her cheeks.

"Happy birthday to me…" she sang, almost feeling optimistic.

Taly felt far more at ease once she managed to escape the Swap. Tipping her head back, she let the sun warm her face as she made her way back towards the main gates and the forest beyond.

Just when she was starting to relax, an unexpected hand clamped down on her shoulder, and she suddenly found herself pulled into a familiar embrace.

"Talya Caro, as I live and breathe. It's been

almost a month. I was starting to worry about you."

Smiling softly, Taly wrapped her arms around the woman and returned her embrace. Sarina Castaro was not put off easily, and truthfully, Taly was surprised she had managed to elude the persistent noblewoman for as long as she had.

"That's not my fault," Taly mumbled into the freshly laundered shoulder of her old governess' shirt. She smelled like soap and perfume, things that still made her think of bedtime stories and goodnight kisses. To Taly, Sarina would always smell like home. She closed her eyes and breathed in deeply before responding. "I've been where I've always been."

Sarina pulled back and studied the younger woman, her bright blue eyes shaded by a wide, floppy-brimmed hat. Highborn eyes could be disconcerting to those who weren't used to seeing the vivid, almost dreamlike colors. Their irises were surreal, like pure unadulterated pigment against a stark white canvas. Any hues that may have overlapped with mortals were so much more intense that it made human eyes look like mud in comparison.

Leaning down so she could look Taly in the eye, Sarina asked, "And where is that? Getting into trouble?"

Taly just shrugged, once again fiddling with the twine on the concealed package. She couldn't really deny it.

"Or perhaps" —the edges of Sarina's mouth lifted— "you've just been hiding in the back of Synna's cart this past month. Skye says he scented you out on the road today."

Taly blushed but kept her mouth shut. Sarina

had no proof other than Skye's stupid shadow senses.

The fey noblewoman shook her head disapprovingly, her copper curls bouncing around her. Then with a weary sigh, she gestured for them to continue down the street. "You are going to age me before my time, Miss Caro."

"Just doing my job," Taly said with a smile. "Besides, you're fey. Even at your age, I'll be old and gray long before you get your first wrinkle. *If* you get your first wrinkle. I have to level the playing field somehow."

"Fair enough, I suppose," Sarina replied, chuckling and throwing a familiar arm around Taly's shoulders as they walked side-by-side. "How is Jay treating you? Any better?"

Taly couldn't stop the groan that escaped her lips. "He needs to reconsider his definition of the words 'leftovers' and 'meals included with rent.'"

She felt Sarina tense beside her as the woman gave her shoulder a curious squeeze, feeling for her slight frame beneath the oversized coat. In a disapproving tone, she said, "I thought you looked thinner. I'll have to have a word with him."

"Please don't," Taly said as she pushed her hair out of her face. "I've already told you—this is my problem. I'll handle it on my own."

Sarina eyed her skeptically. "How many meals has that man given you in the past week? Including the rotten ones?"

Taly looked away, fidgeting with a lock of hair that had fallen across her eyes. "Laurel's been sick," she hedged, wincing when her stomach decided to protest, quite loudly, at that very moment. "Once she's back on her feet, Jay will go back behind the bar where he belongs, and the issue should resolve itself."

Sarina sighed, and the hand at Taly's shoulder gave another squeeze. "While I understand your need for independence, little one, this is a matter of public health. I've told Jay before, saving coin here and there is all well and good, but he's going to make someone sick with his 'leftovers.' If not you, then somebody else, and that simply won't do. So, until I can have another chat with him, why don't we try to get some meat back on those bones?"

Taly suddenly found herself steered off the dirt path towards a tiny food stand. This place was familiar. She'd visited it countless times as a child, and the owner, a kindly lowborn, always used to give her an extra dollop of frosting on her sweet rolls. Now, however, she avoided coming anywhere near the booth. The owner's son had taken over two months ago, and the young man ran a disdainful eye over Taly as Sarina pulled her over. The baker glanced pointedly at a sign hanging off to the side—bright, red letters sloppily spelled out "NO SHARDLESS."

"No, I couldn't." Taly raised her hands to protest as she pulled against Sarina's firm grip.

"Nonsense," Sarina argued, shooing away her complaint.

"Sarina," Taly mumbled through gritted teeth, trying to back away. "I can't be here."

Sarina stopped, her brow crinkling in confusion before her eyes alighted upon the sign. Sighing, she ran a motherly hand over Taly's hair before approaching the booth and shamelessly ripping the offensive notice off its tack and tearing it in two. A look of stark disapproval colored her delicate fey features as she stepped over to the counter and tossed the remains at the shopkeeper. The man wasn't yet 30, but he at least had the good sense to hang his head. There wasn't a person on the island that didn't know and respect Sarina. "I'll be speaking to your father about this," she said, honeyed venom lacing her words.

Taly felt a tightness in her chest release and give way as Sarina pulled her over to stand in front of the counter. Some of the loneliness that had settled deep inside her started to ease. Even though the way Taly had left the manor had been unintentionally abrupt, Sarina had never stopped fighting for her.

Sarina made a show of dusting off her hands before handing the flustered man two gold coins. He fumbled, dropping the coins and dipping behind the counter to pick them up as Sarina began stuffing several pieces of the most decadent, ripe fruit Taly had ever seen into a small burlap bag.

Handing Taly the sack, Sarina raised a perfectly manicured brow. "And did you really think I'd forgotten it was your birthday today?" A glazed sweet roll suddenly appeared in Taly's open palm.

Taly couldn't help but smile as she stared at the steaming pastry. She had expected her birthday to go by completely forgotten. As she accepted the bag, she did her best to school her expression into something that said, *You don't have to do this but thank you anyway, and I'm doing just fine.* Failing miserably, she settled for trying not to look too hungry as she took a bite of the roll. The delicious combination of butter and sugar burst onto her tongue, and she had to suppress a moan of pleasure. She'd always had a sweet tooth, especially when it came to pastries. "Thank you," she mumbled through a mouthful of bread.

Sarina laughed and gestured for them to continue. Taly chewed thoughtfully, savoring each bite of the sweet treat, as she allowed herself to be led down the street.

"You know," Sarina said quietly, interrupting her thoughts, "everyone misses you back at the manor. You could always come back—even just to visit."

Taly winced, the lie she'd repeatedly told herself and others slipping past her lips mechanically: "You know why I can't do that. You and Ivain were far kinder to me than you needed to be, but I'm still mortal. I'll start aging faster than you all very soon, and I need to establish my own life before that happens. Like I've said before, it's easier for everyone involved if I just completely cut—"

"Shards, I know," Sarina interrupted, waving her hand. "You've told me all this already. And while I still don't agree, I'm well aware that you're an adult now—even by fey standards—and you can do whatever you please. But my brother and I… we've lived on this island a long time. We knew the dangers of entangling our lives with mortals when we took you in."

"But Skye doesn't," Taly replied, swallowing her last bite of bread and licking away the remaining frosting from her fingertips. "At least, not in any *real* way."

Sarina looked at the younger woman sadly. "No. He's young and still very naïve in that respect. But in his defense, I don't think any of us truly know what it means to lose someone until it happens. All mortals die. Skye will eventually have to come to accept that."

Taly stopped and stared moodily at her feet. While the story she had fed Sarina didn't reveal her true motivations in leaving the manor, it still had some truth to it. Her mortality was a problem—one she felt acutely, if not for the reasons she had just stated. While she had always known that she would eventually outpace those closest to her—she would grow old while they stayed young—she had never realized just how differently fey society viewed her. A human. To most fey, she was little better than an animal, and after spending almost her entire life under the Marquess' protection, that had been a hard lesson.

Doing her best to ignore the sudden tremble in her hands, Taly finally mumbled, "I don't want to talk about this."

Sarina stood there for a long moment, hooking a finger underneath Taly's chin as she observed the younger woman quietly. Taly's cheeks burned, and her eyes felt oddly damp as she focused on the spattering of freckles on Sarina's nose, unable to look her directly in the eye. She had been on the receiving end of that furtive stare too many times, and though she had gotten much better at hiding her emotions over the past year, she knew Sarina would see right through her.

Finally, seemingly satisfied, Sarina waved her forward. "I have a job for you."

"What kind of job?" Taly muttered, wiping at her eyes discreetly and hoping that her voice sounded more confident than she felt.

Chuckling, Sarina replied, "I thought that might pique your interest. I have someone that needs to be escorted to the Aion Gate."

"What kind of someone?" Taly asked suspiciously as she followed Sarina around a corner. The evasive tone in her old governess' voice was all-too-familiar, and it immediately put Taly on edge.

"The kind that wants to go to the Aion Gate. It's been a tough year, and our regular guides have all been hired out. You know the area as well as anyone else, so I gave him your name." Taly eyed her skeptically, noting how Sarina had yet to tell her this mysterious someone's name. Seeing her dubious expression, Sarina added, "He's offering to pay you—and provide food and equipment. It's a good deal."

Taly absentmindedly chewed on a hangnail as she considered the offer. She could use the work. And while the Aion Gate was dangerous, it was less than a day's ride there and back.

It's fast coin.

Completely absorbed in her thoughts, she didn't notice when Sarina reached over and pushed her hand away from her mouth. She had always hated it when Taly chewed her nails. Looking at the woman in startled irritation, Taly asked, "What's the catch, Sarina?"

Sarina ignored her question. "I told him you'd want to speak with him before agreeing to take the job," she said with an evasive smile. "We're almost there, actually."

There's definitely a catch, Taly thought, fighting the urge to turn around and walk the other way.

They were nearing the southern edge of town now, and in the distance, a man paced back and forth restlessly.

Taly squinted her eyes against the bright

sunlight. She couldn't make out his face, but she could clearly see that his clothing was expensive. His blue waistcoat looked to be made of silk, and the clean white shirt underneath was crisp and pressed. He wore black, loosely fitted slacks, a style that was currently favored among the highborn gentry, and a navy greatcoat trimmed in gold trailed out behind him.

At least it looks like he has coin.

Something was off, though. The way he moved was familiar. The way he would scuff at the dirt with his heel. And how he kept running his hands through his hair—almost like a nervous tic? She'd seen it before.

The realization hit her hard.

"No." Taly stopped abruptly and glared at the traitorous woman beside her.

Unsympathetically, Sarina grabbed her shoulders and pushed her forward, paying no mind to the villagers that had to dodge out of the way. Leaning down to whisper in her ear, she said, "Think about it. Do you really have the luxury of saying 'no' right now?"

"I'm not sure if you heard, but we didn't exactly part on good terms the last time we spoke." Taly dug her heels in as Sarina continued to push her forward. That was, perhaps, a bit of an understatement. Skye had tracked her down just a few weeks after she had left the manor, and the exchange had become… heated. They had both screamed some things in anger that could never be unsaid.

"I'm sure it won't be that bad," the older woman replied airily. Even though she didn't have shadow magic, Sarina was still highborn and, therefore, far stronger than even the strongest mortals. She easily rebuffed the younger woman's struggles.

Taly leaned back, trying to use her weight to slow down their progress. "I don't know. 'Fine. Die for all I care. I never want to see you again,' seems like a pretty straightforward way to wash your hands of someone."

She felt Sarina pause behind her and used that as an opportunity to push back. She actually managed to gain a foot or two before Sarina renewed her efforts. "Hmmm. He left that part out."

"Yeah? I'm not surprised. In light of this new information, I think it's clear why you should just let me slink off into cowardly anonymity. If you think about it, it's really best for everyone involved." Taly, to her great dismay, was still losing ground.

"It's for your own good," was all Sarina said before giving her a hard shove.

Taly released a muted squeak as she stumbled forward. Trying but ultimately failing to find her footing, she started to fall, helplessly flailing as the ground rushed up to meet her. But instead of finding herself face-down in the dirt, her cheek collided with soft linen. Her eyes scrunched tight, and she braced herself. It seemed today was a day for reunions.

"Hi Skye," she mumbled, her voice muffled in the fabric of his shirt. Taly made a mental note not to trust Sarina anymore. Not only had the older woman gone back on her promise not to interfere in her life, she had just tossed her and walked away. From the corner of her eye, Taly could see Sarina's retreating form disappear around a corner.

"Hey there, stranger," Skye said softly. His fingers flexed in the fabric of her coat, steadying her, and for a moment she thought he was going to embrace her. She felt a small pang of disappointment when he didn't.

When she finally found her feet and pulled away, irritation quickly took the place of disappointment. He looked exactly the same. The same vibrant green eyes. The same lanky, muscled frame. The same pale, flawless skin. Sure, his hair was a little longer, but the dark locks were still just as tousled and unruly as she remembered.

Jerk, she thought petulantly. Really, how was it fair that he looked just as he did the last time they spoke while she probably more closely resembled a half-drowned alley cat than she did a human girl at this point?

Okay, Caro. Just remember—this man is not your friend anymore. Taly forced herself to take a step back. She didn't miss the flicker of pain that flashed across his face. In a blink, it was gone, leaving her to wonder if she'd imagined it.

"So, I see you're still alive," Skye teased, breaking the awkward silence.

He shifted his weight as he ran a hand through his dark hair, revealing the delicate, sharpened point of his ear—as if she needed to be reminded of his parentage. His every feature, his every movement *screamed* highborn. This small group of ruling-class nobility could trace their lineage all the way back to the Faera—the long-dead gods from which all fey were said to be descended. All of the most powerful magic users in this and all other known worlds were highborn. And Skye, known at the Dawn Court as Lord Skylen Emrys, was the heir to one of the oldest, most powerful families on the fey mainland—House Ghislain.

Shoving her hands into the pockets of her jacket, Taly scuffed the dirt at her feet. "Try not to sound so surprised."

Skye laughed, easy and relaxed, and a fond smile curved his lips. "I'm not surprised. You were always a lot tougher than you looked." Hesitating, his expression sobered. "And I'm sorry about the things I said the last time we spoke. I was out of line, and... I didn't mean any of it. I was worried about you, and I just wanted you to come home." He shrugged and hung his head sheepishly. "You know how my mouth gets away from me sometimes."

Taly huffed and pursed her lips. She didn't know what to do with that. He wasn't supposed to apologize. Seriously, since when did he apologize? She held up a hand and opened her mouth, hoping the words would come to her, but nothing came out. She tried again. Still nothing. Closing her mouth with a click of her teeth and letting her hand drop, she gave an exasperated sigh.

And that's when she saw it—that telltale smirk she knew all too well. He managed to quickly school his expression, but not before she'd already seen through his act.

That asshole! He had always known how to get under her skin and leave her floundering. He wasn't sorry about what he said. He just wanted to fluster her. Scowling, Taly muttered, "Yeah, well. Mind telling me why you and Sarina decided to ambush me this morning?"

"Ivain has a job for you."

"I don't want it," Taly said abruptly, turning on her heel.

She heard Skye jog after her, so she quickened her pace. He could catch her easily if he had a mind to, but hopefully, he would take the hint and go away.

A hand reached out and grabbed her arm, and she instinctively twisted her body and drew her blade in a single, fluid motion. By the time she had managed to process the situation, her knife was already pressed against Skye's stomach.

His eyes widened slightly in surprise. "Put that thing away before you hurt yourself," he said, his voice low.

Clenching her teeth, Taly deftly flicked her blade, cutting off one of the gold buttons on his waistcoat and catching it in the palm of her hand. She promptly flung it at his face. "You shouldn't sneak up on people." Once again, she turned to leave.

"Would you just wait?" he called after her, frowning as he pulled at the loose threads on his coat. He sounded more desperate this time. "You don't even know what the job is."

Taly rounded on him. "You want me to take you to the Aion Gate. Sarina already made the pitch, and since I'm not really in the mood to take on any guide work at the moment, that doesn't leave us much to talk about. Now, if you'll excuse me, I think we're done here." She really shouldn't have enjoyed how out of sorts he looked. He was almost pouting.

Taly turned to leave again, but he wasn't done quite yet.

"Would you just come to the manor and talk about it? I promise it's official Gate Watcher business, and Ivain is willing to pay you good money." When she paused, he added, "Please,

Taly. We're in a tough spot. Ivain and I haven't been to the Aion Gate since the last time it opened—almost five years now—and you know how unreliable the roads on the northern part of the island can be. We need a guide, and Sarina says that you've been making the trip pretty regularly."

"I don't think it's a good idea, Skye." Taly kept her back to him but made no further movement to leave.

He sighed and stared at his feet. "It's your birthday, right? Just come to the house. I'm sure Eliza would make lamb and noodles for dinner. The kind with cream and garlic. Your favorite."

Taly remained silent. Despite the melancholy and loneliness that still burned deep in her belly, it wasn't really her birthday—just a random day they had chosen to celebrate every year. Since she couldn't remember anything from before the fire, she didn't know when her "real" birthday was. Still, real or not, she couldn't deny that it might feel good not to spend the day alone. And it had been a lean month. If there really was a job, she could use the coin.

No! the rational part of her mind screamed. *No, no, no…*

Going back to the manor just wasn't a good idea. She had worked too hard trying to separate herself from her old life to walk right back into it. She needed to walk away. And she would.

Any minute now.

Skye took a step towards her, slowly rounding on her like he would a wounded animal. "You can take a bath. We have hot water." He watched her closely and smiled when he saw her lips quirk. He had her attention, and he knew it. Bending at the waist, he caught her eye. "Remember how Ivain had the fire and water crystals in your bathroom replaced? You could run enough hot water to last a week. I think Sarina even has some of that fanged rose oil you used to like so much."

Taly bounced on her heels, conflicted. She couldn't remember the last time she'd been able to take a proper bath. And hot water would feel so nice right about now. Especially since she was still soaked through and shivering.

Damn wyverns. If she wasn't careful, she would end up getting sick. That would make earning coin even more difficult.

Taly growled and kicked at the dirt. "Okay. Fine. But just to be clear. I'm in this for the coin. *And* the hot water, but mostly the coin." She shook her head. She was getting distracted. "I'll listen to the pitch, but I can't waste all day there. I've got other things I need to do today."

"Understood." Skye smiled, standing to his full height.

He offered her his arm, but she pointedly ignored him as she marched ahead. She was irritated, and she wanted him to know it. True, most of her irritation was directed at herself for giving in so easily, but he didn't need to know that.

Skye blew out a slow breath and watched her despondently. After a moment, he jogged to catch up, falling into step beside her as they walked towards the manor. He didn't press her to speak, and when Taly glared up at him, he just grinned and shrugged. It seemed he was wise enough to keep his mouth shut now that she had agreed to accompany him.

As they approached the city gate, Taly spotted a flash of gold in her peripheral vision. Her heart began to race, beating a deafening rhythm in her ears, but she didn't dare turn her head to look. Out of the corner of her eye, she could make out the ghostly golden forms of a family walking past them as they made their way into the village. They were ethereal, almost translucent, but no one on the street reacted to their sudden appearance. The villagers went on about their day, completely unaware.

Moments later, a barghest appeared on the road, pulling at its master's leash. The dog and its owner unknowingly barreled through the spectral procession. The golden haze stuttered for a moment but then reformed around the disturbance, the edges of the strange hallucination even more defined than before.

Closing her eyes, Taly took a deep breath, willing the vision to disappear. *Please, please go away. I don't need to deal with this right now.* She swallowed past a lump in her throat, silently pleading with whoever might be listening. When she opened her eyes again, she was relieved to find nothing out of the ordinary.

Skye nodded his head in greeting as they passed a farmer and his young family coming in through the gate, turning when a loud peal of childish laughter pierced the air. Taly didn't have to look back to know that the little boy sandwiched between his parents had run ahead to pet the barghest as it waited on its master at a nearby fruit stand or that the gentle beast had proceeded to cover the child in slobber. She had already seen the scene play out in its entirety only moments before.

I hope this isn't a mistake, she thought, staring straight ahead as they turned down the road that would lead them to Harbor Manor.

CHAPTER 3

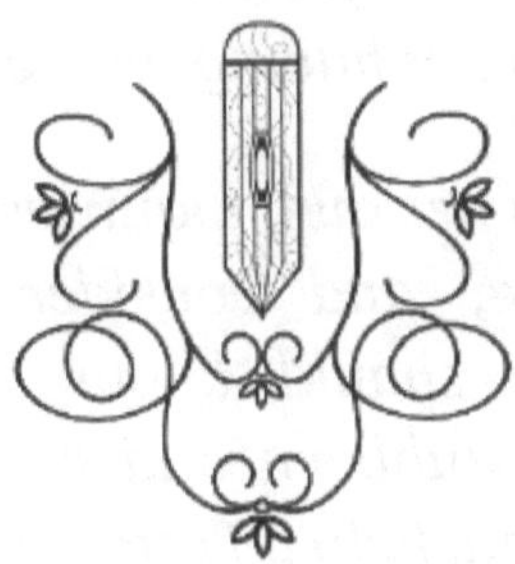

-From the personal notes of Ivain Castaro, Marquess of Tempris

The 32nd day of the month Meridian, during the 250th year of the Empty Throne

It's been a long time since I took the time to write down my thoughts, but today is one of the worst days I can recall in recent memory. Taly, my little one, is gone. She ran away during the night while everyone was asleep.

I've always known that she would want to assert her independence one day. Human lives are so fleeting, and they leave their families so young, so much sooner than any fey could ever dream of sending away a youngling. I knew that when we took her in. I knew and yet now that the moment is here—I wish we'd had more time.

We are all devastated, but Skye is taking her departure the hardest. He believes that the incident in the training yard yesterday afternoon is to blame and set out to find her. Those two have always had a very special bond, ever since we first brought Taly back to the manor. I fear he may have a difficult time adjusting to not having her here.

Sarina is making her own inquiries into where Taly may have gone, and considering my sister's connections, we should know something soon. Though Taly is stubborn and headstrong—would probably refuse my help if I offered outright—I have no intention of letting her leave my care completely unaided.

Skye let out a sigh of relief as he watched Taly march ahead of him. He'd done it. He'd actually managed to sweet-talk the little hothead into coming back to the manor. When Sarina had suggested he hire Taly as a guide, he'd thought she'd finally lost her mind. And when she still insisted on going through with her plan even after Taly had hidden underneath a tarp just to avoid talking to him, he'd thought the noblewoman was just in denial—too stubborn to accept the fact that the two children she raised together were no longer friends. However, not for the first time, he realized he needed to stop doubting his old governess' schemes.

Falling into step beside her, Skye eyed the girl walking next to him nervously. Taly was clearly irritated with him, but that wasn't anything new. When they were growing up, she was always mad at him for one reason or another. And to be fair, he had usually done something to deserve her ire.

He shouldn't have goaded her today—that was on him. Granted, his apology for what he said all those months ago was completely sincere. When she had first left the manor—no explanations, no goodbyes—he had said some things that he truly regretted when he finally managed to track her down. She had refused to come with him, and he had not taken it well. Still, his own remorse aside, that didn't mean he hadn't enjoyed seeing her get flustered when he took away her reason to be mad at him before her anger was completely spent.

"So," Skye said, plastering on a smile as they turned onto Harbor Manor's private drive. Taly walked beside him, her hands stuffed in the pockets of an oversized coat that made her look far younger than her 21 years. "How have you been?"

"Fine," she replied in a clipped tone.

"That's good," he said, unfazed by her surly attitude. At this point in their relationship, he was well acquainted with her moods. "I heard you took up salvaging. How's that working out for you?"

"Great." Again, she kept her eyes trained on the road ahead, and her voice held a note of irritation.

Skye's smile faltered, but he quickly recovered. "Good to hear." When she still showed no indication that she was going to pick up the thread of the conversation, he tried again. "I tried writing to you at Jay and Laurel's tavern, but my letters got sent back. Did you move? Where are you living now?"

"Nowhere," she said immediately, still refusing to look at him.

"Really?" Skye exclaimed with feigned enthusiasm. He smiled when he saw her start in surprise. "What a coincidence! I *love* Nowhere. My family has business dealings with the Noones—lovely people, by the way—so I visit all the time. There's this little bakery at the corner of None of Your Business and Uncomfortable, Stony Silence that sells the best pie. I really think you'd love it."

He thought he saw the corners of Taly's mouth twitch, but he also could've been imagining it. Her posture remained stiff and tense, and she continued to stare straight ahead, pretending to ignore him.

Kicking at a rock on the side of the road, Skye sighed as he pulled at the lapels of his greatcoat. They were approaching the outer edge of the manor grounds, and tiny bell-shaped blooms blanketed either side of the gravel road. Though it was a little late in the season for snowdrops, it seemed even the manor itself was trying to thaw the girl's icy demeanor. Taly had always had a special appreciation for the little flower. For years, Sarina helped her plant countless bulbs at the first signs of spring, and they had eventually enlisted Skye's help as well. As time passed, the snowy blossoms had completely taken over the surrounding area.

Looking down at his silent companion, Skye felt a twinge of irritation. Maybe he'd been wrong earlier. Maybe the little brat did need goading. After all, if she wasn't going to make any effort at playing nice, why should he?

"You're not in the talking mood. I get it," Skye said, waving a hand. "That's no problem. Since it's been a while since we've gotten a chance to catch up, why don't I tell you about everything that's happened at the manor since you've been gone?"

Taly huffed as she finally turned to glare up at him through narrowed eyes.

"I'll take that as a yes!" Skye proclaimed enthusiastically. "Let's see... where to start? Sarina took up knitting a few months ago. That's been interesting. There's yarn everywhere now. I know you were always a bit allergic to wool, so watch out for that. And then... oh, shit! Oh no..." Skye brought a hand up to cover his smile when he saw Taly glance over at him before whipping her head back around to stare at the road. "I just remembered. Our hot water went out this morning."

Although Taly's expression remained stoic, she couldn't fool Skye. He had been using his magic to read her reactions since they were children. While most shadow mages liked to channel their aether in order to increase their stamina, speed, or strength, Ivain had taught him that aether augmentation could be an even more effective tool when wielded with a slightly subtler hand.

Skye bit back a sharp bark of laughter when his magically enhanced ears picked up a sudden spike in her heart rate. *That got her attention*, he thought, making a show of clearing his throat as he tried to suppress another chuckle. If there was one thing that Taly Caro felt strongly about, it was hot water.

Skye rubbed the back of his neck sheepishly. "Yeah... sorry. I probably should've mentioned that before. There was an aether surge this morning, and it overloaded the shadow crystals powering the primary water heater. There's no hot water at all, and the plumber that came out said it would be *at least* two weeks until he could get around to replacing the shadow crystals in the damaged circuit."

"You're lying," Taly muttered. "You and Ivain are both shadow mages. Either one of you could fix it."

Skye did his best to suppress the wide grin he could feel tugging at the corners of his mouth. At least she was talking to him now. "True, but we're both *so* busy right now with the Gate Watchers—what with the Aion Gate connection and everything that goes along with it. This is my first charging cycle acting as a full-fledged Watcher, and I've got so much... *stuff* that I need to do. And don't get me started on the things. Shards, the things! And then after the things, more stuff." Skye peeked at Taly from the corner of his eye, noting the way she fidgeted with the sleeve of her coat. She was agitated now.

"Let's see, what else?" Skye tilted his head and then snapped his fingers. "Oh! Your room. You might notice a few changes. I was getting tired of having to go *all the way* out to the workshop when I needed to work on something, so I converted it into a secondary crafting space. I mean, you weren't using it anymore, and it was right across the hall."

"Sounds reasonable," Taly ground out through clenched teeth.

"I was hoping you would say that," Skye said with an exaggerated sigh of relief. To his growing amusement, he could see that one of her eyes had started to twitch. "I'm actually really excited for you to see what I did with your bed. It's a weapon rack now. When I started the project, Ivain said that you still needed to be able to use the room in case you wanted to stay the night. So, here's what I did—the rack folds down into a bed. Genius, right? Granted, I'm still working out some of the kinks. For example, you might feel something poking you in the back if you try to lie down. If that happens, don't worry about it. That's a known issue."

Skye scratched the back of his head. "No... actually, on second thought, you probably should worry. Because it might be a dagger. Or a sword. And Shards, you humans are so fragile. One cut, and you just bleed all over the place."

Taly's hands fisted at her sides, and she opened her mouth to say something before thinking better of it.

"*You* especially," Skye continued. "I mean, you were always kind of small, but now? I'm starting to think you moved out just so you could go on a diet. I think you even lost height. Yeah... you're definitely shorter." He held out a hand just above her head, laughing when she slapped it away. Taly had always been self-conscious about her height. Even when she was stretching, she barely came up to his chin. "I guess that means we won't be sparring anymore. You're just too... what's the word? Dainty? Yes, *dainty* is a word I would use to describe you now."

Taly let out a frustrated growl before muttering under her breath, "No, he's not worth it." Skye was pretty sure he wasn't supposed to hear that, but, oh well. It's not like she wasn't well aware of how aether augmentation worked.

Skye tilted his head as he pretended to consider something. "That might explain why Sarina has been shopping so much lately. Just the other day, she was telling me that she was just *dying* to get you into a ballgown. I know you used to hate formal wear, but I really think satin and lace will suit you much better now. You know, because you're so *dainty*. And delicate. Yes! *Delicate* and *dainty*—that describes you perfectly now."

Taly's cheeks were starting to get red. When she blew at a piece of hair that had fallen into her face, Skye's eyes were once again drawn to the tangled mop that curled around her shoulders. Truthfully, he had been a bit startled when he saw that she'd cut her hair. For as long as he'd known her, she had kept it long, either falling in loose waves down her back or pulled back into a tight plait. Now, the short, flaxen strands stuck out in a style that strangely suited her.

Unable to resist the urge, he tugged on an errant lock. "I don't know what Sarina is going to do with this mess, though. Did you cut it yourself or something?"

Taly's face scrunched up, and she rounded on him. "Shards! Shut up! Shut up! Shut up!" she cried as she started punching and shoving him. "You're a jerk!"

"Finally!" Laughter bubbled up out of his chest as he fended off her assault. "I was starting to think I'd picked up the wrong girl!"

"I am *not* dainty!" Taly let out another scream as Skye grabbed her fists.

"I'm sorry," he managed to gasp before he doubled over.

"No, you're not!" Taly stumbled when he let go of her fists, and the look of embarrassed outrage painted across her expression before she started trying to pummel him again just made him laugh harder.

"I am! I swear I am," he howled, the tears streaming down his face somewhat belying his words. "I'm sorry!"

"Liar!"

"Okay. Okay!" Standing to his full height, Skye held his hands out in supplication. Taly's eyes were wide, her cheeks flushed, but she backed off slightly when she saw that his laughter was starting to die down. "You're right," he conceded, a devilish smirk curling his lips. "I'm not sorry. Not even a little bit. You're just so *dainty* now! It's adorable!"

With an indignant cry, Taly renewed her efforts, sending Skye straight into another fit of uncontrollable laughter. After letting her get in a few good hits, he easily seized her wrists in one hand and wrapped an arm around her waist, pulling her in close so she couldn't kick at him. She continued to struggle for a few moments, each trailing chuckle that rumbled through his chest fanning the flames of her ire.

When she finally started to quiet down, he loosened his grip and released her fists. Her shoulders were still heaving from the exertion, but she made no move to push him away.

"Hi," he whispered, already moving to give her some space. But before he could step away, she gave an unexpected sigh of defeat and wrapped her arms around his waist.

"Hi," she said, burying her face in the crook of his neck.

Skye's chest felt uncomfortably tight as he folded his arms around her tiny frame, the feeling growing stronger when she gave another soft sigh and relaxed into him. She didn't speak, and neither did he, and for a little while, it was easy enough to pretend that everything was still okay.

"Quick question," he said when he felt her start to pull away. He waited for her to look up before giving her damp hair a playful tug. "Why are you wet?"

Taly shoved him as she stepped back. "That's a long story," she said with the ghost of a smile. Staring out over the sea of white blossoms blanketing the side of the road, she toyed with the pendant around her neck and scuffed the dirt with the toe of her boot. When she spoke, her voice held an edge of uncertainty. "That stuff about the hot water wasn't really true, was it?"

That prompted another fit of laughter from Skye, made worse when she huffed and started walking ahead of him. "Taly, wait!" He started jogging after her, still chuckling. "It's not true. None of it," he said as he fell into step beside her. Shrugging off his greatcoat, he draped the heavy garment around her shoulders. Something inside him sighed in relief when she reached out and pulled the small peace offering more tightly around her. "Except for the part about Sarina shopping. She's always had a problem, but it's been a lot worse lately. I have no idea why."

He saw her trying to fight it, but despite her best effort to maintain a neutral expression, her lips began to quirk to the side. She let out a frustrated sigh, chewing on her bottom lip as the corners of her mouth continued to twitch.

"Don't do it," Skye whispered loudly. "Don't laugh. You know it just encourages me."

A muted snort escaped, followed by a giggle. Looking up, Taly finally gave him a real smile. "You're an ass," she said with a shake of her head.

"Thank you," Skye replied automatically, a

wide grin splitting his face. This was more like it—more like them.

Eventually, they came upon Harbor Manor itself. It was a sprawling stone structure, built when the Time Queen was still in residence on the island—a monument to an era of splendor that had long since passed. Thanks to the Marquess, the home had been kept in good condition. The gray stone facade was regularly repaired, and ivy crawled across the exterior. Ivain had given up long ago trying to contain the plant's chaotic sprawl, and now the willful creeper was as much a part of the manor as the blanket of snowdrops that covered the front lawn.

As they ascended the gray-stone staircase, a tall, lanky man rushed down to meet them.

Ivain Castaro, the Marquess of Tempris, had lived on the island for over 700 years—ever since he bought Harbor Manor as a wedding gift for his late wife. He was at this point in his career one of the most renowned shadow mages in the fey world, and it was for this reason that Skye had been sent to train with him when he was only nine years old.

Laughter bubbled up out of the fey noble's throat as he took the stairs two at a time, and his hands raked through a shock of blonde hair so bright it was almost white. His high forehead only served to accentuate his long, slender face, and despite his highborn heritage and the nearly eternal youth that it granted, lines forged from a countless number of gentle smiles creased his skin.

"There she is!" he called out in the cultured accent of the mainland fey. "My little one has finally come home!"

Ivain embraced Taly, picking her up and

twirling her around before depositing her back on the ground. Holding her out at arm's length, he appraised her with a critical eye, no doubt noting the way she still shivered beneath Skye's greatcoat. His nostrils flared, and his eyes flicked down to the bloody tear in the leg of her trousers. It wasn't the only bloodstain that peppered the worn and faded garment.

"Hello, sire," Taly said, her tone uncharacteristically formal.

"Sire? Since when do *you* call me sire?" he questioned with a scowl. Taly bowed her head out of habit. Though the Marquess was a kind man, he had learned by now how to cow his mischievous wards with just a look. Skye still squirmed just thinking about being on the receiving end of that stark, blue gaze.

After a long moment, the Marquess' stern façade cracked, and he affectionately ruffled Taly's wild hair. "I jest. I jest. Shards, you are skin and bones, little one. We're going to have to fatten you up. Tell me, Skye—did you manage to convince her to stay for dinner?"

Taly opened her mouth to reply, but Skye cut her off. "She said she had other matters to attend to, so I wouldn't want to presume." He bumped her shoulder and gave her a smirk as he moved to stand next to the taller man.

"I see." Leaning down to look Taly in the eye, Ivain whispered conspiratorially, "I approve. You shouldn't make things too easy for him."

Skye snorted. "When has she ever made anything easy?"

Taly smiled serenely. "I've always told you, Skye. You'd have a much easier time if you just stopped arguing back."

Ivain laughed loudly as he reached over and slapped Skye on the shoulder. "Truer words were never spoken! Skye, my boy—take that advice to heart. You really will be happier when you learn to stop arguing with the women in your life." Smoothing back a lock of wispy, white-blonde hair, Ivain announced, "Well, I need to get back to work if I'm going to be able to take this evening off, so I'll leave you to convince her, boy."

Turning to Taly, the Marquess ducked down to look her in the eye. "Just in case, I've already instructed Eliza to prepare lamb and noodles tonight. Still your favorite, I hope. And even though I told her that you wouldn't want her to make a big fuss, our Eliza *insisted* on making a sugarberry pie. The kind with the candied walnuts on top. I believe I also saw her making brown sugar ice cream this morning. Apparently, 21 is supposed to be something of a milestone for young mortals, and she would not be deterred. *Not* that you should let that influence your decision. No. You have your own life now, and we respect that."

Ivain made to leave but briefly turned to add, "*Although,* Eliza did have to go all the way to the mainland to find sugarberries that were in season. Poor dear—she's had a terrible time this past winter. She's just now getting back on her feet after a nasty case of dowsing fatigue, but she simply would not listen to reason. It had to be sugarberries because that was the little one's favorite."

Skye laughed at the retreating noble, chancing a glance at Taly. She didn't seem pleased.

"I'm starting to think I should've just walked the other way," she said, her nose scrunched up like she was trying to figure something out. "Shards, that's low. Fine. I'll stay for dinner, but only because there's pie. You guys know how I feel about pie."

As he turned to follow her inside, Skye added sheepishly, "I swear, there really is a job."

"Skye! Come in here," Ivain called as Skye passed by the open door of his study.

Skye's footsteps creaked as he walked across the wooden floor. While Harbor Manor couldn't compare with the grandeur of his family's estate in Ghislain, it was far more comfortable. Homey. Whenever he was forced to visit his family on the mainland (twice a year, every year), he always found himself craving the warmth that seemed to emanate from the very stones of the aged mansion. He wasn't looking forward to the day when he would be expected to take up permanent residence on the mainland as his role as future Duke of Ghislain would eventually require of him.

The Marquess stood near the back of the study, a fire crackling merrily in the great stone hearth beside him. He set down the book in his hand, turning to face Skye. "Where's Taly? I didn't think you would let her out of your sight now that you finally managed to drag her back here."

"She's taking a bath. It seems she still has a weakness for bubbles and hot water," Skye replied with a smirk, coming over to stand beside his mentor. "And I have an aversion to being punched, so I let her be."

"It's good to have her back," Ivain said with a sigh. "This old place seems so empty without the two of you screaming back and forth at each other from across the hall."

"Yes, but she won't stay. She's out to prove something." Skye frowned, staring moodily into the fire. "Whatever that may be."

"I know. I didn't expect her to come back for good," Ivain said with a chuckle. "We might not like it, but Taly has her own path to follow. The only thing we can do is step aside and offer our assistance when she needs it. At least that's what Sarina keeps telling me. My little sister is generally right about these sorts of things."

"Yeah, Sarina has told me that too. 'Let Taly find her own way,' and so on," Skye grumbled irritably. "The only way Taly's going to find is her way into an early grave. Did Sarina tell you she took up salvaging? *Salvaging,* of all things. It's like she's trying to get herself killed."

"Oh, I know," Ivain said, placing a comforting hand on Skye's shoulder. "That little detail did not escape me either. But you and I both know that if you try to dissuade Taly from something she's set her mind to, you'll just end up pushing her further away."

When Skye remained silent, Ivain continued with a faint note of sadness, "Besides, whether you choose to believe what she's told Sarina concerning her reasons for leaving or not, the fact of that matter is that Taly is not like us. She's mortal, and a little distance will ease the inevitable pain that always comes with those associations. We may not like it, but humans die, Skylen."

"We both know there are ways around that," Skye said, giving Ivain a pointed look.

"True, but she would never consent to joining the Feseraa," the older man replied, his mouth set in a grim line. "And to be frank, that's not the life that I want for her."

"But it's just 50 years," Skye argued stubbornly. "50 years of breeding services in exchange for immortality."

"I understand," Ivain conceded in a measured tone, "but even if the breeding term is only temporary, her children would be taken from her arms as soon as they're born, and she'd be passed around from noble to noble like some broodmare. I don't want that for her, and neither do you."

Skye stuffed his hands into his pockets. "It wouldn't have to be like that. My mother has already offered to buy the full term of Taly's contract, and she's given me her assurances that Taly wouldn't be forced to uphold the breeding requirements. The contract would just be a way to bring her under the protection of my family. Taly would be safe, she would be respected, and most importantly, she wouldn't have to grow old and die. That bullshit she fed Sarina about trying to get some distance before she starts aging would be moot."

Ivain hesitated but then shook his head. "I can't say that the same idea hasn't crossed my mind a time or two this past year—execute a sham breeding contract purely as a means to receive the necessary authorizations required to perform the Rites of the Imorati and grant her immortality. But I still don't like it. The Feseraa have far more rights and privileges now than they did before the

Schism, but that might not last. Anti-mortal sentiment has been on the rise lately. If the situation continues to sour, at least Taly, as a human, still has the option to retreat to the mortal realm. As a Feseraa, she wouldn't be able to survive in an aetherless environment. She would be trapped here."

Skye blew out a sharp breath. As much as he hated to admit it, the older fey noble made some valid points. And it was for those very same reasons that he kept telling his mother "no" whenever she broached the subject. Clearing his throat, he asked, "Was there a reason you called me in here?"

"Ah yes!" the Marquess exclaimed. "Has Taly accepted the job yet?"

Skye barked out a laugh. "What do you think?"

"I see," Ivain said tiredly, drumming his fingers on the mantle. "That's a *no*, then."

"You know, it doesn't help that she probably thinks the job was just a ruse to get her here. You and I never go to the Aion Gate this far out from the actual bridging date."

Ivain sighed and ran a hand across the stubble on his chin. "I am, *perhaps*, being overly cautious, but I just can't shake this feeling that something's off. I'd feel much better if you went and confirmed the last set of readings the Gate Watchers sent us."

"The readings looked fine to me, but I'll go where you tell me," Skye conceded easily. "With or without Taly, I'll make do."

"Taly *will* agree," Ivain insisted. "Just keep at her. I don't care how much coin it takes—make sure she takes the job. If this works out, I'm hoping to offer her a permanent position. Guides are just going to become more and more scarce the closer we get to the bridging date. True—Taly is young and inexperienced, but Sarina assures me that our little one knows her way around the island. With a little training and the right resources, she could be far more skilled than any guide for hire—a valuable addition to the manor staff."

"Wait." Skye arched a suspicious brow, chuckling softly when the Marquess feigned confusion. "As part of the manor staff, wouldn't she need to move onto the main property?"

Ivain shrugged. "Yes, that would be the most convenient arrangement. And since she's been very clear that she no longer wishes to reside within the main house, there just happens to be a little cottage on the eastern edge of the estate I think she would like—very secluded but still inside the manor's wards. As luck would have it, I've just had it freshened up."

Skye turned away from the fire and stepped over to the large oaken desk stuffed into the far corner of the room. Picking through a stack of papers, he asked, "This wouldn't have anything to do with those three mortal girls that went missing last week, would it?"

Ivain's face was impassive as he stared into the fire. After a long moment, he said, "Tempris is always a much more dangerous place when the Aion Gate is charging, but I'd be lying if I said that it didn't seem worse this cycle. The number of missing person reports that have crossed my desk this year is... troubling. Especially considering how many of them have been either mortal or magicless. I know my sister keeps a close eye on our little one, but I'd feel much better if Taly moved closer to the manor."

"What happened to *'humans die,'* and *'a little distance will ease the inevitable pain that comes with those associations?'* Hmm?" Skye glanced at Ivain from the corner of his eye. "C'mon, which is it, old man?"

Ivain pulled away from the fire, scratching at the back of his neck as he came to stand next to Skye. "The cottage is all the way over on the eastern side of the property—how much more distance do you want?"

A rumbling peal of laughter erupted from the older fey's throat, and he clapped a hand on Skye's shoulder. "Now then, come along, boy," he said as he ushered Skye towards the door. "Go get ready for dinner. This is the first time our little family has been together for a very long time, and Sarina will want you looking presentable."

With that, the door to the study closed behind him with a soft click. Skye smiled as he headed towards the stairs that would lead to his quarters on the fourth floor. It seemed Sarina wasn't the only Castaro sibling playing games.

As he approached his bedroom door, he heard another voice calling out to him. "Skylen Emrys! Get in here!"

Skye grinned. It looked like he had already managed to piss Taly off. At least he hadn't lost his touch.

"How may I be of service, Miss Caro?" he asked, walking into the spacious suite just across the hall.

Unlike his quarters, which had been outfitted in dark, masculine hues of green and brown, Taly's personal apartment was all air and light. Draped in varying shades of blue and cream, it was like walking inside a cloud. The last of the evening light was streaming through a nearby bay window, casting shadows across the various pieces of mortal tech that lay scattered across every available surface. For as long as he could remember, Taly had always been fascinated by anything that came from the mortal realm, and though Sarina had tried, the noblewoman had never been able to get the girl to stop tinkering with the random bits of junk she would sometimes find at the Swap. As a result, Skye had taken to calling her "Tinker," and then eventually just "Tink."

Taly was sitting at an ornately carved wooden vanity, and their former nanny and teacher stood behind the fuming girl, trying to tame her rebellious mop of hair with a brush and a pair of scissors. It seemed Sarina still hadn't given up on trying to turn her into a proper lady.

"Sarina? Any idea what I've done now?" Skye gave the auburn-haired noblewoman a pleading look.

Sarina, smiling coyly, replied, "I believe you forgot to mention our visitors."

"Oh." Skye did his best to maintain a neutral expression. When it came to managing Taly's ire, it was important never to show any signs of weakness.

Taly whipped around to glower at him. "Yes '*oh.*' Aimee barged in here while I was bathing. She didn't even knock."

Of course, she did, Skye thought, suppressing a groan. Aimee Bryer, Ivain and Sarina's great-grandniece, was the heir to a lesser barony on the fey mainland and had been visiting Harbor Manor every year since Skye had turned 20. Even though it seemed like it had been far, far longer since he'd first met the prissy noblewoman, this would only be the fifth time that Skye had been forced to endure her presence at the manor.

Studiously ignoring the places where Taly's white shift had become slightly transparent underneath her damp hair, Skye muttered, "Well, Aimee always did like your room better than the guest quarters."

Skye sheepishly rubbed the back of his neck when he heard Taly scoff. That was, perhaps, a bit of an understatement. Less than an hour after being introduced for the first time, Aimee had tried to have Taly evicted from her own room, arguing that a "mortal pet" shouldn't have nicer quarters than a fey noblewoman. That, of course, hadn't sat well with Skye. Or Sarina. Or Ivain—who had promptly shown Aimee back to the guest wing.

"Don't worry," Skye said smoothly, doing his best to mollify the irate girl. "Even if you hadn't come to dinner, we wouldn't have let her use the room. It's still yours."

"That's not the point," Taly replied, glancing at Skye over her shoulder. Her scowl deepened.

"*Talya*, if you don't stop squirming, I'm going to cut an ear off. And it might not be accidental." Sarina placed a firm hand on the top of Taly's head and twisted her back around to face the mirror.

Taly stared at Skye's reflection, her arms crossed. "Why didn't you tell me that Aimee was coming to visit so much later this year? She and Aiden usually come at the end of Yule."

"Because then you wouldn't have come. Can you blame me for trying to increase my odds?" Taly's eyes narrowed, but she remained silent.

"And besides," he said, trying to look contrite, "she and Aiden just arrived this afternoon. They'll probably be too tired to come down for dinner. I doubt you'll have to see her again."

That seemed to somewhat abate her fury. *Somewhat* being the operative word. Taly was still scowling, but at least it was no longer at him. Deciding to keep his mouth shut while he was ahead, Skye wandered into the adjoining room, absentmindedly inspecting the random collection of disassembled mortal tech that lay scattered across the surface of an old worktable. Countless hours of his childhood had been spent within these walls. He knew almost everything about this collection of rooms.

For example, he knew that the board by the main door creaked, so it was important to be careful and step over it when sneaking around after everyone had gone to bed. And that crack in the doorframe—that had *mysteriously* appeared after an unfortunate incident with an experimental catapult that Taly had fashioned out of gate tech. There was a matching crack in the door leading to his quarters just across the hall that had *mysteriously* appeared around the same time.

"There! All finished," Sarina proclaimed, stepping back to admire her handiwork.

Skye turned and couldn't help but smile. He had always known that Sarina was a miracle worker, but she had outdone herself this time. She had somehow transformed Taly's unruly tangle of hair into something far less chaotic. It was still quite messy by fey standards, but the wilder flyaways had been tamed and now curled gently, cascading out of a loose twist at the base of the young woman's slender neck. A few rebellious strands had already managed to escape and framed her face.

"Now, where is that cosmetic glamour?" Sarina said mostly to herself, picking through a small jewelry box. Finding what she was looking for, she reached for Taly.

Taly stubbornly waved her hands away. "No. I don't like glamours. They itch."

Ignoring the girl's feeble attempts to ward off her advance, Sarina firmly grabbed her chin and turned her head. Despite Taly's squirming, she expertly clipped on a pair of small silver earrings set with blue water crystals. The glamour shimmered as it activated, and in the mirror, Skye could see that Taly's cheeks were now just a little rosier and her lashes a little darker. "Lovely," Sarina said, turning back to the vanity and reaching for a flowered jar. "Still, I think it's missing something. Maybe just a little kohl around the eyes?"

This time, Taly jumped out of the chair and crossed the room. It seemed she was done being cooperative. "Nope. That's where I draw the line."

"But, Taly. You have such pretty eyes. Gray eyes are so rare, even among the fey."

Skye chuckled as he made his way back into the main room and leaned against the doorframe. He had seen this battle play out time and time again. It always ended the same.

"Absolutely not," Taly said heatedly. "You always poke me *in* the eye. I'm lucky I still have both of them."

"Now, Taly—"

"No."

Seeing that she wasn't going to win, Sarina

held up her hands in surrender. "Well then, it seems my work here is done," she declared. Gesturing towards the bed, she added, "I've already laid out a dress for you. Skye, I need to get myself ready. Would you mind helping her with the laces?"

"My normal clothes are fine," Taly said through clenched teeth, her fingers twisting in the fabric of her shift.

Sarina turned and gave her a motherly stare. "Oh, of course, dear. But, I'm afraid I already sent them to the laundry. They were quite damp. You're lucky you didn't catch a cold."

Taly wasn't buying the act. "I'm sure there's something else in my closet that I wouldn't find quite so… offensive."

Smiling evasively, Sarina replied, "Oh, I'm afraid I sent your old clothes to the laundry too. I was dusting in here today, and I noticed that everything needed to be laundered. Everything except that lovely lavender dress you never got a chance to wear." Not waiting for a reply, Sarina turned and swept out of the room with a swish of her skirts, confident in her victory.

"I hate it when she does that." Taly looked crestfallen as she considered the offending garment draped across the foot of her bed.

"You left me all alone with her and her scheming when you left. It serves you right," Skye teased gently, coming to stand behind her.

Taly looked at him over her shoulder, her eyes narrowed. "Yeah, but you're a guy. She hasn't tried to make you wear a dress."

"Yet," Skye snorted. "She was getting close though. She hasn't had anyone to dress up in a long time. In fact, you probably saved me a lifetime of embarrassment today. Between you and me, I don't think I have the figure to pull off a corset."

Taly sighed dramatically and approached the bed, running a finger across the jeweled beading that peppered the structured bodice. To be fair, the dress was very pretty—at least Skye thought so. It was just far too elaborate and "poofy," as Taly used to say, for her liking. She had always hated the voluminous ballgowns that seemed so popular among the fey nobility.

Carefully picking up the dress, Taly held it up to her body for appraisal. She almost looked scared of the pale lavender mass of satin and lace. "Might as well get this over with."

"Should I hum a funeral dirge or something? You know, to set the mood?"

"Shut up!" came the curt reply along with a string of muttered cursing as she disappeared behind the dressing screen.

Deciding it was in his best interest to let her fight this battle on her own, Skye plopped himself down on the bed. A small, brown package bounced and landed beside him.

This must be Taly's.

Curious, he reached for it.

"Don't touch that."

Skye jumped, startled. Looking at the screen, he didn't see any indication that she had been watching him. "What is it?" he asked.

"It's none of your business," she snapped back in between muffled sighs and grunts. "Damn it. Why is women's clothing so complicated? It makes no sense."

"Taly, what have you gotten yourself into?" he asked, now staring at the package suspiciously.

"It's nothing," she said, stepping around the

screen. “Just a little something I wanted to try out.”

Skye could tell she was hedging. Making a mental note to revisit this issue later, he decided to drop the subject for now. Their relaxed, casual banter almost made it seem like the events of the past year had never happened, and he was loath to break whatever spell had managed to revive the easy familiarity.

He looked up as he heard her bare feet padding across the expanse of the room and felt his breath catch in his throat. The pastel fabric perfectly complemented Taly’s fair skin, and the bodice tapered elegantly into the folds of the skirt, revealing a narrow, feminine waist. Skye was suddenly having a hard time remembering if she used to fill out her other dresses quite so well.

“You know, for the fuss you put up, the dress isn’t half bad,” he said, feeling slightly awkward. He took a deep breath as he moved around to tighten the laces on the back of the bodice.

Taly stood up a little straighter as he pulled the laces taut, absentmindedly fiddling with the teardrop pendant around her neck. It was a plain little piece—polished, pink quartz and no bigger than a thumbnail—and she still wore the delicate silver chain he had given to her years ago as a birthday present. As she twirled her wrist, Skye caught sight of a crescent-shaped scar at the base of her palm. Reaching out, he stilled her hands, rubbing a thumb across the blemished flesh.

It was a magical burn—evidence that his worst fears were true. He’d actually hurt her that day in the training yard. Except for their disastrous confrontation in Ryme a few weeks after she’d left, that incident marked the last time he'd seen her.

"Was this... did I do this?" Skye whispered, staring at the little scar intently. In the aftermath of her departure, he had never been able to figure out just what had happened. They had been sparring, and when he began to discharge the dagger in her hand—just like he'd done countless times before—she had dropped to the ground, screaming in pain. He had rushed to help her, but she wouldn't let him. Instead, she had run inside and locked herself in her bedroom. Nobody knew she was gone until the next morning.

Taly chewed at her lip. "It's not your fault," she finally replied, equally quiet. "That's just the price I paid for trying to use an enchanted weapon in a fight against a shadow mage. Really, I'm the one to blame." She attempted a laugh, but it died in her throat.

Skye wanted to ask her the one question he had been repeating to himself over and over since she left. *Is that why you ran away?* He opened and closed his mouth several times, trying to form the words.

Sensing his hesitation, Taly said, "That's not why I left. At least, not completely." For a moment it looked like she was going to say more, but she didn't. Instead, she closed her mouth with an audible click of her teeth.

He continued to stare at the mark. Even after a year, it was still there—an angry, purple welt.

Pulling her hand away, she asked, "Are you finished?"

"Uh... not yet," Skye stammered as he turned back to the laces on the back of her dress. He worked quickly, making sure to carefully conceal the white shift beneath the delicate silk of her gown.

"There. All done," he said stiffly as Taly turned around to face him. The lighthearted atmosphere had dissipated, and she wouldn't look him in the eye. He cleared his throat uncomfortably. "Well, since Sarina and Ivain seem intent on making this a formal affair, I should probably go change. I'll see you in a bit."

Skye turned and made for the door. His throat felt tight, and he wanted nothing more than to retreat to the quiet solitude of his private chambers.

"Hey, Skye. Wait a minute," Taly called as he crossed the room to leave. "Does Sarina still send the laundry out?"

Skye paused and then let out a rumbling laugh. She had finally figured it out.

"Just now catching on?" he asked, a little too pleased.

He didn't need to turn around to see the dawning look of horror on her face as she started to realize the full extent of Sarina's manipulation. The laundry wouldn't be delivered until the next morning.

"You cagey bastards trapped me here."

"See you downstairs," Skye responded in a sing-song voice as he excused himself.

CHAPTER 4

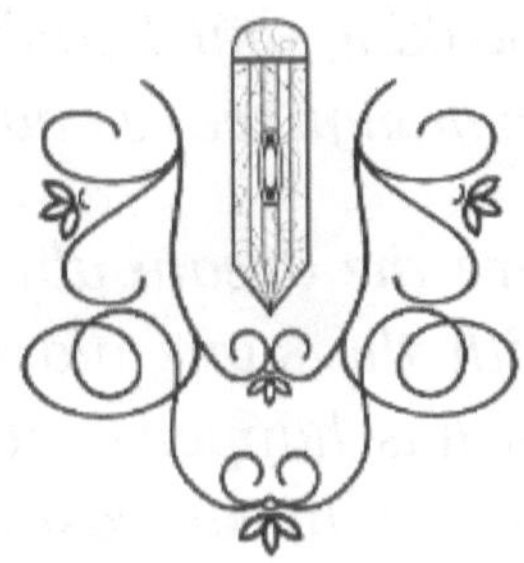

-From the personal diary of Talya Caro

I had the dream again last night. The dream about the fire.

It began differently this time. Rather than being shaken awake as the fires blazed outside, it started out peacefully. I was standing in a garden with a man that seemed so familiar to me. His face was scarred, but his eyes were kind. He made me feel safe. But when I tried to focus on anything else about him—the color of his hair, the clothes he wore, or even his name—the more difficult it became to stay present.

We were walking a circuitous garden path, and my hands danced through an intricate series of gestures. Gold dust started to materialize and weave itself around my fingers, and in my dream, it almost felt like that energy was a natural part of me—an extension of something deep inside that I've somehow forgotten.

The dream skipped forward at that point. No matter what, no matter how many times I relive this same nightmare, I always end up face-to-face with a woman. She's speaking, but I can't quite make out her words. It's as though we're underwater.

And that is where the dream always ends. Every time, I wake with the same alarming sense that something awful has happened to that woman. I dream so often of her. In contrast to the man, I can recall every detail about her. Her face. The dimple in her cheek. Even the spatters of blood that dot her fingernails as she strokes my hair. I don't even know if she's real, and yet, I'm always left with an inexplicable sense of loss.

Taly gasped, startled awake by a familiar sense of dread. The illusory sting of smoke still clouded her eyes and sweat beaded on her brow as she emerged from the already fading memory of the blistering heat.

Taking a deep breath, she sunk into the mattress as the rapid beat of her heart began to slow. This particular nightmare was nothing new. She'd been reliving the night of the fire that stole away her old life for as long as she could remember, so the initial terror, though acute, was fleeting.

With a sigh, Taly stubbornly pulled the impossibly soft quilt over her chin and flopped onto her side, wriggling until she was fully ensconced inside a cocoon of fluffy blue blankets. How could it be morning already? It felt like she had gone to bed only moments ago.

I guess that's what a soft bed will do for you. Shards, I miss soft beds. And food. And champagne. Shards, how much coin did Ivain and Sarina throw away on just champagne last night?

She tried cracking open her eyes again, flinching away from the bright light streaming in through a gap in the curtains. A quick glance around her old room immediately confirmed her worst fears. She really had agreed to come back to the manor.

Taly still wasn't quite sure how she had ended up here. She had successfully avoided coming back home for nearly a year, and then Skye had somehow talked her into returning within the span of a few minutes. It was almost pitiful if she really thought about it.

That doesn't matter now. What's done is done. As nice as it had been to be reunited with all the people she loved most—eating and laughing together like she had never walked out on them—she needed to leave. She would finish the job today and then go back to her new life. Even if nothing bad had happened in the past year, she was no longer comfortable staying here. Not with her... *condition.*

As if to reinforce that thought, a gossamer fog fluttered across her vision.

Not again, Taly thought, bringing her hands up to shield her eyes. Most of the time, if she just took a deep breath and willed the visions to go away, they would.

When she dared to peek through her fingers, it became clear that wasn't going to be the case today. The golden mist was still there, hovering in the far corner of the room. It flickered, its edges hazy and undefined until, finally, it molded itself into the ghostly likeness of a woman. As Taly continued to stare, the specter listlessly drifted across the perimeter of the room before coming to a stop in front of the door. It raised a hand as if to knock but then paused, its edges already blurring as the image dissolved.

These visions—*premonitions,* as she had started thinking of them—used to frighten her, but she had become accustomed to their sudden appearances at this point.

At least... that's what she was still trying to tell herself.

In the beginning, she had hoped, prayed, *pleaded* with whatever might be listening, that she was just going crazy. After all, humans weren't supposed to have magic. And every time an earth mage came to the island, she had considered going to see him, desperate for this strange power to be nothing more than an affliction.

But she never did. Because if it wasn't an illness, easily cured with magic and medicine, if she really was seeing some version of the future...

The Sanctorum would not be kind to her. Or anyone stupid enough to try to protect her.

Taly listened closely, straining her ears for signs of movement. It was faint, but she could just make out the sound of measured footsteps as they echoed down the hallway. They came closer and closer, coming to a stop right outside her door. After a moment of hesitation, there was a soft knock.

"Taly?" came Sarina's gentle voice from behind the door.

Her voice still raspy with sleep, Taly replied, "Yeah. I'm up."

"I'm leaving your things outside the door. The others aren't up yet, so take your time. Eliza's already put on a pot of coffee—it's downstairs when you're ready." With that, she heard Sarina turn and walk back down the hallway towards the stairs.

Stretching, Taly decided it was time to get out of bed. She was just postponing the inevitable at this point, and she had coin to earn. She had finally managed to corner Ivain and Skye the night before to get the details of the job. It was real. And while she knew they were overpaying her, she was desperate enough not to care.

When she went to retrieve her clothing, she wasn't surprised to see that Sarina had taken it upon herself to make some substitutions—meaning that Taly had a completely new set of gear waiting for her outside her door. Not that she was going to complain. The leggings were a deep royal blue and lined with wool, and the ivory tunic was made of lightweight silk with sleeves that buttoned at her wrists. She had a new jacket too—black, waterproof canvas with a brindle fur trim around the hood.

She dressed quickly, admiring her reflection in the full-length mirror set against the wall as she tightened her belt holster. Even though her old wardrobe didn't fit her nearly as well as it had only a year ago, she couldn't help but preen—just a little bit. The coat pulled in at the waist, accentuating what was almost an hourglass figure, and even her hair had chosen to behave this morning, lying flat with only a very slight curl at the end. For the first time in months, her cheeks had color, and the circles under her eyes seemed a little less bruise-like.

"Not bad," she murmured. It was remarkable how a single night of good food and even better company could transform a person.

Pulling herself away from the mirror, Taly dropped to the floor, groping underneath the bed for the brown parcel she'd hidden there before dinner last night. She really hoped this little project didn't turn out to be a waste of coin. Eyeing the door warily, she stepped over and turned the lock before settling back onto the bed to unwrap the package. The paper came away easily, revealing two translucent hyaline pistols.

When the first firearms had started coming through the Aion Gate from the mortal realm, the shadow mages didn't know what to make of them since even the smallest amount of aether could render human gunpowder completely inert. It had taken a few years, but eventually, a particularly industrious crafter managed to mimic the human firing mechanisms using fire crystals.

Unfortunately, the transition wasn't completely seamless. The smaller handguns that Taly preferred just didn't have enough room for both a shadow crystal large enough to power the circuit and the necessary focusing crystal required to transform the raw aether drawn from the power source into fire aether. Even under the best circumstances, the shadow crystals completely discharged after only a few shots, making the converted firearms impractical in combat scenarios.

With this new design, however, Taly was hoping to change that. Despite their drawbacks, she had always had a fondness for pistols. Guns felt solid, more so than a simple bow. And as a human, if she could avoid getting into close-range with a fey combatant, all the better.

She glanced in the mirror one last time, making sure that the illegal firearms were well hidden beneath the hem of her coat, before setting out.

Taly tiptoed through the house, easily navigating the familiar path out the back door and through the training yard to the workshop, a spacious single-story structure situated at the back edge of the main property.

The door to the shop was a great massive thing, old but sturdy. She hadn't been able to open it on her own until she was fourteen, and even then, she had trouble. Setting down a steaming cup of coffee she had grabbed on her way through the kitchens, Taly leaned against the door and pushed hard. It groaned in protest but eventually slid to the side. A blast of cold air immediately rushed out of the open doorway, and she shivered as she stepped inside. She took a sip of coffee, relishing the warmth.

The inside of the dusty workshop was a welcoming sight. The forge in the back corner was unlit, so the air inside the main room was unusually crisp. An array of hammers, tongs, and files hung neatly to the side, and she could see the anvil and quench tank tucked into a corner.

She slowly made her way to the back of the room, trailing one hand across the various crystals, quills, and other enchanting tools that had been left strewn across the benches.

Skye's personal workbench was chaos (nothing new there). Evidently, all the hard work she'd done trying to bring order to his crafting station had completely disintegrated in her absence. There were random piles of crystals, the odd piece of scrap metal, dirty inkwells, and discarded pieces of crumpled parchment littering every available surface.

In the middle of it all sat a polished longsword. The blade was made of a dull, gray metal that almost seemed to absorb the light around it, and blood-red crystals had been embedded in even intervals along the ornately swirled hilt and cross. Taly ran a finger along one of the gemstones set into the flourished sweepings. The rich color and startling clarity made the fire crystals shine like rubies in the dim light of the workshop.

A cup extended below the sweeping curls of metal encircling the guard, and an intricately carved relief of House Ghislain's crest, a dragon surrounded by violet tendrils of coiling shadow magic, had been etched into the surface of the metal. Black leather cord enveloped the grip, parting in even intervals to reveal three deep violet shadow crystals.

The artistry of the blade came as no surprise to Taly. Skye had always had a special talent for etchings and carvings. When they were younger, he used to practice by whittling little animals out of wood that he would then present to her whenever she needed cheering up. No, what truly made this sword unique was the row of glittering air crystals embedded along the length of the blade.

Taly remembered when Skye had first shown her the plans for the sword. She thought he was crazy at the time, but it seemed he had gone and done it anyway.

Tucked beneath the weapon, Taly spied a small slip of paper, the edge of what looked like a glamograph. Glamographs were pictures created with aether-infused paper and a glamera—a small device programmed with a simple water enchantment. The humans had created something similar called a *camera*, undoubtedly copied from the fey device after its inventor had accidentally stumbled through the Aion Gate.

Taly immediately recognized the picture as she pulled it out from beneath the clutter. She had an identical copy hidden away in her room at the tavern. It was from her 18th birthday, and Skye's arm was slung around her as they sat on the front steps of the manor, laughing. Though she had been reticent at first, he had convinced her to let him take her into town that night, insisting that he should have the honor of buying her the first beer she would drink as an "adult." Sarina had made them stop as they were leaving, and they had sat down on the steps, waiting for the older fey noblewoman to return with the glamera. Skye had been telling her some stupid joke, and Sarina had snapped the picture when they weren't looking.

"I see you found it already," a voice drawled from behind her.

Taly hastily tucked the picture back underneath the sword. She hadn't expected Skye to get up before early afternoon. "What? The sword? Yeah. It's beautiful. How did you keep the fire crystal from overheating the circuit? With the enchantment diagram you showed me originally, you would've had to route the aether flow through the fire crystal first. Air focusing crystals are so finicky when it comes to internal temperature."

Reaching for the sword, Skye hefted it and

gave it an experimental swing. "That's my little secret. Although, I did break a lot of crystals in the process. Ivain threatened to disown me on more than one occasion."

Taly snorted. "I can imagine." Then, with an appreciative smile, she said, "But you did it. So, I will gladly concede that I was wrong. In this case, at least."

Skye grabbed his chest in mock horror. "Now, I've seen just about everything. Princess Tink can be wrong?" He held up a hand to her forehead. "Are you sure you're alright? I think we need to get you back to bed immediately."

"I'm not that bad," Taly muttered, shoving him away. It seemed some of the familiarity they had recovered the previous night hadn't completely disappeared. She probably had Sarina to thank for that. She had kept their champagne glasses quite full. "I'm usually quite agreeable. You're just an ass."

Chuckling to himself, Skye turned to sheathe the sword in a scuffed, leather scabbard while Taly started absentmindedly tidying the bench. She was just finishing sorting the crystals by type when she jumped back and said, "Oh! I almost forgot." She reached for her dagger. "Since you were complicit in trapping me here—"

"Yes—*trapping* you. In a place with hot water, ample food, and soft beds among people who care about you, your well-being, and your safety. I'm a truly awful person, I know." Skye made no attempt to hide the sarcastic edge to his voice as he turned to glare at her. "But go on."

"Yes, all of those things," she replied, unaffected by his teasing. "I was hoping you could repay me by repairing my dagger." She held out the weapon for his inspection. It was a plain little thing. There was a single, dull air crystal embedded in the blade and a shadow crystal mounted on the hilt. When he continued to stare at her blankly, she added, “Please? It stopped firing last week.”

With a beleaguered sigh, he took the dagger and held it up to the window behind his bench. “I can’t believe you still have this thing. It’s so awful.”

“Hey! Don’t talk about Zephyr that way. She’s sensitive.” Taly punched him in the arm for emphasis.

“Terribly sorry. I forgot that Princess Tink’s special power is granting sentience to inanimate objects,” he responded drolly. The crystal in the hilt flashed as he used his magic to push a small amount of aether into the circuit. “The shadow crystal is fine—shitty but fine. Here,” he said, handing the dagger back to her, “show me what it’s doing.”

Skye tossed a wadded-up piece of parchment into the air, and Taly held up the dagger, depressing the tiny toggle mounted beneath the guard. She tensed as the blade lurched in her grip, and a pitiful gust of wind sputtered out of the tip. It didn’t even reach the little ball of paper as it landed and rolled off into a corner.

Skye looked at her with a smirk. “Wow, Tink. I used to be jealous of your aim, but now? I don’t know.”

Taly pursed her lips and threw the dagger on his workbench. “You watch your mouth, Em.” She didn’t miss the small smile that tugged at his lips at her use of his old nickname. She was only six years old when she came to the manor, and she hadn't been able to pronounce his last name—Emrys. So, she had taken to calling him *Em*. "This has nothing to do with my aim, and you know it."

Skye laughed as he turned and started to rifle through a stack of parchment. Finding a page that had a series of crimson runes inscribed down the side, he sat down on the bench and set to work. "You know, I'm much better at setting air crystals now. I could make you a new dagger. This thing—it's just a stain on my reputation at this point."

Taly shrugged noncommittally as she leaned against the table. She had always liked watching him work. Skye might be arrogant, but no one could deny that he had the skills to back up the ego.

Choosing a quill, he pricked his index finger and held it over the page. A single drop of blood dripped onto the surface. Before the wound managed to heal itself, he held his hand over a clean inkwell and let the remaining fluid trickle out. Since shadow mages didn't need to refine the aether they absorbed from the air into a specialized form, they had raw aether dissolved in their blood. That meant the more traditional uses of their magic tended to be tied up with bloodletting. As a child, Taly had been surprised to learn about this little quirk in their magic, but she had become accustomed to it over the years. She only felt a little squeamish now whenever she saw Ivain and Skye slice open their hands with ceremonial daggers.

Skye gave her a knowing look as he placed the dagger directly over the crimson stain and touched the quill to the shadow crystal inlaid at the base of the blade. The script on the edge of the page began to glow as it pulled aether out of the surrounding air.

"The rune on your air crystal is starting to fade. At the very least, it needs to be re-inscribed, but I'm thinking the entire crystal is probably going to need to be replaced eventually. From what I can tell, you're still getting aether feeding in from the shadow crystal, but the air crystal just isn't converting it to air aether efficiently enough. For now, I can increase the amount of aether that's getting pulled for each shot—overload the circuit—but that's going to drain your shadow crystal pretty quickly." Skye glanced at her briefly before turning his attention back to the dagger. Dipping his quill into the inkwell, he penned a few additional crimson runes around the base of the grip before setting down his quill. "While I'm at it, do you need anything else looked at?"

"Let me check," Taly replied, pulling out her new pistols from the holsters hidden beneath her coat and placing them on the bench for his inspection. She also retrieved a small drawstring pouch from her pack and dumped its contents out on the table. "I think that's it. I just had the fire crystals for my lamp re-inscribed, so they should be fine, but it can't hurt to check."

He began picking through the little pile of crystals, occasionally holding one up to the light and running a finger over the runes carved into the surface. As he finished examining each one, he carefully placed it back in the bag. "These are fine—for now. They won't last long, though. Whoever inscribed these runes did a piss-poor job. I'd try to fix these for you, but this is beyond my ability to patch. I'd need to get a fire mage here to look at these." He handed the pouch back to her and then moved his attention to the pistols. "Is this what was in that package last night?" he asked, picking up one of the crystalline handguns and turning it over in his hands.

"Yup." Taly shifted her weight nervously. "I'm testing a new theory."

"Is this what I think it is?" he asked, scowling. He tapped the crystal frame and looked at her pointedly.

"If you were thinking hyaline, then yes," Taly said shakily, fidgeting with one of the stray crystals on the bench. She knew Skye would have a *small* conniption once he found out she had been meddling in a few harmless, illegal activities, but she was hoping his curiosity would win out in the end. She really wanted his feedback on her latest idea. "And before you freak out, I only used hyaline for the frame. And the magazine. And the slide. And the barrel. Okay, it's mostly hyaline."

"Talya Caro!" Skye exclaimed, running an anxious hand through his hair. "What the hell were you thinking?! Hyaline? Are you crazy?"

Taly rocked back on her heels. "I know you're mad, but you're also curious, right?"

"Shards." He placed the gun back on the bench with a thud. "Yes. Yes, I am. So, go on. You have one minute."

"I can work with that," Taly said enthusiastically, shoving him over as she sat on the bench beside him. There was barely enough room for both of them, so she had to lean into him to keep from sliding off the edge. "So, you already know that the problem with guns is the same problem with any other enchanted weapon. Once the shadow crystals expend their aether, there's no way to charge them back up quickly unless there just happens to be a shadow mage hanging around. On top of that, any shadow crystal small enough to fit into the circuit for a handgun is only going to be able to store enough aether to fire off a few rounds—meaning that after seven or eight shots, the gun is useless. I figured out a way to fix that problem."

Smiling, Taly depressed a small button below the barrel. A hidden compartment in the frame slid out. Carefully removing the capsule inside, she held out the rectangular piece of metal for him to see.

"What is this?" Skye held up the metal object to the window, running a finger along the surfaces of the embedded shadow and fire crystals.

"It's a cartridge," she explained. "This piece and the inner spring are made from an aether-conducting metal—viridian. With these, instead of installing the crystals in the gun itself, both the shadow crystal and the fire crystal for the firing mechanism get set into the cartridge. That way, when the shadow crystal runs out of power, the cartridge just pops out, and you can replace it." Reaching into her pack, Taly pulled out a handful of identical cartridges.

Skye took the cartridges and laid them side-by-side on the bench, studying each one with rapt interest.

Resting her chin on her hand, she continued, "This way, the gun keeps firing. And then when you drag your still-alive ass back into town, your resident shadow mage can do all the necessary handwaving and such" —she paused to demonstrate, earning a snort from Skye— "and the newly charged cartridge fits back into the chamber. The viridian still conducts aether the same way any enchanted weapon would, but the cartridge makes it interchangeable. Carry enough cartridges around, and suddenly you have a weapon that's good for more than a few cheap shots."

"So why use hyaline then? Why not use a metal that conducts aether?" Skye started disassembling the handgun, turning each piece over in his hands before he laid it on the bench in front of him.

Taly shrugged. "Because you don't really need to use a conducting metal for every piece of the gun. The first firearms were made from metals because that's just how traditional enchanted weapons are made. But this is different from, say, a sword or an ax. The entire pistol doesn't need to conduct aether—just the firing mechanism. And since aether can't move through hyaline, I thought it might make the aether transfer from the shadow crystal to the fire crystal more efficient. Plus, hyaline is harder than the metals used in the vast majority of weapons, and it doesn't conduct heat."

Skye sat stunned for a moment. "Taly, I..." He stopped, unsure how to go on. "Where did you get the idea for this?"

Taly reassembled the handgun with a few practiced motions before placing it back on the table. "Remember when Sarina taught us how humans had figured out a way to store energy in these little metal cylinders and use them as interchangeable power sources? Kinda like shadow mages and shadow crystals? It was an interesting idea, so I tried to replicate it with our materials. If there had been more interest in guns when the first enchanted firearms hit the market, I'd be willing to bet good coin the crafters in the Shadow Guild would've come up with something similar—eventually. But everybody just sort of lost interest in guns small enough to be carried."

Skye remained quiet for a long moment as he considered the two pistols laid side-by-side on the benchtop. "You know what would make this even better?" He paused, waiting for her to look at him. "The cartridge needs an air crystal. There's more than enough room for one, and that would decrease the load on the fire crystal. You're going to have a problem with heat buildup inside the frame. The way this is constructed right now—I bet you're going to get some kickback."

Taly stood up from the bench and stretched. "Yeah, I thought of that. But *most* shadow mages for hire can't make fire and air crystals work together in perfect harmony. Not like *some* people." She half-heartedly punched his shoulder, glancing at the sheathed sword that sat on the table behind them. "Plus, that would've been way more expensive. I spent three months eating sludge just to save enough money to get the metal for the cartridges. Don't ask me how much it cost to have them made."

"Yeah. There's so little surface area on the cartridge—if you had used anything cheaper than viridian, you wouldn't get nearly enough aether to the focusing crystal. Why didn't you ask me? I could've made these for you, or at least given you the metals."

Taly shrugged, looking away. "We didn't exactly part on good terms the last time we spoke. Plus, you probably would've lectured me."

"Yes. Yes, I would have," Skye snapped. "Granted, this is kind of amazing, but hyaline mining is regulated by both the Genesis Council and the Dawn Court. There are some *heavy* penalties for illegal mining. How did you even get enough dead crystal to make these?"

Taly bounced in place. "I... *found* it," she said with a secretive smile.

Skye looked like he wanted to say something else, but instead, he held up his hands in surrender and turned back to the bench. "So why didn't you want to show me the guns last night?"

"Because you already looked like you wanted to lecture me about—well, knowing you—everything. I could see it in your eyes," Taly replied, waggling her finger. "Plus, they're my new toys, and I wanted to spend some alone time with them before I let you manhandle them."

"You are so weird," Skye chuckled, his irritation seeming to evaporate. "I hope you know that." Holding one hand over the parchment and dagger that had been pushed to the side of the table, he said, "Well, my work here is done. Zephyr should be good as new in about an hour. Are you sure you don't want a better dagger? Maybe even a short sword?" He jerked his head towards the door to the armory at the far side of the room. "Ivain and I have stuff in there that we literally haven't touched in years. You can take your pick."

Taly smiled and shook her head. "Nope. I like Zephyr."

"Okay." Skye stood and started heading towards the door of the workshop. "What do you want to do while we wait?"

Taly followed him out into the training yard. The sun had chased away some of the chill, and the smell of early morning dew saturated the air.

Taly leaned against the wall of the workshop. "Do you have everything you need for the trip to the Aion Gate?"

"You act like this is my first time outside of the city, Tink." Skye's voice carried just a hint of derision, but mirth colored his expression.

"Okay, okay," Taly acquiesced easily. Pushing herself away from the door, she rounded on him, pretending to inspect him carefully. "We could spar. We used to do that all the time when we got bored."

"Or Sarina just wanted us out the house," Skye added with a laugh. His good humor was short-lived, though, and a look of pain flitted across his expression. "I don't feel like sparring."

Taly snorted indelicately. "Since when? You've never turned down an opportunity to kick my ass."

"Just… I said no." Grabbing a dagger from the rack on the wall, he stepped over to one of the training dummies.

"Oh, come on."

"No, Taly. The last time we sparred, I hurt you, and then you left." His eyes were hard as he swung the dagger in a practiced motion.

Way to ruin the mood, Caro. She knew Skye still blamed himself for what happened during their sparring match that day, but it wasn't his fault. After all, it wasn't the first time he had discharged a dagger while she was holding it. There was no reason it should've hurt her the way it did, and no way they could've known that it would. Really, it was what happened after that was the real problem. Just after she'd dropped to her knees screaming in pain, her vision had clouded with gold, and she had started seeing things that hadn't happened yet.

I need to fix this, she thought. It was one thing to push him away. It was another, entirely, to let him think it was his fault.

Well, Skye had exploited her weaknesses to get what he wanted. Turnabout was fair play.

Dirt crunched underneath her boots as she entered the training yard, circling him thoughtfully. When he lowered his dagger, she sauntered towards him, trying to muster some bravado. "I get it. You're scared." She punctuated the statement with an arrogant smile.

Skye frowned. "Scared of hurting you, yes." He grabbed her hand and held it up between them. "Here's the evidence, right here." His thumb grazed the small scar centered at the base of her palm. "You're too fragile, Tink." When Taly arched a brow in response, he said, "Don't give me that look. You know exactly what I mean. You're human, I'm fey. I could kill you without even trying."

He had a point there. Still...

"This?" Taly squeaked, jerking her hand away. "This was just a fluke. You know that. I know that. But if it makes you feel any better, you could *not* use your magic. I hardly think it'll be a fair fight, though." She pursed her lips and shrugged in mock sympathy. "You always were a little slow when you weren't using aether."

She knew the exact moment she had him. That narrowing of his eyes. That smirk. She had to consciously fight the urge to crow victoriously.

He raked an appraising eye down the length of her body. "Okay, *Caro*. But first—*terms*."

"Oh, so you're a betting man now?" she taunted, taking a few steps back as he started to round on her. "Name them."

"If I win..." He paused, making sure she wasn't going to say anything cheeky. She gave him an *innocent* smile, so he continued, "If I win, you have to come to the manor once a week for dinner."

"No deal."

"Fine, once every two weeks."

"Skye," she warned. "No."

"I'm not backing down on this. You've lost too much weight since you moved out." Taly grimaced, but either Skye didn't see it, or he chose to ignore it. "And you have to start using me for all of your weapon crafting and crystal maintenance. Exclusively—none of that overpriced back-alley shit anymore. Whoever inscribed your fire crystals ripped you off. You need to start using better vendors, which I happen to have access to."

Taly opened her mouth to speak, but Skye interrupted her. "*And,* you have to let me give you a better dagger."

Taly stared him down, quietly considering his terms. She knew that she shouldn't take this bet. Skye was fey *and* a highborn. Even without magic, a highborn's reflexes, strength, and speed were far superior to their lowborn brethren and orders of magnitude above what a mortal could manage. Taly had been sparring with Skye for almost ten years, but as a human, no amount of training would ever allow her to match his natural gifts. As much as she hated to admit it, she couldn't beat him. Not without help.

Of course, she wasn't completely without help, now was she? Taly smiled when she saw a gold aura materialize around Skye. His ghostly shadow peeled away from his body, walking one step ahead of him as he circled her. If she knew *what* he was going to do, *where* he was going to be, before he did, that skewed the odds in her favor. And while it was probably a little stupid to encourage this ability to manifest, she would *really* enjoy being able to beat Skye without having to wonder if he'd let her win. Just once—just to know what that felt like.

She opened her mouth to speak, but not before pausing momentarily to make sure Skye was finished with his extensive list of demands. When he nodded his assent, Taly said, "Wow! You want a lot. You're going to have to let me think about this a minute. Let's see. What do I want? What would even be comparable?" She stopped, pretending to consider his potential punishment carefully.

Oh, she thought excitedly. *That would be fun.* She had the perfect punishment for Skye. It was a little mean, but he'd probably done something to deserve it.

While Ivain entertained the Bryer siblings every summer because they were family, Aimee had never hesitated to make her true intentions known. She planned to marry Skye in the hopes of becoming the future Duchess of Ghislain. However, throughout the years, her clumsy and aggressive attempts to woo the future duke had not gone quite according to plan. In fact, she had only been successful, so far, in making Skye dread her presence at the manor only slightly less than Taly did. In this particular case, Taly could use that to her advantage.

With a snap of her fingers, Taly announced, "If I win, then you, Skylen Emrys, have to tell Aimee that you're in love with her."

Skye stared at her with wide eyes for a long moment, his mouth slack. Just when she was starting to think that she had broken him, he doubled over, his body shaking with uncontrollable laughter. As much as she tried to remain serious, Taly felt herself start to smile. "That's so mean," he gasped, glancing up at her. "You know if I do that, she'll never leave. She will be here forever. *Forever*. A resident, overzealous, annoying pest."

"Oh, I'm aware," Taly said with a poorly suppressed chuckle. "But if I win, I won't be here to witness that. I'll just get to sleep soundly at night knowing that *I* was responsible for your future marital bliss."

"It'll be a cold day in hell," Skye replied with a grimace. He hesitated for a moment, running a hand along his chin as he considered her proposal. A slow smile emerged. "Okay, Caro. You're on," he said, already confident in his victory. "I take it the usual rules apply?"

"No weapons and no magic. Three hits or a pin to win," Taly agreed with a nod. She shrugged out of her coat and threw it off to the side. Then, pulling her old pistol from her boot, she tossed it onto the pile.

Skye followed suit, depositing his dagger and greatcoat with her gear, before stepping back and eyeing her up and down. Taly did the same. Even if she could predict his attacks, she shouldn't underestimate him. He was bigger, faster, and better in close combat. A single mistake would cost her.

She watched him carefully, waiting for him to make the first move. He sidestepped around her, looking for an opening. Then she saw it. A faint golden specter—almost an afterimage—lunging forward. Even before Skye began to move, she shifted her weight, narrowly avoiding his attempt to grab her. He looked slightly taken aback, but he quickly recovered, twisting his body as he reached for her again.

He's trying to grapple me. That was his best strategy, with his superior weight and strength.

Taly dodged his second lunge easily. She could sense his confusion—his ghostly aura was chaotically dancing this way and that in her peripheral vision as he planned his next move. He wasn't certain what to do. Taly had always been quick on her feet, but he'd always been quicker.

Sensing his hesitation, she sprinted forward, punching him in the gut. He managed to slip to the side, partially deflecting the blow, but that didn't matter. Even a partial blow counted. Those were the rules.

"That's one!" Taly cheered, dancing backward out of his reach.

"Not bad, Caro," he replied grudgingly.

Skye took a step back, and the golden mist crowded around him. She could see the moment he made his decision. The mist shifted, taking on a more corporeal form, and it shot out to her right. So she dodged left, laughing lightly. "You're going to have to do better than that, *Emrys*." Taly couldn't help giving him a cocky grin as he grasped at empty air.

"Okay." He stopped to wipe the sweat from his brow. "You're definitely better than you used to be. I guess I can get serious now."

"You weren't serious before?" Taly taunted. She couldn't help but goad him a little. It was just too much fun. "Remember, if you lose, Aimee's going to be moving in. And this time, I'll gladly give her my room. I know you're going to want her close by."

Instead of replying, Skye abruptly charged.

But Taly was watching his gilded doppelganger, and she anticipated his advance. She waited, letting him get close, before relaxing her body at the last moment, successfully ducking out of his grasp just as he reached for her. His fingers grazed her sleeve, but not enough to grab her. She rolled away, putting some distance between them.

Skye was starting to look frustrated now. He wasn't used to being beaten. Not by a mortal, at least. He considered her stance, watched her movements—and Taly waited, her eyes trained on the glimmering aura only she could see. While her newfound ability had saved her life more than once on a salvaging run gone wrong, this was the first time she had ever used it in hand-to-hand combat. It was exhilarating.

"Giving up, Emrys?" she challenged.

"Not by a long shot, Caro. I'm going to be seeing you for dinner in two weeks' time."

Taly saw the psychic aura shudder restlessly, flickering in and out, starting to take form and then shifting back into a chaotic assembly of particles. He was thinking about flanking to the left, but he wasn't sure yet.

Let's help him make up his mind, she thought devilishly. She lowered her arms and stood a little straighter, just enough to relax her defensive posture and create a small opening. Just as she predicted, he took the bait. The aura condensed into a solid form and leaned to the left.

Taly braced herself when she saw him charge, waiting until he came a little closer to dodge. She made a slight miscalculation, however. Skye was fast, even for a highborn. She stepped to the side, but his hand shot out and found purchase in her collar. He dragged her in close, but she wasn't going to be caught that easily. She twisted her body, grasping at the thin fabric of his shirt as she pulled herself forward and slammed her forehead into his nose. He released her as he rocked back and fell to one knee.

Taly giggled as she easily regained her footing and circled him. "That's two!" she sang.

Wiping away a trickle of blood from his nose, he snapped, "That was a cheap shot, Caro."

She ignored him. "So, tell me. How exactly do you intend to express your love to the young Miss Bryer? Flowers? Chocolate? Oh, I know," Taly said, hopping from foot-to-foot. "You'll probably take her to Halcyon Hill. That's where you used to take all your dates in Ghislain, right? Oh, Shards—that is so sweet, Skye. I always knew you were a romantic."

Skye looked up at her, his gaze cold and angry. The golden haze roiled and seethed around him. Taly tensed as she waited for him to determine his next move. She knew him. He was most likely going to charge her again.

A slow smirk began to surface, spreading his lips, and then he sprang forward. But this time, his specter kept pace with his movements.

What's he doing?!

The aura split as he approached, darting to both the left and right simultaneously. It converged right where she stood. Taken aback by the sudden change, she hopped back a few steps, hoping to dodge his attack, but it wasn't enough. He feinted right, and then flanked her from the left, grabbing her arm as he shoved her to the ground.

Taly fell, hitting the dirt hard. She had seen him pull back at the last moment, but she was still a little disoriented. Skye was much stronger than her, even when he pulled his punches.

He was crouched over her now, and he seemed far too pleased. As she started to regain her bearings, she tried to move, first her arms and then her legs. No luck.

Damn. He had her pinned.

Refusing to go down without a fight, she tried again, putting a little more effort into her struggle, only to be rewarded with a smug laugh from her captor.

"You're going to have to do better than that, Tink." He smiled as he extended one of her arms, reminding her that she was well and truly stuck. "Do you surrender?"

"I know the rules as well as you do," Taly dodged, her brows knitting together in a frown.

Skye laughed and pulled at her other arm. "I know. But I want to hear you say it. C'mon, Tink. Let me hear those three little words I love so much. '*Em, you won.*' C'mon. You can do it."

He was uncomfortably close as he searched her face, waiting for her to capitulate. She could feel the heat from his body even though they were barely touching, and the way his muscles flexed when she struggled against him made her stomach clench in a very confusing way. When she still didn't submit, he shifted, letting more of his weight press against her as he pushed her into the ground. All she had to do was surrender, and he would help her up. Everything would go back to normal, and they'd have a good laugh.

She hated losing, though. Especially to him.

"Skylen!"

Taly saw his face fall just before he hung his head. Still unable to move, she whispered, "And there's your biggest fan."

He snorted humorlessly, his hair tickling her nose as he lifted his head to look at her. "Well, at least I managed to save myself from the horror you would have inflicted upon us all."

Standing, he reached down and pulled her up with an ease that left her slightly off-balance. His hand hesitated at her waist as he waited for her to find her footing before he reluctantly turned to greet the girl that had just emerged from the house. "Good morning, Aimee."

"And to you, Lord Emrys." Aimee lowered herself into a deep curtsy, artfully arranging the voluminous, velvet folds of her skirts around her in a crimson halo.

Taly didn't miss the subtle roll of his eyes. Gesturing for the young woman to rise, Skye asked, "What can I do for you?"

Aimee looked up, shock gracing her delicate fey features. "Oh! Talya. You're here too?" She reached up to fidget with a raven curl, unable to completely conceal her irritation behind her schooled expression.

Really? Taly thought, recalling their unscheduled and uncomfortable meeting the night before.

Taly took a step forward, coming to stand next to Skye. She made no move to subserviate herself as the noblewoman's superior station demanded. "Yes. I believe I had the pleasure of your re-acquaintance last night. I'm pleased to see the Shards blessed you with a safe journey." Taly tried to smile, but it came off as more of a pained grimace.

Aimee smoothed her hands over the bodice of her gown, no doubt trying to draw Skye's gaze towards the feminine dip of her waist. Even though the fey noblewoman didn't participate in anything unladylike like sparring or being outdoors in general, her highborn blood still granted her a natural fitness and tone to her body that Taly had only ever been able to achieve after years of training in the ring with Skye. Seeing as how Taly had lost more muscle mass than she cared to admit over the past year, the disparity between the two girls was stark.

"I had no idea you were still... *in residence.* I offer you my sincerest apologies for any discomfort I may have caused," Aimee replied in the cultured accent of the mainland nobility. The look in those inhumanely blue highborn eyes was anything but sincere.

Taly took that as her cue to exit and gave a curt nod. Skye grabbed her arm as she moved away. "Please don't leave me with her," he whispered desperately.

Prying away his fingers, she said through gritted teeth, "No. This is your problem. Not mine. So play nice, have fun, and keep her away from me."

Walking back towards the workshop, Taly smiled when she heard Skye's barely suppressed groan of pain. Since she had lost the sparring match, she wouldn't get to see her little prank play out—but this would be almost as much fun.

CHAPTER 5

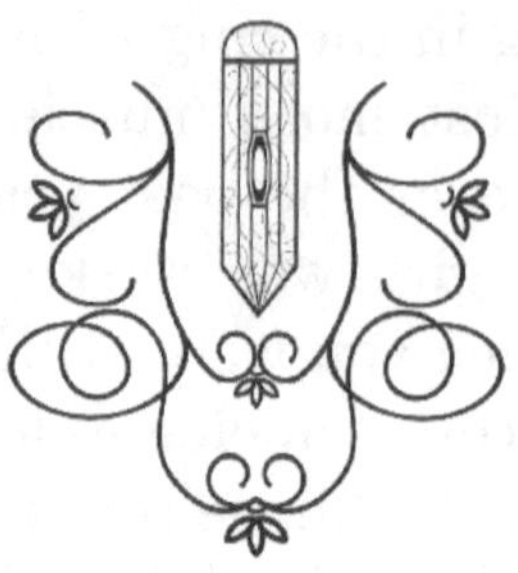

-An excerpt from The Fey Imperium: Institutions and Policies

The Genesis Council was originally made up of the six fey mages chosen to wield the Genesis Shards and functioned as the primary ruling body in the Fey Imperium. Chosen by the Shards—those six objects of ultimate power believed to house the souls of the slumbering gods—each mage was granted the title of High Lord or Lady of their respective magical discipline, and they were responsible for legislating and enforcing the rule of law within the confines of the Lycian homeworld and its territories.

The High Lord and Lady of Shadow and Time carried an added burden. Ruling under the titles of King and Queen, they were the peacekeepers of the Council. In times when the Council could not come to an agreement, their word was law.

In the wake of the Schism, the Genesis Council was effectively dissolved. The High Lord and Lady of Water and Fire as well as the Shadow King moved their courts to the mortal realm, and though the Council members have refused to comment, scholars believe that this division was the result of a disagreement concerning the Sanctorum's brutal treatment of time mages. As a result, the Dawn Court is now the effective ruling body of both Tempris and the continent of Lycia.

Having finally extricated himself from the clutches of his overambitious, female suitor, Skye was now searching the manor grounds for Taly. He wasn't exactly surprised that she had abandoned him when Aimee showed up, but he was irritated. And he planned on letting her know it—assuming he could find her.

The sun had finally melted away the last of the early morning frost, leaving crisp green grass in its wake. Skye tugged at the collar of his leather breastplate. Age had molded the hide armor to his frame, broken it down until it no longer protested and groaned with each movement. The heady scent of beeswax, oil, and saddle soap now clung to his skin beneath the heavy wool of his greatcoat. Even though he wasn't expecting trouble at the Aion Gate, it was always a good idea to wear armor when venturing outside the main cities. The creatures of the island were dangerously erratic when the aether was thin, and even small amounts of the right venom could be devastating to the fey.

Coming around the corner of the house, Skye

finally spotted Taly. She had found herself a sunny spot and was stretched out on the front staircase like a lazy cat. He should've known. This wouldn't be the first time he'd found her napping on the wide, stone steps. She made no indication that she heard his approach. Her eyes remained closed, and her chest rose and fell evenly.

"What are you doing?" Skye asked with an exasperated sigh.

Her lips quirked ever so slightly. Opening one eye, Taly replied, "Waiting. You were taking forever."

"No thanks to you." He took a seat on the step below her and leaned back. He was going to enjoy this next part. Without ceremony, he dropped a small dagger on her chest. "As per our agreement."

"Shards. You're not actually going to hold me to that, are you?"

"Yes. Yes, I am," he replied mercilessly. "Every word of it, you little brat."

Taly looked up at him and pouted, and there… there was a look he knew all too well. When they were younger, it used to get her whatever she wanted. "That's not going to work this time. I'm immune to your tricks." Skye laughed and tugged playfully at her hair, enjoying the look of frustrated defeat on her face as she slapped his hand away.

"Fine!" Taly theatrically hoisted herself into a sitting position and settled next to him. Picking up the dagger, she studied the ornate scabbard. Filigreed metal swirls swam across the surface, sheltering opalescent flower petals within their silvery tendrils. As she unsheathed the dagger, the sharpened blade gleamed in the morning light. The crossguard was thin and nimble, and a tiny row of shadow crystals peeked out of the poplar handle. The pommel was carved out of a single, glassy air crystal.

"It's beautiful," Taly murmured. "But I can't accept this. It's too much."

Skye pushed her hands away when she tried to return the dagger. "You can accept it, and you will. The bet was that you would let me give you a better dagger. That one's better."

"But this dagger is pure viridian! Even the scabbard! And these are all A-class crystals, Skye. How am I going to find someone that can repair a dagger with A-class crystals? This isn't practical."

Skye chuckled. Crystal quality was important when it came to spellcasting and magical crafting. Though higher-class stones could channel aether more efficiently, they could be temperamental. Every increase in crystal class required an exponentially more powerful shadow mage to perform the necessary repairs, and at the present point in time, Skye and Ivain were the only two shadow mages in Ryme that had enough magic to properly maintain a weapon with A-class crystals.

"I don't see a problem," Skye said. "I can take care of it when you come to dinner because… Oh! That's right. I won. And that means that in addition to letting us feed you occasionally, you have to let me, and only me, maintain your weapons from now on. And your crystals—that was part of the deal too." He draped a companionable arm around her shoulders, ignoring the way she groaned and buried her face in her hands. "What day works best for you? I'll need to let Eliza know to set an extra place at the table. And I'm sure Sarina's probably going to want to make sure she coordinates the laundry."

"I was so close. So close to beating you!" Taly elbowed him in the side, but he just tightened his grip, laughing. With a sigh, she exclaimed, "You know what? I don't care. I'll take your stupid dagger. But I want Zephyr back too."

"Oh, *come on*. What is it going to take for me to get you to let that thing go?" Skye asked, releasing her and pulling her beloved dagger from his boot. "It's embarrassing."

She accepted the dagger eagerly. Holding it up to her cheek, she gently stroked it and cooed, "It's okay, baby. He doesn't mean it. I know he still loves you."

"You're weird, Tink."

"Says you. I like to think that I'm 'adorably quirky.'" Taly stood and gave him a friendly punch on the arm. "You ready to go? If we leave now, we can be at the gate by" —she pulled out a beat-up pocket watch— "midday? If we make good time. That'll put us back here with plenty of time for me to get back to Ryme before dark."

Shit. Skye cleared his throat uncomfortably and averted his gaze. In the short time since they parted ways at the training yard, he had messed up. Badly.

"Uh..." His mouth suddenly felt very dry. Ducking his head, he mumbled, "Yeah. So, Aimee asked to see the Aion Gate, and I might have" —chancing a glance at Taly's face, he could see the dawning horror in her eyes— "told her that she could... come."

Taly didn't say anything immediately. She just stood there with her back to him, her shoulders tensed, staring straight ahead.

That made him nervous. Channeling just a tiny bit of aether, he heard the rapid flutter of her heart. “You know,” he stammered, wincing when her hands fisted at her side, “to be nice? I mean, Aimee *is* a guest.”

Taly exhaled forcefully and pinched the bridge of her nose.

“I’m sure it won’t be that bad,” Skye continued. She still wasn’t saying anything, and she hadn’t started hitting him yet. That made him *really* nervous. “I tried pawning her off on Sarina already, but then Sarina kinda disappeared. Ivain—well he just laughed, and then he disappeared too.”

Jerking her head, Taly finally looked down at where he still sat on the steps. The sunlight enveloped her slight form, casting a long shadow across her face. Skye braced himself, expecting her to release the full force of her fury.

But that didn’t happen. Instead of ranting and fuming, Taly took a deep breath and rolled her shoulders. “The price just doubled,” was all she said before turning to walk away.

Skye could hear Taly quietly grumbling beside him as they made their way to the stables. He wasn’t happy about the situation with Aimee either, but he couldn’t exactly do anything about it now.

He had messed up. He knew that. When he had been walking with Aimee back to the manor, she had started prattling on about the Aion Gate, but he had only been half-listening. At the time, his mind was somewhere far away still replaying the events of the sparring match. So naturally, when Aimee had asked to see the Aion Gate, he had stupidly and unknowingly mumbled, "Uh-huh." It seems years of just nodding along to her babbling had finally come back to haunt him. Before he could try to dissuade her, Aimee had let out a squeal that should've made his ears bleed, said something about going to change, and then ran off.

"You've got to be kidding me," Taly muttered.

Following Taly's stare, Skye could see that Aimee had somehow managed to beat them to the barn. The noblewoman stood in the center of the training yard issuing instructions to a very agitated groom. And while she *had* changed clothes, Skye wasn't sure he saw any more utility in her new wardrobe. She wore a traditional ladies' riding habit, complete with tapered sleeves and a bustled skirt. Gold cord adorned the front of the green velveteen gown in swirling loops, and a small, black dressage hat sat atop her immaculately coiffed hair. She tapped her foot impatiently as she watched the groom finish adjusting a sidesaddle on their most docile mare.

That's odd, Skye thought, squinting to make sure he had seen that correctly. Out of the vast array of riding equipment and horse tack that Harbor Manor's stables had acquired over the years, he had never seen a sidesaddle among the collection. As far as he knew, there had never been a need for one. While Taly would've outright laughed in the face of anyone who dared suggest she ride sidesaddle, even Sarina—a proper fey lady worthy of the title of Matriarch—chose to sit astride.

This was not going to be a good day.

"Skye," Taly whispered, "you need to tell her to stay here. She's going to get hurt."

"You know that's not going to work. She's just going to whine and pout until she gets her way," Skye replied. His irritation from before was starting to resurface.

Taly huffed and angrily shoved her hands into her pockets. "Oh, Shards forbid she might complain. You really need to learn to stand up to your girlfriend, Skye."

"You know what?" Skye snapped, trying to keep his voice low and stabbing a finger at Taly. "This is partly your fault too. You left me alone with her. You know that never ends well."

Taly turned on him, halting their advance. "Really? That's the argument you're going to go with? You're a grown man, Skye, and I'm not always going to be around to be your chaperone."

Her careless words made something inside him snap, but Skye did his best to hold back the surge of anger he could feel threatening to break loose. "Oh, believe me. I got that. You've already made that point loud and clear."

"What the hell is that supposed to mean?" Taly shot back accusingly.

"Are you kidding?" Skye asked in disbelief. "Have you just completely forgotten about the fact that you up and left last year with no explanation whatsoever?" Taly's eyes widened. Since she'd returned, they had both been dancing around this subject, trying to avoid the pain and awkwardness. But the hurt, the resentment, was still there—a gaping wound that had yet to heal.

When Taly continued to silently stare at him, her expression unreadable, Skye finally allowed himself to give into his anger. "What's the matter?" he hissed, the edges of his mouth curling up into a sardonic smile. "Having a hard time remembering how you just ran away from home without so much as a 'goodbye' or even a 'hey, I'm stepping out, so don't wait up?' It's okay. I get it."

Taly opened her mouth to make a retort, but Skye cut her off. "After all, why should it matter that I spent three weeks unable to do anything but hope that you weren't dead? That's on me, right? Because I worry too much? It's not like you were screaming in pain the last time I saw you. I must have imagined that."

"Stop it, Skye," Taly whispered.

"No," Skye growled in reply, taking a step towards her. He ignored the way his eyes began to sting, the way his breath caught in his throat, as he charged ahead, channeling all of his pent-up frustration into words. "Not until you tell me how you could just throw everything away without any regard for anyone's feelings but your own. The girl that I knew—my Taly… she never would've done that. She *never* would've cut everyone that gave a damn about her right out of her life with no explanation whatsoever."

"Skye—"

"Why did you leave, Taly?"

"I've already told you," she said quietly. "I'm mortal. You're not. That's going to end up being a problem when we're older."

"That's bullshit, and you and I both know it," Skye replied, his voice equally quiet. "All the years that we've known each other—when has that *ever* mattered? Just tell me the truth, Tink. Please…

just tell me something that's true."

Taly regarded him for a long moment. If he hadn't been watching her so closely—reading every breath, every heartbeat—he might've missed the almost imperceptible shake of her head. "I'm sorry, Skye." She tore her eyes away from his, wiping at her cheeks with her sleeve. "I'm sorry I hurt you. I… I *never* wanted to hurt you. But me leaving? It was for the best. And I know you want a better reason—a *different* reason. You want something that you can fix so that you can bring me home and we can go back to the way we were. But that's just not going to happen, Em. I'm not coming back. You need to let me go."

Skye wasn't sure what he had been expecting, but it hadn't been that. His shoulders slumped forward. He had asked for something true, and she had given it to him. She had no intention of coming home. He could see it in her eyes.

Taking a deep breath, he pinched the bridge of his nose, trying to regain his composure. "Look, I messed this up today. I wasn't paying attention to what I was saying while I was with Aimee, so that's on me. But I can't tell her not to come at this point. For the time being, we need to keep the little twit happy. Ivain is trying to get a loan from the Dawn Court so we can finally begin repairs on Tempris' fast-travel system, and for whatever reason, House Thanos currently has the favor of the High Lady of Air. If Aimee goes home and whines to her family, Ivain likely won't get the loan."

Taly frowned. "Why can't you endorse Ivain at the Dawn Court? Doesn't your family have more political sway than House Thanos?"

"Yes," Skye replied evenly. "Significantly

more. But I didn't attend court last year, and the High Lady of Air decided to take that as a personal snub. As you can imagine, that puts House Ghislain at a bit of a disadvantage right now when it comes to currying personal favors from the Air Guild."

"You skipped the court season?" Taly asked, her eyes widening in surprise. "Why? You always go to the Dawn Court in Arylaan when you visit the mainland."

Skye rubbed the back of his neck. Taly's departure was just one of many reasons he was in no rush to reminiscence on the events of the past summer. Deciding to ignore her question, he just shook his head and said, "Everything will be fine, Taly. I spoke with Ivain already, and even he didn't see a problem with bringing Aimee along. He just quoted that mortal saying he likes so much: 'there's strength in numbers.' You're worrying too much."

"And you're not worrying enough." Grabbing his arm as he moved past her, Taly whispered, "There's been a lot of talk around the Swap this week. Some of the traders are saying that people are going missing. No one really knows why, but I'm starting to think it might be the beasts. Whatever the Gate Watchers are doing differently with the gate this cycle is making the magical beasts even more erratic than usual. I know this trip might seem routine, but we really should be careful."

"And we will be, Tink," he said, trying to sound reassuring. "I promise. But if worst comes to worst and something does happen, let's not forget that Aimee *is* a mage. She might be a twit, but she's not completely defenseless. Who knows?

She might even be useful."

Taly sighed and pursed her lips, but she didn't say anything else.

"I hope you're not going to leave without me!" a deep baritone voice called from behind them.

Taly and Skye turned to find Aiden Bryer, Aimee's older brother, approaching. Though not wearing armor, his clothes were sturdy and well-suited for riding, and he wore a leather baldric with a polished ebony short sword sheathed at his waist. His hair had been shorn off since the last time Skye saw him, and his eyes were the same exotic shade of blue as his sister—a trait they had inherited from their human mother.

Catching up with them, Aiden wrapped his arms around Taly's waist and swung her off the ground. Laughing, he exclaimed, "I didn't know if I was going to get to see you this year! Aimee told me you'd moved out."

Taly let out a girlish squeal, and she was grinning when he set her back on the ground. Standing on her toes, she reached for his head and ran a hand over the closely cropped, red down. "When did this happen? You're so fuzzy now!"

Skye felt a strange pang lance his chest when he saw the friendly, unguarded smile Taly gave Aiden. Stepping closer to her and standing up straighter, Skye said, "Aiden just finished his initiation into the Crystal Guard. He's been assigned to the regiment in Faro where he'll be protecting the High Lord of Water."

"That's fantastic! Just like your dad, huh?" Taly was still smiling, completely at ease.

Aiden grinned back. "Yup. And unfortunately, this haircut is mandatory for anyone with a burning desire to protect the Genesis Shards and their chosen—at least for the first five or so centuries while the Knights are still training the stupid out of their new recruits."

Under normal circumstances, Skye would have no problem with Aiden and Taly's friendship. But as he continued to watch the two of them chattering away just like old friends should, he frowned. Where he'd had to coax and cajole and coerce just to get a few words and a reluctant smile out of her, for Aiden… for Aiden, there was no awkwardness, no animosity—just friendly teasing and easy laughter.

Taly looked like she was going to say something else, but Skye cut her off. "What are you doing here, Aiden? I thought you'd be at the clinic today."

Aiden's sapphire eyes widened in surprise. Skye's voice had come out a little gruffer than he intended. Recovering quickly, Aiden replied, "Not today, no. Apparently, there hasn't been an earth mage coming through town in a while, and the clinic had more patients request healing services than they expected. The menders decided to use today to try to get a little more organized before bringing me in."

"Lucky for us," Taly quipped. "Your sister is being a pain in the ass."

Aiden grinned, ducking down to look Taly in the eye. "That's not surprising. And, as it so happens, that's why I'm here. Ivain mentioned that Aimee managed to insert herself somewhere she didn't need to be, so I thought I might tag along to keep an eye on her."

"Or you could just escort her back to the manor," Taly replied pointedly.

"I *could* do that," Aiden said with a shrug. A

devilish air crept into his expression. "But I'm just so worried about what Skye would do without me there to protect him."

"Say what now?" Skye asked, arching a brow.

Aiden grinned. Being the same age as Skye, the two men had become natural rivals, and it seemed like they were always vying for something, be it women, prestige, or anything in between. However, as they matured, their relationship had evened out, and they tended to get along more times than not.

Of course, they did still like to poke at each other on occasion.

"Now, c'mon, Skye," Aiden drawled, crossing his arms and widening his stance. "You know that I've always thought of you as a little brother—emphasis on the *little* part. It's my duty as the *bigger* man to make sure you get to the Aion Gate safe and sound."

Skye rolled his eyes. Aiden had grown to be just a hair taller than him, and he never let him forget it. Well, two could play that game. "Yes, that extra fraction of an inch is quite intimidating. Although, now that I look at you, I think it may have been all hair. We might need to re-measure."

Skye smirked when he saw Aiden's smile falter slightly. And before the earth mage could formulate a response, he pivoted, saying, "Also, I've been meaning to say that I'm sorry I missed you at court last summer. I heard that you and Lady Aliya were seen together. I also heard you couldn't quite close that deal. If you'd asked, I could've told you she only goes for shadow mages now." Skye gave an unapologetic shrug. "That's my fault, by the way."

As Aiden was opening his mouth to make a

retort, Taly stepped between the two men. "No!" she snapped, waving her hands. Turning to Skye, she gave him a stern look that he knew all too well. "We are not starting up this bullshit again. Shards! Sometimes I really wish the two of you would just whip 'em out and get it over with already."

Aiden laughed and ruffled Taly's hair. "Nah, I wouldn't want to ruin you for other men." Looking towards the stable, he suddenly exclaimed, "Oh Shards! That poor groom. I should probably go save him from my sister's wrath." He gave them a sheepish smile and then jogged off towards the stables.

Skye scowled after him. "Why don't you have a problem with Aiden coming?"

Taly crinkled her nose as she glared up at Skye. "Because he's not a dumbass."

By the time the pair arrived at the stables, the groom had finally managed to saddle Aimee's horse to her satisfaction and had brought around two others. Ignoring the tittering woman, Taly sidled up to the smaller of the two unsaddled animals. The little gelding nuzzled her cheek with its nose as she pulled an apple from her bag and reached out a hand to stroke its neck.

"He missed you, you know," Skye said, leaning down so only Taly could hear him.

She raised an eyebrow, glancing at Skye from the corner of her eye as she ran a hand down the white stripe on the horse's nose. "Well, with only you for company, who could blame him? Isn't that right, Byron?" She inclined her head, pretending to listen before turning back to Skye and saying, "He said *yes*."

"Princess Tink can still talk to animals?" Skye

asked with a laugh.

"She can."

Feeling a little awkward after his outburst, Skye placed a tentative hand on Taly's shoulder, smiling when she reached up and twined her fingers with his. After a moment, he moved to start saddling his own horse.

"Aiden. What are you doing here?" Aimee asked as her brother led another horse out of the stable.

"You're not the only one interested in the Aion Gate, dear sister. I'm crossing over to the mortal realm in a few weeks to join my regiment, and I figured I would go take a look before that happens. I hear the Aion Gate is quite a sight, even when it's closed." As the groom approached Aiden to assist with his mount, he waved the man off. "I can saddle my own horse. No need to worry."

"Talya," Aimee began, inspecting Taly's clothing and equipment distastefully, "you could almost be pretty if you tried. I will never understand why you *insist* on dressing like a man."

"And I will never understand why you *insist* on dressing like a cupcake," Taly replied with a smirk. Seeing that Aimee was opening her mouth to make a retort, she quickly added, "You're certainly not dressed for a trip to the gate. That outfit" —she hesitated, looking Aimee up-and-down disapprovingly— "is entirely impractical."

"Well," Aimee huffed, sensing that she wasn't going to be able to get underneath Taly's skin, "I would rather be pretty than practical." Taking a deep breath, Aimee ran her hands over her velvet bodice and smiled serenely. "For what it's worth, I liked your hair better when it was longer. That haircut and those clothes? You look like a child."

As Aimee walked away, Taly gave Skye a meaningful look. Not knowing what else to do, he just shrugged and smiled apologetically as he continued readying the bay stallion standing restlessly in front of him.

As their small band passed through Ryme, Taly spurred her horse into the lead, setting a brisk pace. Skye could see that she held a stack of papers in one hand and a map in the other, the reins wrapped around the horn of her saddle. Between the two of them, she had always been the better rider. While he was far more comfortable in the saddle than most, she could ride literal circles around him.

A densely wooded forest separated the town of Ryme from the wasteland that surrounded the Aion Gate. The air was slightly cooler in the shade of the massive trees, and Skye couldn't help but admire the austere surroundings. In a few weeks' time, this area would be teeming with life as the animals awoke from their winter slumber and the plants reemerged to start a new cycle.

Alongside the road, a flash of steel caught his eye, and when he looked closer, he could just make out the outline of an old set of air tram tracks peeking from beneath the underbrush—the remnants of a direct line that used to connect

Ryme to the Aion Gate. When the Time Queen was still alive, the air tram made it possible to travel the entire length of the island and back in only a matter of hours. But the fast-travel system was just one more thing that had fallen into disrepair after the Sanctorum ravaged the area. The Marquess had tried again and again to have the air rails restored, but there just never seemed to be enough tax revenue to fund the project.

"Tell me about the Aion Gate, Skylen," Aimee said suddenly, her tone dripping with false sweetness. "I'm sure you're an expert."

"Huh?" Skye hadn't been listening again. He really should stop doing that. "Oh, right. What would you like to know?"

"Well? Why is everyone so eager for it to open? I've heard such horrible things about the mortal realm. All of those *humans* that don't even believe in magic. I don't know why anyone would want to go there." Skye had managed to get a few steps ahead of her, so Aimee urged her horse forward. It promptly ignored her and continued its slow, deliberate pace.

Skye slowed his horse. The stallion's ears twitched, and it pulled on the reins. "Well, I suppose the primary reason most people look forward to the Aion Gate opening is because there are three members of the Genesis Council that have chosen to make the mortal realm their home. It certainly benefits us all if we can maintain contact with our rulers."

"Why don't those Lords come over here then?" Aimee asked. "Staying in the mortal realm—I've always felt that was very irresponsible on their part."

She was falling farther behind, so Skye

reached back and grabbed the lazy mare's bridle, pulling it forward. "Not necessarily. A significant portion of our population is on the other side of the Aion Gate. The Council has as much a responsibility to those people as they do to the people on the mainland and Tempris."

Aimee hummed disapprovingly. "Well then, please correct me if I'm wrong, but I was told that each gate on Tempris used to lead to a different kingdom—all of which resided under the Genesis Council's jurisdiction. Is that accurate?"

"Yes," Skye answered with a nod, already knowing where she was taking him with this line of questioning. "Before the Schism, the fey empire was vast, sprawling out across all the known worlds. Tempris was the crossroads that connected them all. Every gate on the island—the Seren Gate, the Aion Gate, and all of the many other gates that no longer function—connect to other realms separated by time and space."

"I don't understand then," Aimee claimed. "Don't the Genesis Lords have a responsibility to the citizens in those kingdoms as well?"

Skye clicked his tongue and gave the mare's bridle another tug. Looking back at Aimee, he continued, "Yes, they do. But, unfortunately, the Gate Watchers don't have the resources to monitor and power every gate on the island, and the Dawn Court has refused to reevaluate our budget. So, we do what we can with what we have."

"Alright," Aimee acquiesced. "If that's the case, then why did the Watchers choose to focus on the Aion Gate instead of any of the others? Why did they prioritize the gate that leads to the mortal realm?"

Skye resisted the urge to roll his eyes. He

knew for a fact that the noblewoman had been educated on the myriad of reasons the Dawn Court had ordered the Gate Watchers to give the Aion Gate priority. What he didn't know was why she seemed to think that playing dumb would appeal to him.

"Several reasons," he replied patiently. "The most important being that we need the mortals that choose to become Feseraa. Even before the highborn birthrate began to dwindle, humans were considerably more prolific than the fey. Over the past two centuries, the noble families have tried to negate the effects of our declining fertility by negotiating breeding arrangements outside of formal marriage bonds, but, as I'm sure you know, that initiative has been met with limited success. Pureblooded fey children are still rare, and most households have had to use mortals to boost their numbers. Hence why we have a vested interest in maintaining contact with what is, for all intents and purposes, a magicless realm. While mortal blood does significantly dilute our magic, the survival of our species may eventually come to depend on our ability to breed with the humans."

Aimee coughed delicately, visibly uncomfortable with the turn their conversation had taken. Her mother was a Feseraa, and though she and her brother had enough magic to be considered a part of the small circle of highborn gentry, they still had human blood running through their veins.

"On the subject of breeding" —the noblewoman gave him a sidelong glance— "I hear that your mother is trying to secure an alliance with House Arendryl by way of a breeding offer. House Arendryl has already recommended a young woman from their estate in Faro. Do you know who Lady Emrys plans to put forward as the sire? I heard your name come up in conversation. Is there any truth to the rumors?"

A muscle in his jaw began to feather, and Skye let out a hissing sigh. His mother's efforts to involve him in her political machinations were the very last thing he wanted to discuss. "You're very well informed," he said, giving Aimee a tight smile, "but my mother would be very cross if I were to reveal all of her intrigues. If you have any other questions about the gates, I'll be happy to answer those. Otherwise..." He looked to the two riders in front of him. Aiden had moved up next to Taly, and the two had started talking quietly. "Otherwise, I should probably go speak with Taly—make sure there are no problems with our route."

Aimee placed a hand on his arm. "You mentioned resources. Why aren't you able to open the other gates? Did the time mages do something to break them?"

"No," Skye replied, dragging his eyes away from Taly. "Most people are usually very quick to accuse the time mages of sabotaging the gates during the Schism, but that's simply not true. The gates aren't broken. They just can't function correctly without a time mage—the Time Queen to be exact."

"That dreadful woman? If that's the case, perhaps we're better off without the gates." Aimee's voice held a note of contempt that didn't surprise Skye in the slightest. Many of the mainland fey were still very quick to condemn the High Lady of Time for her actions during the Schism, regardless of the lack of any physical evidence. "You know, our stepfather says that the time mages were nothing but power-hungry tyrants, never willing to work with anyone. He says that the Schism finally gave us definitive proof that they were simply too dangerous to be allowed to live."

Skye grew quiet. Although he hadn't been alive when the great disaster occurred, he had studied it. No one had ever figured out why the Time Queen had forcibly shut down every gate on the island. Thousands died when the bridges between the worlds collapsed, and they'd lost contact with all of the gated realms—over half their population.

"While I can acknowledge that the Time Queen's actions were reprehensible," Skye said carefully, "I'm not sure I agree that executing every new time mage for what they *could* be capable of is either fair or just."

"And I disagree," Aimee said with a practiced sigh. "After all, if there are no time mages, then the Time Shard can never revive. There will never be another High Lord or Lady of Time… or another Schism. It's a small sacrifice to make."

Skye's lips thinned, and he couldn't help but think that Aimee reminded him of a rather annoying bird he had once seen in the mortal realm—imitating and echoing whatever words were fed to her, regardless of their merit.

Aimee waved a dismissive hand as she prattled on. "The Sanctorum may have become a little overzealous during the Hunt, but their actions have always served the greater good."

"Perhaps if you spent more time on Tempris, you would feel differently," Skye replied, forcibly reining in his burgeoning ire. "The Sanctorum's cruelty was felt far more keenly here, and you'll find that most of the island's citizenry still hold a great deal of resentment towards their order."

Aimee huffed, then smoothed back a dark curl. "Well, *perhaps,* if the Time Queen and her followers had simply come forward rather than running away to wherever it was they went, the Sanctorum wouldn't have been forced to resort to such drastic measures during the Hunt."

Skye raised a disapproving brow. The Hunt was still a sensitive subject in most circles. After the Schism, it took the Genesis Lords on the fey mainland almost a year to pry open the Seren Gate and regain access to Tempris. By that time, the Time Queen as well as every time mage under her command had inexplicably vanished. So, the Sanctorum was formed, and the Hunt began. The newly anointed officers were given a single directive—find the High Lady of Time and her followers.

However, when the time mages couldn't be found—ultimately presumed dead when the time crystals began to lose their magic—the Sanctifiers, rather than surrender the power they'd been granted, created for themselves a new purpose. They convinced those still in mourning that "drastic measures" were needed to prevent another calamity. They fanned the flames of panic and hysteria, soaked the soil with innocent blood.

When Aimee opened her mouth to make some other careless remark, Skye cut her off. "The Schism and the Hunt were both tragedies." His voice held a hidden edge, and he gave Aimee a meaningful look. "And they resulted in the deaths of far too many innocent people. People who had no connection to the Schism or the Queen. People without even the faintest trace of time magic, whose only crime was being in the wrong place at the wrong time. You would do well to remember that—especially if you have any intention of travelling to the mortal realm when the Aion Gate opens. I should not need to remind you that the Genesis Lords beyond the gate have publicly condemned the Sanctorum and the Dawn Court for continuing to support it."

Aimee faltered, visibly surprised by Skye's rebuke. This was the closest he had ever come to being rude, despite her repeated unwelcome and overly aggressive attempts to woo him. Clearing her throat uncomfortably, she stammered, "Forgive me, Skylen. I spoke out of turn." Her cheeks flushed, the color dampened somewhat by the heavy cosmetic glamour she wore. "How... how is the Seren Gate different from the Aion Gate? They lead to different realms, so I assume there must be some differences in the way they function."

"No," Skye answered curtly. His eyes slid to the riders ahead of him, and he frowned when he saw Taly turn to Aiden and laugh at something the other man had said. "The Seren Gate and the Aion Gate function in exactly the same way. They just open on different schedules."

"And what exactly does that mean?" Aimee looked to see what had captured Skye's attention. When Taly glanced back, a broad smile on her face, the noblewoman turned her nose up into the air.

Skye shook his head, looking away from where Taly and Aiden rode side-by-side and refocusing on Aimee. "That means that time runs at a different pace in each of the gated realms. Since we don't have the ability to force the timestreams to align, we have to wait for time in the bridged realms to sync up with time here on Tempris. The fey mainland and Tempris are very similar—a year spent here is almost the same as a year spent on the mainland, give or take a few days. That's why we're able to open the Seren Gate several times a month.

"In contrast, the Aion Gate connects to the mortal realm. Time in the mortal realm generally runs far more slowly than on Tempris, so we have to wait for the rare moments when the two timestreams synchronize. When that happens, we charge up the gate and try to keep the power steady enough to stabilize the connection."

"Stop," Taly called out from the front of the procession. They were approaching a fork in the road. Aiden had stopped beside her, and Skye saw him whisper something as he tugged on the sleeve of her coat. Taly nodded, the tightness around her eyes melting away as she smiled back at him.

Skye walked his horse up to where Taly had halted the group. "What is it?"

She didn't look at him. She just gazed off into the distance where the road veered right.

"I'm not sure yet. Stay here." She gave the gelding a kick and trotted ahead of them.

Skye scowled as he watched her leave, but he decided to follow her lead. He had agreed to hire her after all. He might as well let her do her job. Straining his ears, he noted that he could no longer hear the echoes of the gypsum sparrows' songs. The whisper of dry leaves was the only sound hissing through the densely packed wall of trees.

That's odd, he thought with a twinge of unease.

Channeling a small amount of aether, he felt

his senses start to sharpen, and he listened. He could just make out the crackling of leaves about a mile east, most likely a deer or a bear, but still no birds or insects. A strange hush had fallen over the forest.

That could only mean one thing—a predator was nearby.

Skye's heartbeat quickened. Looking behind him, he could see that Aiden and Aimee talked quietly amongst themselves, completely unaware of the potential danger. And why should they be frightened? The main roads had magical wards put in place to protect travelers from the beasts that roamed the forest.

Feeding more aether into the augmentation spell, Skye focused on the arch of overhanging branches that Taly had disappeared through earlier. He could just make out the faint scent of iron and soap wafting on the air, and the crunch of dirt thundered in his ears. A horse pawed at the ground nervously.

Taly—she was no longer on horseback. She wasn't even on the road. No, she was wading through the underbrush between the trees, past the protection of the wards.

Shit, Skye thought as he let go of the spell. His heightened senses dulled, and the world around him blurred before snapping back into focus. It was just as he feared—Taly had sensed something and set off to track it.

His first instinct in this situation was to go get her and drag her back to safety, willing or not. However, that would most likely destroy any goodwill he still had left after their little spat earlier that morning. He knew he should stay back—demonstrate that he trusted her to do her job. But he had spent 15 years trying to protect her. Those habits were hard to break.

Just as Skye was about to ride after her, Taly returned. "We can't go this way."

"Why not?" Skye asked gruffly, relief washing over him.

Taly raised an eyebrow. "Because a harpy passed through. Not too long ago by the looks of it. It's not too surprising since it's their mating season. This is the only time of year they ever really come out during the day. I set out some lures to try to push it farther east, but we should still go around."

Taly started to ride off in the other direction, but Skye grabbed her arm, pulling her up short. "Are you absolutely sure? We should be fine if we stay on the main road. The wards were repaired last month."

Taly sighed impatiently. "Which would be fine if those drunken assholes in the Fire Guild hadn't burned through a large chunk of them just ahead. How do you think the harpy got through? The wards on the back roads are spotty at best, and it's going to add several hours to our ride. Still, I think it's safer."

"Damn it," Skye cursed quietly. "Are you sure you're not just messing with me?" He glanced back at Aimee and gave Taly a pleading look. The absolute last thing he wanted to do was spend more time with that silly noblewoman than he had to. "Is this revenge?"

Taly's expression softened, and her lips quirked to the side when she saw his pained grimace. "I'm not happy about it either, but I know how to track a harpy. *And*, I know what a busted ward looks like."

Shaking her head, she exhaled sharply and pulled out the same stack of papers she'd been reading earlier. "Scouting notes," she mumbled distractedly when she saw Skye's questioning stare. "The harpy was already headed east, so we should be able to stay out-of-range if we skirt around from the west. There was a kelpie sighted in that direction a few days ago, but it's probably moved farther north by now—back to the coast. Just make sure you stick close to me and don't get ahead. Some of these side roads are pretty overgrown, so we're going to have to take it slow. I take it you brought the aether concealment charms?"

Sighing and falling in beside her, Skye said, "I handed out the charms before we left." He held up his arm and showed her a simple silver band. Water and shadow crystals were set in the center of the bracelet.

"I meant to ask you what these did," Aimee gushed with false enthusiasm, picking at the band on her arm. Being a water mage, Skye was sure that Aimee knew *exactly* what they did. "Tell me, Talya. Why don't you have one?"

Taly mumbled something unintelligible under her breath and signaled for her horse to go faster. Louder, she said, "Because I'm mortal. I have no aether and, therefore, no magic." Skye didn't miss the slight quaver in her voice or the way her shoulders slumped forward. Glancing back, he saw an arrogant smirk twist Aimee's lips as she pulled on the reins of her horse, deliberately slowing her pace.

As Aimee's mare once again fell behind, Skye ignored her calls as he urged his own horse to keep pace with Taly.

CHAPTER 6

-An excerpt from When the Bridges Fell: Letters from a Lost Island

The 32nd day of the month Septane, during the 8th year of the Empty Throne

Hey Lea,

We still can't figure out why all this stuff keeps falling through. Since the gates went down, it's just started accumulating in places where the veil is thin. A new wave of junk came through last night over at the Odyssea Gate, and there's enough now that it's starting to affect our ability to access the gate controls.

When you see her, can you ask Diantha where she wants us to put it for the time being? There's a lot of metal, so maybe the fire mages can do something with it.

-Pasha

Late into the afternoon hours, the small band of travelers arrived at the northern edge of the forest. The trees began to thin, allowing rays of sunlight to peek through the branches, and the horses grew restless as the scent of sand and metal saturated the air.

Taly raised a hand, signaling for them to stop at the tree line. “Stay here. Something’s not right.” Without looking back, she pushed her horse forward and skirted silently along the border of the desert surrounding the Aion Gate.

No matter how many times he visited the Aion Gate, Skye was always shocked by the swift transition from lush forest to arid wasteland. The Aion Gate was by far the largest gate on the island, built directly on top of a tear in the veil between the worlds. It required a massive amount of aether to function, and after the Schism, it had started leeching the aether out of the surrounding area. As a result, the land around the gate was uninhabitable. No plants would grow, and the animals knew to steer clear. Only the magical beasts dared to venture out of the forest, drawn by the massive power of the gate when their thirst was at its worst.

Skye could just make out the smooth planes of the gate several miles in the distance. Mountains of junk and scrap metal surrounded the base of the monument, spreading, thinning and scattering out across the barren landscape.

“It’s dirtier than I thought it would be.” Aimee’s lips turned down into a frown. “What is all of that… stuff?"

"Since the Aion Gate leads to the mortal realm, most of what falls through the veil in this area is mortal tech," Skye explained. "Sometimes, we'll see a few items that look like they came from somewhere else, but not often."

"Shards, I don't know what half of that stuff is," Aiden said, his eyes wide. "I suppose I'll have to learn, though. I hear that Faro is quite progressive in the way that it's chosen to incorporate mortal culture and technology into its infrastructure."

Skye shrugged, his eyes trained on where he had last seen Taly. "I wouldn't feel bad about it, Aiden. Mortal technology has been advancing very quickly in recent years. It's hard to keep up."

"What do you do with it all?" Aimee asked, a hint of genuine curiosity lacing her words.

"The Fire Guild will take most of it," Skye replied. "Mortal salvage contains a lot of metal, so they'll smelt it down."

After a long moment, Taly returned. As she dismounted her horse, she said, "A fresh batch of scrap came through, so there's not a straight path to the gate. That means we leave the horses here and go in on foot. Also, there's a harpy about a league west of here, circling."

"Is it safe to approach?" Skye asked, his shoulders tense beneath his armor. The harpies on Tempris were a special kind of nightmare, one of the few things the highborn fey had cause to fear.

"I believe so," Taly replied with a decisive nod. "We'll be in full view as we make our approach, but it's still far enough away that we won't draw its attention if we're careful."

Taly absentmindedly scratched at her horse's

neck as she gave them all a pointed stare. "Keep the talking to a minimum and watch where you're going. Move *slowly*. Some of this mortal tech is sharp, and if you get cut, that concealment charm won't do shit to cover the smell of your magic. If something does happen, then run for the tree line and pray that the harpy doesn't pursue. It's female from what I can tell—which means it's venomous. Just in case you all need a reminder, the venom of the Tempris harpy is one of the deadliest poisons known to the fey. One scratch, and you *will* die without a healer. And on Tempris when the aether is thin like this, you might die even with a healer. It's a tossup. So, in conclusion, if the harpy comes for you, do not engage this thing. If you see it so much as twitch, run the fuck away, screaming if need be."

"So vulgar," Aimee grumbled. "Aiden, be a dear and come help me."

Skye watched Taly closely as she tied off her horse and grabbed her pack. She was all business as she checked the pistols holstered around her waist and secured the new air dagger he had given her that morning in a sheath strapped to her thigh. Shaking himself, he followed suit, effortlessly swinging himself out of the saddle.

Skye felt inexplicably uneasy as he watched Taly start into the wasteland. She scanned the area around her carefully, a hand resting on one of the pistols at her waist. Even though Sarina had told him again and again that Taly had found her footing in the salvaging trade, he had never fully believed her. Until now, that is.

"Grown up, hasn't she?" Aiden commented as he came to stand beside Skye. He too was watching Taly as she threw down some ashewa dust across the trail to mask the scent of the horses. This close to the Aion Gate, the risk of encountering a non-magical predator that might attack the animals was minimal, but the dust was still a good precaution to take. The strong smell of the powdered ashewa bark would ward off pretty much anything with a nose.

Skye glared at Aiden from the corner of his eye. There was something about the way the earth mage's eyes raked over Taly, top to bottom and back again, that rankled him. Clearing his throat, Skye said evenly, "Yeah. Took me by surprise too."

They carefully picked their way through the debris, making their way towards the gate. Skye could just see the harpy in the distance. It was at least twice his height, grotesque and flea-bitten, and the skin on its bald head was almost the same color as the bronzed dust that collected around the gate. Great feathered wings protruded from its back, and its body was covered with rows of glassy scales. Lifting its head, it sniffed the wind with its strangely flat nose, its head cocking to the side when it caught sight of them. For one breathless moment, it considered them, trying to decide if their little party was tempting enough to pursue.

"Give it a minute," Taly whispered when she saw Skye's hand instinctively reach for his sword. "It's just sizing us up. If those aether concealment charms are working like they're supposed to, it'll lose interest."

Skye nodded in acknowledgment but still kept his hand on his sword as he continued to stare down the harpy. He let out a slow sigh of relief when the great beast eventually shook itself and turned away, just as Taly predicted.

It was a long trek across the field, made even

more arduous as the layer of scrap littering the ground began to thicken and the mountains of metal grew taller and more menacing. Aimee would occasionally try to voice a complaint about a tear in her dress or how uncomfortable the ground felt underfoot, but halfway through each attempt, Aiden would promptly shush her. Taly eventually split off from the group, never taking her eyes off the harpy as it listlessly circled in the distance. Every so often, she would bend down and inspect something of interest, sometimes tossing it back into the piles of debris and other times stashing it away in her bag.

A salvager's paradise, Skye thought with a low chuckle. While the fey had little use for most of the junk that tended to accumulate around the gates, every now and then, valuable gems and metals, even the occasional magical object, would fall through. That's why salvagers like Taly were always rushing to the areas on the island where the veil was thin and digging through rubble and trash.

Finally, after what seemed like far longer than it should've taken, Skye found himself standing at the base of the monolith. The Aion Gate was a thing of frightening beauty. At thirty feet wide and at least a hundred feet tall, it was almost three times larger than any other gate on the island. It towered over him, shooting up into the sky and disappearing into the clouds.

The outer hyaline pillars practically glowed, deflecting the afternoon sun in a chaotic, rainbowed array of shattered light—silent crystalline sentinels surrounded by rolling hills of rust. Slotted inside the translucent obelisks stood two solid sheets of shadow crystal, sanded and polished so that the glittering violet surfaces reflected the ruddy wasteland. The Gate Watchers had been tirelessly pouring aether into the crystals over the last few months, and they thrummed with a pulsating energy that seemed to vibrate the very air. Skye could feel the aether reach out to him as it swirled restlessly behind the smooth wall of crystal. He trailed a finger along the surface, watching the glowing eddies of whirling magic shadow his movements.

Between the massive amethyst panels rested a single strip of gold, about two fingers wide—time crystal. The Gate Watchers had just barely managed to preserve the time crystals in the gates after the Schism. The glittering, golden stones had all gone dark when the Time Queen died, and with no one left to wield the Time Shard, they would most likely remain that way.

"Feel free to look around," Skye said to his companions as he ran a hand across the control panel. It was a small rectangular piece of shadow crystal set into one of the hyaline pillars, and a network of inscribed runes flashed and stuttered to life as he keyed in the proper commands. Though hardly spoken by anyone except scholars, the ancient Faera language, by its very nature, could channel and bind magic. Their technology, their magic, their crystals—the very foundations of the modern fey's way-of-life depended on this ancient, arcane typography they'd inherited from a dead race that most had all but forgotten.

"Just be careful with the shadow crystal," Skye added as an afterthought. "At this point in the charging cycle, it tends to spark."

Aiden and Aimee broke away and started circling the base of the gate. Aimee had to lean on her brother's arm, her skirts bunched in one hand as he helped her navigate the debris. They spoke to each other in hushed voices as they surveyed the stacks of salvage with wide eyes.

Skye moved with practiced precision around the gate, stopping here and there to make a notation in a small journal. Although it had been several years since he'd had to take readings on the gate, he'd performed these same tests so many times during the final days of the last charging cycle that the movements were still second-nature. Everything seemed to be in order, so it didn't take him long.

With the measurements from the shadow crystals squared away, Skye approached the time crystal. Without a time mage, they had no way of knowing exactly when the separate time streams would sync, but they could make a guess. Skye blew out a slow breath as he ran a hand over the strip of gold. Even dark crystals, crystals that could no longer focus or refine aether, retained faint traces of magic swirling about their inner depths. There was information in that energy—if one knew how to find it. Closing his eyes, Skye attempted to tease out that tiny ripple of aether still lingering inside the crystal, tried to guess its secrets.

Jotting down a few notes, he closed the notebook and slid it back into his pocket. It seemed Ivain was right to be worried. Their original estimate was off. These readings were telling him they needed to move up the timeline for the gate connection by at least a week, two if they wanted to play it safe.

Just enough time to create more paperwork.

"Is everything alright?"

Skye jumped at the sound. He hadn't heard Aimee and Aiden come up behind him. "Yes. It's nothing we can't still correct," Skye said to Aiden in a low voice. "I'm done here. If you want to start heading back to the horses, I'll go get Taly."

Taly had scouted around to the far eastern perimeter of the scrap field where she stood motionless, scanning the area the harpy had been guarding earlier. As Skye approached, she said aloud, "I think we're okay now. It was watching us for a while, but it seems to have lost interest. It's moving away."

"Just in time." Skye came up to stand beside her. "I'm finished if you're ready to head back."

"Yeah," she said, nodding stiffly.

Skye turned and waved at Aimee and Aiden. Aiden was almost carrying his sister at this point, and the two had fallen behind. They moved slowly, taking deliberate steps and occasionally stopping to peer into the piles of mortal waste.

Taly and Skye walked back in silence, deftly picking their way across the uneven terrain. She kept her eyes trained on the ground, her lips pursed in a frown. The tension from their argument at the stables still hadn't dissipated completely, and if her previous words and actions were anything to go by, he knew she would be walking out of his life again in a few hours. He couldn't let her go like this.

Hesitantly, Skye reached over and flicked her on the nose, just like he used to do when they were children and he wanted her attention. She started, her eyes narrowing in irritation as she gave him a questioning look. But then to his great relief, instead of pulling away, she cocked her head to the side and smiled.

At least that was one thing he could still count on. They could bicker and fight until they were blue in the face, but they were still friends in the end.

"You did good today," he remarked casually, placing a hand on her shoulder.

Taly eyed him skeptically. "Try not to sound so surprised... *jerk*."

Smirking, Skye pulled her to his side, reaching around her as he tried to wriggle his hand into her bag. "So, what did you find? Anything good?"

Taly laughed and slapped his hand away. "Not really. Just a few pieces of old jewelry—absolutely garish, but still gold. If I'm lucky, I might not be forced to eat Jay's cooking this month. Even on a good day, that guy makes Sarina look like a gourmet chef."

Skye covered his mouth, trying to suppress the laughter he could feel bubbling up. His stomach still turned just thinking about the few times he'd been subjected to Sarina's cooking. "Shards... that's bad. That's *really* bad."

Eventually, they approached the edge of the debris field where the scrap started to thin. Glancing behind them, Skye could see that Aimee and Aiden had stopped, and Aimee was crouched on the ground reaching for something.

"Hey, about earlier..." Skye started to say to Taly. He hesitated, unsure of how to finish that sentence. He felt a pressing need to address their argument before they headed back, but at the same time, he meant every word he had said earlier that morning. She had hurt him, and he still didn't quite know how to move past it.

"Don't worry about it," Taly sniffed.

"Whatever hatred or hostility you feel towards me, I deserve it."

"What?" Skye stopped, standing motionless as he stared after her. She thought that he hated her? Where the hell had she come up with that crazy idea? "I don't hate you, Tink." Taly walked the few steps back to him, ready to argue, but he held up a hand to shush her. "Don't get me wrong. I'm angry. And hurt. And I wish you would just tell me what the hell is going on with you since, as I've told you before, I can't read your mind. But hating you? I could never hate you."

"I wouldn't blame you if you did," Taly mumbled as she kicked at a stray piece of scrap. "Because you were right this morning. What I did—the way I left—it was selfish. Ivain, Sarina, you—you've never been anything but kind to me, and I threw it away."

Skye felt his heart clench almost painfully, and he took a deep breath, trying to find his voice.

Taly's eyes flicked up to his face. She must have mistook something in his expression for anger because she turned away, her cheeks reddening. "You want answers… I get that. But that's not something that I can give you right now. I know that doesn't make a whole lot of sense, but that's just how it is. Still, whether you believe me or not, I am sorry. The last thing I ever wanted to do was hurt you. If my word still means anything to you at all, then I promise you that much is true." She took a deep breath before looking up at him uncertainly.

Skye shoved his hands into his pockets as he considered her words, tried to measure her sincerity. After a long moment, he felt a smile tugging at the corners of his mouth. "Say it again," he commanded softly.

Taly looked away before meeting his eyes. “I’m sorry, Skye.”

“No.” He waved his hand dismissively. “No, no, no. The other part. The important part.”

Taly just stared at him, her brows pinched together in confusion. Skye knew the exact moment that understanding finally set in. She gave him an icy glare, and a long-suffering sigh fell from her lips. “You were right?”

“Yes!” Skye exclaimed. Clapping a hand on her shoulder, he gave her a gentle shake. “Shards, that’s twice in one day. You know,” he mused, glancing back to make sure that Aimee and Aiden were still behind them, “I changed my mind. I think you need to run away more often. If I’d known that was all it took for you to finally accept my superior wisdom—”

“Oh, please,” Taly grumbled.

“Shhh…” Skye held a finger up to her lips. “Superior wisdom is being imparted. Have some respect.”

Taly slapped at his hand, a wide, only somewhat reticent smile on her face. “The only thing superior about you is your ego.”

“It is very impressive,” Skye agreed readily. “Thank you for noticing.”

Taly arched a brow, opening her mouth to make a retort, but she never got the chance. Aimee ran up behind them, fastening herself to Skye’s arm and using her body to shove Taly out of the way. Unable to channel his magic, to increase his speed and make a dive for her, he could do nothing but watch as Taly, thrown off-balance, lost her footing in the scrap and went down hard.

“Damn it, Aimee!” Skye cursed, shaking her

off roughly. He grabbed her shoulders when she started to stumble. “What do you think you’re doing?”

“I found… Oh! I’m so sorry, Talya. I didn’t see you,” Aimee said with false sympathy. She didn’t even bother to turn around as she tried to press herself against Skye.

“Skye!” Taly groaned, still on the ground. “I think I’m hurt.”

Sidestepping around Aimee, Skye rushed to Taly’s side and fell to his knees beside her. She was clutching at her leg—her face scrunched up in pain. As he pulled her hand back, he felt bile burn his throat. A jagged, rusted piece of scrap metal protruded from the back of her thigh.

“Oh, Shards!” Aimee exclaimed, her hands flying to cover her mouth. “Oh, my… Talya… you’re… that’s blood! I’m sorry! Shards! I’m so, so sorry!”

The apology was real this time, but Skye didn’t care. “Shut up, Aimee!” he barked.

The sharp, metallic scent of human blood filled the air, and Taly winced as he gently nudged the shredded fabric of her leggings away from the wound, trying to get a better look. Blood trickled out of the gash, coating his hands. “Aiden! We need you!” Skye shouted frantically. He heard the hurried patter of footsteps as Aiden quickened his pace.

“Skye, you have to pull it out,” Taly moaned through gritted teeth. Her breathing was growing ragged, and she stared at the metal with wide, fearful eyes.

“No, Taly. Aiden is coming. He can heal you.” Skye grabbed her shoulder, both trying to reassure himself and to get her to focus on him instead of the wound. When he pulled his hand away, flecks of blood clung to the fur trim lining her coat.

"We don't have time for that." She turned her head and pointed behind them. "Look."

The harpy had circled back around and was watching them. It was closer than before—close enough that Skye could see it shift restlessly as it perched on a pile of rusting metal.

Skye turned back to Taly. "Come on. I'll carry you back. Aiden can look at you behind the tree line."

Taly cried out as Skye tried to lift her. "No! Damn it, that hurts. Put me down."

"Don't move her!" Aiden called as he finally reached them. Pushing Skye out of the way, he carefully turned Taly's leg so that he could see the wound. His expression grave, Aiden produced a green earth crystal from his pocket and placed his hand around the shard of metal protruding from her leg.

"Aiden," Aimee cried. She stood off to the side, watching the proceedings with tear-filled eyes. "I didn't mean—"

"Not the time, Aimee." The green crystal in his hand flashed, illuminating the veins and arteries that tunneled through the layers of flesh beneath Taly's skin.

Taly grabbed his hand. "No," she warned. "No magic. Not here."

Aiden blew out a sharp breath. "Taly," he stated, his calm tone belying the stern set of his jaw, "this piece of metal is too close to the artery. I cannot in good conscience move you in this state. It's too risky."

"Do whatever you need to do," Skye stated, placing a hand on his sword. He crouched next to

Taly, watching the harpy.

"I won't use much magic." Aiden's voice was soothing as he continued to prod gently at the wound. "Just enough to stop the bleeding until we can get far enough away to treat it properly."

Taly was breathing harshly, unshed tears glinting in the corners of her eyes. "Okay."

Aiden carefully placed the crystal in the palm of the hand that still touched her injured leg and then gripped the metal fragment. "I'm sorry, but this is going to hurt."

Skye swung an arm around Taly as Aiden gave a quick tug, easily unsheathing the piece of scrap. Skye winced when she screamed—the sound muffled as she buried her face in the fabric of his coat. Blood was now gushing freely from the gash, but Aiden was already shaping a small cloud of earth magic around the wound. A soft green glow emanated from his fingers, slowing the crimson ebb as the flesh knitted itself back together. Skye watched Aiden work and breathed a sigh of relief when the radiant wave of earth magic once more swept across Taly's skin. The fragment of metal had just missed the artery.

"That should buy us some time," Aiden declared after several, long moments.

"Good," Skye said in a clipped tone. "It's time to go." He pointed to the horizon. The harpy was advancing. "Taly, I'm going to pick you up now."

"Yeah," she said with a weak nod. Her eyes were slightly unfocused as she wrapped her arms around Skye's neck, and she let out a small whimper of pain as he lifted her.

Aimee stood off to the side, her head bowed in shame. "Talya, I'm so sorry. I didn't mean for—"

"It's still not the time, Aimee. Move!" Aiden

snapped, taking his sister's arm and pushing her forward.

They made good time as they rushed back towards the forest. Even without channeling his aether, Taly weighed next to nothing, and Skye carried her across the field easily. Aiden and Aimee were behind them, and Aiden had an arm around his sister's waist, lifting her over the larger pieces of scrap. Despite his aid, Aimee still clutched at her skirts as she tried to navigate the debris field.

Taly's breath came in gasps as she pulled on Skye's collar. "Put me down. We're moving too slow."

"Absolutely not," Skye protested vehemently.

"We can't waste time." Taly pulled on his collar more forcefully, pulling Skye's eyes down to hers. "The harpy's gaining on us, and Aiden and Aimee aren't moving fast enough. It's already after Aiden, so if you and he can lure the harpy away, that'll give Aimee and me enough time to get to the tree line. We just have to get far enough into the forest so that it won't be able to dive."

Taly had a point. He could get her back to the forest easily, but that would leave Aiden and Aimee out in the open. And Aimee kept tripping over that damned dress.

"Okay," Skye conceded reluctantly, his footsteps slowing. "You hear that, Aiden," he called over his shoulder.

"Yup," came the curt reply. "And I agree with Taly. Let the girls get to safety. You and I can hold our own."

Stopping, Skye looked down at Taly. Her face was pale, but her eyes shone with grit and determination. Every instinct he had rebelled against him as he gently set her down on the ground. She winced when she tried to put weight on her wounded leg, grasping at his hands as she tried to find her footing. When Aimee and Aiden caught up, Aiden stopped long enough to release his sister but otherwise kept moving forward, trusting Skye to catch up. Without hesitation, Aimee slung an arm underneath Taly's shoulders.

"Go," Aimee insisted. Her face was streaked with sweat, and she'd lost her hat. "I'll take care of her. You have my word."

Giving them one last look, Skye gave a low growl as he forced himself to run ahead. He easily caught up with Aiden, and they both started running at a diagonal across the field. To Skye's great relief, Taly's hunch had been right. The harpy immediately changed direction, following them and moving away from the girls. They still weren't moving fast enough, though. At this rate, the harpy would catch up to them before they managed to escape into the forest on the far western edge of the wasteland.

Using magic around the Aion Gate was never a good idea, but Skye didn't really care about that anymore. There was barely any aether in the air around him, so he pulled a crystal from his pocket. All it took was a slight mental tug to release the stored aether from its stone prison and push it directly into his bloodstream. He felt the change immediately. The magic seeped into his muscles, soothing away the burn and fatigue as the augmentation spell took effect.

"Aiden!" Skye panted. "I'm really sorry about this, but you're just too slow!" Without waiting for a reply, Skye stooped down, hoisting Aiden up and over his shoulder as he began to run in earnest.

They flew across the field, great plumes of dust trailing after each footfall.

Still not fast enough. Pumping more aether into his legs, Skye smiled when the landscape started to blur. He felt Aiden clinging to a strap on his armor, but if the earth mage made a complaint, it was lost on the wind.

Approaching the southern edge of the tree line, Skye started skirting around the perimeter, trying to give the girls as much time as possible. He slowed his pace when he heard a pained cry, coming to a stop completely when he looked back and saw that the harpy had turned and was no longer pursuing them.

"No!" Skye shouted, setting Aiden back on his feet. Aimee was lying on the ground, grasping at that damned skirt. It had caught on something. She tugged at it frantically, but the fabric wouldn't give. Taly lay on the ground beside the struggling fey noblewoman, her face scrunched up in pain as she grasped at her leg.

"Go!" Aiden barked, still stumbling. "Get them out of there! I'll be fine!"

The harpy was getting closer. Giving Aiden a jerky nod, Skye turned and started running back towards the two women at a full sprint. He saw Taly pull Zephyr from her boot and start to cut at the green velvet of Aimee's dress. Taly's movements were stiff, but she managed to free the other girl. Now back on her feet, Aimee pulled Taly to a stand, and they began to run for the tree line once more.

They're not going to make it.

Taly was having trouble. Her leg was practically dragging behind her at this point, and the harpy was almost upon them. They could no doubt hear its mad screams as it streaked through the air.

Channeling more aether, Skye sharpened his vision. He saw Aimee's lips moving as she said something to Taly, who nodded in reply. They stopped completely, and Aimee lowered Taly to the ground. Aimee tore off her ripped gloves, and a soft blue light coiled between her fingers as she channeled her aether and took on a defensive posture in front of the wounded girl.

But he didn't see… damn. Aimee hadn't brought any water crystals, and he doubted she was skilled enough to cast an offensive spell without a focusing talisman. Her primary study had always centered on glamours.

Skye kept pulling aether from the shadow crystals in his pocket, but it wasn't enough. Desperate to go faster, he tapped his body's aether reserve, forcing the magic into his legs. His feet barely touched the ground as he raced to reach them in time.

"Damn it!" Skye screamed, ducking his head and willing his body to move faster. The harpy had caught up, and it loomed over the girls as Aimee formed a long ribbon of water between her hands. She slung it forward, whipping the harpy across the face, but the lash of water glanced off the beast, nothing more than an annoyance.

Just a few more minutes and Skye would be there—he just needed to buy some time. Pulling a dagger from his belt, he ran his hand along the blade. "Hey!" he screamed, waving his bloodied palm in the air. The aether in his blood would be more than enough to lure the beast away. "Over here!"

The beast gave him an uninterested glance

before reaching out a feathered claw and smacking Aimee to the ground. She fell and started backpedaling, thinking the harpy would pursue her. But it didn't. Instead, it turned its eyes on Taly.

What is it doing?! Taly was mortal, and Aimee had just used magic. Harpies craved aether, not flesh. None of this was making any sense.

Three gunshots rang through the air as Taly pulled out a pistol—the old metal firearm he had made her last year—and fired. The harpy stumbled back and screeched manically. Three more shots. Skye knew she was aiming for the beast's vulnerable points—head, heart, and knees. And while Taly was a good shot, harpies were notoriously hard to kill. Their skin was like iron, and the bullets most likely just embedded themselves beneath the beast's scales. Nothing more than an irritation.

Taly lifted the gun to fire off the last two shots she'd likely get before the shadow crystal powering the gun's firing mechanism depleted itself, but the harpy had already recovered. It slapped the pistol out of her hands. Scrambling away, Taly rolled and somehow managed to stand, but her leg immediately gave out beneath her.

Aimee hadn't given up yet. She was back on her feet, feebly flinging whips of water magic at the enraged beast. But it still wasn't enough aether to tempt the creature. Its rage-filled eyes never wavered as they followed Taly's retreat. It took a step, shaking off a spray of mist as Aimee continued to pelt its retreating form with long ribbons of water. Taly's scream carried on the wind as the harpy reached for her, raking a claw across her back as it dragged her across the ground.

Skye was starting to run low on shadow crystals—he'd stupidly left his pack back with the horses. His legs began to burn as he pushed himself to go faster, trying to drag out every last ounce of magic that he could muster as he clung to the augmentation spell. "Hey!" he screamed again. His palm had already healed, so he dragged the dagger over the mended flesh, deeper this time. The harpy finally looked at him, its unblinking eyes riveted on the blood dripping from his fist.

That's right. Come and get me. You want me, not her.

But once again, the creature didn't do what Skye expected. It just gave him a disinterested snort as it turned back to Taly, and the pained wail that tore from her lips when it dug its claws into her back cut him to the core. It started to beat its wings, lifting her into the air just as Skye finally got close enough to reach for her. He jumped, just managing to grasp at her fingertips.

"Skye!" Taly cried, struggling to hold on. But her hand, slick with blood, slipped away, and he began to fall.

Skye slammed a fist into the dirt as he landed, the ground trembling from the force of the blow. The entire field shook, and small fissures opened and branched out across the surface of the red dirt. "Taly!" he screamed, despair in his eyes.

But there was nothing he could do.

Sinking to his knees, he watched the harpy carry her across the field and out of sight.

CHAPTER 7

-An excerpt from the Bestiarium Compendium: A Practical Guide to Staying Alive When Vacationing on Tempris Island

Though small, Tempris is home to a wide and varied array of wildlife. Wyverns, basilisks, grendels—as a result of the many dimensional gates found on the island, populations of creatures that were once separated by both time and space have migrated and now live side-by-side.

Those traveling from Lycia to Tempris for the first time may be particularly surprised to see that this island is home to one of the few remaining undomesticated populations of harpy. It is highly recommended that tourists refrain from approaching these animals. While the Glynadwyr and Lycian harpies are inordinately docile creatures, making them popular household pets among the nobility, Tempris harpies exhibit high levels of aggression and are extremely venomous. A single scratch could prove fatal if not treated properly.

Taly felt weak.

There wasn't a single part of her that didn't ache. The back of her body was completely soaked with blood, both from the puncture wound that had reopened during their mad dash back to the forest and from a new gash that ran across her back.

The pain was excruciating as it pulsed and throbbed, keeping time with her erratic heart.

The harpy's claws were still wrapped around her, and she winced when she felt one of the rigid talons pierce the flesh of her shoulder, burrowing deeper and deeper with each flap of its wings. The forest canopy loomed below her, looking more like a woven tapestry than a real forest. Leaves of all different colors—varying shades of brown, green, yellow, even red—all woven together in a chaotically beautiful display of imminent springtime renewal.

Shards. This couldn't be real, could it?

But the bile rising in her throat, as well as the continuous swells of pain assaulting her senses, told her that this was indeed very real.

Questions bounced around Taly's mind. Why had the harpy chosen her? Why hadn't the creature gone for Aiden or Aimee? Or even Skye when he cut open his hand and waved it around like a big, red target?

Idiot.

She didn't even try to convince herself that

they would find her at this point. While they might have been able to pursue her on horseback around the Aion Gate, skirting around the uneven terrain, they had almost certainly lost the trail after the harpy veered off over the forest. The tree cover was too thick, and there were no roads on this part of the island. It would be impossible to track the creature's path from the ground.

Well, if she was going to die, at least she had the satisfaction of knowing she was right. Bringing Aimee was a terrible idea. And that outfit was ridiculous. They might have made it to the safety of the forest if her skirt hadn't caught on a stray piece of scrap, forcing them both to stumble and fall to the ground. The harpy had been pursuing Skye and Aiden until it heard Taly's cry of pain and turned.

Taly groaned as the harpy readjusted its grip and jabbed a talon in her side. "Watch it!" she grumbled weakly.

The harpy's head swiveled, and it eyed her in irritation before giving her a rough shake.

Taly cried out as she felt her wounds deepen. "I'm going to turn you into a feather duster, you heinous bitch!" she screamed. The screaming helped—helped her fight against the wave of blackness that threatened to drag her under. It would be so easy to give in—to let herself drift off and leave the pain behind.

But sleep meant death.

Another long stream of cursing tore from her lips followed by an enraged shout when the harpy gave her another jolt. Apparently, it didn't like its meals to talk back.

The harpy was headed east, towards the seaside cliffs on the northeastern edge of the island. Taly had only been there once, shortly after she had taken up salvaging, and she'd vowed never to go back. The harpies nested on the far side of the cliffs, and there would be hundreds of them out right now as they waited for dusk to fall. If she ended up there, Taly knew that she would die slowly and painfully as her flesh was ripped from her bones. Her last moments would be spent screaming in agony as she prayed for the painless peace of oblivion.

Personally, she would rather take her chances with the ground.

Taly wriggled in the harpy's grip, trying to jerk her arm forward. The beast's claws dug into her back, and each movement only intensified the excruciating bite of those razor-sharp talons. Her skin ripped, her muscles tore, but she kept at it. She didn't have any other choice at this point. She needed to make the creature drop her.

Finally, she just managed to grasp one of the hyaline pistols holstered around her waist. She didn't even know if it would shoot, but she had lost her old handgun back at the Aion Gate. This one would have to do.

Taly tried to turn her head, but she still couldn't see well enough to aim. So she pointed the pistol up and over her shoulder, trying to guess where the center of the harpy's body might be. Murmuring a short, earnest prayer to the Shards, she pulled the trigger.

It was loud. That was the only thing she could think as she felt the harpy falter and loosen its grip. A sharp, almost painful ringing pierced her deafened ears, momentarily drowning out the beast's enraged yowl. She shot again, smiling when she felt a wave of heat wash across her skin.

Moments later, a guttural scream tore from the harpy's mouth as it burst into flames. She barely had time to register the sound of ripping fabric before she felt the unmistakable sensation of falling.

The incendiary rounds work! Taly thought excitedly as the wind whipped at her clothing and hair. She had grabbed them from her old workbench on a whim that morning—an experimental ammunition she had developed last year but never gotten a chance to test.

For one breathless moment, she was mesmerized by the sight of the harpy exploding midair, flaring bright as a newborn star. But when leaves and sprigs started tearing at her skin and clothing as she shot through the forest canopy, she quickly turned her attention back to staying alive.

She reached out an arm and desperately grabbed at the scattered branches, trying to slow her descent.

She landed flat on her back—the air rushing from her lungs. Wheezing and gasping, slightly dazed, she stared up at the broken branches above her, blinking furiously as she tried to refocus her blurred vision.

She was bruised and bleeding—but still alive.

As she regained her breath, Taly managed to push herself to a sitting position. She patted down her body, taking stock of her injuries. By some small miracle, she didn't seem to have any broken bones, just a web of scratches and lacerations that coated every visible patch of bloodied skin. Some of the cuts looked superficial, but others, like the slashes ripping open her palms, had cut deep. Of all her injuries, her left leg was by far the worst, but her right arm—her dominant hand—wasn't in much better shape. A long, angry gash bisected her forearm, starting at the back of her hand and ending just above her elbow. She must have caught it on a branch when she fell.

With a crazed shriek, the harpy landed about 15 yards away, rolling around on the ground frantically to put out the flames. While the effect of the experimental rounds had been painful, the fiery blaze was already starting to fade.

Shit! Hurry…

She had two options at this point. She had landed near the edge of the forest where the tree cover was still thin. She could try to retreat further into the woods, but she had no doubt that the harpy would easily catch her before she managed to make it to the safety of the thicker underbrush.

The cliffs were option number two. She wasn't very far away—maybe 20 feet. The cliff face towered over her, blotting out the sun and casting a long shadow. She would have to cross a narrow, treeless space where she would be vulnerable, but she could just make out a small gap in the wall of stone. If it was deep enough, she might be able to wedge herself inside and wait out the harpy. After all, she had no aether, so it would likely lose interest in her eventually.

Taly blinked, trying to summon the premonitions—something that might give her a hint about which choice to make. All she saw was an erratic haze of indecision, her golden, spirit-like body flickering as it considered her options. Meanwhile, the harpy was wild, driven mad in its thirst for aether and screeching as it whipped its head to and fro. Gold dust encircled its body in a roiling cloud. It wasn't making conscious choices at this point. It was just acting.

She had better do the same if she wanted to live. The beast was already starting to regain its footing. It was decision time.

Pushing herself to her feet, Taly bit back a cry as she began hobbling toward the cliffs, praying she would make it before the harpy completely recovered. Every step she took was agony, but she kept going. She felt her flesh tear as the wound in her leg deepened, and a trickle of fresh blood streamed down her thigh, staining the ground behind her.

The harpy let out a shriek as it shook its body. It had caught sight of her as soon as she moved, its head swiveling in a way that should've been impossible as its mad eyes homed in on her.

Although Taly had dropped her original handgun during her descent, she still had her backup. The twin hyaline pistol only had standard slugs, but at least it would slow the beast down. She winced as the grip of the pistol dug into the cuts on her palm, biting her lip as she tried to curl her finger around the trigger. Turning her head, she clumsily aimed over her shoulder and shot blindly, ignoring the sharp jolt of pain that raced up her arm as the gun shuddered in her hands. She heard a howl as the first bullet made contact.

She shot again.

Missed.

Again, and she heard another injured cry.

Taly was at the cliff face now, and she groped for the narrow opening. She tried to re-holster the pistol, but her hands were slick with blood, and it clattered to the ground. Deciding to leave the gun, she pulled her body between the narrowing walls. It was uncomfortably tight, but she kept going, trying to put as much space between her and the entrance as possible.

Before she knew it, she was out of time. The harpy slammed its body against the cliff, setting off a concussive wave of sound that seemed to vibrate the very stone. It jabbed its face through the gap and sniffed, saliva dripping from its decaying grin. It could sense her vulnerability. It stretched, its claw raking against the stone walls and stopping just a hair's breadth short of her bloodied shoulder.

The harpy, newly enraged, threw itself at the crevice. A rain of stone and sand shook loose, coating Taly's body and mixing with the blood on her skin. A flurry of bronzed scales ripped from the beast's body and fluttered to the ground as it desperately tried to wedge its gangly form inside the gap. Even in its emaciated state, it couldn't fit.

Undeterred, it reached for her, writhing and moaning in a hideous dance. Every so often, it would manage to graze her arm or her cheek, and it would pull back to frantically suck at its claw.

It wasn't losing interest. No… if anything, each drop of blood it managed to collect just made it renew its efforts to reach her.

I must smell like magic after staying at the manor. That was the only explanation. With two shadow mages in residence as well as its own aether core, Harbor Manor had more aether than anywhere else on the island.

The rock face tore at her skin as Taly pushed herself farther back, and she twisted and squirmed, groping for the daggers still strapped to her thighs. But no matter how hard she tried, she couldn't reach. Her arms and legs were pinned in place, and the harpy was still tearing at the walls.

She was going to die here. The realization

made her feel cold. Up until that moment, she hadn't truly believed it. She thought maybe—just maybe—she might find a way out. She always had before.

Not this time it seemed.

"Please stop!" Taly screamed hopelessly, pounding her fists against the stone. "Stop! Just stop!"

As she shrank away from another sharp rake of the harpy's claws, her skin began to tingle. It was faint at first, easy to ignore, but the prickling sensation soon began to intensify, morphing into a dull burn that started at her fingertips and radiated all the way up to her shoulder. The searing pain continued to surge, overpowering the collective agony of all her other wounds and adding to her desperation.

"*Please!*" she wailed. "I don't want to die here! Just stop! Please stop! Stop! *Stop!*"

The scar on her palm started to glow an angry violet, illuminating the small space as strange markings flickered to life across the skin of her arm. The pain pulsed, setting her blood on fire as she tipped her head back and let out an agonized scream.

And then, as if in reply to her desperate pleas, everything went quiet. Her ears rang in the unexpected silence, and she wondered briefly if she was dead. But the pain still wracking her body with every tortured breath quickly told her that she was still very much alive.

For now, at least.

When Taly finally opened her eyes, she saw that the beast stood frozen before her. Its gnarled arm was still extended, its claw fixed in place as it raked across her shoulder. But all movement had ceased. Delicate golden threads spanned the narrow divide, tangling together as they encircled the harpy's body in a gilded, flickering web.

"What the hell?" Her voice was barely above a whisper, but the sound was deafening in the strange silence.

She had no idea how or why this was happening, but she wasn't going to waste this chance. She looked for a way around the beast. Maybe with enough time, she could climb over and out? If she could get her legs to work, that is. She tried to push herself up, but the stone raked against her wounds, momentarily paralyzing her as a fresh wave of agony shuddered through her.

She didn't have time to try again. A feeble whimper fell from her lips as the harpy started to move, exaggerated and slow at first but quickly gaining speed as it shook off whatever magic spell had stopped it in the first place.

Taly's body started to shake as she finally gave in to the hiccupping sobs. The tears rolled freely down her cheeks, streaking the patina of blood smeared across her face. If she were lucky, maybe the harpy would puncture some vital organ, killing her before it managed to drag her back to its nest. Or perhaps she would bleed out, stuck inside this stone prison.

Closing her eyes, Taly pressed her face against the rock face, trying to force her mind to think of something happy. She didn't want her last thoughts to be filled with pain and fear. There had to be something that would take her away from this hell. Like… like the first time she bested Skye in the sparring ring. That was a good day. She was pretty sure he had let her win, but even now, she still didn't care.

She did her best to recall every detail about that moment. The color of the sky. The smell of the grass. The look on his face when she'd tackled him during her victory dance.

Slowly, the harpy and the pain melted away as she lost herself in the memory.

Her consciousness began to fade, and a soft darkness crept in at the edges of her vision. It beckoned her, its honeyed voice promising a blessed release from the pain and fear.

This is it, Taly thought as she embraced the icy tendrils twining around her thoughts. These were her last moments in this world. She'd had a good life with no real regrets save one—Skye. She wished she could have told him the truth—given him the answers he so desperately wanted. At the very least, she had gotten to see him again. She had gotten to spend one more perfect night sprawled out next to him in the space between their rooms, playing chess and nursing a bottle of champagne long after everyone else had gone to bed. That thought brought her a small amount of comfort as her eyelids fluttered closed.

A loud crunch punctuated the chaotic din, startling Taly awake. The harpy stopped reaching for her as it went quiet, its mouth gaping and its body twitching. The tip of a sword peeked out of the creature's chest, and flames lapped at the edges of the wound. As Taly looked into the beast's mournful, glassy eyes, she felt a small pang of sadness as the light slowly dimmed and then faded away completely. The harpy was dead, its thirst finally sated.

She heard a grunt from beyond the opening as the harpy's limp carcass was forcefully removed and thrown to the side.

"Taly?!" came a panicked voice.

Taly wanted to cry in relief. It was Skye. She had never been so happy to see that arrogant bastard in all her life. "I'm here," she croaked, her voice barely above a whisper.

"Thank the Shards!" His face came into view, sweat and blood streaking his skin. "Take my hand!"

Taly shifted, trying to extend her arm, but her body didn't want to obey her commands. She tried again, but the tight space and sudden lethargy pinned her in place. "I can't," she said, her words starting to slur together.

Skye crammed his body farther into the gap and reached for her. His fingers grazed the tattered remains of her sleeve, and he attempted to pull her forward. "Please, Taly! You have to help me!"

"That hurts, Skye," Taly murmured tiredly as he continued to tug at her. "Stop... that hurts." Despite her protests, when his searching hand found hers, she grasped it instinctively.

The rock pulled at her clothing and skin as he edged her forward.

"How did you find me?" she asked as he gently laid her against the cliff face. The cool air felt wonderful as it wafted across her bloodstained skin. "There are no roads on this part of the island."

Skye barked out a mirthless laugh. "Aiden was able to cast a locator spell once you hit the ground. I followed you on foot. Aiden and Aimee are behind me with the horses."

Now that the danger had passed, everything seemed much less urgent. Even the pain had started to fade into the background. For some reason, Taly was having a hard time remembering why Skye looked so concerned. Her eyelids fluttered as her exhaustion started to overtake her.

"Don't fall asleep on me," Skye said, tapping her cheek.

"Stop it," Taly mumbled as her head tipped forward. Couldn't he see that she was tired? "Just… leave me alone."

"No," he whispered, tucking a finger beneath her chin and pulling her eyes back to his. "I'm not going to leave you alone, I won't *ever* leave you behind, so you forget that nonsense right now. You're tired—I know that. But you need to stay awake. Please, just stay awake. Don't go to sleep."

He was pleading with her now, pressing his lips to her hair, her brow. His hands trembled as he wiped blood from her eyes. "Please, Tink. Aiden's almost here. Just stay awake—that's all you need to do. I'll take care of the rest. I promise."

"Skye?" Taly tried to look at him, but her eyes didn't want to stay open.

The world was starting to go dark now.

Her vision narrowed.

No! her mind screamed, thrashing against the pain, the lethargy, the inky blackness that had started to creep in around the edges. There was something she still needed to tell him. Something important.

Her lips tried to form the words. "Skye… Em, I…"

And then it was gone. The thought just slipped away from her, like water through outstretched fingers.

"Aiden! Over here!" Skye looked back towards the tree line and waved an arm before turning back to her. "Taly, wake up!" He started to shake her. "You're not allowed to leave me yet! Understand?! Damn it! Come on, Tink. You just have to hold on a little longer."

Taly felt a new set of hands poking and jabbing at her. She feebly tried to wave them away.

"This is bad. She's going into shock." The newcomer forcibly opened her eyes. "Taly!" he shouted.

"Aiden?" Taly couldn't really see him. Her eyes just wouldn't focus. Still, the voice sounded familiar.

Aiden pulled an earth crystal from his pocket. The symbol for cocin was inscribed onto the surface—an enchantment that would allow him to use the crystal as a focusing talisman. Though the fey didn't need crystals to perform magic, a focusing talisman could exponentially increase a mage's power—take a simple spell and turn it into something lifesaving.

"What are you doing?" Skye grabbed Aiden's coat when the healer's hands began to glow. "What about the venom?"

"She's lost too much blood," Aiden replied hastily. "If I try to bleed the venom out, she *will* die. Our best bet is to stop the bleeding now and deal with the venom later. She's mortal. It won't have the same effect on her as it would on us."

Skye still looked skeptical, but he let go of Aiden's coat.

Aiden's hands began to glow once more, sparkling green as he summoned the spell. He took deep, even breaths, waving his hands through the air, forming and shaping the growing fog of earth magic.

Taly knew the moment the restoration spell took effect. Her skin itched as her wounds began to knit themselves back together, and her vision slowly refocused. The strange sensation of being sewn back together was excruciating, and her back arched as undulating waves of heat seared her from the inside out. Leaning against the rock face, her breath came in heavy, ragged gasps. Even after her wounds had closed, the blood in her veins felt like fire.

"Taly?" Skye asked tentatively. He rested one hand on the back of her neck and turned her head to face him.

Taly took a breath to reply but winced when she felt something sharp lance her chest.

"Why isn't she getting better?" Skye demanded, turning to Aiden.

Her limbs felt heavy, but as Aiden continued to heal her, the pain slowly began to fade. She somehow managed to reach up and grasp the hand that rested on her neck. "It's been a hell of a day, Em. You'll have to give me a minute."

The sound that came out of Skye's mouth was somewhere between a choked laugh and a sob. His eyes were red and glassy, but he was smiling as he wiped a trickle of blood off her cheek.

"She's lost a lot of blood," Aiden said, mostly to himself. He waved a hand over her, watching the bright pulse of earth magic as it searched for injuries. "No major breaks, but she's cracked a few bones. Amazingly, no concussion." Turning to Skye, he asked, "Do you have any more shadow crystals? These restoration spells are taxing, and the aether in the air is so thin—my magic isn't regenerating as quickly as it would normally. If you can feed me a little more aether, I might be able to cast a second spell."

"Of course! Why didn't you ask sooner?" Skye frantically dug into his bag, pulling out a palm-sized shadow crystal. His fingers grazed the faceted surface as he began to prod at the magic stored within, and a violet haze gradually materialized in the surrounding air.

It didn't take long for the aether to saturate the area. In all her life, Taly had never smelled anything so sweet. The air felt richer, more vibrant somehow, and she took in several deep, shuddering breaths, allowing the heavenly draft to soothe the burning pain that riddled her body.

As she leaned her head back, Aiden continued to work on the spells. If she were to open her eyes, she knew she would see threads of earth magic, almost like ley lines, crisscrossing her skin.

When she could finally take a breath without flinching, she mumbled, "Hey guys?"

The two men went silent, staring at her expectantly.

"We need to move," she grunted as she made a half-successful attempt to push herself up into a sitting position.

Aiden was the first to regain himself. "No. You shouldn't exert yourself. The restoration spells need time to work before we try to move you."

"That may be so," Taly replied with a groan, "but there are only a few hours of daylight left. I don't know if you're aware of this, but there's a harpy nest just on the other side of this cliff face, and harpies hunt at night. We need to go. Now."

"Where's Aimee?" Skye asked.

"I'm here!" the fey noblewoman called as she emerged from the forest. Her skirts were hiked up around her hips, her dirtied bloomers peeking out from underneath the tattered hem, and she rode astride Taly's horse. She held the reins of the sidesaddled mare as it struggled to keep up with the nimble gelding.

"Well look at that," Taly muttered tiredly. "She *can* ride."

Skye laughed as he put his arm around her and helped her stand. "At least your sense of humor is still intact. That has to be a good sign."

Taly leaned heavily against him. Though the wounds on her leg had closed, the limb felt like dead weight and refused to respond to her commands. She tried to take a step but lost her footing and stumbled.

Without hesitation, Skye reached down and hooked an arm under her knees, effortlessly hoisting her up. "She can ride with me. Aiden, is there anything else you can do for her right now?"

"No." Aiden paused, thinking. "Just monitor the spells—they'll last longer with a steady supply of aether. Once we're back in the forest, I can check to see how she's doing."

"Wait," Taly said, tugging on Skye's collar. "The harpy… I want its feathers."

"What? Why?" Skye asked, pausing to look at the harpy's rapidly cooling carcass. Its head had been cleaved from its body, and its arms and wings still twitched sporadically.

"My trophy," Taly replied, smiling when she felt Skye's bark of laughter. "I promised that bitch I was going to turn her into a feather duster. Don't make me a liar, Skye."

Skye sighed before glancing at Aiden. "Will you…"

"Yeah, I got it," Aiden said, chuckling to himself.

With Aiden's help, the two men managed to get Taly seated in the saddle, and Skye placed a protective arm around her waist, tucking her safely against his chest as he settled in behind her.

The journey back to Ryme was far shorter this time around. The harpy had carried her southeast of where they had originally emerged at the Aion Gate, so they were able to cut through the forest, heading south until they found an old, forgotten back road. The path was overgrown and cracked, but the horses managed to pick around the broken stones.

As they rode, Taly tried to take stock of the damage to her body. Most of the bleeding had stopped now. She could still feel blood trickling down her leg from the puncture wound, most likely from where the saddle rubbed against the delicate layer of newly grown skin, but it was minimal. The gashes and lacerations from her fall through the trees had closed, and though her skin was still red and swollen, Aiden was a skilled healer—she doubted she would even have any scars left over from this ordeal.

The sun began to slip behind the horizon, plunging the forested road into darkness, but Taly barely noticed. She made no complaint when Skye gently lifted her out of the saddle so that Aiden could check the spells, and she remained silent when they set out again. A single image was burned into her mind's eye. The harpy—it had just stopped. Like it was frozen in time. That wasn't a spell she recognized. It couldn't have been Skye, and there had been no one else around to help her. That left only one conclusion.

I did that, she thought. *I used magic. Real magic. Time magic.* She pressed her eyes closed as her body began to tremble. Skye shifted in the saddle, and the arm around her tightened as he tucked her more firmly against him.

"Everything's okay now. I've got you," he whispered in her ear. For a moment, she almost believed him. As he rested his chin on the top of her head, his fingers absently caressing a patch of skin peeking through the shredded fabric at her waist, she wanted so desperately to believe him.

But he was wrong—everything was far from okay. If a Sanctifier had witnessed what happened today, she would've been immediately sentenced to die for the crimes of a Queen she'd never met. No trial. No mercy. Because that's what the Sanctorum did to time mages or anyone they suspected of having time magic. They hunted them, killed them, and then erased every trace of them from this world. And anyone stupid enough to try to protect a time mage… they got to share in their fate.

"Here," Skye said, jolting Taly out of her thoughts. He looked back at Aiden and jerked his head toward an overgrown path that veered off the main road. "It's a shortcut. Should take us around the back of the manor property."

No! Taly shook herself, trying to dispel some of the overwhelming fatigue that weighed her down. She couldn't let them take her back. She was even more dangerous than before.

"Let me down," she ordered weakly as Skye steered his horse toward the side road.

"What?" Skye asked, confused. Nevertheless, he complied, easily sliding out of the saddle and gently placing her on the ground.

She pushed his hands away, but her knees buckled as soon as he let go, and he quickly pulled her back against his body to keep her from falling. A growl of frustration ripped from his throat as she continued to struggle against him, but when she managed to wriggle out of his grip a second time, she finally found her feet.

"I'm going back to town," she mumbled, trying to ignore the way her words slurred together. Her heart fluttered rapidly in her chest, and a strange shimmer had crept in around the edges of her vision, making the world around her dance and sway.

"Are you kidding?" Skye sputtered in disbelief. "No. You were practically *dead* not two hours ago. You can't even walk!"

Skye reached for her, but she shrugged out of his grasp, still stumbling and listless. "This may come as a surprise to you, but you don't dictate my actions, Skye. I did my job—I got you to the gate and back. We're done now."

"Taly," Aiden said, swinging himself out of the saddle and coming to stand beside Skye, "I don't think—"

"You don't get to tell me what to do either, Aiden." The earth mage simply stared at her, his mouth hanging open in surprise.

Skye wasn't just agitated now. He was fuming. "Taly. You're acting like a crazy person. A very bloody, very injured crazy person. Come home."

"I am going home." For emphasis, Taly added, "*My* home."

"Talya?" Aimee had been uncharacteristically quiet the entire journey back, and when she spoke, her voice was soft and uncertain. "If this is about me, I'll stay out of your way. I didn't mean for any of this to happen. I didn't think." Tears, delicate and ladylike, started to stream down her face, and she worried the reins of Taly's horse between her fingers. "I *never* think. This is all my fault. I am so, *so* sorry."

Taly looked up at her. In that moment, she knew that she had never really hated the girl. Not really.

"I don't blame you, Aimee." Taly took a deep breath, struggling against the wave of dizziness that crept up on her. Despite the chill wind that whistled through the trees, she had started sweating. "If anything, today just showed me that I was right the first time. This was all a mistake. It's too dangerous." A violent shiver shook her shoulders, and her tongue felt clumsy. "I'm... it's all too dangerous now."

"What is she talking about?" Aiden whispered to Skye.

Skye shrugged. "Your guess is as good as mine," he replied, his voice equally quiet.

"Shit," Aiden cursed. "I think I know what's happening."

When the healer approached her, Taly took a step back, then another. She was wasting time. She just needed to go.

"It's okay," Aiden said gently. "If you want to go back to Ryme, that's fine. I'll help you get there. Just let me check the spells one more time. Maybe give you something for the pain?"

Taly hesitated, and Aiden used that as an opportunity to close the distance, slinging an arm around her waist when she tried to backpedal. His hand came up to her forehead.

"Shards, she's burning up." Aiden turned to Skye, who was watching them with wide eyes. "Which is closer? Ryme or Harbor Manor?"

"Harbor Manor," Skye replied readily.

Aiden started pulling her towards the horses. "Then we need to get to Harbor Manor."

"No!" Taly thrashed, trying to shake him off, but she was too weak to do anything but tire herself out. She felt the skin on her thigh tear as one of her wounds reopened, releasing a fresh flood of warm blood. "Let me go!"

"Hey!" Skye snarled, confusion and anger evident in his expression as he pulled Taly away from the earth mage. "You're hurting her!"

Skye's hands were gentle as he grabbed her fists and pulled her against his body. Her wounded leg gave out beneath her, but still, she writhed, resisting whatever help he tried to offer.

"Let me go," Taly pleaded weakly. She was just trying to protect them. Why couldn't they see that?

Aiden's hands began to glow. "We need to get her back to the manor right now. I think an infection is starting to set in." Ignoring Taly's feeble pleas, he began weaving and shaping the spell around her. His eyes found hers, and although she saw nothing but kindness and concern shining through, she shrank back. "Can you tell me your name? Do you know where you are?"

Taly opened her mouth, but her words got caught in her throat. His questions didn't make any sense.

"Tell me your name," Aiden repeated calmly. "Can you do that? Tell me your name, and Skye will let you go."

Taly shook her head. "Let me go," she whimpered, renewing her struggles. Her name didn't matter. Nothing mattered except getting away.

"Aiden, what's happening?" Skye snapped.

"I don't think she's in her right mind." Aiden's hands glowed brighter, and his fingers began prodding at her face, forcibly opening her eyes as he examined her. "Between the fever and the healing spells, I'd be surprised if she even knows who she is, much less who we are."

Skye sighed in defeat, readjusting his grip when she tried to elbow him in the side. "Taly?" His fingers grasped her chin as he tried to pull her eyes to his, but she couldn't see past her own panic. "Taly, you're sick. We're just trying to help you."

"Please let me go." She was getting desperate now, and tears started to stream down her face. "Let me go… *please.* I can't go back. Please don't make me go back. Just leave me here. Just leave me…"

"Oh, Shards," Aimee cried softly. "Shards, this is my fault."

Taly almost managed to wriggle out of Skye's grip, but he tightened his hold on her, his arm looping around her waist as he lifted her off her feet. "Hurry, Aiden," he grunted when Taly managed to kick him in the shin. "She's reopening her wounds."

"Got it." Tendrils of earth magic lapped at the healer's skin as he cupped Taly's face. "Shhh… it's alright, Taly. I'm just going to give you something for the pain. Everything's going to be alright. I promise."

"Please don't do this," Taly tried one last time, her eyes wide and frightened. She was having difficulty focusing on Aiden's face now. Images of the harpy, motionless and still, clouded her vision, pushing away all other thoughts. She saw its gaping mouth, felt the sting of its stationary claw as it raked her skin. Time had stopped. She had done that. She had made time stop. "You don't know what you're doing. Leave me. It's better if you leave me."

The last thing she remembered before the world faded to black was the feeling of Skye's lips pressed against her brow and his whispered words of comfort as he gently lowered her to the ground.

CHAPTER 8

-A letter from Lord Aris Thorne to his stepdaughter, Aimee Bryer

Dearest Aimee,

I hope this letter finds you well. Alas, I was very disappointed to hear of your lack of progress with the young Lord Emrys. A girl with your charms should have no problem seducing a young man—especially one with the Duke-to-be's "reputation." You will have to try harder if you're to become the future Duchess of Ghislain. I should not have to remind you of the political sway his family carries at court or how it would benefit our household to secure such an auspicious and enduring alliance.

Also, your mother is pregnant again. She has been put on bedrest in the hopes of avoiding another miscarriage. I can only hope that this pregnancy will not prove to be as much of a disappointment as the others. She anxiously awaits your return.

Respectfully,

Lord Aris Thorne of House Thanos

No matter how hard she tried, Aimee was having trouble mustering any enthusiasm for her needlepoint this morning. It was a beautiful day outside. The sun was shining high overhead, and the cool breeze ruffled her hair where she sat in front of her open window. But despite the picturesque scene, she couldn't shake the melancholy that seemed to hang over her like a cloud.

Throwing down her embroidery hoop, Aimee leaned back, letting her head dangle over the back of the damask settee. Who was she kidding? She knew why she was upset. While she had never been particularly fond of Talya, she had never wanted to see her hurt.

It had been absolute chaos when they arrived back at the manor. Ivain had already smelled the blood, and he and Sarina were waiting for them at the stables when they arrived. Between the yelling and the crying and the frantic rush of servants back and forth as Aiden snapped orders at them, it had taken the better part of the evening to finally get Talya stabilized. Her brother had been working tirelessly ever since, barely stopping to eat or sleep, but even now, almost a day later, the girl had yet to wake up.

Aimee sunk down further into her seat. Although she had been doing her best to stay out of the way, curiosity had taken her by the girl's room the previous night when everything had finally gone quiet. For as long as she lived, she would never forget just how frail Talya had looked, pale and unmoving, as she lay in her bed surrounded by a sea of blankets. The image of that dark room, of Skylen kneeling by the young mortal's bedside silently pleading with her to wake up—that would always be with her now.

Aimee turned her head when she heard footsteps echoing down the hall. Smoothing the wrinkles out of the pale blue satin of her dress, she stood and turned to face the door. When Sarina appeared in the doorway, an unreadable expression on her face, Aimee dropped down into a deep courtesy. "Lady Castaro."

"Shards, girl," Sarina grumbled, waving a dismissive hand. "How many times do I have to tell you? We don't care if you use formalities here." Shuffling across the room, Sarina fell back into the plush velvet chair opposite Aimee and let out a weary sigh. The woman's usually immaculate auburn hair fell around her shoulders in tangles, and she was still wearing the same wrinkled muslin dress Aimee had seen her in the previous day.

"I'm sorry, Aunt Sarina," Aimee mumbled as she took her seat, her back stiff and straight. She knew that neither the Castaros nor Skylen cared much for court formalities, but she found she could never completely abandon her training. Her stepfather had been very strict about observing stations of rank when she was growing up. Aiden always had a much easier time fitting in when they came to visit the island. "How is Talya this morning?"

Sarina shook her head sadly. "No change, I'm afraid."

Aimee picked up her embroidery hoop, needing something to keep her hands busy. "I… I know I've said it already, but I *am* sorry."

Sarina studied her, and it was all Aimee could do not to shrink back. When her aunt had heard the full account of what happened at the Aion Gate, she hadn't said anything. She had just stared at Aimee for several agonizingly long moments, silent and stony, before turning to walk away.

"Are you?" the older noblewoman asked, an unfamiliar edge to her voice. "Are you *truly* sorry?"

Aimee stared at her hoop and the tiny blue flowers she had been embroidering around the edges. "How could you even ask that?" she whispered, discreetly wiping at her eyes.

Sarina gave her a withering glare. "Darling, do you think my brother and I are stupid? We know you don't come to Tempris to visit us. You come to see Skye. And considering how close he and Taly are, it's not unreasonable to assume that you might think having her out of the way would increase your chances of finally wooing him."

Aimee turned to look out the window, swallowing hard past a sudden lump in her throat. She couldn't deny that when she heard Talya had moved out, she had thought that she might finally be able to get some alone time with Skylen. During her previous visits, he and the little mortal were hardly ever separated.

"Tell me something, Aimee," Sarina said, pouring herself a cup of tea from a pot that had long gone cold. "Why do you bother? You and Skye are completely unsuited for one another."

"And who is suited for him?" Aimee snapped without thinking. "Some shardless?"

"Watch your tongue, dear," Sarina said with a dangerous smile. "We don't use that word in this household. You would also be wise to remember that even though she is not bound to me by blood, Taly is my child. If you are going to speak ill of her, you will promptly remove yourself from my home."

"I'm sorry, Aunt Sarina. That was unkind of me." Aimee sighed despondently. Her shoulders began to slump forward, but she quickly straightened. "And... I'm not blind. I can plainly see that Skylen barely tolerates me. I've told my stepfather over and over again that I don't think it's going to work, that Skylen will never consent to an offer of marriage, but... he never listens. Lord Thorne insists that I'm just not trying hard enough. Some of the things he tells me to do..." Her voice trailed off as she remembered her stepfather's parting words: *Just get the boy drunk and mount him already.*

"I know," Sarina said, sipping her tea. Her nose scrunched up, and she placed the teacup in her palm. Her fingers began to glow, almost like embers, and wafts of steam rose from the liquid's surface as the warming spell took effect. Taking another sip, she nodded before refocusing on Aimee. "I'm well acquainted with how Lord Aris Thorne's mind works. That man is vile, and it makes me sick that your household's Matriarch gave your mother to him when your father died."

"My mother is just a Feseraa," Aimee murmured. Her stomach turned. "And our father was wrong to have stolen her away from the family in the way that he did—to have invalidated her breeding contract by taking her as his wife after my family was kind enough to grant her the privilege of immortality. My brother and I are lucky that our family chose to honor our father's widow by giving her such an advantageous match, regardless of the fact that she's human."

"You don't believe that," Sarina said sadly.

"That is what my stepfather tells me I am to believe." Aimee turned back to her embroidery and began stabbing the needle through the cream silk. "The same way he tells me that I am to marry Skylen. And unlike my brother, I don't have the luxury of escaping to Faro to join my regiment. I have no other choice but to stay in Picolo and, as my stepfather says, fulfill my familial duty."

Aimee jumped when she felt an arm drape around her, pulling her into a warm embrace. Her chest felt uncomfortably tight, and her shoulders trembled, but it wasn't until Sarina started gently shushing her that Aimee realized she was crying. "You don't really believe I would deliberately hurt Talya, do you?" she quavered, giving in to the hiccupping sobs and burying her face in Sarina's shoulder.

Sarina gently rocked her back and forth, smoothing a hand over her hair. "No, my dear. No. I know it was an accident. And once we figure out what sort of infection Taly has, I'm sure the two of you will go back to passive-aggressively bickering over Skye just like you've always done."

Aimee huffed out a laugh, pulling away and wiping at her eyes. "You want to know the truth? Talya can have him for all I care." Throwing her needlepoint off to the side, she slouched down to match Sarina's relaxed posture. It only felt a little awkward and unnatural. "If Skylen and I were to begin courting, my stepfather would probably make me move to the island. And while I enjoy visiting Tempris, I prefer the city. I like attending court. I've heard rumors that Skylen's mother is doing everything within her power to lure him back to the mainland, but he... well, I think he wants nothing more than to stay on this island for the rest of his life. On the rare occasions that our paths cross at court or at his family's estate in Ghislain, he looks so miserable—like he's counting down the days until he gets to leave. Something tells me that if he could hand over his duties as the heir of Ghislain to his older brother, he would've done so already."

Sarina chuckled softly. "You're probably on to something there. Ivain and Skye are cut from the same cloth, I'm afraid. If those two could get away with it, I'm pretty sure they'd spend every day of the rest of their lives out in that dusty workshop, drinking cheap beer and working on things that are better done sober."

Sarina's eyes took on a faraway look, and Aimee knew that the noblewoman's thoughts had drifted back to the girl upstairs. "Skye told me what you did at the gate," she said after a moment. "That you tried to protect Taly with your magic. That was very brave."

"I couldn't even do that right, though." Aimee stared down at her hands. "My father was one of the greatest water mages of his generation. He was a Knight of the Crystal Guard, trained by the High Lord of Water himself. I can't even form a basic water whip."

Sarina reached for her forgotten teacup. "Your father didn't become all of that overnight. He practiced—usually on his little sister. Of course, she was a shadow mage, so she always managed to get him back. Shards, those two…" A small smile tugged at the older woman's lips. "You could be just as good as him if you wanted to be. You have the talent."

Aimee sighed. "My stepfather says that offensive magic is unladylike and that I am to only focus on those skills that will help me to secure a match. Like my glamours."

"Last time I checked, your stepfather wasn't here," Sarina mumbled into her teacup.

Hurried footsteps echoed down the hallway, and a moment later, Aiden poked his head in the room. Dark smudges stained the skin underneath his eyes, and his clothes were streaked with blood that had long ago faded to black. "Sarina? I need you upstairs."

Sarina set her teacup aside with a clatter as she shot to her feet. "Is something wrong?"

Aiden's eyes flicked to Aimee and back. "No. Nothing's wrong. But… I do need your assistance."

Sarina gave Aimee a tight-lipped smile before following Aiden. Aimee listened, sighing when she heard their footsteps taper off as they hit the stairs that led to the fourth floor.

Eyeing her needlepoint in irritation, she threw the hoop across the room and repositioned herself in front of the window. She held out her hands and began channeling her aether. A long ribbon of water materialized between her outstretched palms, but it sputtered and evaporated after only a few seconds. Her stepfather's words came to her mind unbidden: *No man wants a woman that knows how to fight back.*

With a very unladylike growl, Aimee jerked open a small drawer on the small tea table next to her chair and removed a pouch of water crystals, spreading them out on a nearby ottoman as she sorted them by size and enchantment. The delicate Faera runes carved into the faceted surfaces programmed each crystal to perform a single type of spell, and in an experienced mage's hands, the simple modification could decrease the mental and physical burden of a spell exponentially. In her case, however, the runes were a training tool. A crutch.

Aimee picked up one of the crystals, feeding a small amount of magic into the stone. Another stream of water coiled between her hands, stronger this time, with tiny eddies of current rippling through the center. She gave the spell a small mental tug, smiling when the water reformed itself into a flock of songbirds that she sent flying through the window. Her father, her *real* father, had taught her that trick. He always used to say that was the spell that made her mother fall in love with him.

For the rest of the afternoon, Aimee sat there, forming and reforming that same ribbon of water, switching over to a crystal modified for use as a simple focusing talisman when she was finally able to cast the spell unaided.

A heavy sheen of sweat coated her skin, and a dull burn settled in her lungs as she continued to use more and more aether. But despite the satisfaction she felt at seeing the curling streams of water that she had set afloat dancing in the space around her, Aimee couldn't stop thinking about Talya.

Nothing's wrong. That's what Aiden had said when he came to fetch Sarina.

Aimee's eyes drifted to the ceiling, and for a moment, she once again saw that dark room and

Skylen kneeling at his friend's bedside, her lifeless hand clutched in his—as if that simple touch was the only thing still anchoring him.

Aimee flicked her wrist, and the swells of water magic drifting around her evaporated into steam.

Nothing's wrong. She sighed as Aiden's words repeated in her head. Why was it that after so many years, her brother still foolishly believed that she didn't know when he was lying?

CHAPTER 9

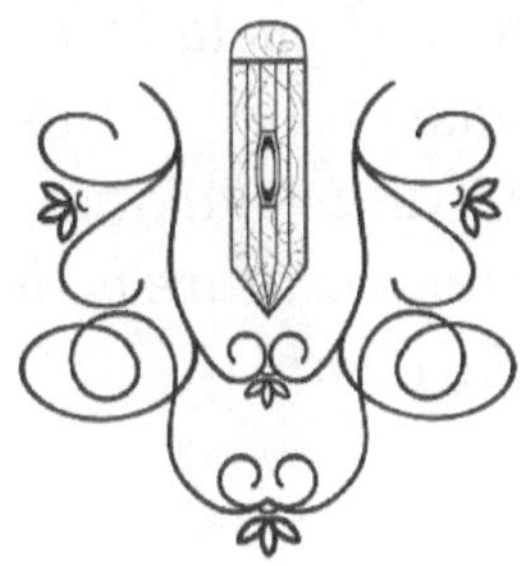

- An excerpt from The Essential Guide to Fey Pathophysiology, 1,263,856th Edition

Though the fey display accelerated healing and immunity to injury and disease, they are still susceptible to certain poisons and venoms. Reactions can vary from mild to life-threatening depending on the individual, the poison, and the time of treatment.

The list of documented poisons and their effects is quite lengthy and will be covered in the next chapter. For now, we will concentrate on some of the deadlier venoms found throughout the fey world.

By far the most dangerous venom is that of the Tempris harpy. Only the females are venomous, and, unlike other creatures which may inject their venom using stingers or fangs, the harpy's venom is produced by a specialized gland located underneath its anterior claws.

If treated immediately, the symptoms will be mild to moderate and may consist of fever, vomiting, and muscle pain. If left untreated, symptoms will rapidly progress and include trouble breathing, chest pain, confusion or changes in cognition, extreme fatigue, and shaking chills. A rapid decrease in body temperature is the final symptom, followed quickly by death.

For Taly, time had ceased to exist. She floated in and out of consciousness, lost in a fog of pain. Every cell, every muscle, every part of her felt scorched and charred. During her few waking moments, she would twist and turn, but she could never stay awake long enough to find any relief from the constant discomfort. At some point, voices started to invade her dreams, drifting across that diaphanous veil between wakefulness and sleep.

"What's... her?" a woman said. Taly could barely manage to catch even a few words.

"... blood loss... harpy venom." A man's voice this time. "... allergic... make her comfortable..."

"When... wake up?" The woman again. She seemed quite distressed.

Taly let out a feeble groan as she turned on her back, no longer able to ignore the burning pain in her arm and shoulder. Her spine arched as a new wave of heat blossomed beneath her skin. Even though her wounds had closed, she could still feel the fiery sting of the harpy's claws.

"Look! She's waking up. Little one?" The worried face of Sarina gradually came into focus. "I'm here, my dear." The frazzled noblewoman sat on the edge of the bed, gently stroking her hair. Taly tried to look beyond her, but there was a strange haze clouding her vision.

"We need to get her to drink some water." Aiden walked into her line of sight. His face looked haggard and drawn in the dim light.

Carefully accepting the etched crystal glass that Aiden seemed to produce from nowhere, Sarina held it up to Taly's lips as the healer moved to lift her into a sitting position. For Taly, everything felt muddled—from the wrenching pain in her neck as she shifted to the pull of skin on her back as Aiden held her up.

She took a tentative sip. The rim of the glass felt cool against her dry, cracked lips, and the heavenly liquid quickly soothed the dull ache that had settled at the back of her throat. Her hands curled around the cup as she started to gulp down the contents in earnest. She couldn't remember ever being this thirsty.

Without warning, Taly jerked forward and promptly emptied the contents of her near-empty stomach onto the floor. Bile burned her throat, and tears sprang up as the pain erupted anew, clawing at her insides, wrapping around her body like a vice. The cup hit the carpet with a dull thud and rolled away.

"What's happening?" Sarina snapped sharply at Aiden, holding back Taly's hair as she continued to heave.

"Her stomach is probably a little sensitive right now. That's all," Aiden explained in a measured tone. He reached down to retrieve the discarded glass and then walked out of Taly's view. He reappeared a moment later. "Here," he said, handing her a fresh cup of water. "I know you're thirsty but try to drink more slowly this time."

With great care, Taly took a small sip, but it made no difference. She immediately expelled the water in the same manner. For the next few hours, Aiden and Sarina tried, again and again, to get her to eat or drink something, but she couldn't manage to hold anything down. Her eyes and nose burned, and her muscles ached as her stomach continued to convulse long after it was empty. She could sense their growing confusion, but she couldn't make her body obey her commands. Something inside her was on fire, poisoning her from the inside out.

Taly soon began to drift in and out of consciousness. Her dreams were vague and disjointed and left her gasping for air, but every time she came to, she could sense Sarina nearby, and some of the lingering fear would slip away. Skye was usually there too, and sometimes she would glimpse him and Ivain huddled over her worktable, whispering quietly.

It was dark outside the next time Taly managed to claw her way back to the waking world. She immediately felt... cold. It was as though the fire in her veins had been replaced with ice. The chill weighed her down, made her limbs feel tight and rigid. Violent shivers racked her body, but she didn't have the energy to pull at the quilt that covered her body. She barely had the strength to crack open her eyes.

Sarina sat beside the bed in a plush wingback chair, looking faded and worn around the edges. Her usually immaculate hair was disheveled, and her eyes and nose were red.

"How much time do you think we have? Do you think that Skye and Ivain will be back before..." Sarina's voice trailed off, and she brought her hands up to cover her face. "This can't be happening," she whimpered, a rough sob ripping from her throat. "We were supposed to have more time."

Aiden sighed, pinching the bridge of his nose. "I don't understand any of this. I've checked for every infection I know to check for. It had to be that metal rod that fell through from the mortal realm. Human diseases evolve so quickly… It must be something that's developed since the last time the Aion Gate opened. Something that we just don't know how to treat."

"Skye and Ivain will never forgive me if they're not here when it happens," Sarina mumbled, her eyes vacant. Reaching over, she pulled the blanket up higher, tucking it around Taly's chin. "Maybe I made a mistake sending them to Litor to get more blood wood. They're supposed to be back tonight, but… Will they make it in time? How much longer does she have?"

"While I think it might be wise to start preparing ourselves for the worst," Aiden said distractedly, studying the various herbs and crystals scattered across the table, "I'm not giving up. Not yet. I have an idea. It's crazy. *Really* crazy. And I'm going to need to go to the clinic in Ryme to get supplies."

"You think she can still get better?" Sarina asked, cautious but hopeful.

Aiden slammed his hands down on the table. "As long as she keeps fighting, then anything's possible. Right? There's one more thing I can try.

It's a last resort measure, but if she's already... well, what have we got to lose? If Ivain and Skye get back before I do, keep them close by. This will be easier with a shadow mage. I'm going to need a lot of aether."

Sarina placed a hand on Taly's brow, her fingers trailing down to cup the girl's cheek. "Please don't let my baby die, Aiden."

Aiden hesitated, swallowing thickly. "I'll do my best." He gave Sarina a curt nod before sweeping a pile of empty vials into a small bag and hastily exiting the room.

The next time Taly awoke, birds were chirping all-too-merrily outside her window. Each happy warble was like a dagger, piercing and razor-sharp to her overly sensitive ears. The scent of herbs and something faintly aseptic tickled at the blistered skin of her nose. Groaning, she turned and buried her head in her pillow. Her very hard, lumpy pillow. She tried punching it, hoping that would make the traitorous sack of fluff fall back into line.

But it didn't. In fact, the feeble blow sent a wave of pain reverberating up her arm and into her shoulders and neck. She writhed, trying to get away from the crest of blazing fire that had been ignited beneath her skin, but the blankets pinned her in place. They weighed her down, and the more she struggled, the more tangled she became.

Someone drew in a sharp breath, and a pair of hands reached out to still her. "Let's not do that," a soft voice murmured. "We don't want your wounds reopening."

"Skye?" Taly rasped. Her throat felt raw, and though she tried, she couldn't seem to work any moisture back onto her tongue. When she cracked open her eyes, Skye's face slowly came into focus. His clothes were wrinkled, and it looked as though he hadn't shaved in several days, but he was smiling.

"Yeah, Tink," he replied quietly, reaching out to push aside a stray lock of hair that had fallen across her eyes. "I'm here."

Taly opened her mouth to speak, but no sound came out. Her throat was on fire, and when her vocal cords rubbed together, it felt like sandpaper. Coughs racked her body, and she whimpered at the fresh surge of agony that accompanied the uncontrollable spasms.

Skye was at her side in a moment, looping an arm around her shoulders as he lifted her. Leaning her against his shoulder, he held a cup up to her lips. "Here."

Taly pushed his hand away as best she could. The memory of the last time someone had offered her water—and the resulting pain—was still too fresh. "No, I don't want that," she managed to choke out between coughs.

Gently pulling her hands away, Skye held the rim of the cup against her bottom lip and tipped her head back. "The healing spells have kept you from getting too dehydrated, but Aiden said we needed to get you to drink water as soon as you woke up. You'll feel better. I promise."

The cool liquid easily slipped down her throat, extinguishing the burning pain, and though it made her stomach turn, she managed to keep it down. When nothing but a faint tickle remained, Taly pushed the cup away. "What happened?" she asked weakly. Her eyes scanned the room, confirming her worst fears. They had brought her back to the manor. A familiar sense of dread stirred in the back of her mind, but it felt far away, nothing but a vague, undefinable fear. "How did I get here?"

"Well, that's a long story," Skye muttered as he gently laid her back down. Setting the cup aside, he settled back into a chair beside the bed. "Let's see... I guess it all started when this little blonde brat decided she had a death wish and tried to hobble off on her own, half-dead and full of harpy venom."

"Hey now, Em. Don't skip the beginning of this story," Taly grumbled when she saw him smirk, clearly amused by his own joke. "Personally, I really love the part about the idiot that brought the twit along that put me in the situation with the harpy."

His smile slipped. "You got really sick, Tink," he said, all traces of playful rebuke melting away. "When you were on the road, you could barely stand, your words were slurring together... you couldn't even tell us your name. Aiden said it was the fever, but... Shards, that was some scary shit. You started panicking, and he had to use a sleeping charm just to keep you from reopening your wounds."

"I remember the road, I think." Taly's head lolled to the side, and she stared at the crack in her curtains. Her mind felt dull, and she was momentarily distracted by the way the dust caught the light as it hung in the air. "Didn't Aiden say it was just an allergic reaction to the harpy venom? Or was it an infection? It's all a little fuzzy."

"We're still not sure," Skye replied with a shrug. "My guess is both."

Taly sighed as she twisted, trying to get comfortable. The pain in her back was becoming a problem.

"Hold on." Rising from his place beside her, Skye retrieved a small, cloth-wrapped bundle from the worktable against the far wall. He lifted her, sliding it underneath the small of her back. The slightly elevated position and the delicious warmth radiating from the pack had her sighing in relief. "Fire crystals," he said when she raised a brow in question.

"How long have I been out?" Taly mumbled. "A day?"

Skye grimaced. "Not quite."

"Two days?" she asked, her eyes widening when he shook his head. "Longer?"

"Try eight."

"What?!" Taly exclaimed shakily. "Eight days? How is that possible?"

Skye stuffed his hands in his pockets. "It took you almost a full day to wake up after Aiden removed the sleeping charm. And no matter what anyone did, your fever just kept getting worse. You were waking up less and less often, and half the time you didn't even know we were there. We tried everything—Sarina even sent Ivain and me to Litor for blood wood. The medicine didn't end up doing anything for you, but I wasn't really expecting it to. I think the trip was mostly just to get Ivain out of the house. He wasn't handling things very well."

Sinking down on the bed beside her, Skye ran a hand along the stubble on his chin. "And then your temperature started to drop the night before last—just a few hours after we got back from Litor. You started shaking. Sarina was casting warming spells for a while, but Ivain and I eventually managed to rig something together to keep your temperature elevated. I think we may have bought every single fire crystal in Ryme in the process. I really thought..." Skye's voice caught, and he stopped. Reaching for her hand, his thumb grazed the pulse point on her wrist, lingering there. The gentle touch felt strange and slightly ticklish, but Taly made no move to push him away.

He stared at their intertwined hands for a moment before continuing. "And then Aiden gave you some sort of draught—he wouldn't say what it was. He just told Ivain and me to keep feeding him aether. Whatever he did, whatever he gave you—it worked. You stabilized a few hours later, and you've been doing really well the past two days. You probably still feel like shit, but Aiden says you're on the mend."

Now that the pain in her back was under control, the aching soreness in her arms and legs was starting to make itself known. She whimpered slightly when Skye reached underneath the blanket and rearranged a small lump situated next to her hip. She heard the clacking of crystals, and then a small burst of heat had her murmuring a soft *"thank you"* as the pain receded.

On his feet again, Skye began checking on other small bundles of crystals carefully arranged around her body. "How's that?" he asked, tucking the blanket back around her. “Are you warm enough?”

“No. It’s freezing in here,” Taly replied, involuntary shivers running up and down her spine.

“Okay. Uh…” Skye clicked his tongue as he looked around the room. “One second.” Taly watched him disappear into her washroom. Still feeling listless and drowsy, her thoughts began to drift as her eyes traced the polished, leafy tendrils etched into the dark wooden surface of the door, and she jumped when Skye reappeared carrying two large bundles. He smiled at her as he arranged what looked like lumpy pillowcases across her stomach and feet. As the warmth of the fire crystals seeped into her, she curled her toes, sighing softly when some of the stinging numbness finally started to recede.

The pain faded to the background, chased away by the heat. “Hey Skye?” she asked, watching as he continued to fuss over her. “There’s something I’ve been wondering.”

“Hmmm? What’s that?” he asked. Retrieving two more quilts from the end of the bed, he spread them over her and smoothed out the wrinkles.

“Aiden,” she said with a yawn. “I had a question about Aiden.”

“What about him?” Skye asked, perching on the edge of the bed beside her.

“Did you…?” Taly paused. Like everything else, the memory felt fuzzy and indistinct. “Did you pick him up and sling him over your shoulder when you were running from the harpy, or did I dream that?”

Skye went still for a moment. It started as a stutter, a choked bark that grew in intensity until the laughter erupted from his throat. For the first time since she'd woken up, the tension in his shoulders melted away, and she couldn't help but join in, albeit weakly. "He was moving too slow," Skye insisted. "I really didn't have any other choice."

"Uh-huh," Taly said tiredly, her eyes starting to droop as her giggles subsided. "I'm not sure I believe you. Are you sure that didn't have *anything* to do with your little pissing match? Because I think you might have just won. Aiden will never live down being carried around like some damsel in distress."

"Was there ever any question that I would win in the end?" Skye asked. Even if he still looked haggard and pale, he was starting to sound more like his old self again. When Taly didn't say anything immediately, he reached over and gently flicked her on the nose. "That was your cue, Tink."

Taly smiled and swatted his hand away as best she could. She didn't miss the way his fingers trailed across her cheek, discreetly checking her temperature. "Of course not. No doubt whatsoever," she replied with a sleepy chuckle. A flicker of silence and then, "That was the answer you wanted, right?"

Skye laughed again as he tucked the blanket tighter around her before gracelessly falling back into the chair beside the bed. Nothing else was said for a while, and eventually, Taly felt herself drifting off to sleep. She could still sense Skye nearby, and a small sigh passed her lips as she snuggled down further into the blanketed cocoon of warmth. For as long as she could remember, he had always been just across the hall, always within reach. She had forgotten just how much she liked having him nearby.

It felt as though she had just nodded off when the sound of hushed whispering invaded her dreams. Feeling warm and lazy, she turned her face towards the noise, blearily opening her eyes.

Aiden and Skye stood over by her worktable, their backs turned.

"When was the last time you slept?" Aiden asked in a low voice, setting down a fresh bag of supplies on the already cluttered tabletop.

"I'm fine," Skye hedged. He ran a hand through his hair. "Really, I'm fine."

"Your general health aside, you're no good to anyone if you deplete your aether," Aiden replied, frowning. "Get some rest. Take a shower. Eat something. She's in the next room, not the next town. If anything happens, you'll be the first to know."

Skye suppressed a yawn. "I know. And, I will. Now that she's woken up, I'll go take a break. I promise. I'd just like to wait until she wakes up again and you get a chance to examine her."

"I'm here," Taly mumbled, her eyes squinting in the morning light. Someone had opened her curtains. "I'm up."

Both Aiden and Skye turned at the sound of her voice.

"Well," Aiden said as he crossed the room. He looked far more put-together than what she could recall from her hazy fever dream. Dressed in pinstriped slacks and a green damask waistcoat, the only trace of the obvious stress the healer had endured over the past week was written in the already fading bruises beneath his eyes. "Welcome back. Dare I ask how you're feeling this morning?" He held a hand up to her forehead and then waved a glowing earth crystal over her body, revealing emerald web-like threads that crisscrossed her skin. Apparently, the earth mage saw something encouraging in the patterns, and he soon backed away with a nod of approval.

"Like I really hate harpies." Grimacing, Taly wriggled as the ever-present pain started to come back into focus. She could still feel the sting of the harpy's claws where the long gash across her shoulders had healed. "I mean, *really* hate them. In fact, I've decided to dedicate the rest of my life to ensuring the extinction of their species. It's a noble cause, and I don't think anybody will miss them."

Aiden barked out a short laugh. "I'll take that as *better*."

"Is she going to be okay now?" Skye asked nervously, coming to stand beside the healer. In comparison to Aiden's immaculate appearance, Skye looked rumpled and worn. His clothing was creased and stained after what must have been a harried trip to Litor and back, and there were lines around his eyes that hadn't been there before. Stooping down, he rearranged the pillow underneath her head, and Taly rewarded him with a grateful sigh as she found a small amount of relief from the almost-constant discomfort.

"Her temperature still isn't where I'd like it to be, but yes, I believe so," Aiden replied, walking back over to the table set against the wall. Taly's collection of mortal tech had all been cleared away, and an assortment of herbs, vials, and medical supplies now covered the oaken surface. "As long as the restoration spells have a steady supply of aether and she continues to take the draught, then I think she'll make a full recovery."

Aiden reached into his bag and pulled out a small packet of black powder. Pouring it into a cup of water, he began to stir absentmindedly. "Skye, I think you should go get some rest now. I can take things from here."

"Yes, you've made your point. I'll take a break," Skye grumbled as he stepped across the room and began checking the bundles of fire crystals laid across Taly's feet. Glancing up at her, he said, "By the way, Sarina's headed into town this afternoon. She wanted to know if there's anything you need from your room at the tavern."

They think I'm here to stay, she realized, guilt welling up inside her.

Taly stared down at her hands, the image of the harpy flashing in front of her eyes. No matter how much she wished it could be different, there was no coming home for her now. Because nothing had changed. If anything, her reasons for distancing herself from her adoptive family had only multiplied, and it was even more imperative that she leave and never come back.

That left her with only one option.

"Aiden?" she asked, trying to push herself up. She fell back against the pillows when a searing stab of pain shot down her spine. "How long until I'm back on my feet?"

Aiden glanced at her over his shoulder. "You'll be hurting for a while yet, but I'd say you'll probably be getting back some mobility by tomorrow morning. Maybe tonight if I give you something a little stronger for the pain."

Taly jerked her head decisively. Then, taking a deep breath, she gathered up her courage and braced herself. "Skye, while I'm grateful for what you all have done for me this past week, I'm not staying. Tell Sarina to leave my things where they are. I'll be leaving first thing tomorrow morning to go back to Ryme."

With a low growl, Skye tucked the edge of the quilt back under the mattress and stood. His eyes found hers, and he said, "Aiden, could you give us a minute?" He didn't turn around as the earth mage quietly excused himself, nor did he say anything once the door clicked closed. He just stood there, quiet and unmoving, staring at her with that molten green gaze until she looked away.

Finally, he huffed out a cheerless laugh and hung his head. "So, let me get this straight. You can't even sit up on your own, but you're already planning to stagger your way back to Ryme? Let me guess—is it because you're mortal and we're not? Hmm? Or is it something else now? C'mon. Let's hear it. What lie have you come up with this time to avoid having to tell me the real reason you decided to leave home?"

Taly flinched at his harsh tone. *You're doing this for them,* she tried reminding herself. Her lip began to tremble, but she shook her head, steeling herself. What she was about to do… it was going to kill her, but she had to do it.

"Shards, Skye!" Taly exclaimed weakly. "Fine. You want to know the *real* reason I left? The reason I'm not coming back? Okay, here it is. I got tired of being treated like some *mortal pet,* so I went to where I could be around my own kind. I'm not like you. You can teach me to walk and talk like some highborn fey, dress me up all you want, but I'm always going to be *shardless.*"

Skye winced—he hated that word. Which was exactly why she'd chosen it. Already winded, her chest heaved from the exertion of these few clipped sentences, and she fell back against the pillow. Her eyes stung, but she viciously blinked back the tears.

Skye paused to take a deep breath and then gave her a tight-lipped smile. “Taly, don’t take this the wrong way, but you’re full of shit. When are you going to stop lying to me and tell me why you’re pushing us away—why you’re pushing *me* away?”

“I just did.”

Skye stepped closer, turning the corner of the bed and coming to stand beside her. “Another lie,” he replied sadly. Taly made to refute his claim, but he cut her off. “Just talk to me, Taly. *Please*.”

“There’s nothing to talk about,” she mumbled, refusing to break eye contact. “You brought me back here when I clearly stated that I wanted to return to Ryme. What did you think was going to happen?”

“Are you kidding?” Skye snapped, his eyes wide with disbelief. “You would’ve died if we’d tried to take you to Ryme. Aiden says we were lucky to get you back to the manor when we did. Another hour and you would’ve been too far gone. I’m sorry, Taly, but you’re absolutely crazy if you think that I should’ve knowingly done something that would’ve endangered you, maybe even resulted in your death.”

He hesitated for a moment, shaking his head in frustration. “That’s it. I... I can’t do this anymore.”

“Skye, I—"

“No, Taly. You’ve said enough. It’s my turn.” Sinking down onto the bed next to her, Skye reached out and took her hand in his. “I’m done fighting you on this,” he said with a heavy sigh.

"I'm just... I'm done, Taly. If you're telling me that you want to spend your life salvaging and barely making enough coin to keep yourself alive—I'll respect that. If you say that you don't want me in your life, then you don't ever have to see me again. Even though I know you're lying, even if I can see how much you want to come home, how much you're hurting... I'll back off."

Skye stopped, and the hand that still gripped hers tightened. His eyes turned glassy. "You're my best friend, Tink. For 15 years, you've been my best friend. And even though I've tried to be there for you, I can't do this anymore. This fucked up back-and-forth, where one minute everything's fine and the next you're telling me that you're just some *pet*? It's not fair. I don't know what your game is, but I don't want to play anymore. It hurts too much."

Taly wasn't sure what to say. Something in her chest felt impossibly tight as she watched Skye wipe at his eyes, and tears were already starting to roll down her cheeks as he slowly stood and left the room.

Aiden was waiting outside the door, but Skye pushed past him. Taly jumped when she heard the door to his quarters slam shut.

Aiden looked between the two rooms, his face impassive, before stepping inside. Closing the door behind him, his hand pressed against the carved surface. A crest of white light swept through the wood and the surrounding walls as the silencing wards engaged—a necessary precaution to preserve any semblance of privacy in a house full of shadow mages.

He didn't look at her as he crossed the room, nor did he say anything as he retrieved the forgotten cup from her worktable and began mixing in an assortment of powders from various jars and vials.

His voice was low and even when he finally broke the silence. "You'll need to drink this mixture three times a day until the soreness goes away." He regarded the brew for a moment before adding another small pinch of white powder and handing it to her. "I'll have to mix it up for you to take with you if you really do intend to leave."

Taly took the cup and drank, wrinkling her nose at the taste. The strange prescription was slimy and bitter, more so than anything she had ever tasted.

"So, what are you two really fighting about?" Aiden's tone was casual, but there was something sharp in his expression.

"You were eavesdropping?" Taly asked, her words mumbled into the cup. She ignored the obvious tear tracks on her cheeks.

Aiden snorted. "I didn't need to eavesdrop. Skye looked like he'd just had his heart ripped out, and you're still crying. I'm no scholar, but I'm not stupid."

"With all due respect, our fights are none of your concern." Shuddering, Taly finished off the foul-tasting medicine and handed the cup back to him.

Aiden watched her closely. "Do you know what it is that you just drank?" he asked, shaking the cup for emphasis.

"No idea, but it's disgusting," Taly quipped, avoiding the healer's piercing gaze. The way he was looking at her—suspicion tinged with curiosity—had her shifting uncomfortably.

"It's faeflower," he replied, setting the cup

down on her bedside table with a thud.

Taly's hands flew to her throat. Faeflower was a common antidote for everything from aether depletion to virago venom—for the fey, that is. The plant was highly poisonous to mortals. In fact, it could kill them almost instantly if the dosage was large enough. "What have you done?" she whispered, her eyes wide.

"I saved your life," Aiden stated tersely. "Over the last two days, I've given you enough faeflower to kill a human three times your size three times over. And yet here you are—back from the brink of death. So tell me, Taly—and you better answer this next question honestly... What exactly are you?"

Ignoring the sudden tremble in her hands, Taly pushed her hair back behind her ear. "What do you see?"

"A human ear." Aiden ran a gentle finger along the rim of her ear.

"That must mean I'm human then." Taly raised her eyes to meet his. "You must've been mistaken about the faeflower. Lucky for me, I guess."

Aiden sat next to her on the bed, his lips pressed into a thin line. "Taly, I treated you with mortal medicine, and you got worse. In fact, over the last eight days, you've presented with all of the symptoms I would expect to see in a fey woman of your size that had been exposed to harpy venom. The progression, the timeline—everything was completely textbook, right down to what would've been the time of death. And then, wonder of wonders, when I treated you with fey medicine, you got better."

He held up a hand when he saw her open her

mouth to protest. "Also, I was watching your match with Skye the other day before we left for the Aion Gate. He's *fey*, Taly, and highborn. Even without engaging his magic—his instincts, his reaction time, his speed... I know you've been sparring with Skye your whole life, but there's still no way a human could dodge a fey's attacks like that. And after hearing about your bet, I can tell you with complete certainty that Skye wasn't trying to let you win that day. If you were truly human, you never would've gotten to two hits. I think you were using magic."

"Stop it, Aiden," Taly croaked, panic starting to set in. Her breath quickened, and she could feel her pulse fluttering at the base of her throat.

"No," he replied harshly. "You stop it. You better level with me right now. If you don't, then it's my duty to tell the Marquess what I know. He needs to know that the girl that he raised as his own, that he allowed to live in his home, isn't who she says she is."

Aiden turned away for a moment, massaging his temples. "Truthfully, the only reason I'm giving you an opportunity to explain is because I've known you for so many years." His voice trailed off, and his eyes found hers. "You have to realize what this looks like. Are you a plant? A spy from one of the other noble houses?" Sighing in frustration, Aiden moved to stand. "I'm sorry, Taly, but I have to tell Ivain."

"No! Just wait." Taly reached out and grabbed his sleeve. She whimpered when her muscles protested sharply against the sudden movement. "Please don't tell anyone. I'm not a spy. I don't know what I am. I really don't. If you look mortal, then you're not supposed to have magic. That's how it's supposed to work, right? This isn't supposed to be happening."

"What isn't supposed to be happening?"

"Last year..." Taly choked back a sob. "Last year, I started seeing... and then the harpy..." She stopped, the words getting caught in her throat.

Could she really do this? Could she really reveal her biggest secret? Looking up, she saw the dogged determination in Aiden's eyes. He had meant what he said. If she didn't tell him, he would go straight to Ivain. They would figure her out, and then she'd no longer be able to protect the people she loved most.

Taly hung her head, a heavy weight settling on her shoulders as she whispered the words she hadn't dared utter out loud. "I have time magic, Aiden."

Aiden's eyes widened, and he stared at her for a long moment, completely still. Then, without warning, he pushed himself off the bed in one explosive movement and started pacing restlessly in front of the bed. "Shards!" he hissed in a low voice. "Just..." A garbled stream of cursing fell from his lips as he raked his fingers through what was left of his hair.

"That was my reaction too," Taly said quietly, not quite able to lift her head to meet his gaze.

Aiden rushed back over to the bed and grabbed her shoulders, shaking her. His grip loosened when he saw her wince. "Are you sure?" he implored. "Are you absolutely certain? What even makes you think...?" He shook his head. "Start at the beginning."

"The visions started about a year ago," Taly mumbled. "Skye and I were sparring in the yard, and I'm still not sure what happened exactly.

Right after he discharged the dagger in my hand, this gold haze, almost like dust, clouded my vision. It wasn't very distinct—not like now—but I could still see enough to know what he was going to do a few seconds before he actually did it. Needless to say, I panicked. I'm still not sure why, but I just ran."

Taly picked at the sleeve of her nightdress. "At first, I only meant to stay away until the visions stopped. But they didn't stop. There were some days when I couldn't see because of the dust. It was all so confusing... I thought I was going crazy!" she insisted. Her chin dipped, and she whispered, "I hoped I was going crazy."

"If there was something wrong with your mind, I would've seen it during my examination," Aiden interjected, his voice low. "Everything seemed normal, but based on what you've described, that would still be more plausible than... but then the faeflower..."

"There's more." Aiden's eyes found hers, and Taly hesitated, recalling the events at the Aion Gate. "What happened a few days ago was different—it wasn't just visions. That harpy was about to kill me. I was dead. There was no way I was getting out of there alive," she said, looking at the healer with a pleading expression. "Then it froze. The harpy just... froze. I told it to stop, and it did." Her face screwed up, and she wiped at her cheeks as Aiden finally released her and sank to the floor.

"I don't know what's happening to me, Aiden. The only thing I know for sure is that the Sanctorum would kill me without a second thought. They'll do anything to make sure that the Time Shard never revives—even if that means killing anyone and anything that displays even the faintest trace of time magic or precognitive ability. And if Skye and Sarina and Ivain… if they tried to protect me, they'd die too."

"I think I understand," Aiden murmured. "Because Ivain, Sarina, and Skye—they *would* try to protect you. They hate the Sanctorum. They love you. There would be no question."

"*Please* don't tell them," Taly begged. "Please, Aiden. The less they know, the less contact they have with me, the harder it will be for the Sanctorum to go after them if I'm found out."

Aiden pulled himself up and sat on the edge of the bed. "What's your plan then?"

"What?" Taly asked, a hitch in her voice.

"Your plan?" Aiden repeated tersely. "You ran away to protect them—I get that. What do you plan to do next? To survive?"

Taly shrugged, fidgeting with the edge of the quilt. "I don't know. Stay out of sight until the Aion Gate opens? Sarina taught us a little bit about the mortal world. I thought I might be able to travel to one of the human cities. Even if I'm not completely mortal, I still look human. I was hoping I could just… disappear."

Aiden stood and began pacing again.

"I'm not your responsibility, Aiden." Taly's eyes followed him as he traversed the length of the room. "You've already done more than you needed to just by healing me."

"Except that's where you're wrong." Turning and leaning against the table, Aiden sighed. "If you have time magic, then it's my duty as a member of the Crystal Guard to protect you." He stopped and ran a hand over his head, scratching the fuzz at the back of his neck. "Whatever you might be—mortal, fey, or something else entirely—the fact is that you're the first indication we've seen in almost 200 years that the Time Shard might be trying to reappear. New mages can't attune to a school of magic unless a Shard calls to them. At least, that's the theory."

Aiden cocked his head to the side, lost in thought. "We have the Attunement Ceremony to force a child's magic to manifest itself," he said, mostly to himself, "but I wonder what would happen if a mage was never taken to the temple. Since you looked human, no one would've thought to give you a ceremony, but what if the Time Shard still made the call? Maybe it just took your magic longer to manifest itself."

"I'm not a mage," Taly argued stubbornly. "I'm human."

Aiden snorted. "Not from where I'm standing. The faeflower aside, do you know why harpy venom is so deadly to the fey? It's because it binds to the aether in our blood. If the venom affected you, that means it found something to bind. Something you needed to survive. You're a mage."

"But I don't look fey," Taly countered. "Even if I'm not completely mortal, I still don't look fey. That would make me a… I don't even know. Something that looks human but has magic? That's unheard of. There are people who would kill me just for that!"

"I'm aware," Aiden replied grimly. He stared out the window, a faraway look in his eyes. "I'll make you a deal. I'll help you. I'll keep your secret, and I'll accompany you to Faro. That's where my regiment is stationed. The High Lord of Water has declared all fey cities in the mortal realm a sanctuary for time mages and their sympathizers.

The Crystal Guard will be able to protect you there. We don't answer to the Dawn Court or their Sanctifiers. Our duty is to serve and protect the Shards—*all* of the Shards."

Taly opened her mouth to respond, but Aiden held up a finger. "In return," he paused, making sure he had her attention, "you have to stay here, at the manor, until the Aion Gate opens."

"Absolutely not," Taly objected.

"Yes," Aiden shot back, "you will. My obligation is to keep you safe. You're either going to agree to my terms, or I'm going to tell Skye and the Castaros what you just told me. Either way, you're staying right where you are." When Taly looked away, Aiden came to sit beside her on the bed. "The harpy venom isn't completely out of your system, and I'm just assuming from this point on that I need to treat you the way I would a fey. That means you're still in danger of relapsing. If you go somewhere where the aether is thin, like Ryme, you *will* die. You need to stay close to an aether core, and Harbor Manor just so happens to have its own private system.

"On top of that, you're not going to be able to get by on your own—not anymore. If you have enough aether in your blood that a harpy would go after you with a water mage *casting* right next to it, you're going to have a very hard time going out to the gates to salvage. The magical beasts are rabid right now and drawn to the same places you would need to go to make your living."

When Taly remained silent, stubborn pride still shining in her eyes, Aiden threw his hands up. "Okay—still not convinced? How about this? The High Lord of Earth's brother has been spreading all kinds of inflammatory rhetoric about humans and Feseraa at the Dawn Court. Tempris is generally pretty isolated, but the effects of that are going to come here eventually. Mortals already have a tendency to go missing when the Aion Gate is charging, but this year is going to be worse. Ivain and Sarina and *especially* Skye can insulate you from that. Believe me when I say that no fey—highborn or otherwise—is going to piss off the heir to Ghislain. His family has too much power."

"I'm not going to endanger Skye and the Castaros so that I can hide behind their noble rank," Taly snapped, reaching up and grasping her necklace.

Aiden sighed, adopting a more placating tone, "Look—you don't have a choice right now. You need the Castaros' help and the protection that being close to Skye will grant you. And it's like you said—if they don't know what you are, it will be much more difficult for the Sanctorum to go after them if you're discovered. While the statutes have never been tested, there are laws that protect those unknowingly harboring time mages."

Taly ran a finger over the pendant, feeling the small divot in the center. "You're assuming that Skye will even want me around at this point. I don't think he's going to forgive me this time. I went too far."

Aiden laughed as he pushed himself off the bed. "I wouldn't be so sure about that. Just talk to him. Be as honest as you can. That's all he wants."

Taly chewed on her lip as she considered Aiden's proposal. It was a good plan—better than any she had come up with so far—and a part of her was desperate to embrace this unexpected ally. After a year of harboring this secret on her own, she couldn't deny that it would feel good not to be alone in this anymore.

I'd get to come home, she thought, fighting back a fresh wave of tears. There would be no more nights spent in a shitty room with a roof that leaked, shivering underneath a threadbare blanket because the heating element in her stove hadn't been replaced since before she was born; no more days where she was so hungry that even Jay's "leftovers" started to look appetizing.

And... she'd get her family back.

She would no longer have to pretend that she hadn't missed Skye, Ivain, and Sarina every single moment of every single day since she'd made the decision to leave.

Taly's voice was shaky and uneven when she finally said, "Okay, Aiden. You win. But if anything happens... anything at all—"

"If the variables change, we'll reassess the plan." Aiden gave her a knowing smile as he moved towards the door. "Now get some rest, and don't worry about Skye. I'm sure everything will work itself out."

Taly leaned back against the mountain of pillows stacked behind her, staring at the closed door long after Aiden had gone. Wiping at her eyes, a slow smile began to emerge, and she couldn't stop the weak peal of laughter that bubbled up out of her chest.

She was home. She wasn't alone anymore, and she was finally *home*.

CHAPTER 10

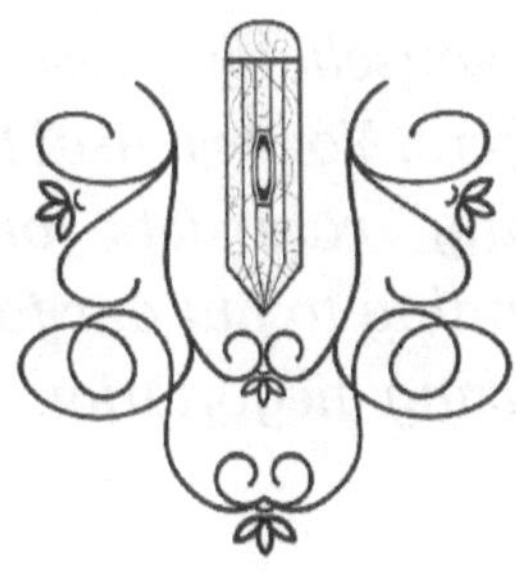

-A letter from Lady Adriana Emrys, Duchess of Ghislain, to her son, Lord Skylen Emrys

The 27th day of the month Yule, during the 250th year of the Empty Throne

Skylen,

As you already know, it was not my wish that you stay on Tempris to continue your training in lieu of attending the University in Arylaan. However, I gave you my blessing when you gave me your assurance that you would not further isolate yourself from the nobility in Lycia. As I sit here in my quarters at the Dawn Court, listening to the sounds of the Yule Ball filtering up from down below and preparing my usual excuses for why my son, the heir, is not by my side, I cannot help but think that perhaps I made a mistake in allowing you to stay.

While I cannot deny that Lord Castaro can give you a far superior education than you would receive here, you need to start attending to your duties as Ghislain's heir—appearing at court with more regularity, forming relationships among the nobility, and at the very least meeting with the ladies the other households present to you before rejecting their offers. Your refusal to even entertain potential breeding contracts or proposals of marriage is beginning to put our family at a severe disadvantage during negotiations with the other noble houses.

You will be receiving another breeding offer from House Arendryl within the coming months. The young lady in question lives in Faro, and I highly recommend that you agree to meet with her when the Aion Gate opens. Otherwise, you and I may need to revisit the matter of where you choose to continue your education.

With all my love,

Your Mother

"Damn it!" Skye cursed, the air crystal in his hand cracking. With a growl, he hurled the offending stone at the nearest wall before slumping over his workbench.

Skye couldn't help but feel antsy and caged after his confrontation with Taly, so instead of getting some much-needed rest, he'd retreated to the workshop, hoping to lose himself in his work. Unfortunately, what was usually a place that let him breathe when he was feeling overwhelmed was only serving to amplify his irritation as he broke crystal after crystal trying to fix a simple dagger.

I should've just gone to bed, he thought sullenly. After three days with no more than a few hours of sleep at a time, his mind was too dull, his thoughts too fractured, to muster the amount of precision that setting crystals required.

Not for the first time that day, his attention drifted to the dusty little bench in the corner. Taly's two air daggers, the handgun she'd dropped at the Aion Gate, and those stupid hyaline pistols had somehow found their way onto her old bench. Surprisingly enough, Aimee was the one that had collected Taly's dropped weapons.

Tearing his eyes away from the bench, Skye stalked to the other side of the room and began picking through the crystal cabinet. Rows upon rows of drawers adorned the massive wooden chest pushed against the wall—just another reminder of the stubborn brat. For years, Ivain had kept all of his crystals together in a single bin—fire, water, earth, air, and shadow crystals of every class and size all mixed together. The jumbled mess had made Taly's eyes cross the first time she'd seen it, and she'd cried and pouted until Ivain finally relented and let her re-sort the crystals by type, class, and then size. Only eight years old, and she'd already had an incessant need to rearrange everything around her.

"Skye?"

"In here, Ivain," Skye answered, retrieving another air crystal and slamming the drawer he'd been rifling through shut.

The door to the workshop slid open, letting in

a blast of cold air and the scent of rain.

Ivain ducked through the small opening. “This storm came out of nowhere,” he exclaimed, peeling off his morning coat and shaking it off. Droplets of water stained the dull gray fabric.

“How did the call with the High Lady of Air go?” Skye tossed the crystal on his bench, watching it roll across the cluttered surface.

Ivain shrugged and tossed the coat to the side as he began tugging at his tie, revealing a row of parallel violet lines that had been tattooed onto the skin of his neck. There were 10 in total—one for each of the primary training designations, or seals, sanctioned by the Shadow Guild. Skye had only completed four so far, and each seal was marked by a thin, vertical stripe drawn beneath his collarbone.

“As good as could be expected,” Ivain said with a sigh. “You know I grew up with that old bat? Horrible woman. Even as a child, she could suck the joy right out of a room.” The older fey noble crouched and reached underneath a cluttered workbench. “Want one?” he asked, glancing over his shoulder.

Skye laughed as he fell back onto his stool and propped his feet up on a nearby bench. “I was wondering where you’d hidden your stash.” Ivain smiled as he stood back up, two bottles of beer and a sleeve of cigars in hand. “Sure, why not? All I’m doing is breaking things over here, so I should probably call it a day.”

“A wise choice, and one my coffers would thank you for.” Ivain twisted the cap off one of the bottles and handed it to Skye before sinking down onto the stool next to him. He sighed as he removed one of the cigars and brought it to his nose. "I've been saving these. It's the last Arendryl tobacco I'll see before the Aion Gate opens. Better to smoke them now, though, before Sarina finds them. Shards, that woman was in a mood when she got back from town today."

"What happened?"

Ivain grimaced. "She finally went by Jay and Laurel's tavern and saw that none of the repairs we paid for had been completed. Jay pocketed her investment and tried to do the repairs himself. Unsuccessfully, I might add."

Skye arched a brow. "Since when does Sarina invest in third-rate taverns in what might possibly be the worst part of Ryme?"

"Since she found out that Taly was having trouble finding someone willing to rent a room to a human." Ivain scowled as he began clipping the cigars. "Jay and Laurel already owed us a few favors, so all it took was a little gold to convince them to ease their policy on mortals."

Skye frowned at the mention of Taly but said nothing. He had always suspected that the Castaros were far more involved in her new life than they let on. It was nice to know his instincts had been correct.

The older man's expression turned wistful. "Anyways, my baby sister went on a tear as soon as she got home. She even managed to find my reserve of Ghislain tobacco and then proceeded to lecture me on how I needed to be a better influence on Taly or something or other. As if that girl's cigar habit is my fault."

Skye took a long sip of his beer, drawing in a slow breath as he finally felt some of the tension in his shoulders start to ease. "Well, you are the one that taught Taly how to blow smoke rings."

"Yes, that was a mistake in hindsight."

"Don't tell me you agree with Sarina now about tobacco smoke being bad for humans." Skye took one of the cigars from Ivain and reached for a fire dagger that lay forgotten on his bench. Depressing the toggle underneath the hilt, he lit the end of the cigar with the flame that zipped along the blade.

Ivain chuckled as he waved the end of his own cigar through the flare of fire magic. "No. It's because as soon as I taught that girl how to blow a little smoke, she was always stealing my cigars. And not the cheap ones either. That girl likes her cigars the way she likes her brandy—expensive and from Arendryl. At least you always had the courtesy to swipe the ones you knew I wouldn't miss."

Ivain took a long drag. Then, tapping his cheek, he blew out three perfect smoke rings in quick succession. "Your mother wrote to me again."

Skye groaned. "Shards, what does she want now?" Flicking the switch on the dagger, he twirled the blade, extinguishing the flame, before tossing it on the bench behind him.

"The same. She's unhappy that you're skipping another season at court."

Skye stared out the window, past the droplets of water streaking the glass. "Sounds about right. She's still mad I ducked out of the winter court season after I cut the summer season so short." His eyes became shuttered as an image of a dark room and a young woman flashed through his mind. The scent of blood filled his nose, and he once again saw that brief flash of steel.

Ivain placed a hand on the younger man's

shoulder, snapping him out of the memory. "What happened last summer was not your fault, Skye. It was a bad situation with no right answers, and you did the best you could."

"I know," Skye conceded quietly. "It just doesn't feel that way. Not yet. And, while I know I can't keep putting it off forever, I'm just not ready to go back to the mainland yet, to my family's estate—especially since Kato insists on reminding me of Ava at every turn. He's even started writing me letters. The last one started with, *'The servants finally managed to get the blood stains out of the tile.'* After that, I asked Eliza to throw his letters into the fireplace as soon as they come in the post."

"Your brother is a prick and just trying to spread around his own misery. You did nothing wrong." Ivain began sipping his beer. "I heard you agreed to meet with Lady Lori when the Aion Gate opens. Are you actually considering accepting House Arendryl's offer?"

Skye huffed out a laugh. "No. But my mother says I can't keep turning down breeding contracts without at least meeting with the lady in question. And since this one is in Faro and wouldn't require me to travel back to Ghislain, I figured I could spend an afternoon with the Lady Lori and her family. Even if I turn down the offer, my mother will be happy."

"House Arendryl is a very respectable family. Good people. If I were you, I would consider accepting their proposal."

Skye snorted. "Are you joking?"

Ivain looked completely innocent as he continued sipping his beer. "I'm concerned for you, boy. If you go on much longer like this, you're going to turn into a monk. You do know that the Gate

Watchers don't require a vow of celibacy, right?"

Skye rolled his eyes. "I do just fine."

"I'd give you the time off," Ivain went on. "I'm sure one of the other Gate Watchers can take over your duties. I say—*go*. Spend a few weeks wooing a beautiful woman while your mother renegotiates Ghislain's trade agreements. Really, I don't know why you're so against the idea."

"I don't know," Skye mused. "Maybe I don't want to be a father. That seems like a perfectly valid reason to turn down a breeding offer."

Ivain waved his hand dismissively. "Those fertility spells they use to bind the contracts never work, especially on fey as young as you."

Skye brought the cigar to his lips, breathing in deeply. "You know, you used to try harder, old man. You think I can't see through this? You just want to use me to get more Arendryl tobacco."

"Now, Skye, you wound me. I would never whore you out just for a little tobacco." Ivain's lips twitched. "I need *brandy* too. I finished off my last bottle of Arendryl liquor last week."

Skye gave the man a withering glare.

"It's not a bad offer," Ivain added with a shrug. "You could break that dry spell."

"It's not a dry spell," Skye muttered irritably. "If I wanted to bed a woman, I could. I just haven't been back to the mainland in a while."

Ivain laughed, stretching out to prop his feet up beside Skye's as he continued to puff on his cigar. "There are girls on the island, you know. What about… oh, what was her name? Lady Shura? Lovely girl. Very smart. I thought the two of you got along quite well when we visited Starfall Estate over in Strio."

Skye took a long swig of beer. "I don't mess

around with girls on the island. You know that." Not that the thought hadn't occurred to him as of late. Since he'd managed to avoid returning to Ghislain for the winter season—claiming that his Gate Watchers duties and the upcoming Aion Gate connection made it impossible for him to travel—it had been *a while* since he'd been with a woman.

Ivain scratched at his ear. "Why not? You're 25—Sarina and I wouldn't mind if you brought women back to the manor. In fact, we were more surprised when you turned 18 and we still hadn't gotten to embarrass you in front of a girl. You really let us down there, boy. What's the point of having teenagers around if you don't get to ruin their lives every once in a while?"

"I don't sleep around on the island for the same reason I've never seen you bring a woman back to the manor." Skye tapped his cigar in the crystal ashtray that Ivain handed him. "For the fey aristocracy, sex and politics go hand-in-hand, and the 'island society' is the same group of catty highborn that vacation here every summer. Like you, I have no desire to get involved in their petty squabbles. Plus, if I were to stray outside the highborn nobility—*stoop below my rank*, as my father likes to say—I can guarantee the rumors would reach my mother's ears before morning. Considering how many breeding offers I've turned down just this year, she'd be so incensed she'd come through the Seren Gate and drag me back to Ghislain herself."

"Valid points." Ivain finished off his beer and tossed the bottle into the rubbish bin across the room. "Still," he mused, a devilish gleam in his eyes, "I can't help but think that maybe your recent reticence to entertain the young ladies might be because you already have a special one in mind."

Skye scoffed, chucking his own beer bottle across the room and into the bin. "I've been chained to my desk this past year, the same as you. When the hell was I supposed to have met someone *special*?"

Ivain chuckled softly. "Still in denial, I see," he murmured, shrugging when Skye arched a skeptical brow. "Oh well. Tell me, did you have any luck contacting the Gate Watchers' compound in Ebondrift yet? With the new timeline in place, we really need them to move to Ryme soon."

"Nope. No luck," Skye said. While there were more shadow mages on Tempris than anywhere else in the fey world, Ivain and Skye were the only two members of the Gate Watchers that chose to maintain a permanent residence in Ryme. The bulk of their forces were stationed at the main compound in Ebondrift near the Seren Gate. "I pinged them on the scrying relay this morning, but I haven't received a response from Commander Enix or his Precept yet."

Ivain scowled. "I realize that the Seren Gate is open and that they're undoubtedly dealing with all of the traders and supplies that are coming through for the Aion Gate connection, but Enix is usually more conscientious than this. Even without the new timeline in place, we should have received at least *some* backup by now."

Skye rubbed at his temples. Just thinking about the stack of paperwork waiting for him on his desk made him feel tired. In a few short months, Tempris would be inundated with people traveling from both the fey mainland and the mortal realm, and the logistical nightmare this presented for the little island left no shortage of work.

The Marquess clasped his hands behind his head. The cigar perched between his lips garbled his words. "*Surely*, they don't expect two people to handle all of the logistics for the Aion Gate connection. I just finished a call this morning with the Master of Letters in the Port of Marin, and the amount of backlogged mail and parcels bound for the mortal realm this cycle is truly staggering. We're probably going to need to open every storehouse between Ryme and Litor just to hold it all when it finally gets transferred."

"Oh, I don't doubt it. I swear if one more person asks me about their package delivery, I might stab someone. And don't get me started on signage. We've already sold every last inch of available promotional space around the Aion Gate. I would send people to start setting up, but the army hasn't arrived to secure the area."

Ivain pushed himself to his feet and began pacing the room, stopping to inspect the two hyaline pistols on Taly's bench. "Unfortunately, the army has been delayed. When I spoke with the High Lady of Air, she confirmed that the regiment that was dispensed is going to be late."

"They need to get here soon," Skye said with a sigh. "I have a feeling the magical beasts are going to put up a fight this year. It's probably going to take several weeks to thoroughly sweep the area around the gate and run the creatures out."

Ivain nodded. "I agree. Although, if the beasts are so rabid that they're attacking humans, maybe that explains why so many mortals are going missing. I had another five missing person reports delivered just this morning—all human. That makes 12 this week alone. Usually, I don't see those kinds of numbers until much later—not until there are enough people coming from the mainland that the illegal Feseraa traffickers manage to slink through unnoticed."

Ivain picked up one of the pistols. "Is this... hyaline?"

"Taly's latest project," Skye replied, grimacing.

"Well, I can see I'm going to have to have another talk with her about not engaging in illegal activities—even if she doesn't think she'll get caught." Ivain shook his head and placed the pistol back on the desk. He smiled when he saw Zephyr. "Of course, she took this old thing with her."

"What do you mean?"

"Hmm?" Ivain looked up. "Oh. Sarina cleared out Taly's room at the tavern today. Apparently, she didn't have much—just a stack of old glamographs and a little bit of gold. Now, I don't know what she took with her when she left, but I find it quite interesting that after a year, the things she held onto were family pictures, the pistol you gave her, and this dagger. Judging from how skinny she is now, she missed a lot of meals, and just the crystals from that pistol could've brought in enough coin to feed her for several months." He gave the dagger a practiced twirl, holding it up to the light. "If I recall correctly, this was the first air crystal you ever set."

"I wish she would just get rid of that piece of trash," Skye muttered. "Throw it into the rubbish bin where it belongs."

"Shards, boy," Ivain laughed. "You really are dense. You're telling me you don't know why Taly likes this old thing so much?" When Skye shook his head, Ivain gave him a good-natured glare. A flick of the old man's wrist was all it took to embed the blade in the workshop door across the room. "When Sarina told Taly that she was too young to learn how to throw a knife, you snuck out to the training yard one night and taught her using *that* blade. You never could tell that girl *no*."

Skye felt a tug at the corners of his mouth, and some of the weight that had settled on his chest in the wake of his confrontation with Taly lifted. "Well, in my defense—when she pouted, she looked like a kicked puppy. You try saying *no* to that."

"Oh, I remember. That look—you know the one—got me into a lot of trouble with my dear sister. I still don't think Sarina's forgiven me for teaching Taly how to fight." Ivain paled slightly before taking one last drag of his cigar and depositing the remains in the ashtray. "Well, I need to get back to work. I put a new stack of files on your desk, but you can set those aside. Something tells me that Enix would enjoy personally overseeing the public latrine repairs, so I think we should save it for him. We can just tell him that we were too busy to get to it since he forgot to send us help."

Ivain shrugged on his coat as he prepared to dash out into the rain.

"Hey Ivain," Skye called out before his mentor could disappear through the small crack in the door. His mind, dulled by stress and lack of sleep, finally managed to catch up with something the older man had said. "What did you mean by 'Sarina cleared out Taly's room?' The last time I talked to Taly, she was adamant about going back to Ryme."

Ivain's eyes widened. "Oh, you don't know yet? Aiden convinced her to stay. Apparently, he got her to open up a little bit, and she decided to move back in." He shook his head, a stark look of relief washing over his features. "At least one good thing came of this mess."

With that, Ivain turned and ducked out of the workshop, running through the rain at a speed that turned him into nothing but a blur of color set against the gray light of early evening.

Sitting back, Skye smashed the tip of his forgotten cigar into the ashtray, a deep frown creasing his brow. Aiden had convinced her to stay. After basically telling him that he could go to hell, she had listened to Aiden—*talked* to Aiden.

But not him. No. After 15 years of friendship, she had stopped confiding in him, stopped talking to him, seemingly stopped trusting him.

Skye's eyes stung, and he viciously swallowed past the sudden lump in his throat. Pushing himself to his feet, he approached Taly's bench and picked up the viridian dagger he had given her after their sparring match. The gleaming swirls of metal shone, even in the unusually dim, watery light pouring in from the window behind her bench.

He didn't tell her at the time, but he'd made this for her 21st birthday. It had taken him six months to get the design right, and he'd lost count of the number of times he'd almost finished only to find some imagined fault that would prompt him to melt it down and start over.

And she hadn't even wanted it. She'd tried to give it back.

With a growl, he turned and hurled the dagger at the workshop door, his chest heaving as he stared at the two blades embedded in the splintered wood.

"It doesn't matter," he tried telling himself, his voice barely above a whisper. "It doesn't matter who she talked to." Because she was home. She would be safe now. That's all that mattered.

Turning back to his bench, Skye resumed his place at his workstation, doing his best to ignore the hollow pit that had opened up inside him.

It was late when Skye returned to his quarters. Closing the door and engaging the wards, he began peeling off his clothes, dropping them on the floor as he made his way to the washroom. The light from the fireplace cast a soft glow, and the carved mahogany panels set into the walls almost looked garish as the shadows flickered and swayed.

He tiredly fumbled for the switch to the washroom, sighing when the light from the swirled glass fire lamp hanging overhead illuminated the cavernous space. Shuffling across the tiled floor, he barely registered the familiar gray-and-white marble that lined the walls as he leaned against the sink and took in his reflection.

His eyes looked sunken, and his skin was paler than usual, making the violet ink that marked the flesh of his right arm seem even darker in comparison. In addition to the four marks symbolizing each of the seals he had earned during his training with Ivain, a dragon surrounded by ribbons of shadow magic hugged his shoulder. Like all highborn nobles, he had been branded with his household's crest when he was only five years old—just before he had been brought before the priestesses of the Faerasanaa for his Attunement Ceremony.

Turning, he studied the tattoo inscribed at the base of his neck, between his shoulder blades. That one he actually liked. He had received the Gate Watchers' crest—a sun rising behind an outline of the Aion Gate—the night he was initiated as Ivain's Precept, his second-in-command.

Suppressing a yawn, Skye splashed some water on his face, pulled on a soft pair of cotton trousers, and then made his way towards the unmade bed that sat at the far side of the main room. Already hearing Sarina's reproach in his head, he gathered up his clothes as he went and tossed them over the back of one of the chairs in the small sitting area by the window.

He needed sleep. Badly. Maybe a full night of rest would make this nonsense with Taly seem a little less… demoralizing.

Before he could fall face-first into bed, a soft knock interrupted his thoughts, and when he turned to see the door edging open, his jaw dropped.

Taly stared back at him through a crack in the door, her skin almost as white as the beaded nightdress she wore. She gripped the doorframe, and she was shaking from the exertion of having walked across the hall. "Skye?" she asked, her voice uncharacteristically timid.

Breaking out of his stupor, Skye rushed

across the room, catching her just before her legs gave way. "Shards, Taly. What the hell do you think you're doing?"

"Well," she started, unsure. She trembled slightly, and he didn't miss the wince that fluttered across her expression when he readjusted his grip, accidentally grazing the newly healed skin on her back. "I wanted to talk to you, but you never came back."

Gently scooping her up, he carried her back across the hall. "You could've just called me. You know I can hear you through the wards if you yell."

Her fingers traced one of the lines beneath his collarbone. "I didn't know if you'd come."

Skye frowned as he laid her back on her bed and tucked the blankets around her. She had already started to shiver. "It hurts me that you would even think that," he muttered, walking over to the fireplace and stoking her fire.

Taly's eyes followed him. "Well, after what you said this afternoon, it seemed like a fair assumption."

Skye smiled humorlessly as he leaned against the marble hearth. A line of little animals he'd carved when they were children were arranged neatly in a row along the mantle. "Well, after what *you* said this afternoon, can you blame me?"

Taly's cheeks flushed, and she turned her face away, intently studying the shadows that danced on the opposite wall. "No. I haven't treated you very fairly as of late, and everything you said was perfectly reasonable," she whispered, her words slightly slurred.

That got his attention, and he turned to face her. "If you're willingly admitting that you were wrong," he said, walking back across the room and sinking down on the edge of the bed, "then that can mean only one of two things. Either the world as we know it is ending, or—" He glanced at the table set against the wall. A truly staggering number of potions and herbs littered the cluttered tabletop. "—you're drugged out of your mind. I take it Aiden gave you something for the pain?"

Taly nodded sleepily. "He gave me a lot of things."

"I can tell," Skye replied, chuckling when her head lolled to the side. She'd gotten distracted by the fire. "Go to sleep, Taly. We can talk in the morning."

Skye started to stand, but her hand shot out and grabbed his wrist. "Don't go yet," she mumbled, already half-asleep. "I wanted to tell you… I decided to stay."

Skye settled back on the bed. "Ivain told me. You seemed pretty intent on going back to Ryme this morning. What changed your mind?"

"Aiden," she sighed. "He's helping me."

Skye bit back a growl. "So you'll let Aiden help you, but not me?"

"You can't help." She drowsily shook her head, and her eyes began to droop. "You can't help with the dust. Only Aiden can help with the dust."

Skye gently flicked her on the nose. Her eyes were unfocused and glazed as she looked up at him. "The dust?" he asked, holding his breath. This was the closest thing to an answer he'd gotten yet.

Taly's brow crinkled in confusion, and then she started giggling. "Oops. I wasn't supposed to say that." When Skye frowned, that only seemed to spur her on. In a sing-song voice, she mumbled, "Dust, dust… can't tell Skye about the dust."

"Taly." Skye snapped his fingers, abruptly shushing her and drawing her eyes back to his. "Focus. Just how much painkiller did Aiden give you?"

"Ummm..." She gazed into the fire for a long moment, almost seeming to forget that he was there. "I think... not enough. So, I took more."

Skye picked up a discarded cup on her nightstand and held it up to his nose. Wyrmwood tea—great for pain, but also a *very* strong sedative. "Well, that explains a few things."

Like drug-induced desires to clean.

Dust, he thought, shaking his head. She hadn't come to his room looking for him. She was probably trying to find a broom.

"Go to sleep, Taly."

"Not until you say you're not mad at me anymore," she argued stubbornly, an almost childish whine to her voice. "I'm here now, so you're not allowed to be mad anymore." A large yawn interrupted her. "I wanted to tell you about the... and the... magic and harpies? I hate harpies... and wyverns... and magic..." Her words became more and more garbled the longer she babbled, and her voice trailed off as her face relaxed in sleep.

Skye stared at her for a long moment before huffing out a mirthless laugh. "Are you kidding me?" he asked her sleeping form. "I'm not *allowed* to be mad? Is that a joke?"

Taly mumbled something incoherent as she turned over.

"I'm not allowed to be mad," he repeated to himself. "That's a good one. But Princess Tink has spoken, so I have no other choice but to obey, right?"

Skye took a shaky breath. "Sorry to tell you this, but that's not going to work this time. After what you've put me through this past year, after what you said to me when I found you in that bunkhouse in Ebondrift right after you left... Shards, after what you said to me this afternoon... I'm *allowed* to feel anything I damn well please. You don't get to decide when I stop being *mad*."

Taly kicked in her sleep, wriggling to get comfortable.

"I thought you were going to die," Skye whispered, reaching up to tuck the blankets back around her. "I've been so angry at you for so long, but the moment that harpy grabbed you, none of that mattered anymore. And after spending a week wondering if I would ever get to hear your voice again, or see you smile, or even have you smack me for saying something stupid—I was ready to move forward. I thought you might be too, but..."

Skye stopped, turning away and hanging his head. "But the first thing you did when you woke up was try to push me away. *Again*. I'm not going to lie—that fucking hurt. And then you know what hurt even more? After telling me to piss off, you go and talk to Aiden. You confide in Aiden. *Aiden* is the one that gets to know why you decided to cut *me* out of your life."

Skye wiped at his eyes. "Mad, Tink? I should be *furious* with you. I should be cursing your name. I should cut you out of my life the same way you did to me—let you see how it feels to suddenly have your closest friend run out on you with no explanation. Because let me tell you—it feels shitty. Really, really—"

Skye started when he felt a hand on his arm.

Turning his head, he found Taly staring back at him sadly.

"I'm sorry," she breathed. She still looked sleepy and dazed, but there was a little more clarity in her eyes now. "I'm so sorry, Em. I'm sorry, I... I don't know how to fix this. You're still mad at me, and... I don't know how to fix it." Her lip began to tremble, and her face crumpled. She swallowed back a sob.

"Don't cry," Skye said softly, wiping at the dampness that was swiftly collecting on her cheeks. "Yes—I'm still angry. I'm angry and hurt and confused and, right now, *tired.* But I'm not going anywhere. You are the most infuriating woman I've ever known, but I've given up trying to deny that I won't keep running back for more."

"Tell me how to fix this," Taly slurred. She was struggling to keep her eyes open as the sedatives and medicine began to drag her under. "Just tell me what to do, and I'll do it."

Skye shook his head. "You need to rest, Taly. We can talk about this in the morning."

"Tell me," she demanded mulishly.

Skye's lips quirked to the side. Even half-asleep, she was still as stubborn as ever. "Okay," he began, hoping to placate her. "Well, I think a good place to start would be honesty. If you don't want to talk to me about something, that's fine. But don't push me away. Don't make up some hurtful lie about how you think you're just some *mortal pet* or go around saying that you need to cut me out of your life *right now* because you're going to die in 60 to 70 years, give or take. That's ridiculous, Tink, and you know it."

Her face scrunched up, like she was getting ready to argue.

"No more lies," he said hastily, tucking a stray lock of hair behind her ear and effectively shushing her. "Just talk to me, be as honest as you can, and tell me to shove off if I start to pry. If you can manage that, we can figure out the rest as we go along. Like I said—I'm not going anywhere."

Reaching for his hand, she twined her fingers with his. A sleepy smile emerged. "Deal," she sighed as her eyes fluttered closed. "No more lies. I promise. I promise I'll..." She abruptly stopped mid-sentence, and soft, kitten-like snores took the place of words.

"And she's asleep," Skye grumbled tiredly, a smile tugging at the corners of his mouth.

It wasn't much, and they still had a long way to go to get back to where they were before, to find that level of trust—but it was a start. And in the end, he supposed it didn't really matter *who* convinced her to stay. Even if she wasn't ready to tell him the truth, she clearly still wanted him around, still valued him enough to seek him out when she was delirious and in need of comfort.

For now, that was good enough.

Leaning down, Skye pressed a kiss to her brow. "Welcome home, Tink," he said as he pushed himself to his feet. "Let's just hope you still remember this conversation come morning."

CHAPTER II

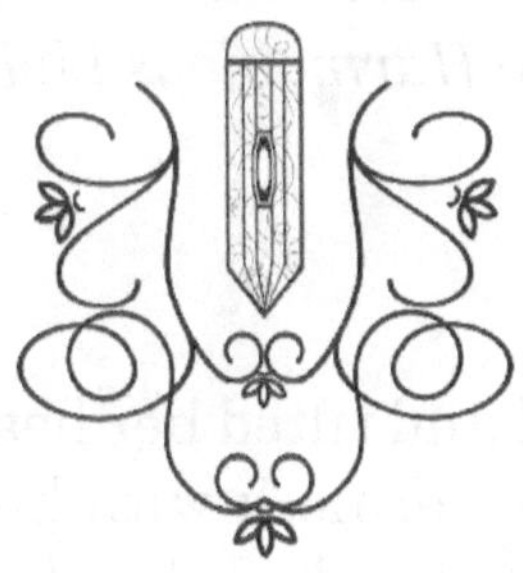

-A relaygram from Lady Sarina Castaro of House Fairmont

The 18th day of the month Meridian, during the 251st year of the Empty Throne

Synna,

If you could, would you please look into acquiring the following texts at the Ebondrift market? Talya has recently taken ill, and it is of the upmost importance. I will double your usual fees if you can deliver them within the next two days. Triple if you can have them here before morning.

- *A Guide to Human Infectious Diseases*
- *Human Cancers: The Complete Works of Doctor Webster Emdee*

- *Ten Signs Your Human Has Cancer: The Newer More Complete Works of Doctor Webster Emdee*
- *Extending Human Lifespans: A Best Practice Guide to the Care and Feeding of Mortals*
- *Rebellious Mortals and How to Tame Them: A Guide to Harmonious Living*

"Look up."

Taly sighed and tilted her head back as Aiden gently probed at her neck with his fingertips. She sat at the end of her bed, her bare feet swaying back and forth as the healer examined her.

"No more swelling," Aiden mumbled to himself. He was dressed casually this morning, choosing to forgo his usual waistcoat in favor of a plain linen shirt. He rolled up his shirtsleeves, revealing three parallel lines that had been inscribed on the underside of his forearm.

"When did you complete the third seal?" Taly asked, eyeing the tattooed lines. Green for earth magic.

"Hmm?" Aiden looked up distractedly before grabbing her wrist and feeling for her pulse. "Oh… a few months ago. The Crystal Guard won't accept anyone that hasn't completed at least three levels of training in their school of magic. Now, hold out your arms."

Taly held her arms out, tensing when Aiden pressed down with his palms to test the muscles in her back and shoulders. She had been through this same routine twice a day since she was able to sit up on her own. "I want out of this bed, Aiden. It's been 18 days now. 18 days since I've been allowed outside this room. And granted, I was unconscious for eight of them, but still… I'm losing my mind!"

"I know," Aiden replied tiredly. "You've told me. Many times." He hesitated, glancing at the door nervously. "And if it were just me," he added in a low whisper, "I would take you off bedrest. But you know what Sarina will say to that."

Taly shuddered. Since mortals were far more susceptible to injury and disease than the fey, Sarina had always gone just a little too far whenever Taly got sick. Needless to say, the incident with the harpy had driven the overprotective woman over the edge.

"Sarina's been a little… *overbearing* the past few days. Still, if you—the *healer*—tell her I'm better, she can't argue with that."

"Really?" Aiden asked, his face the picture of skepticism. "You've met Sarina, right? She's the one that literally dragged you back to bed just this morning when you tried to go downstairs for breakfast."

Taly picked at the delicate strip of blue satin binding the sleeve of her tunic as she remembered the early morning encounter. She had little doubt that the traders in Ryme had no problem hearing Sarina's screams that morning when she discovered Taly out of bed.

Rolling back the cuffs of Taly's leggings, Aiden gently rotated her ankles. "Do you still have any pain in your joints?"

"Nope."

"Good," he said with a nod. "I don't know if you know this, but Sarina's bought three new books on human diseases since you first fell ill. She made me read *all* of them."

Aiden reached for her arm, waving his hand

and revealing the glowing threads of healing magic crisscrossing her skin. When he pushed back the sleeve of her shirt, he frowned as he ran a finger over a dark, purple welt. A smattering of bruises peppered her arm, and if she were to remove the pale lavender tunic she currently wore, she knew the welts would extend all the way to her shoulder. Her body had healed at a remarkable pace under Aiden's care, but not all of her injuries from her encounter with the harpy had completely disappeared.

"Sarina's convinced herself that your extreme reaction to the harpy venom, the initial difficulty we had getting you to gain weight, and these bruises mean that you've caught some mortal disease called cancer," Aiden went on. "Now she thinks that we need to keep you in bed until she can bring in a special healer from Faro."

"That's absolutely ridiculous," Taly replied, pressing her lips into a thin line. "Mortals don't *catch* cancer. And even if they did, I'm pretty sure harpies wouldn't have anything to do with it."

"I've tried telling her that, but she won't listen. She insists it's cancer." Aiden stood to his full height and massaged the back of his neck. "How are the premonitions? Better? Worse?"

"Better and worse," Taly replied with a shrug. "The premonitions are popping up more often, but I'm having an easier time making them go away now."

Aiden nodded. "That means you're starting to gain some control over your magic, so I'll take that as good news. For what it's worth, I still think we should tell the others about your... *condition.* I can't begin to stress how much easier that would make these next few months. Hell, Ivain and

Sarina's older sister was a time mage—they might be able to give you some rudimentary training."

"For the last time, my answer is no," Taly replied firmly. "I don't want to tell them. Our deal was that if I stayed here, you'd keep your mouth shut. I held up my end, Aiden, so don't go getting any ideas."

Aiden gave her a pointed look but held up a hand in surrender. "Okay," he conceded with a weary sigh. "I still think you're being a stubborn idiot, but okay. For now, I'm going to keep you on the faeflower until the bruises on your arm go away. Other than that, I don't see any reason to keep you on bedrest." Taly squealed excitedly but quieted when Aiden held up a hand. "Sarina's not going to feel the same way, but I'll let you handle that problem on your own."

"That's bullshit, Aiden! She'll just think I'm lying to get out of bed. *You're* the healer. *You* have to tell her."

Aiden shrugged. "No. She scares me."

"Please!" Taly pleaded, trying her best to make doe eyes at the healer. "She's not going to listen to me. At this rate, I'm going to be stuck in this bed until I die of old age!"

"Uh-oh," a new voice interjected. The door creaked open, and Skye appeared, a smirk on his face and a half-eaten piece of toast in hand. Knowing him, that was already his third meal of the morning. "I hear complaining—which must mean Taly's up."

Taly scowled. "Ha, ha… very funny, jerk."

"I thought so," Skye replied, lazily shuffling into the room. "Hey, Aiden—Ivain and Sarina are about to leave. They wanted to know if you needed a ride into town."

"Probably," Aiden answered, turning to face Skye. "The hospital was supposed to receive the new medical provisions for the temporary clinics this morning, so I should go and help the menders sort through it. There's no telling where it all will end up otherwise." Aiden bent down to start gathering up his supplies, neatly arranging everything inside a small black bag. "You know, I'm really starting to regret offering to help you and Ivain with preparations for the Aion Gate connection. The amount of work these temporary clinics are taking to set up is truly astounding."

Skye stifled a chuckle as he sat next to Taly on the bed. "I tried to warn you."

"Yeah, I know. I didn't listen." Standing, Aiden leveled a glare at Taly. "Please take it easy. And whatever you do, don't get me in trouble with Sarina. I've been good to you this week, so try to have a little mercy." When Taly rolled her eyes in reply, Aiden just shook his head and gave her a fond smile. Then, with yet another tired sigh, he turned and disappeared through the open doorway, his footsteps echoing down the hall as he muttered to himself.

"What was that all about?" Skye asked, scowling when Taly plucked the toast out of his hands and finished it off.

Licking the remaining jam off her fingers, she smiled broadly, bouncing on the bed as she turned to face him. "Aiden took me off bedrest!"

Skye huffed out a laugh. "He must have a death wish. Ow!" He flinched when Taly punched him on the shoulder. "Geez, I don't know what kind of extra magic Aiden weaved into those restoration spells, but you hit way harder than you used to."

Taly's eyes widened, and she gave him a sly smile. "Awww," she cooed. "Is the big bad shadow mage scared of the teeny human?"

"No," Skye grumbled, the irritation in his voice undercut by the wide grin that threatened to break through. "But maybe try to pull your punches a little. I'm very delicate."

Taly snorted indelicately. "So where were Ivain and Sarina headed?" she asked, moving up the bed and stretching out on her belly.

Skye fell back on the mattress beside her. "Litor—Ivain said he needed to go check to make sure the storehouses had been repaired."

"Why is Sarina going?"

Skye shrugged and closed his eyes. "Not sure. She didn't seem happy about it, though. I have a feeling Ivain may have concocted some reason for her to go just to give you a break."

"If that's the case, then that man is a saint," Taly said, turning her head and studying Skye's profile. The two of them had done a lot of healing since she'd decided to stay. Once he promised to stop prying, and once she stopped trying to push him away, they had found some middle ground—managed to mend the bond she had tried so hard to break and come out the other side, stronger than ever.

Tapping his cheek, she smiled when he cracked open one eye to give her a good-natured glare. "So what are we going to do?"

"Come again?"

"Don't you get it?!" Taly pushed herself up and then used the mattress to bounce into a sitting position. Skye gave an indignant yelp when she almost landed on top of him. "I'm free! So please, for the love of all that is good and holy, get me out of this house."

Skye groaned, wrapping an arm around her waist and tugging her back down beside him when she continued to bounce. "While I'd love to break you out, Tink, I can't right now. Ivain asked me to go to Ebondrift today. We still haven't heard anything from the Gate Watchers stationed there, so I'm going to go check on them."

"Ebondrift works too." Taly wriggled out of his grip and hopped off the bed. Putting on her best pout, she pleaded, "Please? I don't care where we go. I just need a change of scenery."

Skye stared at her from where he still lay on the bed, his expression warring between amusement and disbelief. "No. Even if I thought that was a good idea, Sarina would kill me."

"If we hurry, we can be back before Sarina ever knows we left."

"Oh, really?" Skye gave her a smug grin as he sat up. "What about Eliza and the rest of the household staff? You don't think someone is going tell Sarina that you just took off for two days?"

Taly growled, rocking back on her heels. He had a point there. Still, she wasn't to be deterred.

"Do you have a guide?" she asked in a clipped tone.

"Nope. Only one came back last night, and Ivain needed him more." Taly glowered at him through narrowed eyes. "What?" Skye muttered defensively. "I don't need a guide to go to Ebondrift. The wards on the central highway have been repaired already."

Taly chewed on her lip for a moment, mulling over her current situation. She *needed* to get out of this room. And while she was sure that both Sarina and probably Aiden would have a few choice words for her when they found out she'd left the manor grounds, she could deal with that later.

An impish grin curved Taly's lips as a plan began to take shape. Approaching the mirror across the room, she pretended to admire her reflection. A week of good food had done wonders for her figure. Her hips and breasts had filled out remarkably, but the curve of her waist had remained slim and narrow. "That is true," she conceded, smoothing out an imaginary wrinkle in her shirt. "You don't really need a guide if you stick to the main roads." When she caught Skye staring at her in the mirror, she gave him a wide-eyed shrug. His face was the picture of confusion as he tried to figure out the cause of the sudden change in her demeanor. "But what's your backup plan if the wards are damaged? Hmm? Remember how the Fire Guild messed up the protective wards on the main road to the Aion Gate?"

Skye's smile slipped, but he quickly recovered. "If the wards on the highway are down, I'll just go around. This close to the Aion Gate connection, all of the main roads have been warded by now."

"Okay," Taly replied casually as she started to braid her hair. It had grown out considerably under the influence of Aiden's spells, and the gently curling waves now spilled over her shoulders, cascading down her back. "If the highway doesn't work, which way do you plan to take?"

"Vale," he replied immediately. "If I can't go through Della, then Vale is the next best option. C'mon, Tink. You act like I haven't lived here most of my life."

"It's been raining for almost a week now, so

the road to Vale is probably flooded," Taly said matter-of-factly, biting back a smile when she saw him hesitate. "I suppose you could head north and then turn south in Bago, but that's going to add an extra day to your ride. Maybe two days if the river's flooded. And before you even say it," she said, holding up a hand and cutting him off, "the eastern roads would be a bad idea. The grendels are starting to come out of hibernation, and everyone knows that wards don't do shit when it comes to grendels. That's all the main roads, unfortunately. There are some hunting trails that are pretty safe—if you know how to find them, that is."

She turned to look at him and couldn't help but bat her lashes a bit. "Do you know how to find them, Skye?" Taly asked sweetly, grinning when she saw the look of defeat on his face. She cocked her head thoughtfully, swaying her hips from side-to-side. "It's too bad you don't know *anyone* that's worked as a guide before, recently gotten off bedrest, and is so bored she'd work for free."

Pushing himself to his feet, Skye rolled his eyes and started making his way back to his room across the hall. Taly followed him. "I take your silence to mean that you know I'm right but just aren't man enough to admit it. It's okay—we all have our shortcomings."

Taly smiled gleefully but quickly schooled her expression when Skye glanced over his shoulder. That was enough pushing. Now she just needed to wait.

He stopped abruptly in the middle of his room, pinching the bridge of his nose. While he stood there deliberating, Taly sat down at his desk and started sorting the scattered pile of shadow crystals on the table by size. Skye had never been the most organized person, but his quarters were even messier than usual. She eyed the cluttered worktable in the adjacent room, and her fingers twitched when she spied a cluster of fire crystals mixed into the bin meant for water.

"Fine," Skye finally conceded. Before Taly could properly celebrate her victory, he held out a hand, shushing her. "But only if we go to the Swap, and there are no other guides available. And I have conditions. If anything happens—and I do mean *anything*—you get behind me. No arguing. Got it?"

"Yes, yes," Taly said in a placating tone, "you're a big, bad shadow mage, and fragile little humans like myself need to stand off to the side and 'ooh' and 'ahh' at your impressive feats of strength. I got it."

"I'm not sure you do," he replied, sauntering over to the desk. "But tell me more about how impressive you think my feats of strength are."

"Almost as impressive as the size of your ego." Taly kicked at his shin—an action that she immediately regretted when she felt the telltale tingle of aether against her skin as Skye activated his magic.

Moving too quickly for her to see, Skye grabbed her bare foot and dragged her forward. His fingers found their mark just at the base of her heel, and his grin widened when she let out a shriek of laughter. "C'mon, Tink! Let me hear you practice your 'oohing' and 'ahhing.' How am I supposed to perform these impressive feats of strength without just the right amount of adulation?" Taly almost managed to twist out of his grip, but he held fast, his hand moving up to a ticklish spot behind her knee. "Stop laughing—this is serious!"

"Stop it, you jerk!" Taly howled. Her sides were starting to ache as wave after wave of uncontrollable laughter crashed into her. When Skye finally took mercy on her and released her ankle, she sighed and sank back into the chair. "I hope you know that you're an ass."

"And you're a brat," he retorted, picking up a crumpled piece of paper from his desktop and tossing it at her head. Taly made no move to dodge, earning her another chuckle from the lanky shadow mage. "Although, my impressive feats of strength aside—"

"Oh, Shards." Taly kicked at him again, recoiling when he made another grab for her.

"You should still be armed," he finished soberly.

Taly stared out the window as an image of the harpy flashed through her mind. That damned bird had made her drop all three of her pistols. "True," she sighed. "You wouldn't, by any chance, happen to have Zephyr, would you? I'm still not sure what happened to her."

Skye reached out and tapped Taly on the nose, prompting her to look up. "I've got something for you," he said with a secretive smile. Stepping through a small antechamber and into the adjacent room in a few long strides, he retrieved a large cloth bundle from his worktable and set it on the desk in front of her. When Taly reached for it, he slapped her hands away. "Patience." She reached for it again, only to be rewarded with another slap and a low snigger. Finally, with exaggerated slowness, he moved the edges of the cloth aside to reveal both of her air daggers, cleaned and polished, and the hyaline pistols.

Taly squealed and reached for a pistol. "Oh! I thought I would never see you again!" Out of habit, she removed the magazine. It had been inlaid with viridian. "I see you made some alterations."

"A few." He was beaming as he leaned against the edge of the desk, clearly pleased by her reaction. "Look at the cartridge."

Arching a brow, she opened the small crystal compartment and smiled. "You added an air crystal. And replaced the metal, I see. You were always such a snob when it came to using alloys."

"And I added more wiring to the interior. Just because you don't technically need more viridian wirework doesn't mean it can't still serve a purpose. That and the air crystal should help with the kickback." Digging around in one of the desk drawers, he pulled out a drawstring sack and handed it to her. "These are your new cartridges. The crystals in these are much higher quality than your last set, so you should get more shots out of each one."

"What's with the color?" Taly asked, turning the pistol over in her hand. The exterior of the gun had been covered in a glossy, black enamel.

Skye reached over and tugged on the end of her braid. "If you're going to walk around with an illegal handgun, at least have enough sense not to advertise it."

"Point taken," Taly said with a laugh, reinserting the magazine. She turned the gun over in her hand, smiling as she ran a finger over yet another of Skye's modifications. An amazingly lifelike tangle of intertwined flowers had been etched along the frame. Snowdrops—the tiny little flower had always been her favorite.

"Oh, and I almost forgot. Here." Skye pulled out a small coin purse from the same drawer and handed it to her. "I never paid you for taking me to the Aion Gate."

Taly waved him away. "Give that back to Ivain. He's probably spent at least that much coin just feeding me this week."

More than that, probably, she thought, grimacing. During her convalescence, her appetite had bordered on the obscene. Humans generally required considerably less nutrition than the fey, but she was starting to rival Skye in the sheer amount of food she could consume.

"You know Ivain's not going to take it back. He'd give you more if he thought you'd take it." Grabbing her hand, Skye placed the coin purse in her palm. "Besides, you earned this. Before Aimee decided to take you out, you were doing a damn fine job."

Taly chewed on her bottom lip, fighting against the smile she could feel tugging at the corners of her mouth. Mumbling a shy "thanks," she took the bag and set it aside as she reached for Zephyr, turning the blade so that the dazzling crystals set into the hilt caught the morning light. Skye had also made some improvements to her beloved dagger. The crystals had been replaced, and the leather around the grip looked new and expensive. She gave the dagger a practiced twirl, before setting it down and reaching for the swirled viridian blade. "You know, this really is some of your best work," she said, admiring the way the pearls set into the scabbard shimmered.

As she stood and looked up, the sincere, unguarded smile on Skye's face as he watched her inspecting her refurbished equipment took her by surprise. That wasn't a look she was used to seeing, and it made something in her stomach flutter in a way that she wasn't entirely certain she wanted to examine too closely.

"Um..." she stammered awkwardly. Her cheeks started to feel warm. "I'm going to go finish getting dressed and maybe get in some target practice. I'll be down in the training yard when you're ready." Standing, Taly scooped up the pile of weapons and beat a quick retreat, her blush deepening when she heard him chuckling behind her.

CHAPTER 12

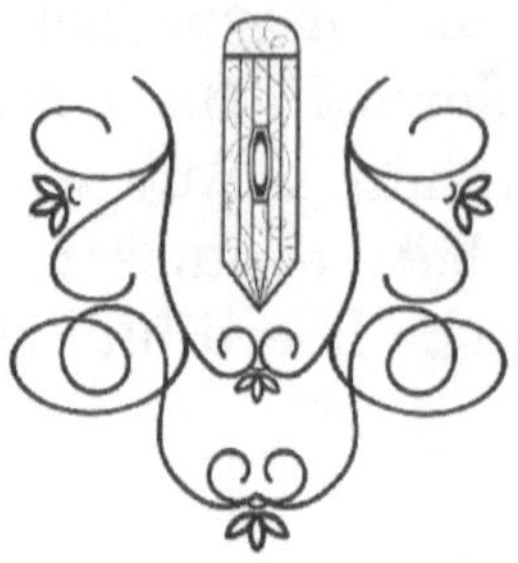

-A letter from High Priestess Melinoe of the Faerasanaa to Lord Auberin Brenin of House Arylaan, High Lord of Earth

The 20th day of the month Luna, during the 250th year of the Empty Throne

Auberin,

We need to talk about your brother. Kalahad was in my office again last night—asking about bodies. While this is hardly the first time this has happened, we had 15 Feseraa go missing last night.

I want them back—alive and unharmed. Otherwise, we may need to revisit our arrangement.

Walk in the Shards' light,

Lady Khanna Melinoe of House Agno, High Priestess of the Faerasanaa

As Taly and Skye walked through the main gates of Ryme on their way to the Swap, Taly couldn't help but notice the extra attention they received from the townsfolk. Well, not "they." Mostly just Skye. The astonishingly rich color of a highborn fey's eyes was always easy to spot, but Skye's practically glowed. Green eyes were rare among the fey, and the members of House Ghislain were known for having eyes that were almost emerald in their intensity. Even to the casual observer, there was absolutely no question as to Skye's parentage.

Taly felt a little uncomfortable standing next to him, but she resisted the urge to hang her head and fall into step behind him where she would be partially obscured. When they were younger, she had been oblivious to the attention they drew walking through town arm-in-arm—a highborn noble and a shardless. Everything had been so much easier then.

Taly fidgeted with the sleeve of her coat, trying to ignore the people around her. The protection spells woven into the fabric tingled against her skin and made her shiver. When she had rifled through her closet that morning, she was pleasantly surprised to see that Sarina had gifted her a new set of leather gear, perfect for salvaging, sparring, or just traveling outside the more populated areas of the island. The charcoal jacket she now wore was soft and pliable, and while it wasn't exactly armor, the hide shell was reinforced for added durability. She had new boots as well. They were tall, ending mid-thigh, and would help protect her legs if she ever got pushed into another pile of scrap metal. As she had learned by now, the mountains of junk that accumulated around tears in the veil certainly didn't lack for sharp edges that liked to reach out and slash through clothing and skin.

"Damn it," Taly cursed as she felt the cuff of her boot start to slip. Sarina had most likely had them made using her old measurements. Exiting the flow of traffic, Taly stood off to the side and inspected the strap buckled around the shaft of her boot. She had already tightened it as far as it would go.

"What's wrong?" Skye asked, coming to stand beside her.

"It's my boots. I'm still too scrawny."

"Scrawny? Shards, you've been listening to Eliza—the same woman that still calls me *scrawny*. You look fine, Tink. You're still a little lean, but you've got plenty of muscle tone." Taly's brows drew together in a frown as she looked up at him skeptically. It wasn't like him to comment on her appearance. Not in a positive way, that is. Skye just shrugged in reply, tugging at the neck of his jerkin and then readjusting the lapels of the dark navy duster he wore over his armor. "What? You've been walking around in flimsy, little nightgowns all week. The restoration spells made your hair longer too. Or was I not supposed to notice that either?"

"Whatever," Taly said, shaking her head. "I'll just pay to get the straps fixed when we get to the Swap."

"No need. I think I have something that may work." Tugging the strap of his bag over his head, Skye crouched down beside her as he began digging through his pack.

Taly sighed, vainly trying to adjust the scabbard of one of her daggers. The harness for her knives was new and stiff, and an intricate border of tiny snowdrop flowers was stamped into the side along with her initials. Looking up, she started when her eyes met the bright violet gaze of another highborn. A sneer was painted across his perfect features. In fact, most of the people passing by were looking at her with icy contempt. She pulled at the collar of Skye's greatcoat. "Get up. People are staring."

"So?" he asked distractedly, still rifling in his pack.

"So, I—"

"What the hell do you think you're doing, shardless?" a gruff voice practically spat.

Taly yelped when a rough hand grabbed her shoulder and twisted her around. She instinctively reached for Zephyr as she struggled against her attacker's grasp, vainly trying to shrug off the hand that was fisted in the fabric of her coat. The man's iron grip didn't loosen. He gave her a vicious shake, throwing her off-balance and wrenching Zephyr's hilt from her grasp in the process. The dagger fell to the ground with a clatter.

She soon found herself face-to-face with a very angry shopkeeper. He was gangly and lean, but his grip on her shoulder was like a vice. He looked down at her contemptuously. "You think to have a highborn shine your shoes, human? Maybe someone should teach you your place." Flames spiraled up his arm, coiling and converging around the hand that held her as he summoned his aether. The smell of smoke filled the air. Bracing herself, Taly waited for the heat of the fire spell to burn through her coat and hit her skin.

But the blistering pain never came. Before she could even blink, Skye was standing next to her. She hadn't even seen him move from his position on the ground behind her. He just appeared next to her attacker, his hand around the fire mage's throat.

"Put. Her. Down." Skye's voice was low and dangerous, and an animalistic growl emanated from deep within his chest. The air thinned as Skye pulled apart the man's spell, quite literally draining away the aether that coursed through the fire mage's veins. There was nothing more fearsome than a shadow mage, especially in close range. Skin-to-skin contact, however, was a death knell.

Taly let out the breath she'd been holding, glad that the heat at her shoulder was starting to abate. Her attacker's grip relaxed, and she scrambled away, eager to put some distance between herself and the angry fey.

The immediate threat extinguished, Taly finally had a chance to look at her assailant. Though his ears were pointed, he looked too much like a mortal to be highborn. Still, the expensive silk of his frock coat and his clean-shaven jaw indicated that he had money.

The lowborn man started to sputter, his face turning red. "I… I thought she was trying to rob you, milord. Her hand was on her dagger."

"So, instead of simply asking, you made a biased assumption and decided to attack a lady unprovoked? And not just that, you attempted to attack her with fire aether—all in broad daylight for an unsubstantiated observation." Skye lifted the man onto his toes. "Apologize."

"Skye, that's not necessary." Taly tugged at

the sleeve of his coat, her other dagger now drawn and held at her side.

"Yes, it is, Taly," Skye replied, glancing at her over his shoulder. "This man needs to learn some manners. Now, *good* sir" —Skye tightened his grip, lifting the man a little higher— "please apologize to the lady."

The man spared a frightened glance at Taly. She could see hatred mixed with the terror in his expression. "I'm sorry," he choked out, "I acted in error."

Skye arched a brow, and his face hardened. Taly tugged at his coat again, and when his eyes found hers, she shook her head. "That's a piss-poor apology, but it'll have to do," he hissed through clenched teeth as he lowered the man to the ground. "You're very lucky, you know. If either the Marquess or his sister had been here, they wouldn't have been so kind."

The man visibly paled as he finally took in Skye's appearance, and Taly could see the pieces start to click into place as he realized just who he had inadvertently picked a fight with. Almost everyone on the island was aware that the Marquess had a mortal ward, even if they couldn't be bothered to remember her name or face. "L-lord Emrys? My deepest apologies, sire." He turned to Taly and bobbed his head before stumbling down the street and back through the door of his shop.

Skye watched the man scurry out of sight before finally turning back to Taly. His jaw was clenched, and his lips were pressed into a thin line. "I think I understand now why you pulled a knife on me the other day in town." He pulled back the collar of her jacket, running a finger over a row of crystals sewn into the lining and checking her skin for burns. "The protection spells in your coat are working, so I guess that's good. Does this happen often?"

"More often lately with so many visitors in town for the gate opening," Taly replied shakily. "Anti-mortal sentiment is always running high when the tourists visit. Seems worse than normal, though. People are on edge for some reason."

Scooping up Zephyr from the pavement, she sheathed both her daggers and then shook out her hands to hide the sudden tremble. While this wasn't the first time she'd been threatened by some lowborn trying to assert his dominance, she couldn't exactly say the experience was improving. "So," she said, taking a deep breath and trying to lighten the mood, "I think this is the part where I'm supposed to say 'ooh' and 'ahh,' right?"

Skye barked out a laugh, and some of the tightness around his eyes started to melt away. As he pulled her over to a bench, he clucked his tongue disapprovingly. "No. The appropriate time would've been *while* I was performing the impressive feat of strength. See—I knew we should've practiced."

Skye pushed her to sit as he fell to one knee in front of her, and Taly's eyes darted from side-to-side, watching the passersby. She started to grow nervous and was about to pull him up to sit beside her until she noticed that he had positioned himself so that if anyone else made a grab for her, they'd have to go through him first. He glanced up, giving her a reassuring smile as he continued to dig in his pack. After a moment, he produced a small leather repair kit and set to work refitting the straps around her boots. Blowing out a slow breath, she leaned back, content to watch as he easily pushed a metal belt punch through the thick leather with nothing more than a flick of his wrist. Every so often, his fingers would graze the inside of her thighs as he adjusted the fit, sending small, not entirely unpleasant shivers down her spine.

Taly shook her head. Skye had helped her with her belt straps at least a hundred times before. This time was no different.

"All done," Skye announced a moment later, patting her knee.

After a long pause, he had still made no move to stand, prompting Taly to look down. He gave her an odd look, his eyes unblinking as they held her gaze. Then, seeming to come to a decision, he abruptly stood, slinging his pack over his shoulder. As Taly moved to follow suit, he reached down and pulled her to her feet, tucking her hand into the crook of his arm and pressing his elbow firmly to his side. Without another word, he continued forward.

Taly's first instinct was to pull away—they were drawing even more attention now as they weaved through the crowd at an unhurried pace. Instead, she found herself stepping closer, a faint blush staining her cheeks.

Thankfully, they weren't far from the Swap now, and she managed to brush aside any lingering unease once they passed through the doors. It was busy that morning, making it easier to disappear into the sea of people. Taking the lead, she started pushing her way to the back of the main room.

"Where are you going?" Skye asked, allowing himself to be pulled along. "Shouldn't we be looking for Sandulf?"

Taly rolled her eyes. Sandulf was the

reconnaissance expert employed by the Marquess. His job was to gather as much intelligence about the island as possible and provide up-to-date information to salvagers and guides. Unfortunately, he was terrible at his job. And lazy.

"I've got someone better," she yelled over the din. "Just let me do the talking. He hates nobles."

"This is going to be good," Skye muttered quietly, smirking when she turned her head to glare at him.

Finally managing to push and shove her way to the back of the room, Taly released Skye's arm as she veered off into a narrow, partially concealed hallway. Back when the Swap was still a lord's manor, this area had been used by the servants.

"Hey Dimas," Taly said in a sing-song voice, approaching a sandy-haired youth. He had a baby-face and freckles, and Taly had mistaken him for a teenager when she first met him. She knew better now not to be taken in by outward appearances. He usually kept them hidden, but she had once spotted the pointed tips of his ears. This "kid" probably had 150 years on her, at least. "Got anything good for me?"

"Hey Taly," Dimas drawled, watching Skye warily as he came to stand beside her. "You're looking *good.* I see you're keeping a little different company these days. What's with the toft?"

"He's a friend." Taly placed a warning hand on Skye's arm. Derogatory terms for the nobility aside, she could already tell Skye didn't like the way that Dimas leered at her. But to be fair, the seedy merchant did that to just about everything female that walked by. "I heard that Marcos came back yesterday. Have any more guides returned?"

Dimas shrugged and started picking at his

nails with a rusty dagger. "If they have, I haven't heard anything. I didn't even get to talk to Marcos before the Marquess snatched him up last night. The last guide I saw in Ryme left for Ebondrift last week. Apparently, Lord Kalahad Brenin decided to make an unexpected visit to the island."

"The High Lord of Earth's brother?" Taly asked, her eyes wide. Turning to Skye, she said, "I wonder if that has anything to do with why the other Watchers have been so unresponsive."

"It's possible," Skye replied. "I've only met Lord Brenin a handful of times, but he seems... *difficult*."

Dimas chuckled. "What a very diplomatic way of calling someone a right royal bastard," he drawled, raking a disdainful eye up and down Skye.

"Cool it, Dimas." Taly stepped between the two men. "Any idea where Brenin was headed?"

Dimas' face relaxed, and he went back to picking at his nails. "Strio, I think."

"Why the hell would anyone go to Strio with the grendels moving in?" Skye asked, unable to hide his surprise. The little village on the east side of the island had been evacuated almost two months ago when the southern grendel population had finally encroached on the town border. The local fire brigade still hadn't managed to put out all of the fires.

"He told his guide he wanted to inspect the farmland, but I don't buy it," Dimas replied. Having grown bored of trying to antagonize Skye directly, he let his eyes drift down the length of Taly's body suggestively. She had no doubt that the smile hovering around the edges of the trader's mouth had everything to do with the way Skye started to bristle beside her.

Taly arched a brow. "Is that so? Well, don't keep us in suspense. What do you think he's after?"

Dimas shrugged indifferently. "Strio is situated near a tear in the veil. Fewer people means better salvage, and some very valuable items have been known to fall through so close to a gate connection. You tend to be the high-risk, high-reward type, *Taly.*" The trader leaned back as he spoke, his coat shifting to reveal a gnarled wand. Judging from the clumsy rune engraved on the scratched surface of the fire crystal, it had probably been illegally modified. His fingers drummed against the shaft, and his eyes flitted over to Skye before landing back on her. "I'm surprised you haven't made an attempt yet."

Taly laughed. "I might be crazy, but I'm not stupid." She saw Skye shift his weight, casually moving a hand to rest on the blade strapped to his waist. Patting the edgy highborn on the shoulder, she said, "Sorry, buddy. No more guides means you're stuck with me."

"Where are you headed?" Dimas interjected, leaning forward.

"Ebondrift," Taly replied as she turned back to the trader. "I need the latest reports."

"Sure." Dimas reached underneath his table and pulled out a small roll of papers. "That'll be three gold."

"I'll give you one," Taly stated simply. She pulled out a single gold coin and threw it on the table.

"No deal." Dimas' eyes dropped, lingering on the swell of her breasts revealed by the slim cut of her leather coat before meeting her gaze again. "I might consider two, but only because it's so rare that I get something so *nice* to look at it."

Skye frowned and took a step towards her. Before he could say anything, Taly scoffed and placed both hands on the table. As she leaned forward, she subtly pushed her breasts together. She knew Dimas could see down the front of her shirt, but she wasn't above exploiting her *charms* if it helped her get what she wanted.

"One gold. And before you give me any more shit, I know that your business has been a little lean lately. Especially since the guides haven't been back in... what? A week you said? More? And I didn't see any other salvagers out front. I'd be willing to bet you'd go as low as 50 silvers, but I don't have the patience to sit here and haggle with you all day. So, you'll take the coin, and I'll take the papers. Deal?"

Dimas grimaced, glaring at her for a long moment. She saw him glance discreetly behind her, most likely trying to ascertain what kind of threat Skye posed. His eyes then flitted to the shiny viridian dagger strapped to her thigh before sliding back up to her chest. After a pause, he laughed, revealing a toothy smile as he placed the papers on the table. "Always nice doing business with you, *Taly*."

"I wish I could say the same, but..." Taly gave the trader a subtle wink, earning her a genuine laugh from the man as she stood. Stuffing the papers in her pack, she turned to leave. Skye followed her as she led them back towards the main room, his hand finding its way to her shoulder as he walked a step closer than he had on their way in.

Taly could tell that Skye was irritated as they

concluded their business at the Swap, but that couldn't be helped. Dimas was the best information broker on the island, and everyone knew he gave better deals to anyone that flirted with him a little. While she might have shied away from dealing with someone like Dimas when she was first starting out, having the lecherous trader in her corner had proven useful on more than one occasion.

When Skye stopped at one of the crafting tables at the front and began negotiating for a new set of quills, she wandered through the rows of stalls, following the scent of food. Despite Eliza's very generous portions at both breakfast and lunch, Taly's appetite was already back.

The harpy meat was by far the freshest offering. As she purchased a large slab of meat sandwiched between two thick slices of bread, she secretly hoped that this was the same bird that had attacked her. That would be fitting.

She met back up with Skye at the shadow crafting booths, and the pair made their way outside. The air was still damp and cool after the rains, but the warm afternoon sun felt like heaven on her skin as she guided them over to a shaded area away from the main thoroughfare. Throwing her pack on the ground, she gracelessly plopped down against the trunk of a nearby tree and started tearing into her simple meal.

"Are you going to stop to chew?" Skye teased as he sat down beside her, leaning back against the old oak.

"Who has time to chew when there's eating to do?" Taly mumbled around a mouthful of food. Swallowing, she said, "Leave me alone. I've been starving all week—even with that awful nutrient paste Aiden's been shoving down my throat."

Skye watched her curiously, one brow raised, but said nothing. A slight frown creased his brow.

"Also, stop judging me," Taly grumbled, turning back to her sandwich and pulling out the papers she'd purchased.

Skye cleared his throat. "So, about... what was his name? Dimas?"

"See, there's the judgment. Right on time," Taly interjected without looking up. She had been expecting this. "Look—Dimas might be a pervert, but he's a useful one."

"I don't like the way he was looking at you," Skye protested. He sat up and peered over her shoulder at the handful of papers in her lap.

"And how's that? Like he wants to sleep with me?" Taly finished off the last of her sandwich and started licking the juice off her fingers. She only half-registered the low growl coming from behind her as she continued to study the newest scouting reports.

"Yes. I mean, no. I..." Skye huffed out an irritated sigh. "I just don't like it. Even if you were already doing that sort of thing, that Dimas guy isn't good enough for you."

Taly let out a loud bark of laughter and turned to look at him, her eyes wide with disbelief. "Are you kidding? *If*? C'mon, Skye—I'm 21 years old. And while I'm not some fey beauty, I'm not completely terrible to look at either. Give me a little credit here," she muttered, turning back to the scouting notes.

The growl was unmistakable this time. "Who?" Skye demanded.

"Why?" Taly asked, unfazed by his obvious disapproval. She wasn't at all surprised by his reaction. She knew he still saw her as some kid he needed to protect, and that incident in the street this morning already had his hackles raised. "So you can go rough them up? Defend my honor? No."

"Wait. Them?!" Skye pulled at her shoulder, turning her around to face him. "Just how many men have you slept with?"

"A lady never kisses and tells." With a wink and a smile, she elbowed him in the side. "Besides, this is all a bit hypocritical coming from you, don't you think?"

"I'm sure I don't know what you mean," Skye replied evasively.

Taly smirked and shook her head as she moved to stand. Skye had always been very tight-lipped when it came to his love life, and she could tell that this was a topic he really didn't want to discuss. For Taly, however, that just made it all the more fun.

"You think I don't know how much of a *'ladies' man'* you are when you go to the Dawn Court? Hmm? You think I don't know that you have a new girl every night? By my estimation, your number is way higher than mine." Skye was about to say something, but Taly interrupted him. "And don't even try to deny it. Just because you were attending fancy balls in Arylaan all those years doesn't mean that word didn't travel. Villagers do *love* to gossip about the highborn nobility. Whether you like it or not, *you*, my friend, have a *reputation*."

"I met a lot of women in Arylaan, but I didn't sleep with *all* of them," he said defensively. "Sleeping around is expected at court." When Taly just continued to stare at him, humor evident in her expression, he threw his hands up. "What?! It is! And Shards, those balls are always so dull. Most of the time, I just pair up with the first noblewoman I meet that can string a few sentences together and then people draw their own conclusions come morning. Regardless of what actually happens, I get to leave the ball, and she gets to use my name the next morning to social climb. Everybody's happy."

"I'm in awe of your generosity, milord," Taly chirped as she gave him a teasing smile. Sobering, she slapped him on the shoulder. "But you still need to get over yourself. We're all grown-ups here. Now come on. It's already well past midday, and we need to get going if we're going to make it to Della before dark."

"Sure," Skye replied irritably as he gathered his supplies. Pushing himself to his feet, he took off in the direction of the public stables where they had left their horses tethered.

Taly frowned as she watched him walk ahead of her. She could tell that he wasn't happy, but, in all honesty, he was just going to have to get used to the fact that she wasn't a kid anymore. It was inevitable that she would end up having relationships with other men. Even though she had lived a sheltered life back at the manor, she was an adult now. With adult desires.

Why was that so hard for him to understand?

CHAPTER 13

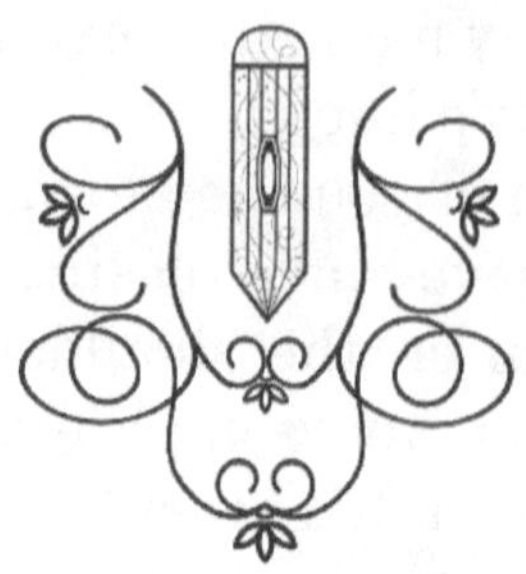

-An excerpt from Della: A Visitor's Guide

The capital city of the Fey Imperium, Della is the ideal destination for your next holiday. From the sparkling waters of the Arda to the glittering spires of Infinity's Edge—the Lucent City boasts a never-ending parade of wonders, ready to delight and amaze.

Skye felt inexplicably irritated as he rode side-by-side with Taly, heading south on the island's main highway. He had no reason to be upset—none that he could articulate, at least. But despite his attempts to redirect his thoughts, his mind kept wandering back to Taly's little show at the Swap that morning.

Taly can do what she wants, he reminded himself for not the first time.

Shaking his head, he tried to focus on the

striking scenery around him. Despite the heavy rains of the past week, it was a beautiful day for a ride—almost annoyingly picturesque. The late afternoon air felt cool against his skin, and scattered rays of sunlight filtered through the canopy, painting the forested road in dappled shade. The plodding of the horses' hooves on the cobbled pavement and the songs of the crickets and sparrows were the only sounds that could be heard echoing through the trees.

Taly had long ago given up trying to draw him out of his bad mood, and she rode on the far side of the road, staring off into the distance as they approached what used to be the outer edge of Della. This tiny township was located almost in the exact center of the island and served as a crossroads of sorts—almost every town on the island connected to Della in some way. Given the amount of traffic it received, Skye was always surprised that the village remained so small. It seemed everyone that passed through just ended up leaving again.

Of course, when the Time Queen was still alive, that wasn't the case. Before the Schism, Della was the capital city of the Fey Imperium and the home of Infinity's Edge, a magnificent crystal citadel from which the High Lady of Time once controlled every gate on the island.

Now, however, in the wake of the Sanctorum's holy quest to eradicate time magic, Della was only a humble village. The last vestiges of this once-sprawling metropolis consisted of little more than a tavern and a few rows of houses that lined the main road. Most of Della's infrastructure had either been destroyed during the Hunt or reclaimed by the forest after the fires were finally extinguished.

"Is it just me, or do the roads seem a little... empty?"

Skye jumped slightly. He had been so lost in his own thoughts that he had failed to notice that Taly was no longer staring off through the trees and was instead looking at him.

"I noticed that too," he said, pulling his horse up beside her.

Wrapping her reins around the horn of her saddle, Taly pulled out her scouting notes. "We haven't passed anyone for almost two hours now. Considering that the Seren Gate is open right now, these roads should be filled with travelers. I've been through my notes backwards and forwards, but I can't come up with a reason why. There was a tree blocking the road south of Della, but that information is a few days old. It should've been cleared by now."

Skye frowned. "That *could* explain it. If the tree damaged the wards, people would have had to cut through to Bago to get to Ryme."

"Maybe," Taly said, frowning. "I still don't like it, but, then again, this part of Della always puts me on edge. I did a few jobs around here with some buddies, Syn and Caleb, and they always liked to tell stories about the ghosts of time mages still haunting the forest around the old palace."

Skye barked out a laugh, his bad mood evaporating. "Don't tell me you still believe in fairy fire. How many times do I have to tell you? The dead can't come back from across the veil."

Taly rolled up her papers and tried to swat him in the face. This only made Skye laugh harder. "It was real! I saw it outside my window every night for a week—a glowing, blue orb of light. I swear to the Shards, I really saw it!"

"Of course you did," Skye agreed sympathetically, his shoulders still shaking.

Taly's nose scrunched up as she glowered at him. "You're a jerk." Picking up her reins, she gave her horse a sharp kick and proceeded to race ahead of him.

The sun had just begun to set when they stopped to board the horses. Taly stopped at the town message board, flipping through the various flyers while Skye paid the stable boys. As he came up behind her, he frowned in confusion. There seemed to be an unusual number of missing person notices. Glamographs of their faces blanketed the board. While there was always a slight uptick in these sorts of issues when the Aion Gate was charging, Skye couldn't remember ever seeing so many sets of eyes staring back at him from the patchwork of leaflets and flyers papering the wall.

"I know some of these people. They're salvagers," Taly said, her forehead puckering. She gingerly fingered one of the notices. There was no glamograph for that person, just a name and a short description.

Skye placed a hand on her shoulder. "Well, salvaging is dangerous work, especially when the Aion Gate is charging."

"Only if you're stupid," Taly replied with a snort. "These guys weren't stupid."

"Even so, I'm glad you're not out there anymore."

Taly's lips quirked to the side. "I was doing just fine until your girlfriend tried to take me out."

"Would you please stop calling Aimee my girlfriend? It wasn't funny the first time, the second time, or the 100th time, and it's not funny now." Skye smoothed out one of the notices for a lowborn man he recognized. He'd seen him delivering meat to the Gate Watchers' compound in Ebondrift just a few months ago. "Believe me when I say that Aimee and I are never going to happen," he added distractedly.

"Really?" Taly asked, and if Skye had been paying attention, he would've seen the sly gleam in her eye. "You and she have never... not even once?"

Skye's head whipped around. "Are you kidding? I can't believe you would even ask me that. You know I can't stand that woman."

Taly shrugged. "Last time I checked, you didn't have to like a person to go to bed with them."

And just like that, Skye's bad mood settled back over him like a cloud. "And you would know that how?"

"Sorry, Skye," she said, enjoying herself a little too much. "You're going to have to buy me a drink before you get to hear about my *conquests*."

Sighing, she gave the pictureless missing person notice one more look before turning and making her way towards the tavern. "I'm sure Caleb's fine. Knowing him, he's drunk off his ass in a bar somewhere and forgot to check in."

"Sounds like you were running with a great crowd," Skye muttered as he followed her down the dusty path.

The tavern in Della was housed in what Skye could only guess used to be a fine hotel. The columns that flanked the entrance were stained but made of marble, and massive blocks of smooth granite formed the exterior walls. An old sign hung out front, and though the letters had faded, he could still make out the words "The Radiance Hotel."

"I need to go see someone before she heads out," Taly said as they ascended the wide stone steps that led to a large, weather-worn veranda. "I'm hoping she'll have more information on whether that downed tree affected the wards."

"Sounds good." Skye reached over and grabbed her pack, slinging it over his shoulder. "While you do that, want me to order you something to eat?"

Taly turned and bounced up and down, her face lighting up with excitement. "Oh, Shards, yes! I'm starving."

"Again?" Skye asked, laughing. She had downed at least three packets of nutrient paste since they had left the Swap. Considering how little nutrition humans generally needed, he wasn't quite sure where she was putting it all.

Taly attempted to glare at him, but the effect was lost when she immediately cracked a smile. "Don't judge me," she said. "I danced with a harpy and lived to tell the tale. I think that entitles me to a few snacks." Not waiting for his response, she gave him a wave as she stepped through the open doorway of the dilapidated hotel and made her way to the bar.

The room wasn't overly crowded, and Skye managed to find a table set against the back wall. Slumping down in an open seat, he watched the patrons as they came and went, patiently waiting for the barmaid to return with their food. A mishmash of people filled the room—some were native to the island, but he noticed quite a few travelers from the mainland as well.

Taly was leaning against the bar in the

adjacent room, speaking with a human woman that, though advanced in years, looked strong beneath the worn leathers she wore.

A hunter, Skye thought, eyeing the bow at the woman's feet.

The old woman scratched at her shorn head while Taly hunched over the bar top, hastily scribbling notes. When the bartender poured two shots from a bottle of what looked like moonshine, the ladies toasted, drank, and then slammed their glasses back on the bar. Taly choked and coughed, and the hunter let out a throaty laugh, slapping the younger woman on the back as she struggled to swallow what was most assuredly an overly strong and foul-tasting liquor.

They exchanged a few more words before Taly started scanning the room for him. Skye gave her a wave before leaning back, his eyes following her as she deftly navigated the narrowly spaced tables.

"Hey! What'd you get?" she asked as she threw herself down into the chair next to him.

"Hydra stew," Skye replied. "Sounded better than bugbear. I also got us some ale."

Taly chuckled and rested her elbows on the table. "Wow. Buying me a drink already? Do you really want to hear about all of my many jilted lovers that badly?"

Skye threw up his hands. "Okay, you made your point. You're an adult, and you can do whatever you want with whomever you want. I get it. I shouldn't have said anything, and I'm sorry." He drummed his fingers against his thigh, fidgeting with one of the buckles on his armor. "What'd you find out about the road?"

"Oh!" Taly sat up and pulled out her notes

again. "I was right. The tree's been cleared. My contact didn't know anything about the wards, though. I figure we can take our chances with the main road tomorrow, but I should still sit down and chart out a few alternatives tonight just in case."

"Let me watch when you do. I want to see these so-called 'hunting trails.' Maybe then I won't get so easily manipulated next time."

Taly laughed as she put away the roll of papers. "Sure thing. Although, I think you might be a lost cause. Your sense of direction was always pretty pitiful."

Ignoring the obvious bait (he'd gotten them lost *one* time), Skye just smiled, content to enjoy the comfortable silence that had settled between them as they waited for their food.

As soon as their meal came, Taly tore into it with an eagerness that was a little disconcerting. He opened his mouth, a teasing comment at the ready, but a commotion from across the room caught his attention.

"Lord Emrys!" a woman called from the doorway. Skye looked up, his eyes widening in surprise as he caught sight of one of the very last people he had expected to see in Della. The great-granddaughter of a high-ranking Countess, the woman currently weaving her way across the room had the kind of elegance and grace that most ladies at the Dawn Court could only dream of—a vision of loveliness, even among the highborn fey. Everything about her, from the demure upsweep of her inky hair to the light brush of color across her cheeks, only served to highlight and enhance her flawless beauty.

"Lord?" Taly mouthed, rolling her eyes.

"Behave," he mumbled under his breath. "Or I'll tell Sarina that your year spent salvaging made you forget your manners." Taly made a face at him, but she complied, schooling her expression and sitting up a little straighter in her chair.

"Lord Emrys, what a pleasant surprise," the woman crooned as she approached, fluttering her unnaturally full lashes. She gave him a deep curtsey and then waited for her manservant, a scrawny lowborn teen, to bring over a chair. Taking a seat, she waved the boy away with a delicate gesture.

"Lady Spero," Skye acknowledged, slipping on his noble façade like a second skin. "Talya, this is Lady Adalet Spero of House Tira. Lady Spero—Talya Caro, the Marquess Castaro's ward."

"My Lady," Taly said, bowing her head as the other woman's superior station required.

Adalet's bright sapphire eyes lit up. "Oh my! You must be *that* Talya!" She placed a familiar hand on Skye's arm. "Skylen's told me so much about you."

"Has he now?" Taly replied cautiously.

"Oh, yes. Skylen and I go way back." Adalet's hand moved down his arm, caressing the skin of his wrist in a way that made shivers go down his spine. Her voice dropped, and a seductive smile curved her lips. "*Way* back."

Taly's eyes flashed and her lips pursed, but otherwise, her expression remained respectfully neutral. "Ah. I see," she replied evenly.

"Oh, Skylen," Adalet said with a sigh, pulling on his arm and leaning in so that he could see the generous swell of her breast spilling out of her pale blue bodice. Her household's crest—a spiraling gust of wind—was artfully tattooed along the length of her collarbone and four thin lines streaked the skin between her breasts. The pale white ink nearly disappeared into her skin. "I dare say I'm not the only one that missed you at court last season, but I can say with certainty that I missed you the most. Where were you?"

Skye laughed lightly. Adalet was perhaps the only thing he had ever truly enjoyed about his visits to the Dawn Court. He had met her when he was 19, during his second season at court, and after their first night spent together, he had continued to seek her out every season since.

"I'm sorry," he replied smoothly. The noblewoman smiled coyly when he intertwined his fingers with hers and placed a soft kiss on her knuckles. He could almost hear Taly rolling her eyes in the background, but he paid her no mind. The lie he'd rehearsed a million times in his head slipped past his lips. "I had matters to attend to in Ghislain. My father was insisting that I start helping with the Mechanica, and then Marquess Castaro called me back early to assist with the Aion Gate."

Adalet smiled, her eyes raking over him appraisingly. Even though Skye knew that she had no personal interest in elevating her current station, he chuckled slightly when he saw the light flush in her cheeks at the mention of his family's claim to wealth and power. The Mechanica was a famed legion of armored knights. Their mechanical suits could grant the strength and agility of a shadow mage to anyone, even a mortal, and House Ghislain alone knew the secrets behind the crystal-powered armor.

"Well, duty calls, I suppose," Adalet replied airily. "Although, now that I've seen it in person, I simply cannot fathom why you chose to stay on this island rather than attending the university in Arylaan. For Shards' sake, everyone still gets around using horses, of all things. I'm surprised you even have running water."

Skye flicked a piece of dust from his trousers. "Now, Adalet. Tempris is not that bad. True, it isn't as grand or progressive as Arylaan, and we're still working on repairing the air trams in addition to a few other things, but if you can look past all that, the island has its charms."

Adalet raised a skeptical brow. "I'll have to take your word for it." Leaning in, she remarked, "You missed out on one of the most eventful seasons to date last winter. Lord Tidas..." Adalet stopped, clearing her throat as she turned to Taly. "I'm terribly sorry. Lord Aaron Tidas. He's the heir to House Corvell."

Taly smiled politely. "I know who he is. You'll find that I'm quite well-versed in both the standings of the current noble houses and their genealogies."

Adalet's eyes widened in surprise. "Oh! How refreshing! It's so rare to encounter mortals with any meaningful knowledge of the nobility. Well, as I was saying, Lord Tidas made a public announcement at the Crystal Masquerade. Apparently, he's planning to form a" —she turned her head from side-to-side before continuing in a conspiratorial whisper— "soul bond."

"Now that *is* scandalous," Skye said as he took a sip of his ale. "But then again, Lord Tidas always was a fool."

"I'm sorry," Taly interjected. "Perhaps I'm missing something. What's so *scandalously foolish* about forming the bond? Exchanging a piece of your soul with the person you love most? I think that sounds romantic."

Adalet looked at Taly pitifully. "Oh, poor dear. How adorably quaint." Skye saw Taly arch a brow, but she remained quiet as Adalet continued on. "I suppose if I only had a century to live, then perhaps I would be satisfied with a single mate too. With our lifespans, however, it makes no sense to permanently tie ourselves to just one partner. There's far too much to do. Too much to *taste*." Here, Adalet turned to Skye, pressing her leg against his underneath the table. Skye covered his smile with his hand, feeling the back of his neck flush slightly at the memories her words evoked.

"So, what you're saying" —Taly paused for a moment, waiting until she had Adalet's full attention— "is that your entire species is afraid of commitment?" Taly's lips quirked to the side when she saw Adalet frown indelicately. "Except, of course, for Lord Tidas."

Skye bit back a laugh. "No, Talya," he said when he heard Adalet suck in a sharp breath, preparing to speak. The woman had a barbed tongue, and the last thing he wanted was to see her turn it on Taly. Reaching for the lessons that had been drilled into him when he was still just a young boy in Ghislain, he said, "The real reason the highborn avoid soul bonds is practicality. The bond is permanent, and almost always precludes the execution of breeding contracts—something that, in addition to helping us mitigate the effects of our declining fertility, is used to form political alliances between households."

When Taly continued to stare at him with that familiar, raised eyebrow, Skye tried to elaborate. "Let's take Lord Tidas as an example.

He's currently serving out the term of a breeding contract with a lady from House Arylaan. If he were to take a bondmate right now, the magic that forms the bond between him and his intended mate would nullify the spells sealing the breeding contract. In other words, the contract would be rendered null and void.

"Also, considering how fiercely possessive bondmates tend to be of one another, his family would be forced to annul his marriage. Hence why soul bonds are so *scandalously foolish,* as you put it. They significantly decrease a household's political maneuverability."

Taly took a sip from her cup. "Well, *Skylen—*" She drew out the syllables of his full name, the look in her eye carrying a thinly veiled note of contempt. She had always hated formalities. "A few comments. Let's start with your point on fertility. Highborn fertility has been declining over the past two or so centuries—ever since the late Time Queen began manipulating the timelines in her favor. That's a given. Still, the fey are an immortal race, and, for all your panicking, you're not sterile. The way I see it, if you could simply learn to stop killing each other, you wouldn't have a population crisis."

Skye coughed, once again trying to hide his amusement. Leave it to Taly to be unabashedly blunt. Adalet also shifted uncomfortably beside him.

"As for politics," Taly continued, giving a practiced sigh, "I'm aware of how breeding contracts work. I'm also aware that where highborn fey are concerned, these arrangements tend to have a very low success rate—around 10% if I'm not mistaken. That means that a breeding contract between two noble households has almost nothing to do with fertility or reproduction. What it really equates to is a temporary ceasefire between families that can't stop bickering unless they're sharing a bed."

Adalet delicately cleared her throat. "I suppose that is *one* way of looking at it."

Taly cocked her head. "If you have a better explanation, then, by all means, clarify my understanding of the matter. However, considering how many additional terms inevitably get built into the executed contracts, I think it's a reasonable assumption. Therefore, in my very *quaint* opinion, the way the nobility view the formation of new soul bonds—almost like a taboo—is completely unfounded."

There was a moment of stunned silence before Adalet laughed abruptly, the bell-like sound carrying over the din of the crowded tavern. "Shards, I always knew that mortals could be passionate, but Skylen—" She paused to run a bold hand through his hair, pushing it away from his face. Taly's eyes narrowed at the gesture, and she quickly looked away. "—you weren't joking when you said she was *feisty*," Adalet said with a giggle.

Skye chuckled, distracted by the way Adalet's fingers trailed across the skin of his neck. "She has her moments."

Taly's ears flushed, but her countenance remained calm as she took another long draught of ale. To Skye, however, she may as well have been screaming. Like most shadow mages, he was usually channeling a small amount of aether at any given time, and his magically enhanced hearing picked up a dramatic spike in her heart rate.

"By the way, Lady Adalet," Skye said, his tone even. "I believe that congratulations are in order. I heard about your engagement to Lord Achard."

Adalet's brows shot up. "I see this island isn't quite as isolated as I thought."

"Adalet, you act as though we're savages out here," Skye said, laughing when she playfully swatted at his chest. He heard Taly shift in her chair, and when he glanced over, her shoulders were unnaturally stiff as she continued sipping at her ale. "I was glad to hear the news, though. The last time we spoke, the match was still in negotiation. I suppose I shouldn't be surprised that you got what you wanted in the end."

"Yes, well..." Adalet said, leaning back and picking at an invisible piece of lint on her skirt. "Our matriarchs finally managed to agree on a set of terms that were favorable to all parties."

"Lord Achard is here with you, is he not?" Taly suddenly piped up. "I believe I saw him a little while ago. I would've greeted him—we were introduced years ago when he visited Marquess Castaro—but he seemed... preoccupied. There must have been something wrong with his room. He was giving one of the maids quite the tongue-lashing."

Skye choked on his ale. Maybe it wasn't Adalet's tongue he should've been worried about.

"That was probably his Feseraa," the noblewoman replied icily.

Taly smiled, sweet and wicked. "I had no idea that House Eno was using Feseraa these days. How interesting."

Adalet picked at her gloves. "Ann is the first they've acquired. She took the Rites of the Imorati just two years ago, and she's already birthed a child. We were, of course, all shocked when it happened. As you can imagine, my family has had several offers to purchase her, but my matriarch saw fit to give her to me as part of my dowry. The girl had been promised to two other men in my household, so the amount of paperwork it took to parcel out the rest of her contract was truly staggering."

"Your family did you a great honor, Adalet. Relinquishing such a treasure just to secure you an auspicious match could not have been an easy decision," Skye replied politely, trying to catch Taly's eye. He didn't know what she was doing, but he didn't like it. "Right, *Talya*?"

"Yes, a great honor," Taly agreed with a simpering nod. "Still, I will never know how you fey do it. I realize this is just my *quaint*, mortal sensibilities getting the better of me again, but, be it a spouse, lover, bondmate, or anything else, I don't think I'd like it very much if my partner was... you know... with other women—even if those women did have the proper paperwork."

Adalet cleared her throat, her gloved hands clenching and unclenching underneath her cloak. She gave Taly a serpentine smile before turning back to Skye. "You know, all this talk of breeding contracts has given me an idea. My household's matriarch has been going on and on about how much she would love to negotiate a treaty with House Ghislain. While you're in town, maybe you and I could" —she paused, pulling her bottom lip between her teeth as her eyes raked his form— "*hammer* something out?"

Skye inhaled sharply when he felt a hand on his thigh. "Perhaps," he replied with a practiced smile. He jumped slightly when Taly placed her mug down on the table with more force than was strictly necessary. When he glanced over, she glared at him pointedly.

What the hell is wrong with her? Skye thought, his irritation from earlier starting to resurface. Taly had gone out of her way to tell him how she had spent the past year sleeping her way across the island, but then she had the nerve to get mad when he engaged in a little harmless flirtation?

Turning back to Adalet, Skye decided to, as the mortals would say, give the little brat a dose of her own medicine. After all, they were all *grown-ups* here, weren't they?

"Now, Adie," Skye drawled, running a finger along Adalet's jaw. He had to forcibly suppress a grin when he heard a low, near-inaudible growl coming from Taly's direction. He didn't even know humans were capable of making that sound. "While that does sound like a very tempting proposition, with that silver tongue of yours, I may be in danger of getting taken for everything I have."

"I was counting on that." Adalet gave him a subtle wink.

Taly's chair scraped against the floor as she pushed herself away from the table and stood. Reaching for her pack, she said, "We've got an early morning tomorrow, so I think I'm going to go see about getting a room." She looked at Skye expectantly. "Are you coming?"

It doesn't have to end here, a small voice in the back of Skye's mind whispered when Adalet's hand became a little more daring.

And… now that he thought about it, he found that he rather liked that idea. Yes—maybe a night with Adalet was *exactly* what he needed. Despite his best efforts, he still hadn't been able to completely banish the memory of Taly leaning over, flirting with that scumbag trader. That incident had stirred up some strange feelings—ones that, upon reflection, felt uncomfortably close to jealousy. But that didn't have to mean anything. It was entirely possible that it had just been too long since he'd bedded a woman. After close to a year and a half with nothing except the touch of his own hand, maybe he had just gotten confused. That seemed reasonable. Right?

"You go ahead, Talya," Skye said, his eyes caressing the gentle curves of Adalet's face. He gave a disinterested wave of his hand. "I think I'm going to stay down here for a bit."

"Are you sure?" Taly pressed. She shifted her weight, readjusting her pack. "I thought you said you wanted to help me go over the map tonight."

"You don't need me for that." Finally sparing Taly a glance, he felt a sharp pang when he saw a flicker of hurt in her eyes. She schooled her expression in an instant, and the icy glare she gave him bolstered his resolve.

"I see," Taly replied tersely. "Well then… I guess this is goodnight." She gave him a saccharine smile before turning to Adalet and inclining her head. "My Lady." Then, without a backward glance, Taly turned and walked away, her head held high.

Skye watched Taly as she made her way towards the front of the tavern. She gracefully navigated the crowd, but… wait. When she turned, dodging a rowdy patron… were those tears? He leaned forward, ready to go after her, but stopped short when Adalet ran a gentle finger along the line of his jaw. The small blip in his attention lasted only a moment, but by the time he looked back towards the crowd, Taly was already gone.

As Skye leaned back, he swallowed down his uncertainty as he tried to find his composure. He was just letting her get to him. Turning back to Adalet, he slipped back into character. He could deal with Taly tomorrow. Right now, he had a beautiful, willing woman practically throwing herself at him, and that was all he needed.

CHAPTER 14

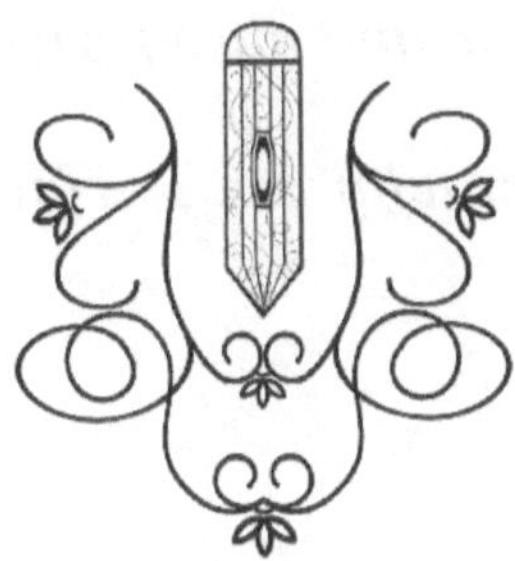

-From the personal diary of Talya Caro

Shards, I hate that man sometimes.

Skye's still down there right now—with Adalet. When I came up to the room, he stayed—just waved me away with that stupid flick of the wrist that I'm sure all nobles sit and practice until it feels appropriately indifferent. Shards, why would he want to stay with that awful shrew? What does he even see in her? Yes, she's beautiful, but the woman has the kind of personality that makes a harpy seem almost cuddly.

I should be angry at him. Anger is the only thing that I should feel right now. After all, he laughed at me tonight. Yes, let's not forget that. After all the times that I've ever had to sit across the table from "Lord Emrys," tonight is the first night he made me feel like I didn't belong there. When that bitch called me "quaint" and "passionate" like I was some poor, mindless pet, he just laughed and agreed with her.

Shards, I want to be angry. Anger would feel so much better than whatever it is I'm feeling right now. Really, what is this? My chest feels tight, I feel sick to my stomach, and my eyes won't stop leaking.

For Shards' sake, why am I crying? None of this makes any sense.

Skye started when he felt a hand brush against his neck.

He needed to stop doing that—letting his mind wander. Thankfully, Adalet hadn't noticed. She was still prattling on about something someone did at court. Or maybe they had said something? Skye nodded, breathing a sigh of relief when she moved on, apparently pleased by his reaction.

If Taly was here... well, she wasn't here, so that didn't really matter. Shards, he hoped she was okay. He was starting to wish he'd gone after her, just to make sure. While he could deal with her anger—went out of his way to provoke it—he had never been able to stomach her tears.

"Skylen, darling, I can't help but notice that you seem a little distracted," Adalet said suddenly, breaking into his thoughts.

Damn. He'd done it again. "Sorry. It's just been a very long day." Leaning back, he smiled when he felt Adalet press herself more firmly against him, her fingers still toying with the collar of his shirt. This felt nice. Familiar. He'd never made a habit of sleeping with women on the island, and since he skipped court last season… it had been a very long time. In fact, his body was already responding to the feather-light touch of her fingers against the skin of his neck. If he could just push all thoughts of Taly to the back of his mind, he might actually be able to enjoy the rest of his evening. After all, Adalet was a very beautiful woman, and even though he knew every curve of her body, she was always finding ways to surprise him.

"You know, I daresay I'm quite impressed," Adalet said, changing the subject. Sitting back in her chair, she unbuttoned her cloak, gracing him with a seductive smile when his eyes dipped down. "The Castaros have done a remarkable job with that little shardless of theirs. Young Talya is going to be worth a fortune once they finally decide to make her a Feseraa."

Skye pulled back from where Adalet leaned against him, his eyes narrowing. In all the years that he'd known her, he'd never heard her speak so tactlessly before.

The noblewoman smirked as she reached for his glass. "Oh, don't give me that look, darling. I know they've denied it for years now, but you can't honestly sit here and tell me that the Castaros don't plan to make her a Feseraa someday. Not after all the time and coin they've invested in grooming their little pet."

Skye felt a muscle in his jaw start to twitch. "You should watch your tongue, Adalet," he said, his voice edged. "I can tell you with complete certainty that the Marquess has absolutely no intention of selling Talya. She is not property. Also, she is my friend, and I do not suffer those that speak ill of her."

"I meant it as a compliment, but fine," Adalet conceded disingenuously. "Oh, Skylen, I know you've always been fond of *that* one, but, at the end of the day, she's just a human. In a few centuries, I doubt you'll even remember her name. Just ask your brother if you don't believe me."

Skye leaned away when Adalet moved a hand up to toy with his hair. If she noticed his growing disinterest, she didn't let on. Instead, she allowed her hand to drop down and rest on his arm.

"You know my household started using Feseraa a few years ago," she continued, still sipping at his ale. "It's been an interesting experiment, to say the least. My cousin is pregnant, but, thankfully, our matriarch stopped making me try to breed with one of those things when it didn't take the second time. Now, I pride myself on being open to new experiences, but that... well, it was like lying with an animal. With any luck, Achard will come to his senses soon. I have a hard time even being in the same room as him after he's been rutting that beastly little creature he wanted so badly."

Adalet went on, and Skye's eyes grew wide as he continued to sit there, listening. Until finally, he couldn't help but ask himself: *What the hell am I doing?*

Taly had just come back into his life not three weeks ago, and now he had gone and pissed her off for... for what? An easy lay with a woman who was quickly revealing herself to be a hateful bitch? A year and a half of celibacy hadn't confused him. It had made him stupid.

"Well," Adalet purred, leaning forward to whisper in his ear. Despite himself, a shiver ran down his spine. "How about we take this upstairs?"

Clearing his throat, Skye carefully removed the hand that had made its way back to his thigh. "Actually, now that I think about it, I do have an early morning ahead of me. Maybe some other time."

"Oh! Of... of course." She sounded surprised. Her perfectly arched brows shot up, and a slight frown tugged at the corners of those bowed lips. "Of course, I understand. You must be very busy right now with your Gate Watchers' duties. However... if you change your mind, I have the top floor all to myself. Please don't hesitate to knock—no matter the hour."

Skye watched as Adalet rose from her chair and glided across the room, heavily suspecting that the exaggerated sway of her hips was for his benefit.

When she was out of sight, he slumped down in his chair and reached for his ale. A deep frown creased his brow when he saw the imprint of a feminine set of lips on the rim. He set the glass down, choosing instead to reach for Taly's abandoned mug beside him. He downed the contents in one gulp.

He needed to go find Taly. She was going to be irate—more than irate—but maybe he deserved that. He didn't know why he felt that way. After all, he certainly hadn't known that Adalet would reveal herself to be so vile, but that did little to alleviate the gnawing sense of guilt that was quickly taking root deep inside him.

"Might as well get this over with," he muttered to no one in particular. Then, with a heavy sigh, he gathered up his things and set off in search of Taly.

Skye didn't know how long he'd been standing outside the door at the end of the hall. He'd had to bribe the innkeeper to tell him which room Taly had taken—one of the cheaper units with one bed instead of two. It had taken even more coin to convince the bartender to sell him an unopened bottle of Arendryl brandy—Taly's drink of choice.

Even through the door, he could still hear the staccato rhythm of her elevated pulse, accompanied by the dry scrape of quill against paper. Not for the first time, he wondered if he should go get his own room and wait until morning for her anger to cool. Years of experience had taught him that it would be far easier to convince her to forgive him after she'd slept it off.

But… that just wasn't what he wanted to do. If he could turn back the clock, he would go upstairs with Taly. Shards, why hadn't he just gone upstairs with Taly? True, he'd spent almost every night this past week with her, but he'd still been looking forward to spending another evening sitting around and doing next to nothing with her beside him.

"It's just Taly," he mumbled to himself. "She'll forgive you. You've been a way bigger ass than this before, and she forgave you then."

That made him feel marginally better.

Steeling himself, he raised his hand and knocked. All movement inside the room ceased, and for a brief moment, he thought she was going to ignore him. He released a harsh breath when he heard the creak of mattress springs followed by the soft padding of bare feet on planked wood.

The door opened and Taly stared at him owlishly. Her hair was wet, and she wore a loosely tied robe that poorly concealed the thin, slightly damp lace nightdress she wore underneath. She crossed her arms as she leaned against the doorframe. "I didn't think I'd be seeing you again tonight. Do you need to borrow a pen or something?"

"What?" Skye's brain had momentarily abandoned him when the fabric of her gown shifted, granting him a teasing glimpse of what lay beneath the nearly sheer fabric. It was always so easy to forget how feminine she could be when the mood suddenly struck her—especially when she spent all day tromping around in boyish clothes, waxing poetic about the merits of pistols over every other ranged weapon.

"You know," she said, a smile hovering at the corners of her mouth, "for all the paperwork. That's what you highborn do before you get down to business, right? C'mon, *Skylen*. You should never skip foreplay. Everyone knows that."

"You're such a brat," Skye muttered, moving to walk past her. He stopped when she held out an arm, blocking his entry.

"I didn't say you could come in. Go get your own room. Or better yet, go back to Jezebel."

"Shards, you and your mortal fables," Skye grumbled, refusing to break eye contact despite the heat of her glare. Since she didn't have shoes on, he towered over her. "That's not her name."

"It is in my head," Taly retorted blithely.

"Well, if that's what you really want" —Skye shrugged as he pulled out the bottle of brandy from his pack— "I'm sure whatever-her-name-is will appreciate this rare bottle of Arendryl liquor I lifted from behind the bar. You know as well as I do how hard this stuff is to find right now."

Taly's eyes flicked to the bottle. Reaching out, she gave him a solid punch on the arm before moving aside. "Your offering pleases me."

Skye followed her inside, closing the door behind him with a soft click. The room was small and unpretentious. There was a bed shoved into the corner and a washroom off to the side, but otherwise, there were very few furnishings.

"You're not staying here," Taly said as she started gathering the papers spread across the bed and stuffing them back into her journal. "Unless you plan to sleep on the floor."

"I know, I know," Skye conceded, dropping his pack. He took a deep breath, rolling his shoulders as he felt some of the tension release. "I'll go down and rent another room later. It's not like they were running short. In the meantime, care to tell me what I've done so I can apologize?"

"Fuck off."

"Actually," Skye said with a huffed laugh, "that's exactly what I'm *not* doing right now, so—" He turned just in time to catch the pillow that had been hurled directly at his head. "Wow. You're in a mood."

"Sorry, Skye. I guess I'm having one of my… how did you put it? Moments?" When she turned around, angrily shoving her journal back into her pack, Skye finally noticed that her eyes were much redder than they should be.

"Shards, Tink." He crossed the room in a few short strides, grabbing her by the shoulders and twisting her around to face him. "You know I have to act like that in front of other nobles."

"That's bullshit," she spat, giving him a hard shove. "I've seen you in front of the nobles Ivain and Sarina hosted, but I've never seen you act like that. I didn't like the person I saw down there."

"You're right," he easily conceded. "I took it too far, and I'm sorry. I don't know what came over me." That seemed to deflate some of her anger, and Skye took a tentative step forward. Although she didn't return his embrace, she didn't fight him when he wrapped his arms around her.

"That woman is horrible, you know," she said, leaning her head against the hard leather of his breastplate. "You should hear the things people say about her."

"I'm starting to get an idea," Skye quietly muttered in reply. "Tell me how to make this better, Tink. You know how much I hate it when you cry."

Taly stepped away, discreetly wiping at her cheeks. "I'm not crying, jerk. Your armor is dusty, and you have horse hair all over you. You're a walking sneeze."

Skye barked out a laugh. She was back to flinging insults and telling him he was filthy. That had to be a good sign. "I get that I can't stay here, but can I at least use your shower?"

Taly nodded, turning away as she settled back on the bed.

Digging through his pack for a fresh set of clothes, Skye decided to take a chance and ask a question that had been eating away at him all evening. "So… Ivain's never hosted Lord Achard, and, as far as I know, you've never met him. How do you know what he looks like?"

Taly laughed, her face lighting up. "I don't." When Skye raised a brow in question, she shrugged. "What? You think I actually saw him?"

"Didn't you?"

"No," she said as though it should've been obvious. "My contact here at the inn told me that Achard arrived last night with his new human consort and that they haven't left their room since they checked in. My contact *also* told me that he asked for this specific Feseraa by name—*before* she'd had her first child—and that he very nearly came to blows with House Tira's representative when he was informed that the girl had been promised out to no less than three other men. Apparently, he knew her before she joined the Feseraa. At least, that's the rumor."

"In other words, you were gossiping with the drunks at the bar. Let's skip ahead to the part where you decided to make trouble."

Taly's smile widened. "Well, I know you were a little distracted back there, but that's a very different story than what Jezebel was trying to sell us. And she was already being such a bitch. I figured that if I was going to have to sit there and watch while she tried to feel you up beneath the table, I should at least get to have a little fun. So, I took a chance. Did you see how angry she got? It almost made having to talk to her worth it."

"Shards," Skye groaned, shaking his head and grinning. "How do you fit so much evil into such a tiny body?" Tossing the bottle of brandy on the bed, he said, "Here. Set up the drinking game while I'm in the shower."

"Drinking game?"

"Yes. I've decided to get you drunk. You're much nicer to me when you're drunk."

"You're less of an ass when I'm drunk." Taly reached for the bottle and popped the cork in a single, practiced move. "Well, if we're doing a drinking game then I want to play Lords and Ladies."

Skye rolled his eyes. "Of course, you do. But let me ask you this—are the cards you brought with you glamoured?" When Taly shrugged, he said, "No. It's no fun if you cheat. My vote's for Coins."

"That's boring."

"Then let's make it more interesting," Skye called out as he closed the washroom door. He breathed a sigh of relief as he peeled off his dusty armor and dropped it on the floor. Lifting his arms high overhead, he groaned as he felt the muscles of his back stretch and shift. "Whoever manages to put a coin in the glass, the other person has to *either*—and here's where it gets interesting—answer a question *honestly* or take a drink."

A loud bang resounded through the thin, wooden partition, making Skye jump. "What was that?"

"I'm practicing," Taly called from the other side of the door. "I'm going to learn all your secrets tonight, Em."

Skye took a quick shower, the dull thump of coins bouncing off of wood followed shortly by the clink of glass spurring him to hurry. Her aim was starting to get a little too accurate.

Dressed in a pair of loose slacks and a casual shirt, he toweled off his hair as he opened the door, gathering up the scattered collection of coins littered across the floor.

"You ready to do this?" he asked as he flopped onto the bed. Taly leaned against the wall, so he pulled himself up into a sitting position beside her. He grabbed the bottle out her hands and took a long swig.

"You're going down," she said, jingling a bag of coins.

They started out easy, asking silly questions that both already knew the answer to. While Taly's aim was pretty good, Skye's was better. He may have been using just the tiniest bit of aether, but, in his defense, they hadn't laid down any rules against using magic.

When Taly's cheeks were starting to look flushed from the alcohol, Skye decided to get a bit more daring. Flicking his wrist, he smiled when the little brass coin landed in the glass. "Okay, serious question now," he said, waiting for her to turn to him. "Why did you run away last year?"

Taly frowned. "I thought you promised you wouldn't pry."

"I never said for how long," Skye replied with a shrug.

Taly held his gaze as she took a generous drink from the bottle. She missed her next turn, and Skye laughed at the forlorn pout on her face when he made his next shot.

"Same question," he said.

Taly took another nip from the bottle. They repeated this cycle two more times until she exclaimed, "You can keep asking, but I'm just going to keep drinking."

Damn. He was hoping that would work. A few more drinks, and maybe it would have.

"You're going to have to tell me someday," he

said quietly.

"Someday is not today," she mumbled in reply.

"Okay, okay," Skye conceded with a sigh, taking the bottle from her. She had gotten way ahead of him, and he wasn't drunk enough to hear the answer to what he planned to ask next. Holding the bottle up to his lips, he said, "New question. Since I've actually bought you *several* drinks now, I want to hear about these conquests of yours. What's little Taly Caro's number?"

"That's it. Give me the bottle. I give up." Taly reached across him, but he held her back.

"C'mon, Caro. This is going to be no fun if you get drunk and pass out."

Taly sat back down looking slightly deflated. Wrapping her arms around her knees, she hid her face. "Shards, I knew this was going to come back to bite me."

"Oh, this sounds fun." Skye took another swig. "Tell me your secrets, Tink. Tell me *all* of your secrets."

Her cheeks were red when she peeked over at him. "So… I may have slightly exaggerated the breadth of my… *experience* with the opposite sex."

"Wait? What?" Skye was sitting up now.

Taly whined, hiding her head again. "Please don't make me do this."

"C'mon, Tink. Rules are rules."

"Fine. It's… it's zero," she said dejectedly, her voice muffled.

Skye choked, the air leaving his lungs in a rush. His mouth gaped; his lips twitched; he said the first words that came to mind. "What the actual fuck? You little *liar*!"

"No." Taly's head popped up. "If you recall the

specifics of that conversation, I did not lie. I simply did not correct you when you made certain assumptions."

Skye could feel the laughter bubbling up. He shouldn't push her any further. He knew that. She was blushing furiously now. Even her chest was red. But he just couldn't resist. She had gotten him all worked up over nothing—needled and poked at him all afternoon. "So, how far have you actually gotten with a man?"

"It's not your turn."

Channeling a little more aether, he tossed another coin without looking. His smile widened when he heard the clink of glass. "I'll let you go twice after this."

"Leave me alone, Em."

"Tell me," Skye demanded, his grin undermining his stern tone. "Those are the rules of the game."

With a growl, Taly grabbed one of the pillows and started pummeling him. "I've gotten nowhere," she cried between strikes. "Never even kissed a guy. Men find me absolutely repulsive. Happy now?" She grabbed the bottle out of his hands, retreating to the end of the bed and leaning against the wall.

Despite himself, Skye was still laughing as he followed her, ignoring her half-hearted struggles as he wrapped his arms around her. "You're not repulsive," he said when his laughter finally started dying down. "That's the silliest thing I've ever heard, Tink. You're the exact opposite of repulsive. You're beautiful, and smart, and funny—"

"And human."

Skye flicked her nose. "And nothing short of

wonderful. Any man that can't see that doesn't deserve you."

Taly stared at the bottle in her hands. "You're just being nice."

"I'm not," he insisted. "You just haven't met anyone that's good enough for you yet."

"Believe me, I've met plenty of people," she said. "Do you have any idea what it's like trying to date on this island as a human? Much less as a human with a magical education and a mainland accent? One word out of my mouth and the other shardless are calling me a toft, but then the lowborn don't want anything to do with me either. And the highborn—all they see when they look at me is a potential broodmare."

"Taly," Skye tried.

But she was already shaking her head. "Don't try to make me feel better. I've already accepted the inevitability of spinsterhood. I'm thinking about getting a cat. I hear that's what lonely human women are supposed to do."

Skye pulled her closer, resting his cheek against the top of her head. He'd never thought about what it must be like for her. How isolated she must feel from other members of her own species. Even if she crossed through the Aion Gate and into the world of mortals, she still wouldn't have a place in that magicless realm that was so different from the one she'd been born into.

"I probably don't tell you this enough," he said after a moment, "but you're my favorite person. I don't care what shape your ears are."

Taly snorted, even as she leaned into him. "That would mean more if you hadn't proven yourself to be such a terrible judge of character."

"What do you mean?"

Another snort. She peered up at him, mouthing a single word: "*Je-ze-bel.*"

Skye barked out a laugh. "*Touché*," he said, planting a sloppy kiss on the crown of her head. "I think I owe you a turn now." He took the bottle when she handed it to him. "Well, two turns."

Taly yawned. "We're out of coins. Someone's going to have to get up."

Skye slumped down, taking Taly with him and tucking her more firmly into his side. "Not worth it. Just ask me something. I'll answer."

"So much power." Her words were starting to slur together as she laid her head against his chest. Her fingers pushed aside the edges of his shirt as she traced one of the seals tattooed beneath his collarbone. "Tell me something about you that I don't know," she commanded, her warm breath fanning out against his skin.

The heat of her lying next to him coupled with the alcohol had him feeling wonderfully languid, and he pulled her in closer. "Technically, that's not a question."

He gave a small whine at the sudden rush of cold air when she pulled away so that she could drunkenly glare at him. "Fine. What's something I don't know about you?"

Skye briefly considered telling her about the events of last summer—about Ava. That night still crept into his nightmares, and on any given day, the scent of blood would unexpectedly sneak up on him.

No, he thought, his heart slightly stumbling when Taly smiled at him. He didn't want to ruin this. Whatever *this* was, it felt too good to tarnish with bad memories.

"Okay. I've got something for you," Skye

finally said. "You remember when you thought you saw fairy fire outside your window?"

"Yes," Taly replied cautiously.

Skye set the bottle aside and braced himself. "That wasn't fairy fire. That was me in the tree with a lantern."

Skye bit back a grin. He had gotten exactly the reaction he wanted. She froze, staring at him with wide eyes as she tried to grapple with this startling revelation. "You..." she sputtered, shaking her head. "How could... why would... Shards, you jerk!" Skye was laughing so hard he barely managed to grab her fists when she started thrashing him. "Why would you do that?" she cried, struggling against him.

"Because it was too good of an opportunity to pass up!" Skye wheezed. Tears were starting to stream down his face as he continued to howl with laughter. "Obviously, you were dreaming the first night you saw it, but every night after? That was all me. I even started moving things around your room so you'd think that the fairies had done it." That prompted another scream of rage, and Skye threw a leg over her own when she started kicking at him. When she finally quieted down, he asked, "Are you done now?"

"I'm going to get you for that," came the muffled reply. She had slumped against him, her face crushed against his shoulder. "When you least expect it, I'll be there."

"And I'll be waiting." Shifting, he pulled her back against him, tucking her into his side. "My turn."

"Wrong. It's still my turn," she said, grabbing the bottle and thrusting it towards him. "I say drink. You still have far too many of your faculties.

It's hardly fair."

Skye took a long draught, almost choking on the liquor when his next question popped into his mind. "Okay then. Like I was saying—my turn. Prepare yourself."

Once again, he set the bottle off to the side and readied himself for a beating. Even though this wasn't where he thought he would be spending his evening a few hours ago, there was no other place he'd rather be right now.

It was going to be a fun night.

CHAPTER 15

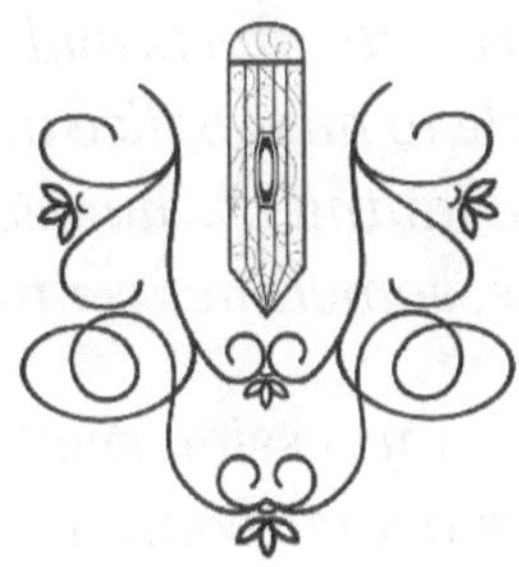

-An excerpt from the 27th Volume of Shadow Magic: A Manual of Best Practice Standards for the Ethical Application of Aether Contamination Spells

The subject of the forbidden rituals inevitably arises when new restrictions on the practice of shadow magic are proposed. Shadow mages, by their very nature, control the flow of aether. By extension, this applies to the aether of those around them. The power to manipulate another mage's personal aether pool grants shadow mages the unique ability to exert influence on other fey.

Aether contamination spells (i.e., spells that require blood to be ingested by the target) are among the most hotly debated branch of spellcasting. These enchantments function by allowing the shadow mage to infect or contaminate another mage's pool of aether with their own. The desired enchantment can then be enacted by penning the correct series of runes onto the subject's skin.

Though there are various accepted methods to anchor a spell, embedding crystals into the subject's body is by far the most common approach. If the spell is not anchored, its effects will dissipate as soon as the target is able to metabolize the foreign aether. An anchored enchantment, however, can remain active for decades, sometimes centuries.

Except for aether suppression spells, most classes of spells that require aether contamination are either regulated by the Shadow Guild or banned by formal ruling of the Genesis Council. Ascendancy, desecration, and necrotic renewal are among those rituals that have been forbidden and struck from the public record.

Taly cracked open her eyes. The curtains were drawn, but a thin sliver of sunlight peeked through a gap in the sheets of fabric, blazing a fiery trail across the dimly lit room. Her mouth felt dry, sticky with saliva, and a dull pressure throbbed behind her eyes. The pain ebbed and flowed, sweeping her closer and closer to consciousness with each undulating wave.

Could be worse, she thought drowsily.

Though her memory of the previous night was a little hazy, Taly did recall that she and Skye had managed to finish off the entire bottle of brandy. While Skye, being both a shadow mage *and* a highborn, probably wouldn't suffer anything more than a fleeting headache come morning, Taly had fully expected to wake up with one of the worst hangovers of her life. But, strangely enough, even though her head felt fit to crack open, it was nothing a little coffee and a greasy breakfast couldn't fix. She'd take that as a win.

Something moved beside her, and Taly froze when she felt an arm tighten around her waist. As she swept away the last of the mental cobwebs cluttering her sleep-addled brain, she became aware of a warm body lying beside her. A very warm, very *male* body. His breath fanned out across the back of her neck, sending small shivers up and down her spine.

What the... How did that happen?! Shards, what's the last thing you remember?

She and Skye had been drinking and... and what? There were large chunks of last night that she simply couldn't remember. She still had all of her clothes on—that was a good sign. So did the man behind her—also a good sign.

Wait—she was starting to remember something, faint glimmers from the evening before. Skye had continued prying embarrassing, personal information out of her, and his questions had gotten more and more pointed as the night wore on. They were both pretty far gone by the time he had started asking her about the butcher boy—an adorably awkward lowborn teen that she had briefly dated when she was 17. The childhood fling had never gone anywhere, and their almost-kiss behind his parents' shop constituted both the beginning and end of Taly's pitiful excuse for a love life.

That was the last thing she remembered clearly, so that meant the man behind her had to be Skye. After all, it's not like she would've been able to pick up a guy with Skye lurking close behind. Overprotective bastard that he was, it didn't surprise her in the least that he had decided to stick around.

Skye shifted, pulling her closer and pressing his face into her hair. As the initial surprise at not waking up alone started to fade, Taly found herself relaxing beneath his touch. The way he had his body almost wrapped around hers, the way their legs tangled together, felt so very, *very* good—warm and safe and...

Woah there, Caro! Taly thought, her eyes popping open. She should *not* be feeling whatever it was she was feeling. This was *Skye*, after all. These butterflies in her stomach were completely unacceptable. The way she thought their bodies fit together perfectly... Nope! That thought did *not* just happen.

She needed to get out of here. Shit, she *really* needed to get out of here.

If he woke up...

She didn't want to think about that. She might actually die from embarrassment. And if by some stroke of luck she didn't expire right there on the spot, Skye would more than likely help her along. Knowing him, he would never let her forget this incident. He would tease her endlessly—*mercilessly*—until she eventually died from humiliation.

Gently uncurling the fingers twisted in the fabric of her nightgown, Taly lifted the arm that was draped across her waist before she attempted to untangle their legs. It took her a few moments, but eventually, she was able to extract herself from Skye's grasp.

Her muscles groaned, stiff and sore, as she

swung her legs over the side of the bed, and the floor was cold underneath her bare feet. She tried to stand, but the floorboards gave a loud creak, eliciting an incoherent grumble from the man beside her. Her heart pounded in her ears as she watched Skye's hand reach out, searching the empty space next to him, and for one brief, agonizing moment, it looked as though he might wake up.

Thankfully, one of the Shards must have been looking out for her that morning. That's the only explanation she had when she saw his face relax as he grabbed at her discarded pillow and pulled it closer, sinking back into a deep, if somewhat fitful, sleep.

As she sat perched on the edge of the bed, Taly couldn't stop her eyes from raking over his sleeping form. He looked almost boyish in the dim morning light, and his mouth curved into a slight frown as he rolled onto his back. The motion tugged at the blanket, pulling it down and revealing a small sliver of skin where his shirt had ridden up. He had always been (and still was) a little lanky, but years of combat training had gifted him with lean, sinewy lines of muscle that flexed when he moved. Even though she would never tell him this, she couldn't deny that he had grown into a very handsome man.

A warm blush spread across her cheeks at the errant thought. When had she started thinking he was handsome?! This was Skye, after all. He wasn't *handsome*! He was just Skye. Stupid—yes. Uppity—check. Attractive—objectively, but not to her.

Shit. She really did need to get out of here.

Rising to her feet, Taly took a cautious step,

and then another, saying a silent prayer of thanks to the Shards that the floorboards didn't give her away a second time.

"Ow! Damn it!" she yelped—her voice barely above a whisper—when she stubbed her toe on a piece of Skye's armor. She hobbled as she tried to find her balance, but her foot caught in the strap of his scabbard. His sword started to tip, and she dove, just barely managing to stop it from clattering to the floor. Carefully leaning the weapon back against the wall, she kept her eyes trained on the bed and Skye's motionless form.

I'll find somewhere else to change into my clothes, she thought, grabbing her pack. Skye had always been a deep sleeper, but there were far too many obstacles and potentially squeaky floorboards between her and the washroom door. She wasn't about to press her luck. Not today.

Just as she was placing her hand on the doorknob, a gravelly voice mumbled, "Wow. Just... wow. After last night, this is what I get? You were just going to sneak out without saying anything?"

Taly froze, and her breath caught in her throat. Her head slowly turned. Skye was no longer asleep. No—he was very much awake and staring straight at her.

"I... I was just going to get coffee," Taly stuttered softly.

"In your nightgown?" Skye asked, a smirk tugging at his lips.

"I... um... well..." Taly pulled at her nightdress self-consciously, wishing she knew where her robe had gotten to. She didn't really have a response to that.

Skye glared at her through narrowed eyes. "And here I thought that last night was *special*," he said moodily. "But, no. I guess I just get the privilege of being your first one-night stand."

"Huh?" Taly shook her head, her mind rebelling against the implication of what he was saying. *Nothing* had happened between them. He was just trying to fluster her. "From what I remember, the only thing special about last night was how especially nosy you were being."

"Wow. And now you don't even remember? That hurts, Tink. That really hurts."

"Stop messing around. There's nothing to remember," Taly retorted, hoping that her voice sounded more confident than she felt.

He sprawled on the bed, one hand covering his eyes. "Heartless woman. One would think that after a night of such *passionate—*"

"Oh no," Taly groaned as she leaned against the door. She didn't believe it. She *refused* to believe it.

"After a night of such *enthusiastic—*"

Taly shook her head. "No… just no…" They both still had clothes on, for Shards' sake! Who did he think he was kidding?

"And then I even got dressed and went downstairs to get you food when you said you were hungry. Because let's face it—you're always hungry now." Skye's head lolled to the side. Those emerald eyes almost seemed to glow in the dim light, unabashedly raking over her form. A slow smile emerged, and he licked his lips. "Although to be fair, I did help you work up an appetite last night."

The pack dropped from her hands, and she covered her reddening face. "Uh-uh. No. No, no, no…"

"The kitchens were closed, by the way. I hope

you know that you're the only woman I'd ever break into a kitchen for. Can you imagine the kind of things they would've said about me at the Dawn Court if I'd been caught? Me? The heir to Ghislain robbing a kitchen at some rundown tavern…"

Peeking through her fingers, Taly spied a small stack of dishes as well as the empty bottle of brandy sitting on the bedside table.

Shit! Her stomach turned, and her knees started to wobble.

"I mean... really!" Skye exclaimed. "After a night of such *fervent—*" When Taly let out an embarrassed whine and sunk to the floor, Skye's shoulders started to shake. "*—drinking*, I thought I'd get a little more consideration. Geez, Tink. Is nothing sacred anymore?"

"What?" Taly snapped, her head popping up.

"Yes, Taly." Skye ran a thoughtful hand along the stubble on his chin. "Drinking. A long night of drinking. What were *you* thinking?"

"Shards," Taly sighed, relief washing over her like a wave. "Fuck you."

Skye pretended to gasp. "Wait… did you think that we…" That slow, irritatingly sensual smirk resurfaced. "*Tinker*," he practically purred, "did you think that I let you have your way with me last night?"

Despite her flushed face, Taly gave him a dirty look.

"Try not to look so horrified," he said, his smile slipping. "You would be so lucky."

"Please stop talking." Reaching for her pack, Taly stood and attempted to retreat to the washroom.

Skye stretched, his head tilting back, and Taly couldn't stop her eyes from following the movement as his shirt rode up higher. The taut muscles of his stomach shifted beneath his skin. "You know," he said lazily, "all the ladies at court used to say that I put the *lay* in *Ghislain*."

Taly felt a tremor pass through her, and she visibly winced. Turning to face him, she gave him her best deadpan expression. "That's the stupidest thing I've ever heard. No one said that. No one has *ever* said that."

Skye had long since given up trying to hold in his laughter. "Okay, if you don't like that one, how about this? *Once you try a piece of the Skye, you'll never want to say goodbye.* Yes? No?" When Taly just rolled her eyes and turned to walk away, he added, "Your face says *no*, but just give it a minute to really sink in."

Though Taly tried to ignore him, his voice followed her into the washroom. "Okay. I've got one more. I just came up with this last night, so it's still a little rough. *When you need a little bliss—*"

"That's it," Taly barked. She bounded back across the room, jumped on the bed, and pulled the pillow out from underneath him. Feathers floated in the air, catching the morning light in their downy tendrils, as she began her assault.

Skye was howling with laughter as he half-heartedly attempted to fend her off. "Temper, temper! What would Sarina say if she saw you right now?"

"She would say 'beat him harder!' That's what she always said because you'd always done something to deserve it," Taly huffed.

Without warning, one of Skye's hands shot out, and his fingers curled around her calf. Taly let out a shriek when she suddenly found herself flipped over onto her back. In one graceful movement, he easily plucked the pillow out of her grasp and seized her fists. She tried to kick at him, but he swung a leg over hers, effectively trapping her.

Pressed against him the way she was, she could still feel the laughter rumbling through his chest when he whispered in her ear, "Three hits or a pin, right? You only got one good hit in, so I win." Taly bucked, trying to free herself, but he tightened his grip. "Calm yourself, Tink. I don't think passing out beside me warrants the amount of shame required to try to sneak out the next morning. After all, it's not like we haven't shared a bed before."

"Sure, but we were kids." Taly wriggled, somehow managing to elbow him in the ribs. She smiled when she heard a low "oof." "I haven't dreamt about the fire in years."

"Now there's a lie if I ever heard one." Skye was still uncomfortably close, and even though his lips barely grazed the skin of her ear, it sent a violent shiver down her spine. "All that time, you have to know that I could still hear you crying when you woke up at night. A closed door and a few wards weren't going to stop me from hearing. Why did you start locking your door at night? Why wouldn't you let me help you?"

"Well..." Taly began, her thoughts drifting to that pervasive nighttime terror that continued to haunt her, even into adulthood. The memory of a particularly violent episode flashed through her mind, and she shuddered. It had taken Skye almost an hour to calm her down—to convince her that she was no longer in that cottage back in Vale and that the heat she could feel burning her skin was only an illusion. He'd stayed with her the rest of that night as well as the one after. Her throat bobbed, and she said, "I started closing my door because the nightmares weren't all that bad anymore—certainly not worth waking you up in the middle of the night."

Skye huffed out a laugh as he released her fists and stretched out beside her. The bed was barely able to hold both of them comfortably, and Taly was all-too-aware of the places where their bodies still touched. "That's not a real answer. If you want me to back off, then say so. Otherwise, stop dodging the question," he grumbled into the pillow. "Something changed that summer. What was it?"

Taly chewed on her lip, unsure. Although they had both shared far more personal information than this only the night before, she almost felt shy now that she no longer had the alcohol burning through her veins, giving her courage. Nevertheless, when he turned his head, his eyes finding hers, she found herself saying, "That was the year your mother decided to introduce you at the Dawn Court, and I realized for the first time that one day when you left to go visit your family on the mainland, you wouldn't be coming back. You're the heir to Ghislain, and it was foolish of me to assume that you were always going to be right across the hall, always within reach when I needed you. That summer, I decided it was time I learned how to deal with the nightmares on my own. I couldn't keep leaning on you."

Skye gave her a lazy smile. "Shards… you really do come up with some of the craziest nonsense when left to your own devices."

Taly opened her mouth, ready to defend

herself, but her retort died on her lips when he draped an arm across her waist and pulled her closer. "I will *always* be there for you, Tink," he murmured, his eyes never leaving hers. "No matter what. No matter where we are. After all these years, I don't know why you still can't see that."

"I... I thought..." Taly stammered, her heart pounding. Skye's fingers had begun absentmindedly toying with the thin fabric of her nightdress, inadvertently grazing her skin through the lace. Taking a stuttering breath, she attempted to change the subject. "I thought I told you that you couldn't sleep here last night."

With a heavy sigh, Skye buried his face in the pillow. "You changed your mind," he said, his voice muffled. "You told me I could stay."

"I did what now?" Taly's heartbeat spiked erratically—something she knew Skye could probably hear with those irritating enhanced senses of his.

Skye let out a low chuckle. "You did. You told me I could stay. You were all, 'Em, please don't go,' but way more adorable. And then when I insisted that I sleep on the floor—just like you told me I would have to do when you were still sober—you climbed on top of me and refused to move."

Taly didn't know what to say to that. Her vague recollection of the event happening exactly the way he described made her distinctly uncomfortable.

"You know," he mused lazily, "I'd forgotten just how cute you are when you're trying to fall asleep. You've got this little frown, right between your eyes—almost like you're trying to *really* concentrate on sleeping."

Taly's retort died on her lips. Skye thought that she was cute? In what universe did *Skye* think that *she* was cute?

"Of course," he added, propping himself up so he could look her in the eye, "I'd also forgotten just how badly you snore."

"What?"

"Yeah!" Skye exclaimed, a devilish gleam in his eye. "Once you fell asleep, it was like there was a herd of cattle moving through here. It was uncanny."

Taly shook him off as she struggled to sit up. "I do *not* snore!"

Skye's hands found their way to her sides, right where she was ticklish. A wide toothy, grin split his face when she gave a shriek of laughter. "Yeah! You do! It was like *mooooo…*"

Working her way free of him, Taly grasped at the pillow and started pummeling him again. "I do not snore!" she cried.

Skye was laughing uncontrollably, and the faint sound of "moo" still sounded from beneath her frenzied onslaught. When he finally quieted, Taly stopped, the pillow still held at the ready. His expression looked strangely calm considering the feathery thrashing he had just endured. His lips moved, and, for a moment, Taly thought that maybe, just maybe, he would apologize.

She should've known better.

"Moo."

That was the point at which Taly decided she didn't care if he died. Bringing the pillow down, she didn't hold back as she tried to smother him.

The rest of the morning was surprisingly uneventful. Once Skye managed to convince Taly to grant him a "stay of execution," they packed up their things, grabbed a quick breakfast, and settled their bill. As they were leaving, Taly spied Adalet and a man she could only assume to be Lord Achard sitting in a secluded corner of the tavern down on the first floor.

"I think Jezebel is trying to get your attention," Taly said, jerking her head towards the pair's table.

"What?" Skye followed Taly's gaze, a slight frown tugging at his lips when he saw Adalet's not-so-subtle wave. He gave a polite nod before turning back to Taly. "You ready to head out?"

Taly raised a skeptical brow. "You're not even going to say 'hello?' In highborn society, isn't that some sort of social heresy?"

"Well, look at that. You do remember your manners," Skye teased, throwing an arm around her and pulling her towards the stairs. "But no. I had more than enough of 'Jezebel's' company last night. As much as you hate 'Lord Emrys,' he at least has enough political sway to get away with snubbing the occasional noblewoman. When my mother hears, I'm sure she'll have a few choice words for me, but that's nothing new."

Despite her reddening cheeks, Taly found herself walking a step closer to him. "Has your mother been pushing you to go back to Ghislain again?"

"That's putting it mildly," Skye said, wincing slightly. "She actually threatened to disinherit me and reinstate my brother as the heir when I said I'd be too busy with the Aion Gate connection to attend my fifth cousin's wedding as well as the summer court season in Arylaan. She took that back pretty quickly, though, when she realized that nothing would make me happier."

Taly smiled. "Skipping court and snubbing Jezebel? If you're not careful, your reputation with the ladies might start to suffer."

"I don't give two shits about this so-called reputation you say I'm supposed to have," he countered as they descended the final stair and hit the first-floor landing. "Besides—between my Gate Watchers' duties and the fact that I'm supposed to be taking the exam to get my fifth training seal next month, I barely have enough free time to deal with *your* nonsense. Where the hell am I going to find the time and energy to entertain other women?"

Taly chuckled softly before giving into temptation and twining her fingers with the hand that rested on her shoulder. When she looked up, the subtle-yet-sincere smile on Skye's face sent a surprisingly pleasant shiver down her spine.

As they stepped through the open doorway of the inn, she glanced over her shoulder and caught Adalet's eye. To Taly's great amusement, the catty highborn's perfect features were screwed up in anger, and her scowl only deepened when Taly gave her a cocky wink.

By the time Taly and Skye retrieved their horses and turned south to head towards Ebondrift, a comfortable silence had settled between them. The forest canopy started to thin, and streaks of buttery sunlight sliced through the trees as a gentle wind rustled the leaves overhead. Leaning back in her saddle, Taly let out a pleased sigh. It was a beautiful day, and the sun felt deliciously warm against her skin. She had always loved lying out on the front steps of the manor during the summer, and when they were younger, Skye used to liken her to a lazy cat.

Maybe he was right, she thought, stretching her arms high overhead.

"Everything alright?" she asked when she heard a low, incoherent curse from the man riding alongside her. Receiving no answer, she glanced over only to see that Skye was staring at her with slightly unfocused eyes. "Do I have something on my face?" she asked, wiping at her chin self-consciously.

Skye started. "Huh? Uh... no. Sorry. It's nothing," he mumbled, shaking his head as he turned away.

"If you say so," she muttered to herself. Shrugging off his strange behavior, Taly pulled out her map. Some of the wards on the side of the road looked damaged. That meant she needed to stay focused. After all, it wasn't like they could depend on Skye's sense of direction if they got lost.

Thankfully, they didn't have to stray too far from the main road, and even though the horses were a little on edge, pulling at the reins and at times refusing to go forward, they made good time on the second leg of their trip to Ebondrift.

"Shouldn't there be more people here?" Taly asked as they approached the outer edge of the small gate town. The main roads were still strangely devoid of travelers, even more so than the day before. In fact, they hadn't passed a single person since shortly after they left Della.

"Yeah," Skye replied. He closed his eyes, and Taly knew that he was channeling his aether, using his enhanced senses to search for those things that were beyond her ability to detect. "This is strange. The Seren Gate opened a few days ago—that's more than enough time for the mainland traders to get set up. The Ebondrift market should be in full swing by now."

"I don't get it," Taly said, dismounting and bringing her horse's reins over its head. "Kaeli, my contact back in Della, mentioned that the market has been a bit slow lately, but I'm starting to think she meant to say it shut down."

"How old was that information?" Skye asked as he slid out of his saddle.

Taly sighed and ran a hand through her hair. She scowled when her fingers caught in her braid. "She said she was here the night before last just before the stalls closed." Glancing around the deserted stable, she reached for the reins of Skye's horse. "I don't see the groom. You go on ahead and check with the Watchers—I'll take care of the horses."

"Thanks." Skye paused when his fingers grazed her palm. His eyes found hers, and he frowned, opening his mouth to speak.

"I'll be fine," Taly said, anticipating his concern. Leave it to Skye to worry over nothing. "And if I'm not… well, I'm armed." She patted the heel of one of the pistols holstered at her waist.

"I know, but I just don't think it's a good idea to split up." Skye ran a nervous hand through his hair. "Especially with that guy in Ryme and—"

"Seriously, would you just go?" She laughed as

she pushed him towards the stable door. "If it makes you feel any better, I'll come straight to the command post after I'm done. No dawdling." She gave a mock salute, something she had learned from a mortal trader years ago.

"Okay! Okay," Skye conceded, holding up his hands. He still didn't look convinced, but he started backing away. "Just *please* be careful."

"I always am." Taly gave him a wink.

Skye stumbled slightly, and she couldn't stop the giggle that fell from her lips. She didn't think she'd ever seen a shadow mage trip over his own two feet. "No, you're not," he muttered, pushing his hair out of his eyes. "Still, I expect you to at least try."

"Will do," Taly said as she turned back to the horses. "Now, get lost, Em."

Tying off the horses, Taly shook her head, still laughing to herself as she heard Skye's footsteps crunching on the gravel path outside. When he was finally far enough away that she didn't think he could hear her, even with those super shadow senses of his, she turned to the little gelding she had been riding and said, "Can you believe that, Byron? No faith. I've done just fine on my own for almost a year now, but he doesn't think I can walk across a village without finding trouble. That highborn jerk is going to make himself go gray if he's not careful."

Byron gave a disinterested snort in reply, which Taly decided to take as wholehearted agreement.

As she wandered up and down the rows of stalls, she shook her head in disgust. She had never had much respect for the grooms in the public stables in Ebondrift before, but this was a new low. Even for them. The stable was near capacity, but there wasn't a man or woman in sight. The stalls hadn't been mucked in over a day, and the animals' water troughs were empty.

Taly had always had a soft spot for animals, so after she stalled her own horses, she started tending to the others—feeding, watering, and mucking. The animals tore into their food, paying her no mind while she shoveled out the trampled hay and manure.

It was hard work, but Taly was grateful for the distraction. After that morning, she could no longer deny that her feelings for Skye were becoming *complicated*, and she needed space to sort it all out. The fact that she had drunkenly invited the arrogant, highborn bastard into her bed last night clearly indicated that her usual strategy of just ignoring whatever made her uncomfortable until it went away didn't seem to be working this time.

When she was done cleaning out the stalls, Taly washed herself off underneath one of the spigots in the training yard, splashing water over her face and arms and picking random pieces of hay out of her braid. She had discarded her jacket when she got too warm, so she dusted it off before pulling it back on. The late afternoon sun beat down on her from above, and she could still feel sweat beading and dripping down her back. Unbuttoning the cuffs of her coat, she rolled the sleeves up and over her elbows, breathing a small sigh as she felt the cool breeze caress her heated skin.

Figuring that Skye would probably be worrying himself into an early grave by now, Taly set off for the village. The stables were situated just outside of town, and instead of taking the main road, she cut through a small wooded area. There was a narrow footpath winding between the trees, a shortcut forged by the passage of people and time that would deposit her just outside the tenements west of the market square. While the western side of Ebondrift couldn't exactly be considered the safest part of town, that didn't worry her too much. If she loosened her braid to cover her ears, she was dressed well enough to pass for a lowborn. She might have to be more wary of pickpockets, but most criminals tended to steer clear of those they thought might have enough magic to put up a fight.

As she stepped off the beaten-down path onto the cobbled street, Taly paused. Something felt off, and her hand instinctively reached for the pistol holstered at her hip. The narrow lane was empty—completely deserted. Though unusual, that wasn't what worried her. The market stalls were just a few streets over. Even if the crowds were a bit leaner than normal, she should've been able to hear *something*—voices carried on the wind or the clang of a blacksmith's hammer. But there was nothing. No sound. Everything around her was still and quiet.

A clash followed by a muted scream shattered the heavy silence. Taly hesitated. This was the part where Skye would tell her to turn around and walk the other way. Unfortunately, the other way would take almost an hour to loop back around to where she needed to be. That wouldn't do.

Taking a steadying breath, Taly pulled her pistol and continued along her original path, heading down the street that would eventually lead her to the market square that bordered the

Gate Watchers' compound. As she navigated the maze-like backstreets, the condition of the homes that lined the narrow thoroughfare started to deteriorate. All up and down the roadway, doors were smashed in, and smoke trailed from broken windows in lazy wisps.

The further she ventured into the slum, circling closer and closer to the market, the more the roads began to narrow. Here, scattered debris littered the streets and some of the buildings had been completely burned to the ground, the embers still smoldering beneath piles of cindered wood. The air around her started to feel hot, and motes of ash drifted on the wind like snowflakes.

There had been fighting here recently. Fire mages—water mages too, if the puddles beneath her feet were anything to go by—had taken up arms. Against whom, she didn't know. There were no bodies, just wide streaks of crimson smeared across the pavement.

Another crash echoed through the empty street, closer this time. Taly crept forward, edging around a corner and ducking behind an overturned food stand. Around a bend in the road ahead, she could see a child huddled against the wall of one of the few buildings that were still intact. Splintered crates surrounded the trembling girl, and she was whimpering pitifully, her hands clasped protectively over her head. Her long, dark locks covered her face like a sheet. Three men, tall but gaunt, towered over her.

Taly couldn't see the assailants' faces, so she had no way to tell if they were fey or mortal or somewhere in-between. If they had magic, that could pose a potential problem if she were to interfere. Judging by the rags they wore, they weren't highborn, and while that was a point in her favor, even a lowborn fire mage could prove worrisome if worst came to worst.

Still, Taly couldn't just let them beat up on a kid like that.

"Hey!" Taly shot her pistol into the air. The sound reverberated harshly through the empty street. "That's the only time I'm going to miss. I suggest you go on about your business and leave the kid alone."

The girl's frightened eyes glanced over at her, searching for the source of the shot. She was fey—Taly could see the pointed tips of her ears from here—but the color of her eyes was too muddy to make her anything more than shardless. Even if by some chance the kid had enough fey blood to be considered lowborn, she wasn't nearly old enough to have completed her Attunement Ceremony. That meant she didn't have any magic of her own. Nothing useful, at least.

None of the attackers turned her way, so Taly fired off another shot. "I lied. *That* was the last time I'll miss. Seriously, guys—you're testing my patience!" Picking up a rock, Taly hurled it at the group of men. One of the assailants finally flinched, and she smiled grimly when three heads swiveled in her direction, the small girl momentarily forgotten. Without hesitation, the child scrambled to her feet and darted off in the opposite direction.

As the three thugs shuffled closer, Taly drew in a sharp breath, and her grip on her pistol faltered. Though they looked like they had perhaps once been men, the resemblance was superficial at best. There was something soulless about them—the way they moved, the way their flesh seemed to sag off the bone beneath pallid, bloodless skin. Each step jerked their bodies from side-to-side, and their eyes… their eyes made her stomach churn. They were flat and dull, almost like the life had been drained away only to be replaced by an immeasurable depth of pain.

One of the creatures' mouths gaped wide, the joints of its jaw creaking in the silence of the abandoned city. Its chest heaved, it gave a feral cry, and before the echo of that tortured wail had ceased, the group charged forward, careening down the street at a pace that shouldn't have been possible.

"Shards!" Taly yelped, backing out of her hiding spot, desperately trying to keep some distance between them and her.

Her finger twitched rapidly, and three pops of gunfire sliced through the air. One of the men grunted as a bullet found its target, but none of the strange undead soldiers fell. She readied her next shot, but her targets were moving too quickly for her eyes to follow, lurching erratically as they ran. The creatures' auras, their golden afterimages, sputtered to life, but even that wasn't enough. At the rate they were moving, it was just a blurry fog that clouded her vision as she tried to aim.

She tried to steady her gun and take aim, but a sudden sharp stinging sensation in her wrist made the pistol lurch in her grip as she fired off another salvo. The shots ricocheted ineffectually off a nearby piece of metal roofing that lay strewn across the street.

"Damn it!" Taly cursed when none of the bullets found their mark. Her pistol clattered to the ground as the sting intensified, morphing into a dull burn. The wave of heat continued to ripple up her arm, a crescendo of agony that grew more intense with each passing moment. The pain dominated every thought, every sense, and she dropped to her knees, clutching at her arm even as the creatures drew closer.

What is this? she thought, tears leaking from her eyes.

As suddenly as the spasm of blazing anguish began, it abruptly released its hold on her. Taly's eyes immediately popped open, and her head whipped around, frantically searching for her discarded gun. When she caught sight of the pistol, she groped for it, whirling to face her attackers.

"Oh, no. Not again," she whispered, coming up short. Her stomach dropped, and she shook her head, unable to decide if the sight in front of her was a blessing or a curse.

The creatures were no longer sprinting towards her. Their movements had slowed, almost like they were running through water. With each decelerated lunge forward, their bodies seemed to hang in the air, coiled in a web of gilded threads. Their cries were long and drawn out and sounded garbled to her ears.

A manic laugh bubbled up out of her chest. *Blessing! Definitely a blessing*, she thought when their ghostly auras finally snapped into focus. They were hazy and undefined around the edges, but the golden specters were distinct enough for her to see. They moved just one step ahead of their physical counterparts, showing her exactly where she needed to aim.

The moment didn't last long. The creatures were already starting to speed back up again, shaking off the gossamer strands that impeded their movements. Not wanting to waste this chance, Taly raised her pistol and fired off six more rounds, using the golden visions to guide her shots. As time once again found its correct rhythm, the men, or things that used to be men, fell to the ground—their knees shattered.

Without warning, the air drained from Taly's lungs, and she doubled over, gasping and desperately clutching at her throat. It felt like something had been forcibly drained out of her. The feeling was horrible—like drowning. She sucked in breaths of air, relieved when the crushing weight on her chest began to lift.

As the pain faded to the background, Taly looked up. Those *things* were still moving towards her, clawing at the ground and dragging their ruined legs behind them. They might have once been human—or fey. She didn't know. It looked as though their ears had been ripped away. Their eyes, sunken and grotesque, swiveled in decaying sockets, and their mouths opened wide as they groaned and gurgled.

Taly's hands were shaking as she gripped her pistol. Three more shots. This time she shot to kill, aiming straight for their heads. All three gave a sad little jerk as their lives were snuffed out. Murmuring a silent prayer to the Shards, Taly hoped that if there was anything with any feeling left in these dead husks, they would find some peace now.

Nearly out of ammunition, she re-holstered her pistol and pulled out her spare. The market square was just around the bend in the road ahead. She took a hesitant step and then another towards the three bodies that lay unmoving in the street. As she came closer, her stomach convulsed. The stench filling the air was, for lack of a better word, *awful*—like decayed carrion. It made the air feel heavy with rot, and she vainly tried to blot out the smell by pressing her face into the crook of her arm.

The street was too narrow to go around. Eyeing the nearest creature warily, Taly gave it a sharp kick, keeping her pistol trained on its body. She gave it another kick, just to be sure it was down, before she started picking her way through the corpses.

Rolling one of the creatures over onto its back with her foot, Taly took a moment to study it. The thing's cheeks were hollowed, and there was a dark, gaping hole where its eye socket should've been—right where she had shot it.

"What the hell?" she mumbled, bending down to get a better look at the dark, coagulated fluid around the ruined eye-socket. The wound wasn't bleeding. In fact, the creature seemed to be covered in lacerations and gashes, but none of them bled. The blood spattered across its body had long ago clotted and congealed.

Beneath the tattered edges of its shirt, a long gash split its abdomen from hip to sternum—another un-bleeding wound with more of the same black, viscous fluid smeared along the putrefied edges of its torn flesh. Embedded in its chest, just above its heart, was a violet crystal. It was large, the size of her palm, and it glowed and pulsed, almost like a heartbeat.

Shadow magic? Taly thought with growing horror. How was that even possible? She had never heard of any kind of spell this heinous.

The thing gave a twitch, and Taly stumbled back, drawing in a sharp breath when a golden haze enveloped her. A hand clamped down on her wrist, the vice-like grip forcing her pistol to the ground. Turning on her heel, she instinctively twisted out of the thing's grip. Years of combat training with Skye made the movements second-nature.

Zephyr was in her other hand in an instant, and she plunged the blade deep into this new attacker's belly. Something cold dripped onto her fist as she felt for the small toggle just beneath the cross-guard. Slamming her thumb down on the crystal switch, Taly braced herself as a rush of air left the tip of the dagger. The gale of wind spiraled outward in an unforgiving blast, and the creature's abdomen exploded, chunks of flesh splattering against the walls of the alley. The thing's body, now torn asunder, fell to the pavement in two pieces.

Taly shook off the fragments of shredded entrails from her blade and wiped at the patina of viscera and ooze that now coated her face and body with her sleeve. There were three more of those creatures moving in behind her now, most likely lured by the sound of her gunfire. They looked different from the ones lying on the ground. Those, even if they didn't look alive, still could've passed for men. The things in front of her had no spark of life left in them. They looked like raw meat that had been left to sit in the sun a little too long.

The one closest to her lunged, forcing her back as she raised her dagger. Her thumb found the switch, but before she could fire off another blast of air magic, something yanked at her foot, and she was pulled off her feet. The world rushed by her in a blur, and her head hit the pavement with a sharp crack as she landed flat on her back. Her vision clouded for a moment before coming back into focus as she felt another tug on her leg.

Coming to her senses, she quickly realized that the creatures on the ground, the ones with shattered knees and bullets in their brains, were somehow moving again. One of them wrenched Zephyr from her hand, so she reached for the shiny new dagger Skye had gifted her. It was still tucked safely inside her boot, well within reach. But before she could grasp the handle, her hands were jerked above her head as one of the creatures standing over her seized her arms, pulling her body taut as it fell to its knees and pinned her to the ground.

The sharp clang of metal against stone followed by Taly's scream echoed between the narrow walls. Another of those strange dead men had dug Zephyr into her side. It was a glancing wound, grazing the flesh of her hip and embedding the blade into the ground below. She thrashed and kicked, but the creatures had her pinned. The metal of her beloved dagger bit into her skin, ripping open the shallow wound.

The creatures on the ground crawled over to her, their bony fingers groping at her skin and clothing. Several more of these strange undead men appeared on the street, staggering out of narrow alleys and side streets, and they crowded around her, their lips pulling back to reveal grim, decomposing grins as they watched her struggle. There was something almost familiar about some of them—something that tugged at tucked-away memories—but she couldn't focus. Not with the sting of Zephyr at her hip and the stench of death filling her nose.

Her body started to tremble uncontrollably. This couldn't be it. She refused to die here.

"No, no, no, no..." Taly whimpered, her head whipping from side-to-side. The dead formed a circle around her as they started pulling her to her feet. Why hadn't they killed her already? What were they waiting for?

Her side throbbed, and she could feel the warm blood spilling across her hip, soaking the fabric of her leggings and staining the cuff of her boot. One of the creatures grabbed her arm, wrenching it behind her at an odd angle, and she could already feel the bruises forming beneath its iron grip. It grabbed her other arm, twisting her wrist as she tried to vainly pull away and eliciting another sharp stab of scalding pain at the base of her palm.

Just like before. Taly's eyes widened.

The familiar pain blossomed and spread beneath her skin as she continued to fight against her captor. Once again, her arm began to burn, setting her blood on fire. She recognized this feeling. The bruises on her arm, the ones that had yet to heal after her encounter with the harpy, flashed brightly, flickering to life and shining with an angry violet light. Golden dust started rippling the air, dancing between her fingertips.

That's it! She clung to the pain, smiling as she felt it stretch and expand.

"Stop!" she cried weakly. Like the harpy. The harpy had stopped. She had made the harpy stop. She thrashed as the undead soldier tried to hold her. Its grip never loosened, and it growled as it gave her a rough shake, its rotted breath fanning out over her face.

"Stop!" More pain. There was so much pain now. She could feel the fire inside her, the flames lapping at the ends of her nerves, struggling to be set free.

The other creatures were crowding around her now, grabbing at her clothing, tugging at her hair. Three more sets of hands seized her arms, and the creatures on the ground tried to pin her legs. They were strong. She could barely move, but she kept struggling.

"Just stop already!" Taly screamed as the pain detonated, reverberating up and down her arm and coursing through her body until there wasn't a single part of her that didn't burn. She felt something inside her shatter, and then a rush of golden light exploded around her, branching out and curling between her attackers.

The world went silent. The ash from the fires hung in the air, suspended, and the trails of smoke from the smoldering, burned-out buildings looked like smears of paint against a frozen landscape. The creatures around her had ceased their assault, their mangled bodies fixed in a ghastly portrait of pain. Everything around her was still.

Time had stopped.

Though her lungs were on fire and every breath felt labored and strained, it was easy to shake off the hands of her attackers now. Taly staggered forward, gasping as she scooped up her dropped weapons and squeezed her body between the crowded circle of motionless undead. She had no idea how long this would last—this strange hushed stillness—and she didn't intend to wait around to find out.

Just ahead of her, she could see the ash motes falling behind a thin, filmy magical barrier. It looked like she'd created a bubble, and the edges of the warped shimmer bent the light, forming a wall of distortion. Ignoring the pain in her side, she ran. She could already hear sounds coming from behind her, stretched groans pulled from putrefied vocal cords as the creatures began to recover, realizing too late that she'd somehow escaped. The tangles of golden strands crisscrossing the expanse of distorted time were already crumbling as the spell collapsed.

Blackness crept in around the edges of her vision as she felt that same drain of… something. It felt like her lungs were ready to collapse in on themselves, and her legs felt shaky, but she forced herself to keep moving forward, one foot in front of the other. She needed to find Skye. Had he run into these things too? Shards, she hoped he was okay.

Taly wiped at her cheek, grimacing when she saw the streak of black blood that stained her hand. Skye *was* okay. He had to be. After all, shadow mages were almost indestructible. If she was still alive, then so was he.

The market square was just ahead now, and beyond that, the Gate Watchers' Compound. That's where he had been heading. That's where she would be safe.

CHAPTER 16

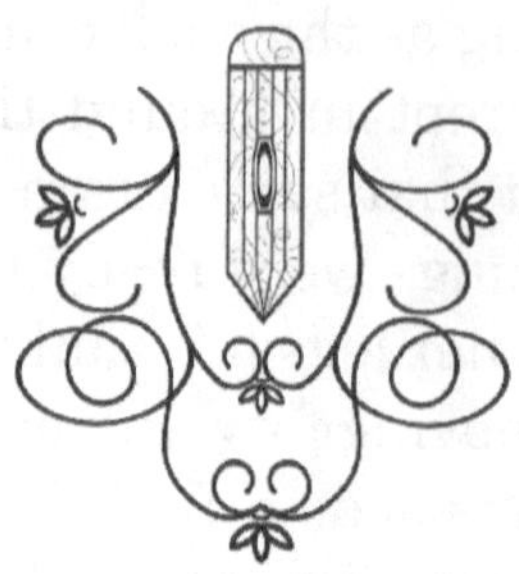

-A letter from Lord Ivain Castaro of House Fairmont, High Commander of the Gate Watchers, to Lord Moryn Enix of House Myridan, Lt-Commander of the Gate Watchers

The 2nd day of the month Dranna, during the 248th year of the Empty Throne

Commander Enix,

I am writing to inform you of my intent to appoint my ward, Lord Skylen Emrys, as my new Precept. Though still young, he has shown great talent and potential, and I believe he is ready to step in as my second.

I realize that this is unorthodox, and we do not usually allow Marshals to skip more than two ranks at a time. However, with the impending Aion Gate connection, I believe the circumstances warrant an exception. Skylen has already been performing the duties of a Precept for several years now. The only reason I held him back from advancing as quickly as he should was so that he would not feel honor-bound to stay with the Order once his primary education concluded. However, he has recently expressed his desire to continue training under my tutelage rather than attending the University in Arylaan, so it is time he was awarded the rank and authority he is due.

I will be bringing Skylen to Ebondrift at the end of the month to complete the written and practical examinations. Please make the necessary arrangements.

Regards,

Lord Ivain Castaro of House Fairmont, Marquess of Tempris and High Commander of the Gate Watchers

The streets were empty as Skye turned onto the main road and headed for the Gate Watchers' compound. Taly had stayed behind at the stables, and he could hear her whistling to herself as she tied off the horses. When the sound of her puttering around the stables began to fade, he channeled his aether, using a small amount of magic to sharpen his senses.

A fond smile tugged at the corners of his mouth. As she was wont to do when she didn't think anyone was listening, Taly had started talking to the various animals in the barn—something about highborn jerks that worried too much. The horses, in voices that sounded strangely like her own, agreed with her and seemed quite sympathetic to her plight.

Skye released the aether augmentation spell and took a long, cleansing breath, attempting to clear his thoughts. The smell of wood, smoke, and wet grass hit his nose, washing away any lingering traces of Taly's scent. If he wasn't careful, he was going to find himself turning around and going back to fetch her, something he really didn't have time to do if he had any hope of accomplishing anything useful.

We should've left sooner. Although he had awoken just before dawn, long before Taly had oh-so-stealthily tried to sneak out of their room, he hadn't been able to pry himself out of bed. Not with Taly curled into his side, clinging to him in a way that almost seemed possessive. Even now, he could still see that waterfall of golden hair glowing in the morning light, still hear the soft kitten-like snores that fell from her lips, still feel her warmth.

Skye stopped, realizing that he had turned and was heading back towards the stables. Shaking his head, he took off for the Gate Watchers' compound at a jog. Maybe he and Taly needed to spend the evening apart to give him time to clear his head. While he couldn't deny that Taly had grown into a beautiful woman (a *very* beautiful woman), he should *not* be having these kinds of feelings for her.

This was Taly. His friend. Nothing else.

And besides, even if he did have *genuine* romantic feelings for her (which he didn't), apparently just the idea of bedding him horrified and disgusted her.

So… problem solved.

As Skye entered the city proper, moving out of the more sparsely populated outer perimeter and into the tenements, all thoughts of Taly were pushed to the back of his mind. Instead, a sense of dread started to take root. Something didn't feel right. The streets were empty. In fact, now that he thought about it, he hadn't seen a single person since he left Taly at the stables.

His steps slowed, and he turned, surveying his surroundings. All around him, the doors to the cramped cottages and apartments hung open, and wagons, still filled with goods and wares destined for the market, were left abandoned. Even the air seemed *off* somehow. Usually, when the Seren Gate was open, he could almost taste the aether flowing in from the fey mainland. But today, the air around him felt dead. Stagnant. Curling his magic between the amorphous, drifting aether, he pulled. Only a few small wisps of energy answered his call—violet threads coiling around his body and then dissipating as he released his hold.

This is bad, Skye thought, increasing his pace. If something were wrong with the Seren Gate, that would throw off their entire timeline for the Aion Gate, and he didn't even want to try to imagine the effects a failed gate connection would have on the island's already fragile economy.

The Gate Watchers' Compound was just ahead. The outer walls were forged from a single block of milky quartz and loomed over the surrounding village, making the patchwork collection of buildings appear shabby and squat in its shadow. The main building, an old, repurposed palace, was housed within, and Skye could just see the towers of the keep peeking over the battlements. Like most traditional fey architecture, every surface of the sprawling assembly was inscribed with stone latticework and ornamentation. The overall effect, though breathtaking, was, in Skye's opinion, exaggerated and just a little too much. But that was how he felt about most traditional fey architecture.

Today, the pale expanse of quartz was marred by smoke and ash. The gates were closed, and the portcullis had been locked. A makeshift barricade of overturned wagons and wreckage had been erected a few yards from the walls.

As Skye crossed the deserted market square, his hand resting on the hilt of his sword, the temperature dropped rapidly, and his breath puffed and hung in the air. He stumbled slightly, his boots slipping as the crunch of ice broke the silence. A thick coating of frost and snow had formed on the ground, and when he took a breath, he could just barely detect the final fading remnants of water magic lingering on the air.

A crackling hiss sounded from in front of him. Glancing up, Skye saw a ball of flame rocketing towards him from the battlements. He ducked, instinctively drawing on his aether to quicken his movements and only narrowly avoiding the fiery blast. The ball of fire struck the spot where he'd been standing, throwing up a cloud of steam and small chunks of ice and rock.

"What the hell?!" Skye snapped, drawing his sword. He turned towards the compound, searching for his attackers. Three mages stood on the outer wall of the compound, peeking above the top of the ramparts and eyeing him warily. Another whirling ball of flame was already being summoned in the air beside them.

“Don’t fire!” Skye screamed, waving a hand in the air. “I’m one of you!”

“Prove it!” one of them called. A man—several centuries old at least. “How do we know you’re not with those things?”

“What things?!” Skye shouted back. “What happened here?”

The mages didn’t answer. Instead, they seemed to look past him, their eyes growing wide. Suspicion and doubt soon gave way to fear. “They’re back,” another man shouted. There was more movement on the rampart, and mages started lining up, taking up defensive stances.

A trickle of dread crawled down his spine as Skye turned. Behind him, an advancing horde of… he didn’t have a name for what he saw. They defied nature—their very existence was an abomination. Dead men. They looked like dead men. Their skin hung loosely on their emaciated bodies, marred by gaping wounds that stained their clothing with congealed blood. Their decaying limbs tangled together as they raced forward. Despite their jerky, uncoordinated movements, they moved with an unnatural speed. Even as he watched in stunned silence, Skye could see that they would be upon him in moments.

“Oh, shit,” he muttered, backing toward the barricade behind him.

Skye raised his blade, adjusting the grip so that his skin was touching each one of the three shadow crystals embedded in the handle. When he flicked a small switch hidden beneath the guard, the stored aether shuddered excitedly as it seeped into the fire crystals embedded in the swirling hilt, sending waves of heat sweeping across his skin.

A current of flame flowed down the length of the blade, lighting the dull, gray metal with a molten glow. Feeling the energy in the shadow crystals start to dip, Skye pulled at the meager supply of aether in the air around him and stored it away inside the shadow crystals.

The advancing wave of corpses was getting closer, their mouths gaping wildly as roars of rage and pain erupted from their rotting throats. Sweeping his blade in a wide arc, the air crystals embedded in the blade activated, blasting out a gale of fire directly at his assailants. Several of the undead writhed and screamed as the conflagration consumed them, but that didn't halt their advance. Although their bodies had been set ablaze, they still stumbled toward him even as their skin bubbled and melted away.

Okay, that's obviously not going to work. There were hundreds of these creatures, and they seemed to be incredibly resilient. He clamped down on the fear that threatened to overwhelm him. He couldn't afford to be distracted right now.

Sheathing his sword and pulling a shadow crystal from his pocket, Skye siphoned off the magic. The aether seeped into his blood, into the muscles of his arms and legs, overcharging the already adrenaline-fueled energy that pumped through his veins.

His eyes darted to the side, catching sight of a ruined wagon resting along the jagged line of debris in front of the compound. The semblance of an idea fluttered through his mind's eye, and then he was running parallel to the walls of the compound, a small group of undead peeling off from the horde to chase him. The world was nothing but a blur as his legs surged, the mangled cries of the approaching throng little more than an unintelligible whine.

A moment later, his boots swept up a flood of gravel and dirt into the air as he skidded to a halt in front of a pile of litter and debris. Skye effortlessly lifted the overturned wagon from the heap, and a grim smile tugged at his lips as he felt the muscles in his arms ripple and surge. It wasn't very often that he got to use the full extent of his augmented strength. Not unless he was sparring with Ivain.

Feeling a tingle of exhilaration, he turned and hurled the cracked, wooden carriage through the air at his attackers. It flew across the square, barreling through the charging horde just as they managed to clear the overturned fountain that used to decorate the center of the market. The force of the blow knocked a dozen of the undead off their feet, severing their limbs and impaling their bodies with splintered wood. Cries of pain and rage promptly echoed above the clamoring din.

Skye grinned as he pulled out another shadow crystal. That was a far more effective strategy.

More of those undead monsters had split off from the main group and were headed towards him. Making a split-second decision, Skye charged at one of the creatures that ran ahead of the throng. These things were fast, but he was faster. Shifting his weight at the last moment, he dodged the creature's blade, grabbing it by the arm and crushing its bones in his iron grip. Its sword clattered to the ground as Skye's other hand swept forward to catch it by the neck. Twisting his body, he hurled the writhing corpse back into the advancing crowd of reanimated dead. They flew back, falling to the ground in a heap.

They didn't stay down long. In fact, Skye could already see that the corpses were beginning to regain their feet. He was only slowing the creatures down. He searched the area around him, frantically looking for anything that could be used as a more effective weapon.

Most of the market stalls that lined the square had been destroyed, the wooden counters hacked apart and the crates of goods and wares overturned and strewn across the ground. Making his way to a stand that was still relatively intact, Skye's hands gripped at a gnarled beam that used to be part of a fruit stand. The post was nearly eight feet tall and rooted in the ground—a product of an obscenely expensive earth spell that could create architectural structures from living trees. He suspected that the awning of the small shop had once been formed from a canopy of leaves, but any and all greenery had been burned away.

He pulled at the young tree, groaning as he felt the muscles in his arms strain. He pushed more aether into the augmentation spell, bolstering his strength, and felt the plant start to give way. With a final jerk, he ripped the tree from the ground in a shower of dirt and rock, giving the end a sharp kick to break away any remaining roots.

"This'll do," Skye said aloud, turning to face the rushing throng of undead. Widening his stance, he swung the makeshift weapon, slamming the fractured tree trunk into one of the creatures. The blow ripped apart the monster's torso and sent the flailing corpse flying into another group of its comrades. Their bodies hit the ground like dolls.

One of the felled undead that had somehow

managed to free itself from the heap of tangled corpses threw a rusted dagger at Skye as he struck at another group with the tree. The metal bit into the skin of his shoulder, embedding into his flesh between a gap in his armor. Blood welled around the wound, but with this much aether flooding his system, it was of no concern. Skye grimaced as he ripped the blade from his arm, watching with detached interest as the flesh knit itself back together.

They're not using poison, he thought with a grin. That was a bad move on their part.

One of the creatures clawed at the ground, inching its way across the broken pavement. Its body had been cleaved in two, but its arms still reached for him. Adjusting his grip on the beam, Skye brought it down, smashing in the thing's head. Its bone and flesh splattered across the pavement, staining the ground black with rotted blood.

Finding a moment of respite, Skye stopped to catch his breath, his eyes taking in the roiling mass of dead men that filled the market square. He stood off to the side of the main fray and could see that the majority of the creatures were scrambling over the debris piled in front of the compound, their mad, soulless eyes focused on the fey on the walls. Giant whorls of flames struck the group as the mages entered the fray, incinerating their bodies and igniting the debris. The fires quickly spread, zipping along the line of the barricade and creating a wall of flame in front of the compound.

Clever. Though the blaze didn't wholly stem the tide, it did slow their attackers down. They stumbled over each other as their flesh turned to ash, revealing cracked and broken bone beneath. The smell of smoke and charred meat permeated the air.

Skye heard a thunderous howl of rage, and his head whipped to the side, searching for the source of the cry. Another group of undead was rounding the corner, streaming in from one of the narrower side streets as they barreled toward the compound. Tightening his grip on the tree, he readied himself for their advance.

There were so many of these… *things*. None of this made sense.

"Back up the shadow mage! He's one of ours!" a voice shouted from the walls.

A hailstorm of ice rained down in front of Skye, blasting him backward and creating a protective barrier of offensive magic. The creatures shrieked as the ice impaled their bodies and severed their limbs. Some were completely ripped apart by the onslaught, and many more were frozen solid, their forms fixed mid-charge in a ghastly portrait of feral rage.

Skye scrambled back to his feet. In an instant, he was in front of the group of undead, each swing of the bloodied trunk in his hands shattering the frozen creatures. Shards of blackened ice rocketed in every direction as he continued to slam the makeshift club against them again and again.

"Shadow mages, reinforce the Gate Watcher!" another shout sounded from the walls.

A group of men and women, other Gate Watchers, jumped from the walls of the compound. Their boots landed with heavy thuds, throwing up a cloud of dust where they hit the ground. They immediately drew their swords and leapt through the flames encircling the compound, wisps of smoke drifting from their armor as they emerged from the fire. Within seconds, they had fallen into line beside Skye.

"These things don't go down easy!" Skye called to the others, brandishing his makeshift weapon. "Fire and slicing weapons only slow them down. You have to bludgeon them!"

The other shadow mages shared a look but followed his orders. Sheathing their weapons, they followed his example, ripping broken beams and girders from the remains of the market stalls as the oncoming swarm raced toward them.

Now that he had backup, the horde of dead men didn't seem so daunting. The shadow mages cut through the enemy's advances, crushing the creatures' already broken bodies beneath the force of their blows and splattering more of that strange, blackened blood across the pavement. Occasionally, a rusty blade would pierce Skye's skin, but the wounds healed themselves before they even had a chance to bleed.

The mob thinned out quickly, and Skye wiped the sweat from his eyes as he watched the other shadow mages pick off the remaining stragglers. The few creatures that managed to regain their feet were quickly torn down and dismembered. Though it didn't stop them from writhing and groaning on the ground, desperately searching for their missing limbs, it did stop their advance.

Skye stared at the still-moving, disarticulated corpses. He couldn't quite wrap his head around what he was seeing. He had a few ideas on how this might be possible, but every single one of them made his stomach churn. Not only that, he couldn't figure out why this unknown, undead force had chosen to attack the compound directly. The front of the compound was fortified and nigh impenetrable when the gates were closed. And while these creatures' movements were uncoordinated and jerky, they worked together far too well to be considered completely feral. It was almost as though they were being directed.

Which left one question—what was their strategy?

He felt it before he heard it. The ground started to tremble, and then a deafening explosion reverberated through the air, drowning out the din of battle.

"The back of the compound!" someone screamed from the top wall. "They're streaming in from the back of the compound!"

"It's a decoy!" Skye shouted, turning and sprinting back towards the wall, the broken trunk still in hand. The other shadow mages turned to follow him.

As Skye leapt through the flames of the barricade, the heat assaulted his skin. Pulling another shadow crystal from his pocket, he yanked out the aether, supplementing it with the small amount he could find in the air nearby. Then, in one explosive movement, he jumped, clearing the edge of the 30-foot wall and landing with a heavy thud on the ramparts. The other shadow mages joined him a moment later, their boots thumping against the dense crystal of the wall in a dull, repetitive rhythm.

From the top of the wall walk, Skye could see a swarm of the creatures streaming in through a jagged, smoking gap in the back wall of the compound. They almost looked like ants, spilling through the narrow opening as they rushed the small contingent of fire mages that tried to hold them back.

While earth mages were rare on the island, there were two standing behind the fiery vanguard, their hands waving through the air as they shaped a green cloud of earth magic. Moments later, vines erupted from the ground, blocking off the gap in the wall and partially stemming the tide. The creatures clawed at the vegetation as they pushed and shoved each other, and the vines were already starting to bend under the strain of their frenzied assault. The flimsy barricade wouldn't hold them back for long.

Despite the momentary respite, dozens of the creatures had already forced their way into the interior courtyard. The corpses of civilians, both fey and mortal alike, littered the ground. Their lifeblood leaked into the dirt as the undead monsters tore into their flesh with gnashing teeth, and each spray of warm blood that spurted across their decayed skin just fed their growing frenzy.

Bile burned at the back of Skye's throat. They were feeding.

The remaining citizens were frantically trying to retreat into the keep as the mages on the wall covered them, but they were moving too slow. A crowd of people surrounded the door, and the feverish undead picked them off from behind, working their way through the mass of panic-stricken civilians.

"Your orders, Milord?" a stern female voice inquired from behind Skye. "The chain-of-command has been compromised. You're now the highest-ranking officer in the compound." At this comment, the other shadow mages eyed Skye with a new appreciation.

Skye turned to find that he was being

addressed by another Gate Watcher, one he immediately recognized despite the blackened blood and congealed gore that streaked her armor. Even in the midst of battle, Eula was a sight—all red lips and dark lashes. She held a rusted, metal pole in one hand, the dents in its surface a testament to her fighting prowess.

"Where's Commander Enix?" Skye asked, an edge of concern in his voice as he rounded on Eula.

"Missing," she answered curtly. "We don't have time to go into the details. We need for you to assume command."

Skye hesitated as he watched the battle raging in the interior courtyard, but his resolve hardened a moment later. This wasn't the time for doubt.

"We need to give the earth mages time to patch the hole," Skye stated decisively. He would have time to reflect on just how he had come to find himself commanding the Gate Watchers' forces when they weren't being attacked. "I'm going to try to hold them off from the inside with the rest of the casters. You and the other shadow mages—loop around and take out these bastards from behind."

"Yes, sire." Eula bobbed her head before turning and stepping off the side of the wall without hesitation. The other shadow mages soon followed her example.

With a shout, Skye did the same, effortlessly finding his footing as he dropped into the interior courtyard. "We need ice! Water mages, to me!"

There was a clatter of boots behind him, and soon the other mages formed a rank in front of Skye. He pulled another crystal from his pocket and tugged at the latent aether in the air, creating a cloud of magic for the other mages to draw upon.

A keen sense of satisfaction washed over him a moment later when a thick layer of glassy ice tangled the creatures' legs, creeping up their bodies until they were completely encased. The frozen soldiers glistened in the late afternoon sun, a horrifying array of sculptures scattered throughout the courtyard.

"Fire mages!" At his command, the fire mages moved to the front of the line. Fiery tendrils of swirling magic coiled around their hands before blasting out in front of them in a blaze. The ice-covered men shattered under the onslaught, their corpses falling to the ground in cindered, bloody fragments. The sound of breaking glass filled the air.

Skye wiped at his face. The smoke from the fire mages' spells stung his eyes. Turning to one of the fire mages beside him, he snapped, "Do we have air mages?"

"No," the boy replied. He couldn't have been older than 16. "There was a small delegation that came through a few days ago, but they've already moved on to Ryme."

"What about earth mages?"

"They're tending to the wounded, sire."

"Unless it's life or death, I want them filling that hole. Go get them and bring them here."

Skye jerked his head, gesturing towards the gap in the wall. The breach was small, but there were still too many of those things breaking through their defenses. The two earth mages tending to the barricade of thick, leafy vines were struggling under the weight of the spells, so Skye redirected what little aether he could pull from the air and sent it towards them in a wave.

Turning back to the young fire mage, he saw

that the boy was staring at the crumbling blockade with wide eyes. "What are you still doing here?" Skye demanded. "Go. Now!"

"Sire." The boy bobbed his head before turning and disappearing inside the keep.

Raising his weapon, Skye moved forward, covering the few retreating fey civilians that still lingered in the courtyard. He couldn't help but say a silent prayer of thanks that most of the remaining mortals and magicless had made it through the doors and were now holed up inside the keep.

The mages still on the wall had managed to staunch the influx of creatures, so Skye swiped at the few corpses that had managed to escape the assault of elemental magic. They fell to the ground, their bodies jerking when he gave them a swift kick to the head, followed by a crushing blow of his club that shattered their bones and splattered their blood across the courtyard. They wouldn't be getting back up.

Then Skye was at the breach. He swung his club wildly as blasts of flame rocketed past him, but the creatures just kept coming, clawing and crawling over their comrades in a desperate attempt to make it inside the interior courtyard.

Skye gave a shout, a wave of relief washing over him when the ground beneath his feet started to tremble. Moments later, the earth cracked as the trunks of newly grown trees erupted from the ground in front of the breach, curling together and reinforcing the swiftly disintegrating barricade. The leafy stems thickened, turning brown as their trunks hardened.

A loud cheer went up inside the keep. The mages still on the wall took out the last few remaining creatures, hitting first with ice and then with fire. More decaying flesh shattered, icy shards tumbling to the ground.

Sweat dripped down Skye's face and neck, and the ache in his muscles intensified as his aether began to dip. For the first time since the attack had started, he had enough room in his head to focus on the smell of these things. It was awful—rank and pungent but mixed with a sort of sickening sweetness. Like rot mixed with perfume.

Skye tried to breathe through his mouth as he pulled another shadow crystal from his pocket. Siphoning off a small amount of magic, he propelled himself onto the back wall, landing with a pained grunt. To his great relief, the other shadow mages had managed to whittle down the remaining creatures outside the keep. Eula stood towards the back, directing the others as they pummeled and smashed the last of the undead force.

It was over. Whatever this was, it was over. The wind changed course, and Skye leaned against the rampart, his chest rising and falling as he drew in heavy gulps of untainted air. He knew he needed to go back downstairs and find the strangely absent Gate Watchers' leadership. So far, Eula was the highest-ranked member he had come across, but, as Ivain's Precept, he still outranked her. That was troubling. Where was Commander Enix? Where were his Precept and his lieutenants?

From the top of the wall, Skye could see decaying corpses that still thrashed about in the interior courtyard, still groping for the feet of those that stepped over them. He could hear crying down below, piercing wails that carried on the wind as fey and mortals alike mourned over their loved ones that hadn't managed to escape to the safety of the keep in time. Desperation and sorrow were written across the faces of those still living, sketched in their frantic movements as they tried but ultimately failed to find that vital, pulsing rhythm in those whose bodies now lay broken on the pavement.

He should go to them—help tend to the wounded and find the Gate Watcher leadership. That was what his sense of duty demanded of him.

But as he pushed himself to his feet, wiping away a trickle of blood from a cut on his chin that was ever-so-slowly knitting itself back together now that he barely had enough aether to soothe his ragged breaths, he could only think about one thing.

Taly. Where is Taly?

CHAPTER 17

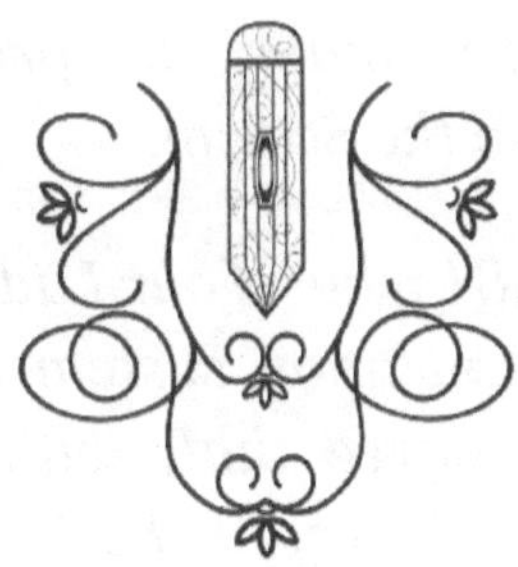

-An excerpt from the Practical Guide to Hyaline Harmonic Analysis

A relic from the Age of the Faera, the scrying relays enable long-range communication by taking advantage of the harmonizing properties of hyaline. Though hyaline crystal does not conduct aether, its frequency can be tuned in such a way that it will connect with another relay set to the same frequency.

Over time, this technology has been adapted to include glamour interfaces as well as data transfer capabilities, and improvements in the harmonizing efficiency of the hyaline crystals have dramatically increased the communication range. Unfortunately, the dimensional gates on Tempris still pose a major problem to long-range signal transmission. When the gates are open, there is no impediment to the relay signals, and communication between worlds is possible. However, when the gates are closed, the discrepancies in the flow of time between realms makes tuning the hyaline harmonizing prisms almost impossible. It has been theorized that the incorporation of a time crystal into the interface might overcome this impediment, but Queen Raine's researchers were unable to produce a viable prototype prior to the Schism.

During the 25,658th year of our Lady Raine, the first handheld communication system was introduced. Most historians agree that, without this device, House Ghislain's victory at the Battle of Raporum would not have been possible.

Taly sagged against the side of a building, one hand pressed against the gash on her hip. She held Zephyr in her free hand, her thumb hovering over the tiny crystal switch that would deploy a gale of air magic at a moment's notice.

She'd finally managed to shake the mob of undead creatures that had been pursuing her, but in doing so, she had ended up somewhere unfamiliar. Just before she'd come upon the market square, she had almost run straight into a veritable horde of those *things,* and she had been forced to duck down a side street to avoid drawing attention to herself. She'd had a hard enough time with the smaller group she'd fought off when she wasn't exhausted and wounded. If the burning in her lungs was anything to go by, she had a feeling she wouldn't be able to muster any more magic if she was forced to face off with another group of those creatures.

Not that she felt she could reliably summon her aether at this point anyway.

The clatter of boots echoed off the walls of the burned-out buildings, drawing closer. Ducking behind a crate, Taly clutched Zephyr in a white-knuckled grip. She saw their shadows first—elongated distortions of obscured light that crept around the corner. Eventually, a group of hooded figures emerged, their swords held at their sides. They were silent as they marched through the middle of the street, their heads darting side-to-side as they surveyed the area.

Holding her breath, Taly shrank back against the nearby wall, willing her hands to stop shaking as she thumbed the small toggle. She had no way to tell if this group of strangers was friend or foe, and she didn't want to risk finding out.

For a moment, it looked as though they were going to pass by her without incident, but as the last of the small troop filed past, the wind changed direction. A cool breeze ruffled Taly's hair, making her skin prickle, and the figure closest to where she hid stopped. He tilted his head, raising a hand as he murmured something to the others. Taly couldn't hear what he said, but his comrades halted and readied their swords.

She depressed the switch—not enough to fire off a blast but enough that she could feel the magic start to stir. She needed to be ready to defend herself, just in case…

In a blur, the hooded figure rushed at her, flinging aside the crates like they weighed nothing. A gale of air spiraled out from the tip of Taly's dagger, hitting the attacker square in the chest. She heard a muted grunt, but he didn't even stagger as he continued moving forward.

Taly didn't have anywhere to retreat, so when he was in range, she thrust her dagger at his belly. She felt the firm resistance of armor beneath the tip of the blade and heard the rip of fabric. Digging her heels into the ground, she threw her weight behind the attack, a grim smile playing at the corners of her mouth when she felt a warm trickle of blood drip across her hand. She moved to depress the toggle again, but the figure's hand shot out in a lightning-fast movement and grabbed her wrist. He gave her a rough jerk, unsheathing her dagger as he twisted her arm around and shoved her against the wall. The shadow crystals in Zephyr's grip started to cool as the aether drained away.

Taly's entire body trembled as the hooded figure leaned in and gave her a long sniff. His breath felt warm, and his sharp exhale ruffled the loose tendrils of hair at her neck.

"Stand down! It's just a human!" a male voice called out.

She felt the man shift behind her as he leaned in and whispered in her ear, "I'm going to let you go now. Please don't stab me again."

As soon as he released her arm, she shoved him off, whirling around and holding her dagger at the ready. The man backed up a step and held up his hands in surrender. In the dim light, she could see that his face, though pale and drawn, was flush with life.

Never thought I'd be glad to see a fey on the other end of my dagger.

"Woah now," he said, his warm russet eyes trained on her blade. "I'm on your side."

"So you say," Taly muttered. "Who are you?"

The man pointed to his hood before cautiously

pulling back the covering to reveal a shock of brassy hair. There was a smattering of freckles decorating his nose, making him look boyish and young. The stark, unnaturally vibrant color of his eyes, however, told Taly that he was probably anything but. "My name's Kit," he said. "I'm with the Gate Watchers."

Taly felt the air leave her lungs in a whoosh. "Thank the Shards," she panted. "My friend, Skye… no, Lord Skylen Emrys… he's with the Gate Watchers. The last time I saw him, he was headed to the compound. I need to find him."

"Well now," Kit drawled, his accent smooth and refined, "it sounds like you have some friends in high places. I know Lord Emrys by reputation, but I can't say that I've seen him. But then again, I haven't been back to the compound since this morning."

"We need to keep moving." A woman moved to stand behind Kit. Her pale violet eyes and white-blonde hair stood out in stark contrast to her flawless umber skin.

They're both highborn, Taly thought warily. In fact, most of the small group of men and women crowding the narrow street stared at her through eyes that were just a little too bright in the dim evening light.

"I'm aware, Adanna," Kit said, glancing at the strikingly beautiful woman. "But the girl is scared. Give me a moment."

"You're from House Bontu, aren't you?" Taly asked the woman.

Adanna gave Taly a dazzling if somewhat patronizing smile. "Yes, little human. How did you know my household?"

"Your eyes," Taly replied, readjusting her grip

on her dagger in an attempt to hide the tremble that shook her hands. "I met your brother once—Charli—when he was trying to negotiate a deal for shadow crystals with Lord Castaro. He had the same eyes."

Adanna leaned in and whispered something to Kit. His lips thinned, and he nodded in response. "You seem to be well acquainted with quite a few important people—for a human, that is. And your diction is too good for an islander."

Taly raised her dagger. "Your point?"

Kit's eyes flicked to her blade and then to the two guns holstered at her waist. "Easy," he said with a low chuckle. "I'm not going to hurt Lord Castaro's ward. I may not be the brightest, but I'm not that dumb. Adanna, assign lookouts. Let's take a short break. I want our weapons recharged and the water casks filled."

Adanna jerked her head in a terse nod, but before she turned to carry out his orders, she caught Taly's eye, her expression softening. "Would you like me to recharge your dagger?"

Taly's eyes darted to Adanna's outstretched hand and then back to Kit before she twirled the dagger in a single fluid motion, gripping the blade as she handed the weapon to the Gate Watcher. "Thank you."

"You probably have questions," Kit said, standing up straighter. Though he was tall and thin, his shoulders looked broad beneath his scaled leather armor. There was a small spattering of crimson across his belly, but Taly could see that the wound below had already healed. "We don't have much time, but I'll answer what I can."

Before she had time to think, the words

spilled from her mouth. "What happened here?"

Kit grimaced. "I think we're all still asking ourselves that same question. In short, Ebondrift was attacked late last night." Taly flinched away when he reached over and picked a chunk of flesh out of her hair. He smiled as he pulled a threadbare handkerchief out of his pocket and handed it to her. "It looks like you've already met our new guests. Friendly, aren't they?"

"That's not exactly the word I'd use to describe those walking nightmares, but yeah. What were those things?" Taly asked, rubbing her face with the cloth.

"I don't know," Kit replied with a tired sigh. "I wasn't assigned to the team responsible for figuring that out. Myself and the men and women you see here were deployed to retrieve a member of the High Lord of Earth's family—Lord Kalahad Brenin."

"I'd heard the High Lord of Earth's brother was on Tempris," Taly said. "I also heard he was in Strio, not Ebondrift."

Kit's mouth quirked to the side. "You're very knowledgeable for a human."

"Try not to look so surprised," she quipped in reply. "If you fey could ever get your heads out of your asses, you might see that humans aren't so bad."

"Duly noted. Please accept my sincerest apologies, dear lady." When Taly arched a brow, the corners of Kit's mouth lifted into a genuine smile. "Lord Kalahad came through the Seren Gate about two weeks ago. His visit was… unexpected. He left the compound several days ago to tour some of the old farms that were destroyed during the Schism and was scheduled to return yesterday evening. At this point in time, we're not sure if he and his entourage encountered these creatures." Kit hung his head. "Since we failed to retrieve him, we were on our way back to the compound. You're lucky we found you when we did."

"Sir," Adanna said, handing Kit a small leather case, "there's a message for you on the comm."

"Thank you." Lifting the flap, he keyed in the proper set of commands on what looked like a scrying communicator—a smaller, handheld version of a scrying relay.

Taly's hand reached out before she could stop herself. "I've never seen a scrying comm with a hyaline harmonizing prism wired parallel to the focusing crystal before."

Kit tilted the communicator so that she could take a closer look. The base of the small device was made of a silver alloy inset with thin strips of hyaline that threw off fragments of diffracted light. Glowing Faera runes were etched across the surface of each strip of translucent crystal, and a single, blinking water crystal was set into the center of the control panel. Her eyes wide, Taly ran a finger over the line of shadow crystals that winked and glittered along the bottom edge.

"I take it you like gadgets?" Kit asked, a wide, toothy grin splitting his face.

Taly shrugged. "You might say that."

Holding up the small device to his ear, he said, "They're new—we just got them in last month. The new design increases the communication range by 50%. I took mine apart as soon as I got it—which is probably how I got stuck on search and rescue duty." Kit winced as a stream of garbled noise sounded from the earpiece of the comm.

"Ma'am," he replied tersely. "No, ma'am. Yes, I understand." Kit's eyes flicked over to Taly. "Describe her. Uh-huh. Yes. So, about three and a half ells, blonde, armed with" —he leaned over, giving Taly a wink as his eyes dipped to her waist— "pistols and two air daggers—both viridian. Okay. Unrelated question—does the look in her eyes say something along the lines of 'if you test me, I won't hesitate to punch you in the balls?' Uh-huh. Hold on."

Kit held a hand over the communicator. "Your name wouldn't happen to be Talya Caro by any chance, would it?"

"Yeah, that's me," Taly replied, her lips quirking to the side. "And your instincts are spot-on. If you test me, I *will* punch you in the balls."

Kit barked out a laugh before replying, "Yeah, I might have seen her around. Tell him not to worry. I'll have her back safe and sound within the hour." With that, Kit pressed a key on the interface of the comm, and the water crystal went dark. Looking up, he said, "It looks like your Lord Emrys is worried about you, Miss Talya Caro."

Taly sagged against the wall as a wave of relief washed over her. Skye was safe. He had made it to the Gate Watchers' compound, and he was safe. And already worrying himself sick, apparently. "That doesn't surprise me. Also, it's Taly—just Taly."

Kit reached out and grabbed her by the arm, pulling her to her feet. "Well, let's not keep him waiting, *just Taly*. I can tell you from personal experience that the members of House Ghislain are not known for their patience."

"Sounds like there's a story there," Taly remarked as she fell into step beside him. She mumbled a shy "thanks" when Adanna handed back her dagger.

Kit gave a signal, and the rest of the Watchers took up formation around them. Pulling Taly to stand in the middle of the large group of heavily armed shadow mages, he wiped a thumb across her cheek, removing a smudge of black ooze she'd missed. "Very astute, Miss Caro. I'm a distant relation of Lord Emrys—a cousin in fact. I've never met the *heir* in person, but I squired for his older half-brother, Kato, before I joined the Watchers. Have you met him?" When Taly shook her head, he gave a low chuckle. "You're not missing much."

They moved swiftly through the silent city. Occasionally, they would come upon a small group of those creatures, but the Watchers were able to dispose of them quickly and efficiently, severing their limbs and smashing in their heads. Even if they couldn't figure out how to completely end their suffering, the shadow mages treated the fallen, undead soldiers with as much respect as possible.

The streets started to widen as they circled back around to the market square. From what Taly could tell, running from those creatures had somehow brought her back to the north side of town.

Kit held out a hand, signaling for her to stop as the other Gate Watchers raised their swords unbidden. No doubt their magically enhanced senses had detected something she couldn't.

"How many do you think?" Adanna asked in a low voice as she came to stand beside Kit.

"Too many," he replied, a faraway look in his

eyes. "Did Eula say anything about another attack?"

Adanna nodded and pulled her hood back, revealing an intricate mass of braids coiled at the base of her neck. "Yes, but she also said that they were able to fend them off."

"Okay. It's most likely the dismembered bodies. They must not have disposed of them properly. Let's keep moving," Kit said, the shadow crystals in his sword flashing. "It's almost sundown. If we want to make it back to the compound before nightfall, we don't have time to send a scouting party."

As they entered the square, Taly felt her breath catch in her throat. The market was unrecognizable. The stalls had been smashed and scattered across the cracked pavement, and severed limbs and broken bodies littered the area. Torsos with no arms or legs, some with no heads, writhed on the ground. A babel of deafening wails filled the square.

"Taly," Kit began, pulling her behind him, "pull those guns and stick close to me. I have a bad feeling about this."

Taly sheathed Zephyr and the yet-to-be-named dagger Skye had gifted her and pulled both of her pistols. "You got it."

"I take it you know how to use those things?" Kit asked with the ghost of a smile.

"Please," Taly replied with a snort. "I can give you a demonstration if you'd like."

"No… no, I believe you." Squaring his shoulders, he turned to each one of the Watchers, catching their eye before giving his order. "Let's move."

They carefully picked their way through the

sea of fragmented corpses. The line of Watchers taking point kicked the still-moving bodies off to the side as the group advanced, and the ground, coated with a thin film of black ooze, felt slick underfoot.

Taly held both pistols at her side, the barrels of the crystal handguns aimed toward the ground. As she followed Kit across the deserted square, tendrils of golden thread began rippling across the pavement, twining between the legs of the men and women surrounding her. Taly blinked, trying to dismiss the vision. The last thing she needed was another explosion of time magic when she was surrounded by shadow mages. But the apparition refused to be ignored, growing in intensity and forcing her eyes up. The market square was now awash in gold, but the glittering magic particles seemed to be concentrating in one area to the south. They clustered together, forming and reforming themselves into something that Taly didn't have the words to describe. It was a colossal mass of chaotically swirling magic, and it was coming right for them.

"K-Kit," Taly stammered softly. "To… to the south."

"What?" Kit asked, his head swiveling around to meet her horrified gaze.

A thundering roar reverberated through the market, completely drowning out the din of the wailing, dismembered dead, and the ground began to tremble beneath their feet.

"To the south!" one of the Watchers called as a hulking beast barreled into the square. Wreckage and debris sprayed into the air as it angrily thrashed about, and a mist of blackened blood stained the surrounding pavement.

This thing—this gruesome fiend—wasn't like the others. Though it might have once been alive, that must have been a *very* long time ago. At least 12 feet tall, its arms and legs were dense amalgamations of striated flesh. Its skin was rotting, stretched so thin it was nearly translucent, and blisters and swollen abscesses covered its bloated body. Countless bony spikes protruded at haphazard angles from its torso, each covered with drips and splatters of tar-like gore.

Except... no.

As the thing lumbered closer, Taly could clearly see that what she had mistaken for spikes were really limbs—arms and legs in varying states of decay that had been randomly planted along the beast's body. And those weren't blisters. They were heads. Some were nothing but skulls with a few remnants of flesh still clinging to the bone, but others looked fresh—recently killed if the crimson blood streaking their cheeks was anything to go by. Their mouths gaped, and Taly suddenly realized that the great wail echoing through the marketplace wasn't a single voice. It was many—a chorus of mournful cries woven together in discordant harmony.

The Gate Watchers were already moving into formation. Flames flared along the blades of swords and daggers, and gusts of wind spiraled out of the tips of wands, lashing at the ground and creating a wall of whirling dust and debris.

Someone grabbed at Taly's arm, pulling her back. "If the human is valuable to House Ghislain, we need to protect her. Get her to safety." Adanna shoved Taly towards Kit. "We'll cover your retreat before we move in."

"Good. I'll join you when I can," Kit said as he

hastily sheathed his sword and dropped to one knee. "Get on," he ordered, turning to look at Taly.

She didn't argue. Holstering her pistols, she wrapped her arms around Kit's neck, tightening her grip when he slung his hands beneath her thighs and lifted her onto his back.

"Hold on tight."

With that short, muttered warning, they were off. The world was a blur, and Taly had to bury her face in Kit's neck when the sting of the wind became too much for her. The sheer force of their momentum was almost enough to make her lose her grip, but she held on, her fingers clutching at the leather strap of his breastplate. Without warning, her stomach lurched, and when she opened her eyes, all she could see was the white marble stone of the compound's wall as they flew through the air. Chancing a glance down, she saw the ground below, the details of the broken carts and shattered bodies blurring as they rose higher and higher.

Kit's boots hit the floor of the ramparts with a heavy thud. As soon as he deposited her on the ground, Taly collapsed against the wall of the parapet, her chest heaving as she desperately tried not to splatter the contents of her stomach across the walkway.

"Shards," she gasped, closing her eyes and turning her face towards the cool breeze drifting over the top of the wall. "How do you shadow mages do that without losing your lunch?"

Kit smiled as he crouched down next to her. "A lot of us do the first few times. I take it you've never run with a highborn shadow mage at full speed?" When Taly shook her head, he laughed and offered her a canteen of water. "Well, I'm honored to have been your first." He gave her a sly wink and a winsome smile.

"Are you flirting with me?" Taly asked as she accepted the canteen and took a long sip.

Kit hung his head. "Maybe. Although, if you have to ask, that means I'm not doing a very good job." When he looked up, his eyes were crinkled with mirth. "Stay here. I need to go take care of that thing out there, but I'll be back soon. Then we can go find your Lord Emrys."

"Thank you," Taly breathed. "And be careful."

Kit gave her another wink as he stood to his full height. "As my lady commands."

With that, he stepped off the edge of the curtain wall. When Taly was able to pull herself to her feet, she could see him sprinting across the market to rejoin the battle. The shadow mages were circling the beast, but it paid them no mind. Instead, it lumbered across the square, its motley collection of limbs grabbing at the mutilated bodies strewn across the ground as it shoved the dead flesh into whichever mouth was nearest.

As Taly tore her eyes away from the sickening sight, someone shoved her to the side. There was more movement around her now as mages streamed in from a set of stairs at the end of the narrow corridor.

"Line up!" a woman called as she marched down the parapet behind the group of mages that were clumsily trying to arrange themselves between the gaps in the wall. Grabbing Taly's arm, she whirled her around. "What are you doing up here... Taly?" The woman's azure eyes widened, and Taly suddenly found herself enfolded in a familiar set of arms.

"Hi Eula," Taly mumbled, returning the

woman's embrace.

"Paravani sora," Eula whispered. "When Skye told me that you were still out there, I thought the worst."

Taly smiled at the old nickname. *Paravani sora* was ancient Faera and roughly translated to *little sister*. Eula had been one of the few Gate Watchers to take an interest in Taly when Ivain let her tag along on his trips to the compound, often inviting Taly to accompany her to the shooting range. If not for Eula, Taly might never have learned how to use a pistol.

"I'm fine. Really," Taly said reassuringly.

Eula raised a perfectly groomed brow, her eyes lingering on the red stain on Taly's hip. Before she could press the matter, Eula's hand flew to her ear, and for the first time, Taly noticed that the Gate Watcher was wearing a scrying comm strapped to her waist.

"Yes," Eula replied tersely into the earpiece, smoothing back a raven lock of hair that had escaped from the braid coiling around her head. "We're not sure, but it's under control. Yes, the search and rescue team have it surrounded. No, sire. I've got her right here. Yes, sire." Eula keyed off her comm before jerking her head, indicating that Taly should follow her. "Come with me."

"What happened here, Eula?" Taly asked as she followed the older fey woman along the battlements.

"Your guess is as good as mine," Eula replied, glancing over her shoulder as they weaved through the crowd of mages lining the walkway. "We've barely had enough time to lick our wounds since this mess started. Skye's arrival was a Shardsend, especially with our chain-of-command in shambles. He may be young, but Ivain trained him well.

"You!" She snatched a young fire mage by the sleeve of his robe, pulling him to his feet. "How many times do I have to tell you?! You're no good if you deplete your supply of aether. Find a shadow mage to help you regenerate your magic."

Eula let out a low growl. "Whelps. Nothing but untrained whelps. Can you believe that?" Eula asked as she stopped on the far side of the battlement. "Almost 200 years old and he still doesn't know how to use his aether efficiently. I'm telling you, I have no idea why these damned noble families nowadays think they're too highbrow to teach their children basic spells. That showy shit is all well and good if you're trying to get laid in Arylaan, but the basics are what keep you alive in a siege. What good are you if you use up your entire supply of aether on *one spell*?!"

Taly jumped when she heard a sharp cry pierce the air. Both Eula's and Taly's heads whipped around to the fight still raging through the market below. The creature had finally turned its attention to the shadow mages, and it looked as though it had managed to catch one of them by the leg. It threw the mage across the battlefield, and the others rushed in to try to keep the beast from charging the wounded soldier.

"Marshal Ora!" Eula snapped her fingers, grabbing the attention of a shadow mage at the opposite end of the wall roughly 20 feet away. The woman was stooped over a table, her hands glowing with shadow magic as she hastily recharged a stack of shadow crystals. The ground around her was littered with crystals centered on pieces of parchment, each surrounded by a faint, violet haze as they pulled aether from the air. "Back them up! They need fresh crystals!"

The shadow mage saluted by crossing an arm over her chest and tapping her fist twice before sweeping the stack of crystals into a bag, stepping off the wall, and darting across the square toward Kit's group.

Eula's eyes followed the shadow mage as she rushed out into the field to join the others. The search and rescue team had managed to herd the beast to the far side of the plaza, and the mages on the ramparts had begun to bombard it with balls of ice and fire, slowly whittling away at its decayed flesh.

Heavy footsteps echoed up the nearby stairs, and Eula turned, crossing her arm over her chest and bowing her head as Skye emerged from around the corner. He had discarded his greatcoat, and his armor was streaked with a thin layer of blackened gore. Smears of crimson blood stained his skin.

"Eula, report. Did the search and rescue team manage to get a handle on that creature yet?" Skye snapped before skidding to an abrupt stop. His brows shot up when he caught sight of Taly.

"Sire," Eula said with a smirk. "Look who I found."

Skye hesitated for a moment, disbelief written across his face. When he remained motionless, seemingly frozen in place, Taly gave him a sheepish wave. The movement seemed to break him from his stupor, and he rushed forward, crossing the distance between them in just a few short strides and enveloping her in a tight embrace. "Thank the Shards!"

Taly didn't hesitate to wrap her arms around

his neck as he lifted her off her feet. After a long moment, he released her, holding her out at arm's length. A frown creased his brow when his eyes flicked down to the gash at her hip. At some point, the wound had reopened, and Taly could feel a trickle of fresh blood running down her leg.

"So, I may have dawdled a little bit," Taly said with a half-hearted laugh, wiping at the tears of relief staining her cheeks. "But it wasn't my fault. These things just won't take 'no' for an answer."

Taly saw the corners of Skye's mouth twitch, but he never got a chance to respond. A shout from down below caught their attention.

"Shards," Eula whispered, her eyes widening in horror.

Taly felt bile at the back of her throat, and she was grateful for the arm Skye had looped around her waist. Her knees felt weak, and she leaned against him, not fully trusting her legs to support her weight as she was forced to watch the nightmare unfolding on the field below.

The monster had become enraged once the shadow mages cornered it, and it gave a feral roar as it whipped its body about, throwing several of the Gate Watchers to the ground. One of its arms, a great giant mass of rotting flesh as thick as a tree trunk, grabbed a mage that was struggling to regain his feet. The creature lifted the Gate Watcher from the ground, and the man let out a shrill scream of pain. Then, bringing its arm back down in a blur of motion, the creature beat the mage's body against the pavement of the square, up and down, over and over again.

A strangled cry erupted from the poor man's throat as his bones were broken and shattered. Violet ripples of shadow magic began coiling in the air around the captured mage as he tried to heal his body, perhaps even bolster his strength as he and his comrades vainly tried to free him from the creature's grip. Giving up, he pulled a dagger from his belt and began hacking away at the leather of his boot, vainly trying to wrench his foot free. But it was no use. The grotesque array of decaying limbs protruding from the monster's distended body groped at the mage's clothing and flesh, drawing him in nearer as it...

"Shards," Taly whimpered. "What is it doing? No, no, no... This can't be happening."

Skye pulled her closer as the creature began to devour its captive.

A heavy silence fell over the rampart when the mage's screams began to echo through the square. Even from here, Taly could see the sprays of warm blood spattering across the other shadow mages as the creature ripped off the man's arms and legs one by one. The mouths of the dead, stolen heads scattered across the monster's body split open, revealing rows upon rows of decayed, broken teeth. With a high-pitched yowl, it began to gnaw on the severed limbs, and bright rivulets of crimson blood dripped down its body as it shoveled fistfuls of muscle, skin, and bone into its gaping, lipless maws.

Taly released a broken sob. The man was still screaming. He was still alive. Skye's grip on her waist bordered on painful at this point, but she didn't care. If she looked up, she knew his face would be painted in the same portrait of stunned shock and horror that adorned the faces of every man and woman witnessing this gruesome scene.

The man's screams abruptly stopped, and Taly's ears rang in the resulting silence.

There was no sound except for the sickening crunch of bones as the beast consumed the last of the shadow mage. The other mages in the square were already backing up, their swords held in front of them.

"I… I don't understand," Eula stammered. "That was Lord Aryn. He was a highborn—that thing shouldn't have been able to overpower him. What is that… *monster*?"

Skye didn't answer. He just shook his head and muttered an unintelligible curse.

As they continued to watch, glowing violet veins of energy flickered to life beneath the beast's waxy skin, and it gave a low groan as its body began to grow. Its skin stretched and tore open, and its arms were already reaching for the corpses of the fallen dead still scattered on the ground. It shoved the putrid flesh into the mouths of its many wailing heads, licking feverishly at the congealed blood that stained the pavement. Sometimes, it would grab a random severed body part off the ground and plunge it into its torso, adding to the gruesome collection of decaying limbs decorating its body. Moments later—be it a head, an arm, or a leg—the new appendage would start thrashing and writhing as the creature continued to feed.

Taly felt Skye start to tremble (or maybe that was her?) as the monster's body grew before their eyes, incorporating more and more dead flesh into its rotted form until it was at least twice the size that it was before.

"It can scale the wall now," Eula whispered. "It's going to come for the compound next."

"Yes," Skye replied, his tone surprisingly even. "Yes, it can. And, it will."

A low growl was carried on the wind as the

creature turned, a lumbering mass of putrefying flesh. Milky eyes swiveled to survey the remaining shadow mages that were now frantically fleeing across the field, their legs a blur as they pushed themselves to go faster.

As a chorus of screams ripped from the throats of a host of dead men rang out, the monster charged. Its massive legs were surprisingly spry, and it quickly began to gain on the line of retreating shadow mages.

Taly turned to Skye, her eyes searching his face as he watched the scene unfolding in the market square. "Tell me you have a plan, Skye. We have to help them!"

"Your orders, sire?" Eula asked, hiding her fear behind a mask of professionalism.

Skye just shook his head, a look of horror in his eyes. His reaction was mirrored by the other mages that lined the walls. "I don't know," he murmured. "I don't know."

CHAPTER 18

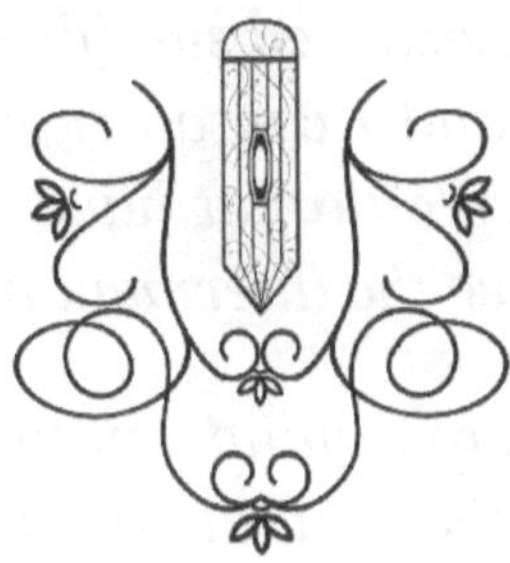

-A letter from High Priestess Melinoe of the Faerasanaa to Prior Keris of the Gravis Somni

The 30th day of the month Ares, during the 35,652nd year of our Lady Raine

Prior Keris,

While I understand that you are very busy tending to the dreamers, I cannot stress how important it is that we all work together to overcome this tragedy. The death of Lord Draco Arrhichion has presented an unusual problem. It has been so long since a member of the highborn court has suffered the final death that we find ourselves unprepared to perform the proper funeral rites. Since the Gravis Somni have traditionally overseen the final interment, I believe that they are the ones that must now be called upon to organize the Night of Lamentation and the burial.

The priestesses of the Faerasanaa have already gone far beyond what is required of them by consecrating the body and arranging for the offerings. The death of a highborn, as well as a shadow mage, has caused significant unrest, and it is all my sisters and I can do right now to quell a city-wide panic. We do not have the time nor the capacity to oversee the interment process.

I should not have to remind you that it is your duty to serve not only the fey that have chosen to take the long sleep but also the dead. I am sending Sister Corienna to act as a liaison. She is a Master Sage regarding the philosophy of Moriah and life behind the veil, so please direct any questions you may have to her. If possible, I would like to start the mourning procession no later than the end of the week. The sooner we can start the funerary rites, the sooner the people will be able to move past this misfortune.

May the Shards bless you,

Lady Khanna Melinoe of House Agno, High Priestess of the Faerasanaa

With a deafening roar, the abomination charged at the retreating line of shadow mages. The piercing wail carried across the square, finally breaking the fey on the wall out of their stupor. With a clamor, they all moved at once, stupefied bewilderment replaced with unmitigated panic.

The death of a highborn, a shadow mage no

less, was unthinkable—a testament to the mortality of an otherwise immortal race. Screams rang out as the fey rushed for the stairwells. Their bodies pressed together, and Taly would've been knocked off her feet, maybe even off the side of the wall, if Skye hadn't kept a firm grip on her waist. He was a steadfast island in the midst of a churning sea of bodies, and Taly had no choice but to cling to him.

"Back to your posts!" Skye roared, his voice carrying over the cacophony of screams and shouts. When that didn't stop the terror-stricken chaos, he reached down and pulled one of Taly's pistols. Three shots rang out, startling the fleeing mages into silence. "I said, back to your posts," he repeated in a harsh tone that Taly had never heard from him before. His face was hard, and his mouth pressed into a grim line. "We will not leave our people out there to die."

"You heard him!" Eula ordered, stomping her boot. The aether-infused blow caused the stone of the rampart to tremble underfoot. "Get moving!"

Taly recognized most of the terror-stricken, tear-stained faces filing past them. She had seen each one of them at one time or another during her many trips to the Gate Watchers' compound with Ivain and Skye. These weren't soldiers. They were scholars and scientists, and she'd be willing to bet that most of them had never seen combat before—much less the final death of another fey. Eula shared a look with Skye before turning on her heel and disappearing into the crowd of mages trying to line up along the wall.

"Taly," Skye said gently, grabbing her by the shoulders, "there's nothing you can do here. I need you to get inside the keep. Go inside Ivain's old room and barricade the door. No matter what you hear outside, don't come out."

"What do you mean?" Taly asked incredulously. "I'm not going to leave you."

"You don't have any magic, and that thing out there is killing trained shadow mages," Skye insisted. When he saw the rebellion in her eyes, he placed a gentle hand on her face. "Please, Taly. I can't lose you. I just... *can't*."

With that, he turned Taly around and pushed her towards the stairs before retreating further down the rampart, bracing himself on the ledge of the walkway as he prepared to leap over the wall.

Rushing forward, Taly grabbed Skye's arm and gave him a sharp tug. "What the hell do you think you're doing?"

"What does it look like I'm doing?" he sputtered as he stumbled back. "They need backup."

Taly punched him on the shoulder. "So you're going to hole me up in Ivain's bedroom while you go out there half-cocked without a plan? Was one shadow mage dying gruesomely not enough for you? You need a strategy to take that thing down."

Skye looked like he was going to argue, so Taly tried again. "Just stop and think about this for a minute, Skye. This creature is as fast as you, as strong as you, and more resilient. How are you supposed to kill something like that?"

"Damn it, you're right," Skye growled in frustration as he raked a hand through his hair. "It has to have a weakness. Everything has weaknesses—even shadow mages."

Taly's eyes drifted back out to the battlefield. "What about the crystals?" she asked after a moment. "The creatures I encountered had crystals. I'd bet good coin that this one does too."

Skye turned to look at her, confusion written on his face. "What are you talking about? What crystals?"

A light drizzle had started to fall, and Taly wiped at the droplets accumulating on her cheeks. "You seriously didn't see the bright, flashing shadow crystals embedded in these things' chests?"

"I was a little busy," Skye replied dryly. "How did you… no, never mind. I don't want to know right now. Still, a shadow crystal would suggest that this thing is being powered by shadow magic. If that's the case—"

"Then taking out the crystal should take out the creature," Taly concluded. They both moved to stand by the edge of the rampart, gazing down at the battle unfolding below. The shadow mages had scattered, and the creature had broken off to chase a group that skirted along the edge of the square. The beast's footsteps created great plumes of mud, dirt, and debris in its wake as it charged after them blindly.

"It's a decoy," Skye muttered, running a hand along his chin. "They're trying to cover the rest of the team's escape." He leaned against the rampart, his eyes narrowed. "I don't see a crystal, though."

The thud of boots sounded from the opposite end of the wall walk. The first group of shadow mages had made it back to the rampart. They were panting and wheezing. Some bent over at the waist while others sunk to the ground, their shoulders trembling beneath their cloaks and armor.

"You there," Skye snapped at a young girl as

she passed. Her bright, highborn eyes widened in surprise, and she ducked her head. "The shadow mages that just got back—take them to the earth mages and see that they get priority. I need them back on their feet and ready to fight immediately."

"Sire." The girl bobbed her head before taking off at a jog, pushing people out of the way as she tried to navigate the walkway.

"How close would you need to be to be able to sense the crystal?" Taly asked when Skye turned back to face her.

"Maybe twenty feet," he replied with a frown.

Taly swallowed against the lump in her throat. That was too close for her liking. "Can any of the other shadow mages do better?"

"No." Skye crossed his arms. "If Ivain, or Commander Enix, or his Precept were here—they could sense the crystal at 30 feet. Maybe 40. But they're not here. I'm the best option."

"I was afraid you were going to say that," Taly muttered. Even though Skye was several centuries younger than the average Gate Watcher, he was strong. Some of the most powerful shadow mages in all of fey history had been born to House Ghislain.

Skye placed a comforting hand on her shoulder, but she shook him off. She didn't want his comfort. She wanted a plan. The cloudy sky paired with the setting sun made the evening unusually dark, and she had to squint to get a better look at the creature raging through the courtyard. "The crystal is probably buried somewhere inside its body. If you have the mages on the wall focus their fire, they could whittle it down so someone can move in and destroy the crystal."

"Except that the fire and ice spells aren't working anymore. Look." Skye handed Taly a small telescope, and it didn't take her long to see exactly what he meant. The mages on the wall were still firing at the creature, but the spells did nothing. Each blast carved away its flesh, only for the skin and bone to knit itself back together in a matter of seconds. The beast didn't even acknowledge the salvo of offensive magic as it continued to charge after the remaining shadow mages.

"Shit," Skye cursed softly, watching one of the decoys stumble. "They're not going to hold out for much longer."

Taly glanced up at Skye before following his gaze. He was right—they were already starting to lag. In fact, the only reason the beast hadn't caught them yet was because they had started skirting along the edges of the square where the layer of scattered debris was densest. The beast, though fast, was far from nimble, and had a harder time pursuing them through the sea of splintered wood.

"You need more firepower," Taly stated decisively. "Something more concentrated than your basic fire or ice spell."

Skye looked thoughtful for a moment, his brow creasing as his eyes scanned the rampart. The mages, a motley collection of Gate Watchers and civilians, had managed to form a sloppy line along the wall. Eula marched behind them, barking orders. "I've got it," he finally said. "Follow me."

Skye took off at a jog, pulling Taly along as he shoved his way through the crowd until they came to one of the crystalline towers overlooking the compound's gate. Tables were set up along the walls of the turret, and mages huddled over the workbenches, some charging crystals and others mixing herbs and salves to help heal the wounded.

Weaving in between the flurry of people darting to-and-fro in the confines of the cramped tower room, Skye dragged her over to a narrow set of stairs set into the corner. When they stepped out onto the tower roof, Taly's head swam, and she had to lean against the balustrade.

"You okay?" Skye asked, placing a hand on her elbow.

Taly nodded. "Yeah—made the mistake of looking down."

Skye glanced over the side of the tower, completely unfazed by the steep 60-foot drop. "I never thought you'd be the type to be afraid of heights," he said, giving her a subtle smirk as he pulled her away from the edge.

"I'm not," Taly retorted. "I just have a healthy respect for things that could kill me instantaneously."

"Well, that is a new but not unwelcome development," Skye said with a chuckle as he approached a large, cloth-covered lump that took up most of the space on the rooftop platform. "Back to the matter at hand, though. You think this will solve our problem?" Skye asked as he pulled off the giant tarp.

Taly felt her breath catch. "Shards," she breathed. "Lift me up." Cupping his hands, Skye boosted her onto the raised platform.

Her eyes wide, Taly ran a hand along the shiny metal barrel of the aged tower gun. It was a great, massive thing, pure viridian and mounted onto a rotating platform that provided a full circular range of motion. Originally based on something the humans called a minigun, this was one of the few mortal firearms that the fey crafters had seen fit to convert and optimize for use with crystal firing mechanisms. Even then, the weapon hadn't really caught on until one shadow mage decided to integrate another human invention—the laser. The result of this single moment of brilliance was what was generally heralded as one of the deadliest ranged weapons known throughout all the fey realms.

"I didn't know the Gate Watchers' compound had flash cannons," Taly murmured. If there wasn't a raging, undead nightmare pillaging the streets below, she could've spent hours studying the weapon. She'd certainly spent far longer than that poring through books and diagrams detailing the crystal circuitry with Ivain. "Why aren't these online?"

Skye bunched up the sheet and threw it to the side. "Two reasons. One—most shadow mages don't know a damned thing about guns. And two—these guns haven't been used since before the Schism. This compound used to be one of the Time Queen's palaces, but it was militarized when the Dawn Court first pried open the Seren Gate after the forced shutdown caused the bridges to collapse. The crystal circuits in the flash cannons require a lot of upkeep, and once the bulk of the fighting stopped, there was no reason to commit the necessary resources to maintain them."

"That's a damned shame," Taly whispered reverently. Her footsteps echoed as she moved about the hollow, metal platform, checking the various toggles and switches on the control panel. She frowned when the machine gave a sad whine, the lights along the barrel flickering before being immediately extinguished. "Oh, my poor, beautiful baby. What did those mean ol' shadow mages do to you?"

"Do I need to leave the two of you alone?" Skye asked, arching a sly brow.

"Any other time, I would say yes." Giving Skye a wink, she jumped off the platform and dropped to her knees. The cover on the side paneling had rusted shut, so she pounded it with her fist until she was able to pry it loose. A tangled web of wiring tumbled out, but she pushed it aside. Skye crouched next to her, holding up a lantern as she stuck her head inside the small opening.

"This one is loaded with ice," she said when she saw the glint of three massive water crystals set into the framework. "But the shadow crystals are missing. The connections to the ammunition chamber are still intact, but someone tried to rewire the firing mechanism at some point. They didn't close the circuit."

"Well, Tinker… it's time for you to live up to your name. If I keep that thing distracted, do you think you can fix this?"

When Taly pulled her head out, she wasn't expecting Skye to be hunched over, peering into the control panel. She felt her cheeks warm when her nose bumped his. "Um…" she stammered. "Yes. The primary circuit for the firing mechanism is the same as the one I designed for my pistols. It'll take too long to set a new shadow crystal into the power conduit and repair the aethostats, but I think I can jerry-rig something if you get me some tools and a shadow mage. Give me ten minutes, and I'll rain icy hellfire down on that thing."

Skye nodded. "If we get the gun up and

running, it might be able to punch a hole in that creature faster than it can heal itself. Then if we get all the mages to hit it at once…" A slow smile drifted across his face, and before Taly could react, he had tangled a hand in her hair and pressed a kiss to her forehead. "I'm counting on you, Tink. I know you won't let me down."

Skye pulled back and gave her a wide grin before he pushed himself to his feet and disappeared down the darkened stairwell. He returned a few moments later with a bag of tools. Setting the toolkit beside her, he helped her remove her pack, throwing it off to the side as she lay on her stomach and pulled the top half of her body into the narrow compartment below the tower gun.

"Here," he said, hooking a comm to her belt and handing her the earpiece. "Let me know when you have the gun up and running. I'm going to have the mages on the wall hold off until then."

"Got it. And Em?" Taly pulled back a moment and caught his eye before he managed to move away. "Be careful. If you die, I'll never forgive you."

Skye chuckled, his eyes crinkling with mirth despite the seriousness of the situation. There was something in his expression, something she didn't have a name for. It made her heart clench and her stomach flip. "I'll keep that in mind," he replied quietly. He opened his mouth to say something else but thought better of it, shaking his head as he stood. Giving her one last smile, he turned on his heel and returned to the battle outside.

Skye's voice filtered in over the comm, a familiar sound among a haze of static. Moments later, the blasts of fire and ice magic began to taper off. The comparative silence that followed felt heavy and tense, and Taly could now hear the beast's screams from the square below. There was a flurry of movement as the mages in the tower room below rushed about, their thundering footsteps echoing up from the stairwell, no doubt scrambling back to the rampart to follow Skye's orders. Taly paid them no mind. Instead, she set to work, pulling herself further into the cramped crawlspace below the tower gun platform, ripping out old wires and trying to reform the connection that would feed aether into the firing mechanism.

There were more voices on the comm now. From what she could tell, Skye had finally joined the battle. The mages that had been keeping the beast at bay were ordered back to the wall, and Skye and his team began distracting the creature, keeping it busy until Taly could back them up with more firepower.

Taly's heart fluttered in her chest, and she had to tamp down on the wave of panic that threatened to overwhelm her. She wasn't having any luck with the firing mechanism. Whoever had tried to repair the gun had stripped the wiring, and moisture had seeped in over time, rusting out the conductive material. If she tried to power up the gun as is, it would probably blow up in her face.

"Think, think, think," Taly muttered, fiddling with a socket that used to hold a shadow crystal. There had to be a way to fix this.

"Taly?"

Taly jumped, banging the back of her head on the edge of the frame. "Ow," she groaned, rubbing at the rapidly swelling lump. The pain, though intense, quickly receded.

Opening her eyes, she saw Kit's sheepish face peering at her through the opening of the control panel. His hair was damp and clung to his forehead, and there was a thin, jagged line marring his cheek. The skin around the half-healed wound was swollen and red, standing out in stark contrast to his otherwise boyish features. "You know, Kit… thirty seconds ago I would've been glad to see you. Now, I'm not so sure."

Kit chuckled, his lips quirking to the side. Even after coming face-to-face with a living nightmare and witnessing the death of a comrade, he could still smile. "You're not the first woman to say that." His face grew serious as the boy melted away and the Gate Watcher stepped in to take his place. "Lord Emrys sent me to assist you. I'm *yours* to command."

Turning back to the control panel, Taly smirked. "You sure you're okay being bossed around by a human?"

Taly felt Kit shift beside her as he dropped to his knees and grabbed the lantern from her hand. "It's funny, but for some reason, I don't find the idea quite as painful as I would've when I woke up this morning. But then again, I've never had a problem taking orders from a beautiful woman—human or otherwise."

"Seriously?" Taly barked out a laugh. "You know, Kit… I'm starting to think the only criteria for making it into your bed is having two legs."

"Well, there are a few other requirements. But you wouldn't be the first woman to accuse me of that," came his reply. Though she couldn't see his face, she could hear the smile in his voice.

The voices of Skye and his team still filtered through over the comm. The creature had deviated from the path they had laid out, but they were starting to bring it back around, circling closer and closer to the wall.

"Okay, Kit. Unless you have a sophisticated working knowledge of firearm-crystal circuits, I need you to shut up and let me think," Taly snapped, staring at the wiring.

"As my lady commands."

Think, Caro. You need to see this from another angle.

Ivain's words from long ago came to her mind unbidden: *If you can only see one way to accomplish a task, little one, then odds are you're not doing it right. No one was ever remembered for doing something the same as everyone else.*

She wasn't going to be able to repair the circuit for the firing mechanism. That was out. *But maybe... Yes! That just might work.* If she could split the aether flow that fed into the ammunition's aether-transformation circuit, she might be able to bring the firing mechanism back online if she got Kit to overcharge the circuit with aether. Without the proper aethostats, the gun would probably still overheat, but she just might be able to eke out a few minutes of steady fire.

Quickly finishing the repair, Taly pushed herself out of the casing and grabbed Kit's arm. "Okay, aether battery—"

"Wait... what?" Kit asked sharply. "What the hell is an aether battery?"

Taly's lips quirked. Apparently, Kit's education hadn't included mortal science. "It's not important. Just be a good aether battery and put your finger here."

Positioning his hands inside the socket for the shadow crystals, she said, "Now push aether into the circuit." Kit's hands began to glow, and Taly couldn't stop the loud, excited squeal that ripped from her throat when she saw the arrow on the power gauge start to move. "Good. We're going to need more than that. I need the arrow to stay here." She pointed to a position on the gauge. "If your hands start to feel hot, don't worry. I'm expecting that. And if the wiring sparks, don't worry about that either."

"Is it supposed to spark?" Kit asked dubiously, his eyes following her as she hoisted herself back onto the platform and started pulling at various levers on the console.

"No," Taly said distractedly. Lights flickered to life across the barrel of the gun, and the platform began to vibrate and hum as the old tower gun powered up for the first time in over two centuries. "But I fully expect this thing to blow up."

"Excuse me?"

Taly wiped at the scope with an old cloth. "Don't worry. Sparks are fine. When it catches on fire, that's when we have a problem."

She heard Kit grumbling in the background, but she paid him no mind. Her eyes were trained on the battle still raging down below. From the top of the tower, she could see Skye and the other shadow mages racing toward the wall, the creature not far behind. They would occasionally switch off, taking turns as they pulled the rampaging beast closer to the compound walls. Eula was next up, running a blade across her palm as the other mages in her team manifested their aether in bright, violet clouds of magic.

The haze of magic around Skye's team abruptly extinguished, and the beast stopped, lifting itself up, almost like it was sniffing the wind. Its grotesque heads swiveled as it trained its attention on Eula and her team, changing course and barreling toward the mages.

It's drawn to their aether. Just like the other magical creatures on the island that went wild from their unquenchable thirst for magic.

Once they had its attention, Eula's team lashed at the monster's body with long whips of water drawn from the tips of wands. The magical attack wasn't nearly enough to hurt the beast, but it did enrage it, kept its attention from wavering.

"Skye," Taly said into the comm. "I've got the gun online. Did you find the crystal?"

There was a screech of static, and then Skye's voice drifted into her ear. He was breathing heavily, and his tone was clipped. "I did. It's dead center—somewhere deep in its chest."

"Of course, it is," Taly muttered. She didn't know how it was even possible, but the monstrous creature had become even more massive as the battle raged on. It had grown at least two or three feet since the unfortunate death of Lord Aryn, and it was still grabbing at the bloodied stumps of dismembered arms and legs scattered across the ground, incorporating them into its body as ripples of shadow magic coiled around its form.

"We're going to have to work fast then," Taly said, holding a hand up to her ear. "I'm only going to have a few minutes of focused fire with this thing."

"Don't worry. I'll make it count," came Skye's curt reply. "Ora, are the earth mages in position?"

"Yes, sire," an unfamiliar female voice replied in Taly's ear.

Taly started turning the crank, rotating the gun around as she took aim at the monster.

"Wait!" Kit kicked at the platform to get her

attention. "Who's going to fire this thing?"

Taly glanced at him, her nose crinkling in irritation. "I am. You think I went to the trouble of repairing this piece of junk just to let someone else do the fun part?"

"But, you're human! You'll break—"

Taly shushed him harshly. "Aether batteries should be seen and not heard."

"But—"

"Don't worry," Taly snapped. "I'm tougher than I look."

Skye's team began to manifest their aether, once more attempting to draw the attention of the beast as they sprinted towards the compound, a trail of mud and rock and magic flying into the air behind them. The creature thrashed angrily, its multitude of heads turning from side-to-side in confusion as the scent of aether changed course. Releasing an enraged howl, it dropped to the ground, propelling itself forward on a legion of stolen, decaying limbs.

"Earth mages! At my signal!" Skye screamed over the comm, his breaths coming in heavy gasps. "Now!"

Even from the top of the tower, Taly could feel the ground start to tremble, a low rumble echoing through the air as the pavement below cracked and splintered. Moments later, a mass of vines erupted from beneath the surface of the square. Their leafy tendrils tangled together, lashing and coiling around the beast's hulking body. Some of its arms and legs were ripped away when the rapidly thickening stems found purchase, sending sprays of blackened blood and gore flying into the air. But others held tight, and soon, the creature fell to the ground, wrapped in a spiraling vice of earth magic.

It struggled, screaming furiously as it writhed and thrashed. Some of the vines had already begun to snap, sending sharp whip-like cracks ringing out over the din of battle. Managing to free some of its limbs, the monster started to claw at the ground, slowly edging its way forward and leaving a trail of oozing tar-like fluid streaked across the cracked stone.

"Mages, ready your fire," came Skye's voice over the comm. A tingle swept across Taly's skin as the mages on the wall began casting. From where she stood, she could see great whorls of fire forming in the air, and a low rumble drifted on the wind as the water mages created shards of ice that glistened in the waning sunlight.

Turning her attention back to the field, Taly started the warm-up sequence on the gun. A cloud of water magic, hazy and faint at first but rapidly growing in intensity, accumulated around the barrel as the water crystals engaged, transforming the massive amounts of aether Kit was feeding into the circuits below into water aether.

Skye's voice was once again in her ear. "Cannons—ready? Aim!"

Taly stared down the sight, bracing herself. Flash cannons had never been optimized for human use, so this thing was going to have a pretty good kick.

With a keening wail, the creature bucked, and more vines snapped and withered.

"Fire!"

The gun shuddered and gave a low whine as the cloud of water aether shivered and condensed. Taly's heart leapt into her throat. For a moment, she thought it wasn't going to work. But then, the gun gave a sharp kick, and a ray of molten, blue energy shot out of the barrel, slicing through the air. The icy beam cut into the beast's hulking form, sending up a cloud of smoke as its flesh froze and shattered. Taly groaned under the weight of the gun, but somehow, she managed to keep it steady. She smiled when she saw a hole open in the beast's side, the edges clean and precise.

"It's working!" Eula cried.

"Mages," Skye snapped. "Aim for the hole. On my mark!"

The creature paused in its struggle, its body falling to the ground as the icy ray of water magic pierced its chest.

"Now!" came Skye's clipped command.

A hailstorm of fire and ice rained down from the sky. Though Taly could no longer see the creature behind the glow of magic, she kept her aim steady. Her arms ached, and her hands went numb, but she held on, throwing her weight against the gun to keep from losing her footing.

"We've got sparks," Kit shouted from below, poking his head over the platform.

Taly's eyes flicked to the console gauges when the beam of energy started to dim. "Give me more power!" She heard Kit mutter a curse, but moments later the aether output stabilized.

A plume of smoke rose from the square below, and blazing streaks of magic continued to rain down from above like shooting stars.

"We've got fire!" Kit screamed, panic in his voice. "There's fire now! You said that was bad!"

"Just a little longer!" Taly shouted back.

"That's it!" Skye's voice said over the comm. "I see the crystal! Cease fire! I'm going in!"

Through the haze, Taly could see Skye reach

into his pocket, pulling out a cluster of shadow crystals. The air around him began to glow as he drained the aether from the crystals, each one dropping to the ground as the light within was extinguished. He kept reaching into his pocket, draining crystal after crystal until a brilliant blaze of shadow magic completely enveloped his form, wispy tendrils of smoke lashing at the air around him.

His head turned, his attention momentarily diverted. Time seemed to slow as his eyes scanned the top of the tower, searching for her. Although she could barely make out his face at this distance, she knew that he could see her clearly.

Turning back to the monster, Skye took a single step toward the creature, his body tensing as he rushed forward. He almost seemed to blink out of existence as he charged the beast, traveling at a speed that Taly's human eyes couldn't follow.

A set of arms grabbed Taly around the waist, roughly pulling her off the platform. She let out a sharp cry as she was thrown on the ground, going still when Kit covered her body with his own just seconds before an explosion rocked the tower.

Taly could feel Kit's harsh breathing fanning out across the skin of her neck as he pressed her into the ground. Lifting a trembling hand to her ear, she listened for voices. All she got was static.

As panic set in, she pushed at Kit's shoulder. "Skye… what happened to Skye?" Wriggling out from underneath the exhausted shadow mage, Taly scrambled to her feet. Thankfully, the explosion had been relatively minor, and only the immediate area around the tower gun had been scorched. Though the wiring underneath the platform was still on fire, it was already burning itself out.

There was no movement in the square below. The shadow mages watched the area where the beast had thrashed about just moments before with wary eyes, massive girders and beams held in their hands as they tried to decide whether to attack or retreat. A heavy silence fell over the fey still crowding the wall as they all waited.

Taly leaned against the edge of the tower balustrade for support. Her heart pounded in her ears, and she grasped at the stone ledge until her knuckles turned white. Kit came up behind her, placing a comforting hand on her shoulder.

"Lord Emrys?" Eula's voice cut through the static on the comm. "Skye, report. Are you okay?"

Taly clasped her hands in front of her. "Please, please, please," she prayed silently as Kit's grip on her shoulder tightened.

Something moved in the cloud of smoke, and the circle of shadow mages took a step back. As the wind picked up, blowing at the debris and dust that hung in the air, a silhouette began to emerge, the edges of his slender form sharpening as the breeze cleared away the last of the fog.

Taly's shoulders shook, and she wasn't sure if she was laughing or sobbing. "Skye," she breathed, covering her mouth with her hands. "Thank the Shards."

Even from the tower roof, Taly could see Skye's chest rising and falling as he gasped for air. He stood over the unmoving creature, his armor and skin covered with gore, violet flames of shadow magic still lapping at his skin. His sword protruded from the beast's charred flesh. Though his arm hung limply at his side and fresh rivulets of blood now streaked his sleeve, Skye clutched at a single shadow crystal, torn from the gaping hole carved into the side of the beast.

"Holy shit, he did it," Kit whispered from beside her. "He actually did it."

Skye moved to take a step, but he stumbled, the crystal dropping from his hand. The other mages rushed forward, grabbing at him before he could fall to his knees. Propping him up, they had to half-carry him off the battlefield.

Taly turned to look up at Kit with wide eyes. "Skye's hurt. I thought shadow mages couldn't get hurt when they're channeling that much aether. What's wrong with him, Kit?"

Kit wrapped his arms around Taly, pulling her closer when her shoulders started to shake. "I don't know. But I promised to deliver you to your Lord Emrys, and that's what I intend to do." Pulling away, he forced her chin up and looked her in the eye. "Let's go find him."

CHAPTER 19

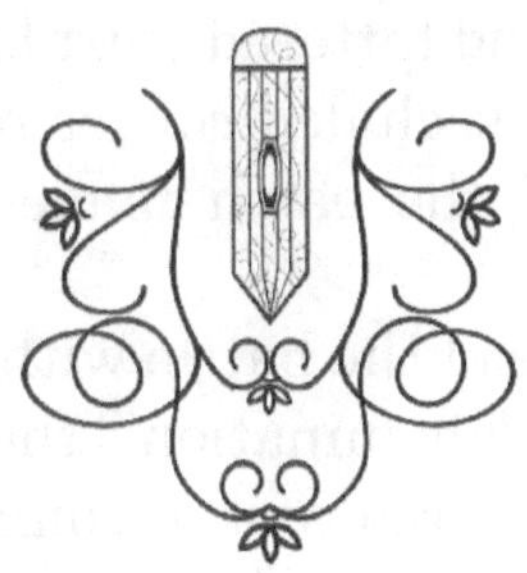

-An excerpt from the Moonfall Morning Post

After a long day of spellcasting, does aether burnout get you down? Try Farris' Flavored Faeflower! With five delicious flavors, you won't even know it's medicine!

Hear from our many satisfied customers:

- *Still tastes like barghest vomit, but with apples.*
- *Slightly less disgusting than regular faeflower.*
- *Goes great with a shot of whiskey... if you drink the whiskey first.*

Try Farris' Flavored Faeflower today! We promise you'll only regret it a little.

"Ow! Fuck!" Skye yelped. A long string of muttered curses fell from his lips as he felt the waves of earth magic lapping at his skin, knitting his broken and battered body back together. His stained armor and tattered shirt lay off to the side, and he sat in a secluded corner of the courtyard, allowing one of the earth mages to tend to his wounds.

In the wake of the battle with what they were now calling the "abomination," the shadow mages' outdoor crafting area at the compound had been turned into a makeshift infirmary. A babel of pained cries filled the air, almost drowning out the steady patter of heavy rain striking the metal awning that sheltered the wounded.

Most of the injured fey sat quietly, their eyes closed in meditation. The fey's natural ability to heal was directly related to how much aether saturated their blood, and nearly every mage in the keep had thoroughly drained their magic over the course of the past day. An assortment of fading bruises and half-healed lacerations marred the immortal bodies scattered throughout the courtyard, their injuries slowly fading as they focused their will on increasing their body's natural rate of aether absorption.

The mortals and weaker lowborn fey, those that couldn't take in enough aether to heal their wounds, were not so lucky. They lay prostrate on the ground, their faces and bodies contorted in agony. The menders, though they could do little more than offer simple first-aid, cleaned and bandaged wounds, offering comfort where it was needed.

Skye let out another low groan as he felt something in his shoulder snap back into place.

"Hold still," the willowy earth mage reprimanded.

The severe woman pushed back a tendril of silvery hair from her face, and she rubbed at her eyes tiredly, the movement pulling at her almost translucent skin. When she looked at him again, Skye felt an uncomfortable shiver run down his spine. The members of House Agno had the most disconcerting eyes he had ever seen. When he wasn't channeling aether, he couldn't distinguish the subtle ring of her pupils from the inky black of her irises, making her eyes seem almost like a bottomless, fathomless void.

"I should be scolding you," she said, her voice full of reproach. Her pale, bloodless lips lifted into a peculiar smile that seemed out-of-place on her smooth complexion. "Using that much aether at one time is stupid, even for a member of House Ghislain. You're lucky you didn't kill yourself." She gave his arm a rough tug as she realigned the joint, paying no mind to Skye's sharp cry of pain.

"Damn it," he hissed. "Could you be a little gentler?! I did just take out some sort of half-dead abomination."

This earned him a skeptical look from the woman. "Technically true, but it doesn't change the fact that you're lucky to be alive. Yes—you succeeded. But your plan was still spectacularly stupid."

Not bothering to wait for his response, the woman checked the bandages wrapped around his shoulder and bicep. "I don't want you channeling aether for the rest of the day. If you need to restore your aether reserves, do what the rest of us do—

meditate and wait for your magic to regenerate naturally. Also, drink this," she said, handing him a cup. "It's faeflower."

Skye took the cup and downed the medicinal draught in one gulp, suppressing a shudder at the taste. Almost immediately, the dull burn in his lungs, a testament to just how little aether he had left, started to abate. "After so many millennia of drinking faeflower for aether burnout, you'd think someone would've found a way to make it taste better."

The healer puffed out a snort as she washed her bloodied hands in a quenching tank. "I have other patients to attend to," she said, ignoring Skye's complaint. "I'll be back to check on you. Sit here and rest—don't move."

"Yeah, yeah."

Skye pulled on his shirt before leaning back, his eyes following the lithe highborn woman as she weaved through the crowd, occasionally bending down to check on one of the wounded.

Meditate. How long had it been since he'd had to meditate?

Closing his eyes, Skye took a deep breath. Every mage, no matter their school of magic, learned to manipulate their aether regeneration through meditation. It was an essential skill, just not one he'd chosen to use in a very long time. After all, why would he need to sit quietly in a corner for hours on end when he could just take raw aether from the air and push it directly into his blood?

Just when he had almost managed to clear his mind, a familiar scent tickled his nose. Even without his magic, he'd recognize her anywhere—Taly.

When he opened his eyes, she was much closer than he would've guessed, but that wasn't surprising. His senses were annoyingly dull at the moment. Already halfway across the courtyard, her worried gaze scanned the faces of the wounded as she searched for him.

"Psst... Tink!" he said when she got close enough to hear him.

Her head whipped around, and when her eyes found his, Skye decided that if he died tomorrow, he wanted that smile to be the last thing he remembered. It made the air around her seem just a little bit lighter, and he could feel the warm glow of her joy and relief slowly seep into him, chasing away the cold.

She rushed towards him, gracefully sidestepping the bodies of the wounded, and by the time she made it to his side, her eyes were red and glassy. "Stupid idiot!" she cried, throwing herself onto the bench and wrapping her arms around his neck. "Arrogant highborn jerk..."

"Hey now," Skye said as he readily returned her embrace. "Is that any way to talk to an injured man?"

Pulling away, she gave him an irritated glare, the severity of which was belied by the tears welling in her eyes. "It's a term of endearment at this point."

"Is that so?" Skye huffed good-naturedly, reaching up to give the end of her disheveled braid a gentle tug. "If that's the case, then your pillow talk really needs work. Don't worry. I'm here to help, and I'm willing to go all night if need be."

"Shards, you're an idiot." She raised a fist to give him a sharp punch on the arm but thought better of it when she saw the bandages peeking out from underneath his shirt. "I thought you were really hurt, but you're fine."

Her fingers traced the edge of one of the strips of linen wrapped around his shoulder. After a long pause, she shrugged and gave him a teary smile. "Although, it's too bad coming face-to-face with whatever that thing was didn't do anything to improve your sense of humor."

Skye let his head fall back against the wall with a thud. "Low blow, Tink. Low blow... You know, you should be nicer to me. After all, I think I'm owed a few 'oohs' and 'ahhs' from my favorite mortal right about now. Those were some impressive feats of strength out there. Some people might even consider me a hero." He lapsed into silence, staring at her expectantly.

Unable to punch him, she flicked his ear, knowing full well that fey ears tended to be more sensitive than her own human ears. When Skye winced, she gave him a satisfied smile.

"Fine. *Ooooh... ahhhhh...*" she conceded with a pained sigh.

Skye grinned despite the physical and mental fatigue that had permeated every cell and fiber of his body. Had it really only been yesterday when he'd laid down his *conditions* for bringing her along? That already seemed like a lifetime ago.

"Thank you," he said a little too sincerely. "You know, when people eventually ask me why I did it, I'll tell them it was for the little people." Even though she was sitting next to him, he held a hand over her head, pretending to measure her height compared to his. "That's you by the way."

Taly slapped his hand away, suppressing an exasperated chuckle. "Seriously, though, are you okay? Why haven't you healed yet?"

Skye tucked a stray piece of hair behind her ear, doing his best to give her a reassuring smile despite the pain the movement triggered. "I'm fine. It's just a little aether burnout."

"Aether burnout?"

"It's..." Skye paused as he tried to think of a way to explain it. "It's like spraining a muscle. I channeled too much aether all at once, so now I need to take it easy—let my magic recover."

Taly released a shuddering sigh, and Skye used the pad of his thumb to wipe away a stray tear. "Tink, I'll be fine after a hot meal and a good night's rest. And you say I worry too much."

Taly shook her head vehemently as she reached up and grasped the hand at her face. "No... I'm just really relieved. For a minute, I thought... when I saw you fall—"

"Taly!" a voice rang out.

His eyes scanned the courtyard for the source of the sound, and Skye grimaced when he saw a familiar brassy-haired mage duck underneath the awning. What was *he* doing here?

"Kit!" Taly waved, drawing the man's attention. "Skye, that's Kit," she said excitedly. "He helped me repair the tower gun."

"Interesting." Skye watched the man approach and found himself sitting up just a little straighter. "And he said his name was *Kit*? K-I-T?"

"Yeah. Is something wrong?" Taly asked when she saw the look of confusion on his face.

Skye shook his head. He would deal with this unexpected *situation* when Taly wasn't around.

"Shards, Taly," Kit said when he was close enough. His hair, wet from the rain, clung to his forehead, and Skye couldn't remember ever seeing the usually put-together noble look so out-of-sorts.

"For a little thing, you're fast."

"Hello, *Kit*," Skye greeted icily. "Taly tells me that I have you to thank for getting the tower gun powered up."

Seeming to notice him for the first time, Kit raised an eyebrow, smirking as he bowed mockingly. "Truthfully, I didn't do much, milord. I am but a humble aether battery." Catching Taly's eye, Kit gave her a subtle wink, eliciting a soft snicker from the girl at the apparent inside joke.

"I see," Skye replied, his jaw clenching.

Taly, oblivious to the tension between the two men, glanced at Skye. "Kit says that he's also from House Ghislain. A cousin, right?" she asked, turning back to Kit.

"That is correct, Taly," Kit replied warmly. An almost genuine smile curved his lips, one that Taly returned.

Placing a possessive arm around Taly's waist, Skye couldn't suppress the cocky grin on his face when he saw the other man's eyes narrow. "You'll have to forgive me. I have so many *cousins*; it's sometimes hard to match the name to the face."

"Our family is quite large," Kit replied with false civility. "But if you're already having trouble remembering things at your age, then you're going to have a real problem in a few *centuries*. You probably won't remember half the people you meet."

A tense silence settled over the two men as they stared each other down. Kit was baiting him, his eyes full of defiance and derision as he silently dared Skye to publicly call him out and sully the image of Taly's new friend. When Skye almost imperceptibly shook his head, an action he knew the other shadow mage's magically enhanced eyes would pick up, Kit's entire demeanor transformed.

"Well!" the copper-haired Gate Watcher exclaimed, his face the very picture of affable sincerity. "I've fulfilled my promise, Miss Caro. I delivered you to your Lord Emrys. I should go see if I'm needed elsewhere."

Rising from the bench, Taly embraced Kit, a gesture he readily returned. "Thank you," she said when she pulled away.

Kit placed a hand on her head, giving her a soft, sincere smile. "Anytime." Turning back to Skye, Kit gave him another mocking bow. "Milord."

Taly watched Kit walk away, and when he ducked his head to dash back out into the rain, she said, "So that was awkward. Kit told me that you two had never met. I take it that's not the case?"

"Oh, we've met," Skye grumbled, leaning back and closing his eyes. When Taly settled back beside him, he frowned. Even without his magic, he could just make out the other Gate Watcher's scent clinging to her. "It's a long story, one I'll tell you later—maybe after a few drinks. Needless to say, we've never gotten along."

"I can see that," Taly replied with a wry smile. "Can't say I'm surprised, though. You're kind of an ass."

Skye chuckled tiredly. "Because it's all my fault, right?" Opening one eye, he just managed to see her nod in wholehearted agreement. "I just can't win with you, can I? I suppose, at the very least, it's nice to know that no matter what I do, I'll always have you here to put me back in my place."

"Well, not always," she replied casually. At Skye's questioning stare, she shrugged, and her expression sobered. "I'll be there for as long as I can, but we're going to have to say goodbye someday. It's kind of inevitable."

Skye's throat tightened at the implication of her mortality. It was always so easy to forget that she was just a human—that she would die. Before he could reply, she hopped to her feet and stretched, her hands flying to her side as her face contorted in pain.

"Ow… I forgot about that."

"Let me see." Skye grabbed her arm and turned her so that he could get a look at the gash at her hip. It was a deep wound, and he could already see small rivulets of pus mixed in with the blood that stained her skin and clothing. "Okay, you're seeing the healer."

"That's really not necessary."

"Iona!" Skye called when he saw the same waifish earth mage from House Agno turn the corner. As the healer approached them, she ran a critical eye over Skye. "I haven't moved," he said, pointing a finger at Taly. "This is for her."

"I'm fine," Taly argued stubbornly.

"Jacket off," Iona commanded, rolling up her sleeves. Those strange black eyes immediately zeroed in on the jagged gash peeking through the tear in Taly's coat. "And" —the healer's hand shot out and grabbed Taly's wrist— "your shirt. I need to see your arms."

Taly gave Skye a withering glare as she stood and started peeling off her clothing, revealing a plain camisole that had been layered over lace underclothes. Under any other circumstance, Skye might have noted the toned muscles of her stomach and arms, but his attention was immediately drawn to her injuries.

"Holy shit!" Skye exclaimed when he saw the angry streaks of purple and red dotting the skin of Taly's right arm. "What happened there?"

Taly looked at her arm in mild surprise. "I guess that explains the soreness."

Iona ran a gentle hand over Taly's skin, her fingers hesitating when they came upon five perfectly spaced patches of discolored flesh.

"I ran into some of those creatures on the way to the compound," Taly explained, a strange twinge of nervousness coloring her tone. She tried to pull her arm away, but Iona kept a firm grip on her wrist. "They managed to grab me. That's all."

"And you still got away?" Iona asked, skeptically. "You're human. How did you manage that feat?"

Taly opened her mouth to reply but winced when Iona poked at a particularly large welt on the back of her bicep.

"Shooting them in the head stuns them," Taly bit out between gritted teeth. "And it's hard for them to chase you if they don't have knees."

There was something evasive in her tone that Skye didn't like. "How many?" When she didn't answer immediately, he asked again. "How many, Taly?"

"Just hold on a minute." She held up a hand. "I'm counting."

"You have to count?" Skye sputtered in reply.

"Three at first." Taly turned when Iona started prodding at her shoulders. The skin of her back and left arm was unmarred. "Then four more came running when they heard the gunshots. Then another three. So, ten at the end. I stopped using my pistols after I got away from that group since they were drawn to the noise."

Skye took a breath, unsure of what to say. *Ten?!* How had she managed to get away from ten of those monsters? From what he had seen, only a shadow mage would be capable of outrunning them.

"You must be quite resourceful," Iona said distractedly. "Still, some of these contusions are quite severe. I'm actually more worried about the bruising than the wound at your hip. Did they grab you anywhere else?"

Taly exhaled sharply. "Yes. My legs, my ankles... I think they may have even ripped out some hair." She frowned, pulling at the tie still holding her hair and combing out the tangles. When she pulled her hand away, her fingers were stained red with blood.

"Arms out," Iona said tersely. When Taly extended her arms, Iona waved a glowing earth crystal over the length of her body. Threads of gossamer earth magic coiled around the healer's fingers, branching off and spiraling around Taly's form in a protective cocoon of healing magic.

"That should do it," Iona said with clinical professionalism a few moments later. "I'll need to see you again tomorrow. Lord Emrys, if you please." She turned to Skye, who dutifully held his arms out in front of his body. The web of healing spells flickered to life, and she nodded. "Good. You may leave now. But remember what I said—no casting until I can examine you in the morning."

Skye nodded in reply, and both he and Taly watched as the healer once again set off to deal with her never-ending stream of patients. Turning to Taly, he said, "They've given me Ivain's old room if you want to go upstairs and get cleaned up." Picking at a fleck of black blood that had dried on the back of her hand, he asked, "Do I want to know how this happened?" He let his eyes rake over the splattered gore that covered her skin and clothing, staring at her pointedly.

"I killed one of them," she replied flatly, pulling on her shirt. "It sort of, well… exploded."

"Come again?"

Taly waved her hand tiredly. "Later. That is a story for much later. What about you? Are you coming up?"

Skye groaned as he pushed himself to his feet, gesturing for her to follow him as they made their way to the main building of the compound. "In a bit. There are a few things I need to see to before I retire for the night."

"Anything I can do to help?"

Skye shook his head. "No. It's mostly just making sure that people are doing what they need to be doing. We need to get a team of mages going through the square and burning the bodies. I also need to speak with the researchers and find out if they've figured out what these things are. Oh, and I should probably set up a meeting with the leadership." Skye ticked off the tasks on his fingers before a large yawn punctuated his train of thought. "Other than that, I think we need to take the night before we decide our next steps. Mourn the dead, tend to our wounded… those things come first."

"Okay," Taly said as she followed him across the courtyard.

The rain had dwindled to a light mist, but they were both soaked by the time they approached the front entrance of the main building. Taly hadn't bothered to put her filthy coat back on, and the stained shirt she wore underneath had started to turn translucent as it clung to her form. Skye could just see the outline of the camisole she wore beneath the damp fabric.

"I'm going to take the longest shower in the history of showers," she said tiredly. "And then when I get the gore washed off, the longest bath in the history of baths. At least the day can end on a positive note."

"Shards help us. Have some mercy and save me some hot water. Please," he begged as Taly rolled her eyes and walked on ahead of him toward the stairs leading up to the upper floors of the keep. He'd had to share a washroom with her on more than one occasion, and he knew from experience that she felt no remorse when he had to start the day with an icy-cold shower.

Turning to glance at him over her shoulder, she gave him an innocent smile. "I'll consider it." With that, she started climbing the stairs, weaving between the people milling about in front of the main building.

Skye stood there for a moment, staring at the place where she'd disappeared through the main doors, and halfway debated running after her. After spending most of the day wondering if he'd ever see her again, it was hard watching her walk away from him.

"So that's little Talya Caro," a cocky voice drawled. "Shame on you, Skye. You never told me how pretty she was."

Damn. Skye had been hoping to put off this confrontation until tomorrow—*after* his magic had fully recovered and he could pummel his so-called *cousin*.

"You told her your name was *Kit*?" Skye asked, refusing to turn around to face the lanky man standing behind him. "And a cousin? What are you up to, Kato?"

"We have a cousin named Kit, don't we?" Kato asked mockingly. "I'm sure we do. Or maybe it was Kat. Kae? No. Kata. It was definitely Kata. See? I told you—old age does things to your memory."

"What are you doing here?" Skye asked in a bored tone, glaring at his older brother. "The last time we spoke, you called the Gate Watchers a group of ignorant, human-loving stooges. Now I find out that you've been masquerading as one for..."

"About 8 months now," Kato supplied, smirking. "And I'm not masquerading. I applied and passed the exams, same as you. In fact, I've already worked my way up to Marshal."

"Why?" Skye pressed.

"I have my reasons."

Skye suppressed a growl as he turned to face the older fey. Though they were both tall and thin, that was where the similarities stopped. Kato had taken after his human father, inheriting his copper hair, freckled skin, and deceptively guileless expression.

"Thank you for what you did today." Skye bowed his head. "And thank you for helping Taly with the tower gun. I probably owe you my life."

Kato's rust-colored eyes widened in surprise, but he quickly schooled his expression into casual disinterest. "I didn't do it for you."

"Of course, you didn't," Skye replied. "Nevertheless, I'm in your debt."

Skye didn't wait for Kato's reply as he started to walk away. If he didn't engage, his brother would eventually get bored and move on.

"She's not how I'd pictured she'd be—your

Taly," Kato remarked suddenly, bringing Skye up short.

"What is that supposed to mean?" Skye asked suspiciously.

The older mage rubbed his chin, softly chuckling to himself. "She's not like other humans that I've met. She's smart... and brave, despite her weaknesses. For a minute there, I thought I was looking at Sarah."

The brief flicker of intense pain and longing that flashed across his brother's face almost made Skye wince. Kato had never volunteered any information about the woman he claimed to have once loved, and Skye had never asked. This was just one more issue they steadfastly avoided talking about.

"Don't pull Taly into your games, Kato," Skye said, a dangerous edge to his voice. "Stay away from her."

"Temper, temper little brother. We're all having fun here." Kato's shoulders pulled up in a good-natured shrug. But then his eyes narrowed, and something sinister crept into his expression. "I wonder... have you told her yet?" he asked, still smiling.

"I'm warning you. Back off," Skye growled.

Kato's head cocked to the side, and then he was howling with laughter. "Shards! After all that agonizing, and you still haven't told her?! Are you serious? You know, I'll do you a favor. The next time I see her, I'll just casually mention—"

Instinctively channeling his aether, Skye rushed his brother, grabbing at his shirt and lifting him to his toes. He wasn't supposed to use magic. He knew that. His head felt like it was going to crack open, but he ignored the pain, enjoying the slightly panicked look in Kato's eyes. "I said… back the fuck off, *brother*."

Kato shook him off, not interested in starting a fight. "Shards! Relax, would you? Everyone's forgotten about that bullshit last summer except for you. It was just a human, Skye."

Scowling, Skye once again turned to walk away.

"Of course," Kato called after him, "that's why it bothers you so much, right?"

Despite his better judgment, Skye replied, "You don't know anything about me."

"I know enough to see the connections." When Skye ignored him and started up the stairs, Kato tried again. "Taly's human. Ava's human. Or, *was* human. It's not hard to connect the two."

Skye stopped in the middle of the stairs, Kato's words bringing him up short.

"Struck a nerve?" Kato cooed mockingly.

Squaring his shoulders, Skye turned to face his brother. "Marshal Emrys. I'm assigning you to funeral pyre duty."

"What?"

"You heard me," Skye said with a deceptively innocent smile. "As High Commander Ivain Castaro's Precept, I'm the highest-ranked member of the Gate Watcher leadership in the compound. That means you're *mine* to command, *Marshal*. And we need people on pyre duty."

Kato chuckled grimly, knowing when he was beaten. "Of course, sire," he drawled, giving Skye a practiced bow. As he marched away, he waved a hand, looking over his shoulder as he said, "Tell Taly I said hi. I assume you'll be keeping her in your room tonight. That's smart. A pretty little thing like that is probably good at finding *trouble*."

Skye didn't grace him with a response. That's what his brother wanted—to rile him. To push him to say something that he would later regret. He wasn't going to give the older fey noble that satisfaction.

With a sigh, Skye retreated into the keep. The sooner he saw to his duties, the sooner he'd be able to retire. And Kato was right about one thing—he had no intention of letting Taly get away from him tonight.

CHAPTER 20

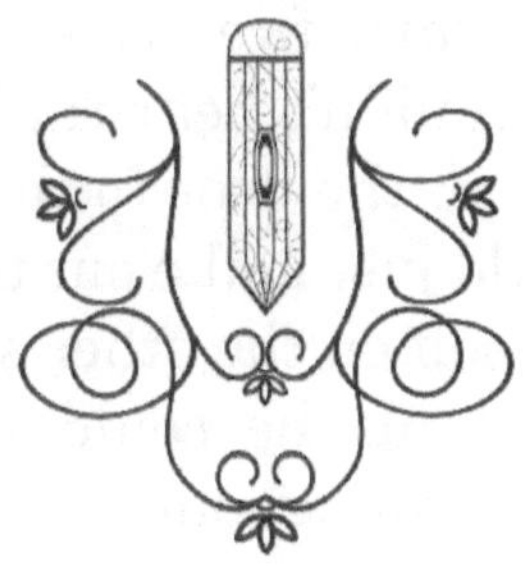

-An excerpt from the Dawn Codex

The anima is what connects us all. It is our essence, our soul, our light. Be ye fey or mortal or beast—the Shards have blessed you with a fragment of eternity and a place in Moriah.

With a groan, Skye fell into one of the chairs situated in front of the fireplace. He had spent the last two hours giving orders to the Ensigns, the newest and greenest members of the Gate Watchers. Then he'd tracked down what was left of the Gate Watchers' chain-of-command, before he finally, *mercifully*, managed to make it up to his room.

Letting his eyes drift over the oaken fixtures, gilded fireplace, and various other flourishes decorating the suite typically set aside for Ivain, Skye almost felt guilty. How many people would be sleeping outside in the rain and cold while he slept in a soft bed with a fire happily crackling in the background?

Another sharp stab of pain lanced his shoulder, chasing away any lingering doubts. If the other Gate Watchers wanted to give him a plush bed and a warm fire, who was he to argue?

Though he couldn't hear the shower running in the background, the door to the washroom was shut, and he could just make out the sound of Taly humming to herself on the other side. In fact, now that he was looking, he could see signs of her sprinkled all throughout the room—small indicators that told him what she'd been doing before he came up.

Through the wide, open entry leading to the antechamber, her things were scattered across a long table set against the wall—both pistols, disassembled and cleaned, as well as the two air daggers. Her jacket and stained clothing had been washed and hung up to dry in the closet, and the remains of a half-eaten sandwich were sticking out of the front pocket of her pack. Like him, it looked like she hadn't been able to stomach more than a few bites of food, just enough to keep her strength up despite the ever-present memory of those sickening creatures. She had even started a fire, and the warmth now permeated every inch of the spacious room.

Though Taly had apparently managed to keep herself busy since they'd parted ways, that did little to explain to Skye just how she was *still* in the washroom. He was suddenly very glad that he'd decided to play it safe and jump in the Ensigns' shower in the bunkhouse downstairs. While using a semi-communal shower wasn't exactly optimal, at least the water had been warm.

Sinking down even further into the impossibly soft, overstuffed chair, Skye decided to close his eyes for a moment, comforted by the gentle, tuneless melody emanating from behind the washroom door. He started when the sound of hushed cries drew him back to the waking world. Slightly dazed, he looked around for the source of the sound, only to find Taly sitting on the floor in front of the fireplace. She stared at her hands, the cuffs of an oversized shirt pulled back to reveal the bruises marring her skin. Her shoulders trembled beneath the billowy fabric.

Dropping to the floor, Skye crawled across the narrow space and wrapped his arms around her. “Hey,” he said gently, twining his fingers with hers and pulling her closer. Taly jolted, drawing in a sharp breath. “It’s okay, I’ve got you.”

“I’m fine,” she insisted. Her shoulders tensed, and she tried to push him off. “It’s just the smoke from the fire making my eyes water.”

“Of course it is,” Skye agreed readily. “Unfortunately for me, though, I don’t have your emotional fortitude, and I could use a hug.” She glared at him even as she leaned into him, and he smiled when he felt her body relax. “Hell of a day, huh?”

Taly barked out a mirthless laugh. “Your ability to understate is truly unparalleled.”

“What can I say? I try.”

Taly sniffed and viciously wiped at her cheeks. “Why do my eyes keep leaking? Every time I turn around lately… Shards, what an annoying habit to pick up.” She shook her head, turning to stare into the fire. “I was actually doing okay until I stopped long enough to think about all of this.

Has it really only been a single day since we left Della?"

"Less than that actually—we didn't leave until midday." Skye moved a hand up to gently comb through her damp hair. "At the very least we'll have some good stories to tell when all this is through. You especially. How many mortals can say they managed to kill one of those creatures? None of the humans downstairs, that's for sure."

When she turned away, her face crumpling as a fresh wave of tears streaked her cheeks, Skye realized his mistake. "Shit. You'd never killed anything before, had you?"

Taly shook her head vehemently. "No. When I was salvaging, I had to protect myself, but most things left me alone if I fired off a warning shot. I think the closest I ever got was about two months ago when I got hungry enough to try to hunt a rabbit."

Skye buried his face in her shoulder, trying to hide his smile. Taly. Hunting. That was something he never thought he'd see. He would never forget the look on her face when Ivain asked if she wanted to learn how to hunt—scorn, outrage, and just the slightest bit of uncertainty since she had been right in the middle of spooning herself out a second helping of Eliza's lamb stew.

"This isn't going to end well, is it?" Skye asked.

Taly wrapped her arms around her knees. "My hands were shaking so badly, I only managed to clip it on the foot—just so it couldn't get away from me. It looked so pitiful, and it was crying, and… I just didn't have it in me to pull the trigger again. I had to sell my coat just to get enough coin to have the menders heal it."

"What'd you name it?" Skye asked knowingly.

Taly's ears flushed. "How do you know I named it?"

"Because this is *you* we're talking about." Reaching for the iron poker near the mantle, Skye stabbed at the fire. "You used to name every chick in the chicken coop. Of course, you named the rabbit. You probably named it before you tried to kill it."

"Fine..." Taly chewed on her bottom lip, looking up at him sheepishly. "I named it Marshmallow."

"Marshmallow?" Skye arched an incredulous brow.

"Yes," Taly replied with a small smile. "Like the human snack? It was a very fitting name, or at least I thought so at the time. Marshmallow lives beneath the tavern now, and Laurel feeds him leftovers from the restaurant. Actual leftovers—none of that shit Jay makes and then tries to pass off as food." When Skye started laughing, Taly tried to glare at him, but it was a feeble attempt at anger. Moments later, she ducked her head, smiling.

"I guess I don't have to ask you the same question," she said, playfully elbowing him in the side. "You used to go hunting with Ivain every spring. And doesn't your family host giant hunting parties every year after the summer court season concludes?"

Skye fiddled with a stray thread on the cuff of her sleeve. "Yes, they do. Still, I don't think a few hunting trips could've prepared me to face an army of dead men. Not even last summer could've prepared me for that."

Taly turned in his arms. "What happened last

summer?"

Damn. He hadn't meant to bring that up. "It's nothing," Skye muttered with a dismissive wave.

"There's a lie if I ever heard one." Her eyes looked unnaturally bright in the flickering firelight as she stared him down. "Tell me," she demanded.

Skye held her gaze. While he would've preferred never to have to tell her what he'd done, Kato had sort of forced his hand. Taly would find out eventually and better she hear it from him than his brother.

"Fine… I… well, I…" Turning away, Skye took a stuttering breath. "Shit."

"Hey," Taly said gently. "It's just me."

"I know. It's just…" A sharp pop sounded from the fireplace, and Skye reached out once more to stoke the blaze. She was right. As he let his eyes take in the soft, familiar curves of her face, he knew she was right. If he couldn't tell Taly about one of the worst experiences of his life, then who could he tell?

"You don't have to tell me if you don't want to," she said after a few moments had passed.

"No, it's alright," Skye conceded, throwing the fire iron to the side and using both arms to pull her closer.

"Last summer," he began, "just after you left, I decided to go back to visit Ghislain a little early. My great-aunt had just had a child—the first highborn birth since I was born 25 years ago—and my mother wanted me present for all of the pomp and circumstance."

Skye stopped, picking out a small tangle in her hair as he tried to find the right words. "So, I'm sure you know that the noble families always hire extra security when new children are born. Even with the decline in our fertility and our dwindling numbers, there's been a rise in the number of highborn assassinations."

Taly nodded. "Mostly from rival families, right?"

"Yes," Skye answered soberly. "One evening, House Thanos was throwing a ball in my great-aunt's honor, so everyone was away from the estate except for the child, the wet-nurse, and the household staff. Just by chance, I came back early that night. My tolerance for what you and Sarina like to call 'courtly claptrap' was running low."

"Personally, I think you should just give in and embrace Ivain's tactic of never showing up to family functions," Taly interjected.

"I've tried. Believe me, I've tried." Skye gave her a tight smile. "Anyways, when I came back to the estate, I could tell something was wrong. It was too quiet, and there were no guards on duty. We're still not sure how it happened, but House Myridan managed to infiltrate the security team with three of their shadow mages. While the family was away, their spies compelled several members of the household staff."

"Compelled?" Taly asked. Her hand had found its way into his, doing her best to offer him comfort. "Isn't that like ascension?"

Skye grimaced. "Yes and no. Ascendancy is forbidden magic. It allows a shadow mage to essentially turn another individual into a thrall by removing a piece of their anima. The person will retain most of their personality, their magic, even some measure of awareness—but their free will is taken from them. Compulsion is... different. Unlike ascension, compulsion only allows for a single command, and it puts the subject into a fugue until they complete their task."

Horror crept into her expression as the implication set in. "Shards. They compelled the servants to kill the child, didn't they?"

"Yes," Skye said with a defeated sigh. "They did. They compelled six of our servants. I managed to subdue five of them, but the wet-nurse... she got away from me. She managed to get to the crib."

Skye braced himself, fully expecting Taly to pull away from him when she found out what he'd done. "I was across the room and never going to get there in time—even with my magic. So, I reached for the first thing I could find. There was a knife nearby. The wet-nurse—Ava—had been peeling an apple. I threw it, and it hit her in the neck. Mortals... even once they're turned into Feseraa, they get hurt so easily. She bled out in minutes."

He heard Taly's sharp intake of breath, felt her body stiffen. *Here it comes*, he thought, closing his eyes. She would likely never look at him the same way again. Not after this. Ava had been so young—completely innocent. And he'd killed her.

"My family decided to try to keep it quiet," Skye mumbled, trying to fill the silence. Maybe if he kept talking, he could stall the inevitable. "All the evidence that pointed to House Myridan was circumstantial. It never would've held up if we took it before the Dawn Court. And when I came back to the island, Sarina and Ivain both said—"

Skye started when he felt Taly's fingers graze his cheek. She turned him to face her, and his eyes found hers. But instead of reproach and fear, he only saw warmth and compassion shining back at him.

Wrapping her arms around his neck, she

pulled him closer. "I'm sorry I wasn't there for you when you needed me," she said, pressing her face into his shoulder. "I'm so sorry."

Skye released a harsh breath. She hadn't pushed him away or recoiled in fear. She hadn't tried to minimize the gravity of his sin because the woman had been mortal. And really… why had he ever expected any differently? This was Taly. *His* Taly. His friend. She had always known exactly what he needed.

"You're here now," he whispered, his voice low and rough. He finally moved to return her embrace, burying his face in her hair and breathing deeply. His shoulders relaxed as the lingering tension of the day melted away.

They sat there for a long while, quiet and content in each other's company. And though he couldn't pinpoint the exact moment, something shifted. Their embrace suddenly became… *more.* His arms tightened around her. Her fingers began to gently toy with the ends of his hair. When she finally pulled away, there was an unnatural rosiness to her cheeks, and Skye suspected that she could feel the erratic beat of his heart where their bodies were still pressed together.

Unable to resist the urge, he trailed a finger along the line of her jaw. Here, with the light of the fire casting a warm glow across her flushed skin, he could almost forget the veritable nightmare they had both just been lucky enough to survive.

When they had set out that morning, completely unaware of the horrors they would each face, he had thought that this irresistible pull he could feel drawing him closer to her was nothing more than some vague sense of sexual frustration, a purely physical urge that could easily be quenched with any woman that was willing.

But that was silly.

Now that he had her here in his arms, now that he'd felt that breathy sigh puff across his skin as he dragged his thumb across her bottom lip, he knew it was completely absurd to think that any other woman could satisfy this craving. There was something in her eyes, something he wasn't accustomed to seeing. Longing, desire, maybe even lust? That thought, the idea that she *wanted* him, shook him to his core.

His heart beat wildly in his chest as he began to lean in, and a violent shiver tore through him when he felt her fingers graze the skin of his neck, twisting in the collar of his shirt as her eyes drifted shut.

A sharp knock shattered the silence, and Taly jumped away, looking anywhere and everywhere but at Skye. Whatever it was that was about to happen between them had ended just as swiftly as it had begun.

Skye sat there for a moment, dazed. His lips still tingled, and he had to fight the urge take her in his arms again—to hell with whoever had chosen this *particular* damn moment to interrupt. He had almost convinced himself to do just that when another heavy knock echoed through the room.

"You should probably get that," Taly mumbled. She didn't look at him, but Skye could clearly see the deep crimson blush that stained her cheeks. Even the tips of her ears were red.

This had better be good, he thought as he pushed himself to his feet and moved to answer the door. A young woman that he vaguely recognized as being Eula's assistant stood on the other side. The timid mage fidgeted with a lock of mousy brown hair, the apprehension falling off her in waves.

"S-sire," she stuttered, sketching out a shallow curtsy. Her hands moved to toy with the sleeve of her robe—a traditional spellcaster's garment that most likely had various crystals sewn into the seams for easy access.

"Ensign Vera. What can I do for you?" Skye said kindly. Yes—he was irritated. But he wasn't going to take it out on the girl. She already looked like she wanted to faint.

Vera ducked her head. "I was told to inform you that the remaining leadership has agreed to your request to meet at ten bells."

"Thank you, Ensign," Skye replied with a patient nod. He opened his mouth to say something else, but the jittery mage was already scurrying down the hall. "And Ensign," he called, suppressing a laugh when he heard her squeak, "anything non-critical? Feel free to slip a note underneath the door."

Vera bowed low, her forehead nearly touching her knees. "Y-yes, sire," she quavered before turning and skidding around a corner.

Chuckling to himself, Skye closed and locked the door behind him. A flash of light rippled over the wooden surface as the silencing wards engaged.

"Where are you going?" he asked when he turned to see Taly sitting in one of the overstuffed chairs in front of the fireplace, preparing to pull on her boots.

"Downstairs," she said as she undid the

buckles. "It's late, and I'm done with this day. I'm going to go find a place to bunk."

Muttering under his breath, Skye tiredly shuffled over to her chair in front of the fireplace, placing a hand on either side of her. When he leaned down to look her in the eye, he was again overcome with an almost violent need to feel her lips pressed against his.

"Or," he drawled, forcefully suppressing the powerful feelings that welled up inside him unbidden, "you could just stay here. I promise I won't bite—unless you bite first, of course. Then I promise nothing."

She tilted her head, her eyes never leaving his as she considered his proposal. A slow smile began to emerge, and when the tip of her tongue darted out to lick at her lips, it took every ounce of strength he had not to close the distance. Their faces were just inches away, their noses almost touching. It would be so easy to just…

Without preamble, she gave him a sharp, unexpected shove, and he stumbled back.

"Thank the Shards!" Taly hopped up out of her seat. Then, sprinting across the room, she threw herself onto the ornately carved bed.

"Huh?" Skye knew that he looked slightly dazed as he watched her stretch out on the bed, her hair fanning out across the wine-colored damask of the coverlet like a river of gold, but he didn't particularly care.

Taly's eyes followed him as he slowly stalked across the room. "Unlike some," she said, unaffected or maybe just ignoring the hungry look in his eyes, "I don't just jump into people's beds uninvited. That's called manners, Em. But then again…"

Her breaths grew shorter and more rapid, the generous swell of her breasts rising and falling beneath the thin fabric of her shirt, as he placed a knee on the side of the bed. Taking his time, he stretched out beside her, getting just a little too close to still be considered strictly *friendly*. He wanted to crowd her, to push her. He wanted to see how far she was willing to take whatever the hell was happening between them. Knowing Taly, she wouldn't hesitate to slap him back into place if he stepped out-of-line. But she didn't. Her cheeks once again flushed a very fetching shade of rosy pink, and her body tensed beside him.

"But then again?" Skye prompted, propping himself up as he began to toy with a stray lock of her hair. The golden strands were mostly dry now and felt like silk between his fingers.

"Well…" Taly licked her lips, drawing his eyes down. And for the first time, he noticed the way she had started fidgeting with the pendant around her neck—a seemingly insignificant gesture, but one he knew well. She was nervous. Maybe even scared. That tiny epiphany was enough to break through the haze of lust clouding his better judgment.

"It's cold and raining outside," she said hesitantly. "A soft bed is far preferable to having to bunk down in wet hay with 150 of my new closest friends. Even if it does have *you* in it."

Skye laughed, a throaty, rumbling sound that vibrated his chest. Even if his body was screaming at him to take this woman immediately and without hesitation, he needed to pull back. Yes—he wanted her. He could at least be honest with himself about that at this point. But he was forgetting one very important thing—she was completely inexperienced.

As that small yet critical detail surfaced in his mind, he realized he would have to slow down—at least for tonight. The part of him that was still thinking clearly knew that this was neither the time nor place to be making overtures. It would be too easy to go too far too fast, and he couldn't mess this up. Not with her.

With an exaggerated yawn, Skye collapsed next to her and buried his face in the pillow, smiling when he heard her sigh in what a part of him desperately hoped was disappointment. "Sleeping next to me is preferable to sleeping in a barn with hundreds of strangers. I suppose that's high praise coming from you."

Taly shrugged noncommittally as she sat up and pulled the blanket over them. Skye's shoulder started protesting, and he was once again struck with just how much he hated not being able to use his magic. He wriggled, trying to get comfortable, but the fabric of his shirt tightened around his wounds uncomfortably. With a growl, he ripped the offending garment over his head and turned to lie on his back.

Taly eyed him in irritation. "Really?"

Skye reached out and pulled her across the bed. She gave a startled squeal, but she didn't fight him. "This is technically my bed, so I get to set the rules. The dress code is *clothing-optional*."

"You're such an ass," came her muttered reply as she curled into his side, apparently not nearly as upset by his half-clothed state as she let on.

"I have one of those, yes," Skye said with a smirk. "And while it's very flattering that you think it should define me, I do have other charms."

She was quiet for a moment. Just when Skye

thought she had already drifted off to sleep, she asked, “What would you have regretted if you died today?”

“What kind of question is that?” Skye asked, slightly taken aback by the sudden change in topic.

Taly snuggled even further into his side, resting her head against his chest. Her fingers began tracing the lines tattooed beneath his collarbone. “It’s something I’ve been thinking about a lot since the harpy. What I would’ve regretted. Funnily enough, it wasn’t the things I did. It’s what I didn’t do. The risks I didn’t take.”

“I get that.” Looking down at the blonde head of tangled hair, Skye felt his chest tighten uncomfortably. After today, he knew exactly what he would’ve regretted. “I guess… well, there’s this girl…”

Taly chuckled softly. “Just one?”

Skye resisted the urge to thump her on the nose. “*Yes*—just one. Trust me, where she’s concerned, one is all I can handle.”

“This must be some girl then.” A wide yawn cut her off, and she stretched her legs, tangling her feet with his.

“She is,” Skye agreed readily. “She really is. I just never saw it before. I don’t know when my feelings for her started to change, but they did. And today made me realize that I would regret not taking the chance to find out if she feels the same way. Even if I just end up making a fool of myself in the end.”

“Please tell me this dream girl of yours isn’t Jezebel.” Taly’s words were starting to slur. She was already half-asleep, the exhaustion of the day finally settling upon her.

"It's not *Jezebel*," Skye replied with a snort. "And that's still not her name, by the way."

"Says you," Taly mumbled almost petulantly in her half-conscious state.

"This girl puts Jezebel to shame," Skye whispered, knowing full well that Taly probably wouldn't remember this part of their conversation come morning. "Hey, Tink?"

"Hmm?" With great effort, Taly turned her head to blearily stare up at him.

Reaching out, Skye tucked a stray lock of hair behind her ear, gently thumping her on the nose when her eyes began to droop. "I'm never letting you get away from me ever again. You're stuck with me now."

She gave him a sleepy smile as she draped an arm across his waist and pulled him closer. "Good," came her breathy reply as her eyes finally closed in sleep.

CHAPTER 21

-An excerpt from the imperial scrivener's records, housed at the Arylaan Archive

The 3rd day of the month Quinna, during the 25,659th year of our Lady Raine

The Genesis Council formally convened at 27 minutes past the 9th bell at Infinity's Edge.

Transcript of the Council Chairwoman, Her Most Supreme Imperial Majesty, Queen Azura Raine's Statements: "Over the course of the past year, this Council has listened to the arguments from both House Ghislain and House Myridan regarding the conflict that many are now calling the Shade Rebellion. What started as a minor territory dispute between two households has now claimed the lives of almost 52,000,000 citizens of the Fey Imperium. Every great race and people scattered across time and space, including our allies, friends, and family united under the name of this Council, all fought and died together, their blood spilled in a pointless war that could have easily been avoided.

It is the unanimous decision of the Genesis Council to lay the full guilt of this tragedy on the aggression of House Myridan and its allies. The members of their household responsible for orchestrating this conflict will have their magic stripped and their bodies desecrated, and any lands they forcibly co-opted will be awarded to House Ghislain.

Additionally, House Myridan's treatment of their dead will need to be further scrutinized. While this Council has always recognized that shadow magic is fundamentally different from any other school of magic, we have been content to allow the Shadow Guild to set the rules and regulations for its practice. However, considering the implications of the spells and enchantments developed by the shadow mages of House Myridan, we will be reconvening at the end of the month to discuss the necessity for a more formal set of restrictions."

For what felt like the hundredth time that morning, Taly sneezed, her body convulsing as she breathed in another plume of dust. Although she had always dreamed of being allowed inside the restricted section of the Ebondrift library, she had never imagined just how dirty it would be.

Dust had collected upon every available surface of the cramped, neglected corner on the top floor of the impossibly vast library, as if even the

Gate Watchers wanted to forget that this part of the collection existed. Peering overhead, she could just make out the faint outline of several months' worth of cobwebs strung between the rows of mahogany bookcases—intricately woven sculptures of silky thread set against the starry backdrop visible through the library's domed glass ceiling. It was almost six bells, and two of Tempris' three moons still swam through the inky sea of the pre-dawn sky.

Suppressing a yawn, Taly turned back to the disorderly stacks of books spread out on the cluttered library desktop, sipping at what used to be a steaming cup of coffee. Why was she awake before six bells again? Oh, that's right. Her subconscious mind hated her. Now, not only did her dreams insist on returning her to the night of the fire time and time again—an unending loop replaying the horrific tragedy that had stolen away every memory from the first six years of her life—but she could also add fighting off an army of dead men to her nightly rotation of things she wished she could forget about.

In sleep, she couldn't escape those creatures' sorrowful, rage-filled eyes as they clawed at her. She could feel their bony fingers, smell the decay and rot that clung to their sallow skin. And perhaps most terrifying of all, her entire body had been awash in a golden haze. It had set her blood on fire as it coursed through her veins, a part of her that was still tethered but begging, *pleading*, to be set free.

To her credit, she hadn't woken up screaming in the wake of this new nighttime terror. After years of facing off against forgotten fears on the battlefield of her dreams, she had merely started awake with a gasp, her face wet with tears. And for the first time in a very long time, Skye had been there with her, already stirring from his own set of nightmares, a warm, comforting presence guiding her back from the dark recesses of her mind.

He shushed her quiet sobs, whispered words of comfort into her skin, all the while telling her stories that grew increasingly more outrageous the longer she let him babble. Needless to say, she did *not* believe that he had snuck into the mortal realm the last time the Aion Gate opened, stumbled upon a lost island, befriended the natives—a species that looked strangely like bipedal bears—and then taught them the way of the shadow mage. Still, despite her refusal to accept his words at face value, Skye had sworn up and down that his shadow bears were now moving across the European continent, spreading the word of the great, all-seeing Em.

He had also decided that he would like her to start calling him the great, all-seeing Em.

So… yeah. That happened.

For as long as she could remember, that had always been Skye's strategy. When the nightmares struck, clouding her mind with terror, he'd just keep talking until he had her laughing so hard she couldn't remember what she'd been afraid of in the first place.

Once the shadows had been banished from her eyes, he'd quieted. They were both exhausted from the previous day, and she had quickly started to drift off again, lulled into a deep state of relaxation by the firm yet gentle stroke of his hand along her shoulder and down the length of her arm. But when he pressed his lips to the back of her neck, his warm breath fanning out across her skin, she had immediately jolted back awake for an entirely different reason.

Even now, hours later, just the memory of having that adorably drowsy, half-dressed shadow mage practically nuzzling her neck had her shifting uncomfortably in the cushioned wooden chair, each creak shattering the early morning silence.

Just friends. You're just friends.

At least that's what Taly had told herself as she made a hasty if somewhat clumsy escape from their shared bedroom, eventually finding her way to the library. And that's what she kept telling herself every time her mind began to wander despite the veritable trove of undiscovered knowledge surrounding her on all sides.

If she found herself smiling as she remembered the way Skye's arm had draped across her waist in sleep…

You're just friends.

When her eyes glazed over as she recalled every detail of how he had held her in his arms the night before, or how she had thought for just one moment that they were about to…

Just friends!

Taly sighed, realizing that she had been staring at the page with unseeing eyes for who knows how long. After *years* of begging Ivain to be granted access to the Vetiri—the collection of texts housed at the Ebondrift library that contained the only remaining written accounts of the forbidden rites—here she was wasting the opportunity by fantasizing about Skye.

"You in there, Tink?"

Taly started, almost spilling her coffee.

Looking to her left, she saw Skye in the seat next to her, a bemused smile gracing his lips. She had momentarily forgotten that he had come with her, refusing to be left behind when she had given him some mumbled excuse of not being able to sleep as she made for the door.

"How long have you been there?" Taly asked, wincing at the slight squeak in her voice. He had shuffled off a little while ago, sleepily muttering something about going to get more tea.

Skye chuckled as he turned back to his book. "Since you started staring at that page about five minutes ago. Must be riveting."

"Yeah... uh..." Taly checked the page, her eyes scanning the sloppily penned lines of Faera script. Most of these texts were just a disorganized compilation of notes and writings—she had yet to come upon a volume that was organized in any cohesive fashion. "Something about desecration. Isn't that the ritual where they take a fey and make him mortal? Neither Ivain nor Sarina would ever say exactly."

Taly didn't miss Skye's slight wince at the mention of the other members of their small family. Although neither of them had dared to broach the subject, they were both worried about Ryme. If Ebondrift was being attacked, then Ryme was the next logical place to strike. And since the scrying relays had inexplicably gone offline before the attacks started, they had no way of knowing what was happening on the rest of the island.

"Understandable," Skye replied, throwing his book off to the side and picking up another one from the stack. "Most fey don't like talking about things that remind them they're not infallible. But yes, that's the gist of it. Desecration strips away a fey's ability to use aether."

Taly nodded, pushing a stray lock of hair out of her face. In her rush to escape, she had forgotten to braid it that morning, something she was coming to regret. The humidity from the ongoing rain just made the golden tendrils stick to her neck. "When did it become forbidden? I feel like I read about it all the time in connection to the Hunt."

Skye leaned back in his chair, sipping from a fresh cup of elfin tea. "About 150 years ago. Ivain doesn't like to talk about the forbidden rites, but my mother told me once that desecration used to be employed as a method of *merciful* execution. The Genesis Council would remove a prisoner's immortality and then send him to live out the rest of his life among the mortals. But then during the Hunt... well, even the Genesis Lords of the Dawn Court found the Sanctorum's practice of desecrating suspected time mages and their sympathizers before publicly disemboweling them rather distasteful."

Taly suppressed a shiver, fidgeting with the cuff of her boot. She hadn't failed to notice the small group of Sanctifiers among the refugees the previous day. "You know, the more I learn about the Sanctorum, the more I hate it."

"You wouldn't be the first person to feel that way."

Picking up another dusty tome, Taly said, "Tell me again why the Ensigns were moving so slowly yesterday. We've already made it through twice as many of these old books in a few hours than they got through in an entire day. It seems like they should've already been able to figure out what those creatures were."

With a yawn, Skye pushed himself out of his chair and stretched. Though she tried, Taly couldn't stop her eyes from following the movement. He was dressed all in black this morning, a color that she had decided she found quite appealing on the lithe shadow mage. It was such a stark contrast to his pale skin, and he'd left the first few buttons of the plain, cotton shirt he wore undone, granting her a teasing glimpse of the flat planes of his chest. She watched him as he walked over to a large pile of books set against the wall, his long legs carrying him across the vast expanse of the library with a grace that made her heart flutter.

Just friends! she screamed at herself mentally. But her heart didn't seem to want to listen to reason as it continued to beat rapidly in her chest. Maybe there was something wrong with it. After all, mortals had been known to die from weak hearts.

As he bent down to examine one of the stacks of discarded books, Skye's words snapped her back to reality. "They were moving slowly because most scholars still like to record everything in Faera—a language that almost nobody speaks anymore. Unlike Ivain, the schools on the mainland don't require complete fluency in Faera, and, as far as I know, House Ghislain is the only family left that still makes it a point to teach even the basic grammar structures to members of the primary bloodline—those set to inherit. Most fey only know the runes required for spellcasting and crystal inscription, so trying to translate full texts..."

"Ah," Taly replied, forcibly tearing her eyes away when Skye started walking back toward the table. "So, the Ensigns had to use a transcription enchantment. What a pain."

"Cé vas'anon, quivanana s'aris," Skye replied in perfect Faera, trusting Taly to know the translation—*indeed, it is.*

"Plus," he sighed, "you're also assuming that those creatures were created using a forbidden rite. All we know for sure is that they were created using shadow magic. It's entirely possible someone came up with some new heinous enchantment and decided to unleash it upon Tempris for… I don't know. A test? Just because they could? Some delusion about time mages rising up to overthrow the Dawn Court? Who knows."

"Time mages?" Taly's head snapped up, and she was suddenly very aware of the bruises on her arm—the ones that flashed when she… "You think this could all be about time mages?"

Skye paused, scanning one of the shelves. "Huh? No, not at all. I was just talking out of my ass. I have no idea why anyone would do this. The only thing I know for certain is that those creatures were clearly *created*, so that means that *someone* is behind it. As for his or her motive, though, I'm at a complete loss."

Taly hummed thoughtfully and did her best to ignore the tremor in her hands as she flipped through what looked like an old lab journal. "Well, at least one good thing came of this mess."

"Really? What's that?" Skye asked absently. He wiped at the spine of a book, squinting as he tried to read the title beneath the grime.

"Sarina being mad at me for tagging along with you is now the least of my worries."

Skye sniggered as he turned his head to give her a playful grimace. "No, I'd probably keep that one up at the top of my list of priorities. If we actually manage to survive long enough to get back to Ryme, she *will* kill you. And me. With fire, I'm guessing. But then again, I knew that when I agreed to bring you."

"Yeah, you're probably right," Taly muttered with a slight shudder. She went quiet a moment, focusing on the text in front of her. "Hey, what about this?" she asked when she came upon a passage that read a little differently from the other pages of dry, arcane language.

"What about what?"

Taly couldn't stop the shiver that ran down her spine. Skye was much closer than she expected, close enough that she could feel the heat from his body as he leaned over her. Resting a hand on her shoulder, his fingers began to absentmindedly brush the skin of her neck.

Damn. He had been doing that all morning. Just when she would finally banish whatever new utterly inappropriate fantasy her subconscious had conjured, he would go and do something that would make the next daydream all the more vivid.

You're just friends. Her mantra; her prayer for sanity.

Clearing her throat, Taly read aloud in Faera, "Though my sister expired at 15 minutes past the tenth bell on the fourth day of the month of Yule, I have successfully managed to trap and stabilize her anima within a shadow crystal. Her body continues to degrade, but the application of the aery and rho rites of preservation in 42-hour intervals has marginally slowed the decay. If I cannot solve the translation error while the body is still serviceable, then I may have to look into acquiring a new one."

"Sounds promising," Skye said distractedly,

reaching past her to turn the page. "Morbid, but promising. What's the date on that?"

"Uh..." Taly flipped the book to look at the spine. "Year 25,657 of our Lady Raine."

"That was during the Shade Rebellion." Skye's fingers, which had briefly ceased their assault on her neck while she was reading, started up again, this time with what felt like a far more deliberate pattern as they pushed aside the collar of her shirt to trace lazy circles on her shoulder. His nails grazed a particularly sensitive area, pushing the straps of both her camisole and bustier aside and...

Taly stood abruptly, sidestepping Skye as she turned the corner and started scanning the shelves. She heard his footsteps following her. "That at least gives us a place to start looking," she said in what she hoped was an even tone. "From what I can tell, the Ensigns have been working backward. Maybe we should start with when the Council first began regulating shadow magic and work our way forward."

Stretching, Taly's fingers groped for a book that was just out of reach.

"Not a bad idea," Skye replied, once again far closer than she was expecting.

Whirling around, Taly almost ran into Skye as he reached over her, effortlessly plucking the desired book from the shelf.

"Um... thank you," she mumbled as he placed the book in her hands.

"Anytime."

Any other day, the cocky smirk on his face would've irritated her, made her suspect that he was up to something. Now, however, all she could think about was how his eyes, those impossibly green highborn eyes, crinkled when he smiled—a small, insignificant detail that somehow made her knees feel wobbly.

Great. Weak knees *and* a weak heart. Maybe the events of the previous day before were starting to age her before her time. Or perhaps it was some lingering effect from the harpy venom. Aether depletion, maybe? Aiden had said that she probably had her own aether supply, and she had drunk the rest of her faeflower the night before when the burning in her lungs had been too much to bear.

When Skye reached up to pull another book off the shelf, Taly ducked underneath his arm, a fierce blush staining her cheeks when she thought she heard a rumbling chuckle. It's like he was trying to fluster her this morning! Usually, she would be able to deal with his teasing, but for some reason, her mind just couldn't come up with the proper words to put him in his place. She wasn't going to be able to get a single, useful thing done this morning if he didn't back off.

Maybe you don't want him to back off, came a sly voice from a dark corner of her mind. *Maybe you like it.*

Taly immediately pushed the voice into an imaginary well, relishing the sound of the receding scream and the splash that came after as she chucked in the bucket and then slammed the cover shut. That little bitch clearly didn't know what she was talking about.

Placing both hands on the desktop, she pretended to study the scattered piles of discarded books as she tried to once again rein in her errant thoughts.

"You seem a bit edgy this morning, Tink."

"Geez!" Taly physically jumped back this time. "Stop doing that!"

Skye just shrugged unabashedly as he sidled up beside her. Too close—closer than he would normally stand. "I can't help but think that your mind might be somewhere else."

"Yeah, on the forbidden rites," Taly retorted, grabbing a book off the desktop and opening it to a random page. Her toe tapped out a faltering rhythm on the marble floor.

"If you say so." That annoyingly suggestive smirk was back, and he stared at the book in front of her pointedly. "By the way, you read that one already."

Taly felt her cheeks warm as she slowly turned the book around to look at the spine. He was right. Slamming it shut, she growled as she swiped at the correct volume and began to march away. Maybe if she went to the other side of the library, she'd actually be able to concentrate.

She yelped when Skye's hand darted out and grabbed her by the wrist, sending the book in her hands tumbling to the floor. Before she quite knew what was happening, he had backed her up against one of the shelves beside the desk, caging her between his arms.

"Are you sure that's it?" There was a huskiness to his voice that Taly wasn't accustomed to hearing, and his chest rose and fell a little too rapidly, almost like he was out of breath. "Are you absolutely *certain* that the forbidden rites are the only thing on your mind this morning?"

"Yes," she replied, feeling a little dizzy. She placed a hand on his chest, meaning to push him away. Instead, she ended up twisting her fingers in his shirt, her eyes eagerly taking in the teasing glimpses of smooth flesh and lean muscle she could see peeking through his unbuttoned collar.

When she dared to glance up at his face, she felt her breath catch in her throat. He was watching her with something akin to… longing? Hunger? She didn't have words to describe that heated gaze, and when his hand moved up to trace her jaw, then her lips, she had to lean against the shelf for support, lest her knees give out.

She *needed* to push him away. If he had his magic, if he could hear the way her heart was racing, she would never hear the end of it. Because surely this couldn't be real. She was misinterpreting the situation. That was the only reasonable explanation. He *didn't* want her. He *couldn't* want her. She was just a human, and he'd already been with dozens of other women. *Beautiful* women. *Fey* women. Women like Adalet—a glittering jewel wrapped in silk and lace, her eyes full of dark promises and her tongue dripping with honeyed venom.

Taly couldn't compare to any of these ladies. She knew this. But she felt rooted to the spot, pinned in place by that inhuman green stare. He was leaning forward now, and, to her great surprise, so was she. Then, before her brain had quite managed to catch up, his lips pressed against hers.

The chaste kiss was impossibly soft—warm, almost reverent. Nothing like the harsh meetings of tongue and teeth that she had read about in romance novels. Far too soon for her liking, Skye pulled away. His expression was strained as he studied her undoubtedly flushed face.

"Is this okay?" he asked, his eyes searching for something, some measure of doubt perhaps. When

Taly hesitated, her words catching in her throat, he took a step back, self-reproach evident in his expression. "I'm sorry. I shouldn't have—"

"No!" Taly tightened her grip on his shirt. Whatever this was, she wasn't ready for it to end yet. Skye stopped, his eyes finding hers. "It's okay. I just… I don't know what to… *how* to… damn it." She looked at him plaintively, praying that he would see what she couldn't find it in her to say.

Skye laughed, relief flowing off him in waves as he gave her a dazzling smile. "Don't worry. I think I get it."

He leaned forward slowly—so *achingly* slowly that it took most of her self-control not to grab him and speed this along. But then his lips tentatively touched hers, and she felt lost as he gently cupped her face, waiting for her to respond. The moment seemed to last longer this time, and when Skye backed away again, it almost felt painful.

"How about that?" he asked, a small grin tugging at the corners of his mouth.

"Umm… that works, I think," Taly murmured. Her cheeks felt impossibly warm, and her lips still tingled.

"Really? You just think?" His smile widened. "I guess I'm going to have to try a little harder then."

With that, his mouth immediately pressed against hers, more firmly this time as one hand came up to tangle in her hair. As Taly began to move her lips in response, hesitant at first but slowly gaining confidence, his kiss became more demanding. His grip on her tightened, but he didn't press his body against hers—not in the way she needed it. The inch of distance he maintained between their bodies was almost… respectful.

Taly groaned inwardly. Of course, Skye would choose *now*, of all times, to start being respectful. Well, if they were already scheduled to have one hell of an awkward conversation when this was done, she should at least enjoy herself in the meantime. At least, that was how her brain chose to rationalize what she did next.

Wrapping her arms around Skye's neck, Taly pressed her body against his. That simple gesture, or maybe it was the sudden skin-on-skin contact as she snaked her palms inside his shirt, seemed to finally break through his restraint. With a strangled moan, he coiled his other arm around her waist, drawing her to her toes as he shoved her against the bookcase. In the distance, through the haze of lust, she thought she heard several books fall to the floor with heavy thuds.

Shards, he felt good. *This* felt good. That was all Taly could think as he pressed himself against her, all firm masculine planes and sinewy lines of muscle.

Eventually, her need for air made itself known, and she had to pull away, gasping for breath. As soon as her lips left his, Skye was at her neck, placing wet, open-mouthed kisses down the column of her throat. Tilting her head to give him better access, she shuddered as the cool air of the library wafted against her moist, overheated skin.

"Skye?" His name came out as a needy moan, and Taly fisted a hand in his hair.

"Yes?" he whispered against her skin, his voice lilting. His hands traced the curve of her waist, up and then back down over the swell of her hips.

She gave his hair another tug, hoping that he'd catch her meaning. All she got was a low chuckle, puffs of air against her skin as he ghosted his lips across the length of her neck.

"Is there something you want?" His tongue darted out to trace the shell of her ear, and she thought she felt a slight tremble shake his frame.

Another tug and she finally pulled his lips back up to hers, but he didn't close the distance. Instead, he teased her, placing soft kisses along the line of her jaw. "You're going to have to tell me what you want, Tink. Word for word—you know I don't take instruction well."

Taly's cheeks flushed an even brighter shade of red. "I…" she stuttered, a breathy sigh escaping when he started to nibble at her other ear. "I… I want…" Another lick. Another nip. "Shards, would you stop being such a tease and just kiss me again?" she finally managed to blurt out in a rush.

Skye's reaction was immediate. With a low growl, he hooked his hands beneath her thighs, twisting them around and hoisting her up on the nearby desktop. His lips were back on hers in an instant, and he used her gasp of surprise to deepen the kiss as he hooked her legs around his waist.

His tongue felt like velvet as it expertly invaded her mouth, but she froze up, overcome by the flood of new sensations. Sensing her hesitation, he pulled back, pressing his lips to hers once, twice. Slow, soft kisses, waiting for her to set the pace. After a moment, she opened her mouth in invitation, and though she fumbled, he was patient. His hands cradled her face tenderly as she tried to match his rhythm, and she felt him smile against her lips when she started kissing him back with increasing confidence and enthusiasm.

Eventually, his hands started to become more daring, moving to caress her waist, her thighs. But when he began tugging at her shirt, palming the bare skin of her back and grinding into her just where she needed it most, she had to pull away.

“Skye, stop,” she gasped, tipping her head back as a strangled whimper tore from her throat. She gripped his shoulders and gave him a slight push.

“Sorry.” Breathing harshly, he pressed his face into the crook of her neck. “Too fast?”

“No… I mean… maybe a little,” Taly stammered. The telltale hardness that was still pressed against her core did little to help her recover what was left of her higher thought processes. “What are we doing?”

“Isn’t it obvious?” He gave a strained laugh, then a groan as he took a step back, putting a small amount of space between their bodies.

“Don’t be a smartass.” She pinched his shoulder, which earned her a sharp nip on the side of her neck. “I mean it. What are we doing?”

Skye finally pulled back far enough to look her in the eye, and his hands moved to encircle her waist, almost like he was afraid she was going to run away. “Well,” he said, a little unsure, “I wanted to kiss you, so I did. Then you kissed me back, and then it… *escalated*.”

Taly licked her lips, and his eyes dipped down to her mouth. She placed a hand on his chest, a warning. “We shouldn’t be doing this.”

“Why not?” His face fell, and she could see a shadow of apprehension creep into his expression.

“Well,” Taly said, her breaths still heavy and uneven, “you’re my best friend, for one.”

“I’m sorry,” Skye broke in. “I’m confused. Is that supposed to be a reason for or against me kissing you again?”

Taly swatted his chest. "Stop it. I know you love the sound of your own voice, but just shut up for one second and listen." Skye didn't look too terribly chastened, but he pressed his lips together as he waited for her to continue.

She took a deep breath before saying, "You're my best friend, and I don't want to ruin that. I don't want to ruin *us* for… I don't even know. What is this? Just a way to relieve stress after a shitty day? Or hell, did you strike out with Jezebel the other night and still need to scratch that itch?"

Skye's arms tightened around her waist. "Is that what you think?" he asked, so quiet, so calm. His eyes turned hard—lethal. "Do you actually believe that I would use you as some sort of *plaything*?"

"No," Taly replied quickly. When she moved a hand to cup his cheek, she felt him relax as he leaned into her touch. "But I do think that this is a little unexpected, and maybe we need to take a step back before we end up making a mistake. Shards know I've already made far too many of those."

Skye snorted a laugh. "Oh, Taly, full of grace, who did flee from the manor in all due haste."

Taly glowered at him as best she could from where she was still pressed against his chest. "How long have you been waiting to use that line?"

"A while," he replied, grinning. "There are other verses if you'd like to—"

"Nope. I'm good."

"No poetry. Got it." Growing serious, Skye sighed as he pressed his forehead against hers. "I don't have every single answer for you, Tink. I wish I did, but I don't. Just know this—I would never risk you, risk *us*, just to *scratch some itch,* as you so eloquently put it. You're too important to me. All I know right now is that I want you. It's a little scary just how much I want you. How much I want *us*."

Taly swallowed past a sudden lump in her throat as she tried to process the open and raw vulnerability that Skye had just laid bare before her.

When she didn't respond immediately, he shifted his weight, his grip on her loosening. "That's what I want, at least. What do you want?"

That was a good question. What *did* she want? What was she allowed to want? She had made so many mistakes, and she still had so many secrets. The least of which being that she had been planning to leave him again in just a few short months. If she were smart, she would tell him she just wanted to be friends. If she truly cared about him, she would end this before she inevitably caused him more pain.

Taly opened her mouth to reply, but Skye shushed her. His head tilted to the side like he was listening.

"Damn," he quietly cursed.

"What is it?"

"We have company. One floor down by the sound of it. I should've noticed him sooner but" —Skye shrugged and sighed wearily— "still no magic."

His eyes found hers, and she knew her expression probably still contained the same measure of sex-addled desire she could see reflected back at her. "This conversation isn't over," he said as he stepped away. Taking her hands in his, he pulled her to her feet. "Just on hold until we see what this asshole wants."

He pressed a soft kiss to her knuckles, his eyes never leaving hers, before gesturing for her to sit. With a groan, he sunk down into the seat next to her, closer than he had been before, and Taly had to suppress a chuckle when she saw him shift uncomfortably. Despite the *problem* she could plainly see tenting his trousers, he let his leg press against hers suggestively as he picked up a random book from the pile littering the table. Several of the stacks had toppled over, spilling out onto the floor.

"What do you want?" Skye said after a few moments, not bothering to hide his irritation.

Taly followed his gaze, her eyes widening in surprise when she saw a familiar face peeking around the corner. He looked far more haggard and worn than when she'd last seen him, but she'd recognize that brassy hair anywhere.

"Terribly sorry," came the guileless response. "I'm not *interrupting* anything, am I?" When Kit's eyes caught hers, Taly found herself looking away, her cheeks feeling even warmer than they had before.

Skye scowled as he threw his book off to the side. "Would it even matter if I said that you were?"

Finding her voice, Taly said, "Good morning, Kit. I didn't take you for an early riser."

Kit's eyes widened, darting to Skye and then back to Taly as his momentary surprise was replaced by something more calculating. "I think you'll find that I'm full of surprises, *Tal-ee*." The way he drew out the syllables of her name, as though he could taste them, had her raising a skeptical brow.

"None of them good," Skye muttered under his

breath.

"Says you," Kit replied with a shrug. "I say we let Taly be the judge of that."

Taly laughed lightly as she reached for her discarded book from earlier. It had been kicked underneath the desk, and she had to duck to retrieve it. "Please don't drag me into whatever *this* is. Because, Kit..." Sitting back up, she stared at him pointedly. "You seem nice and all, but you're not going to win that fight." Skye's brows shot up, and he smiled. Before he had a chance to say something cocky, she jerked her head in his direction, muttering, "After all, I've got to live with this asshole."

"Hey!" Skye exclaimed, his grin widening.

Kit cleared his throat, suddenly serious as some of that sly wit melted away. "Eula was looking for you, S... sire." His tongue tripped on the last word, as though he weren't used to saying it.

"Of course she was," Skye replied with a sigh.

"C'mon, Skye," Taly said as she scanned the page. "Did you really think something as insignificant as an undead army rampaging through the town and possibly ending life as we know it was going to stop Eula from getting up at six bells on the dot?"

Skye laughed lightly, his eyes still tinged with a lingering heat that set Taly's heart racing. "I suppose that was silly of me, wasn't it?" he said smoothly, just a hint of that usual teasing humor peeking through. "I should go see what she wants."

"Take your time," Kit said innocently, the look in his eyes anything but. "Taly and I can keep ourselves *entertained*."

Skye's eyes flashed, his irritation flickering to

life as quickly as it faded. "And I'm sure Taly can handle herself, even when it comes to *you*." Skye gave the man a meaningful look before turning back to Taly. "Kit is also fluent in Faera, in case you need any help here. And if he gives you trouble, feel free to push him over the railing."

"I'll keep that in mind," she replied, her eyes raking over Kit appraisingly. There was something about the older fey, something about the veiled animosity she could see creep into his expression every so often that didn't sit well with her.

Skye gave her one last longing look, sighing softly. Then, in a single fluid movement, he stood, his hands in his pockets as he sauntered past the freckled Gate Watcher leaning against the shelves. The tension was almost palpable as Kit continued to watch Skye long after he had disappeared around the corner.

"What's his problem?" Kit asked suddenly, all hints of aggression immediately evaporating.

Turning back to her book, Taly said, "I think you know very well what his problem is."

"So I *did* interrupt something." Kit's eyebrows waggled suggestively as he claimed Skye's abandoned seat.

"Don't get cute," Taly replied, staring at him pointedly, "*Kato*."

That good-humored expression never budged. "Ah. I see he told you."

"Nope." Taly smiled a feline grin. "*You* just did."

The aforementioned Kit balked, his mask finally cracking. Then, a loud peal of laughter erupted from his chest, the sound echoing through the cavernous library. "I must say I'm a little stunned, Miss Caro. If my dear baby brother didn't tell you who I was, what gave me away?"

Taly shrugged as she continued to casually flip through the book. "It wasn't hard to figure out. You're a member of House Ghislain, a shadow mage, and you speak fluent Faera—something that Skye said is only taught to members of the primary bloodline. That would include Skye and his siblings, maybe a handful of cousins. Certainly not a distant relation, which you claimed to be when we first met. You also managed to get underneath Skye's skin well enough to get assigned to funeral pyre duty." She grabbed one of Kato's hands. Though his clothes were clean and his skin had been washed, there was ash underneath his fingernails. "That's Ensign work. And I'd guess you're at least a Marshal since you were commanding the search and rescue team yesterday."

Kato's grin widened. "Beautiful *and* clever. I can see why my little brother likes you so much."

"So why did you lie to me?" Taly asked, ignoring his attempt to flirt with her.

"And blunt." Kato looked slightly uncomfortable now. "In my defense, I didn't *exactly* lie to you about my name."

"Go on."

Kato sighed, running a nervous hand through his hair in a way that was strangely similar to Skye. There were seven violet lines tattooed on the underside of his wrist—each one a testament to his training as a shadow mage. "Kit used to be a nickname. It was given to me by the last woman that managed to stab me, and I haven't used that name since we... parted ways. Considering that you were standing there with my blood on your dagger and the world had just gone to hell… I don't know. It seemed fitting at the time—almost poetic."

Taly snorted. "I'm not sure I believe all of that, but since you were such a good aether battery yesterday afternoon, I'll give you the benefit of the doubt." Kato sagged in relief but tensed when Taly added, "And the cousin bit?"

"Split-second decision?" he said sheepishly. Taly gave him a withering glare, and his shoulders slumped. "Fine. When you said that you were traveling with Skye, I figured out pretty quickly that you were more than likely the little mortal companion that my brother hasn't shut up about since he was ten years old. And considering that the two of us aren't what you'd call *close*—"

"You mean belligerent, bordering on hostile?" Taly interjected.

Kato snapped his fingers. "She has a way with words—I'll add that to my list." He gave her a sly wink before continuing, "Since I figured Skye had probably already told you some things about me, none of them good, I thought it would be safer to lie about our relationship until I got you back to the compound. While we were out in the open, still in danger of being attacked, I needed you to trust me."

Taly pretended to read the page in front her, suppressing a grin when she heard him shift uncomfortably. After a long pause, she said, "You do see the irony in that, don't you? Lying to make me trust you?"

Kato held up his hands in supplication. "Like I said when we first met, I'm not a smart man."

"There's another lie." And it was. Taly could see cunning behind that boyish facade.

"I take it you're not mad?" Kato reached for Skye's discarded cup of tea. "According to my brother, your temper is something to behold. I figure if I'd committed some grievous sin, I'd be splattered across the tile by now."

"Well, Skye would certainly know a thing or two about my temper." Taly threw the book she was reading into the growing pile of rejected tomes. Leaning back, she let her hair hang down past the back of the chair as she rubbed at her eyes. "But I'm too tired to be mad right now. Anger takes energy. If you give me a few hours and ten more cups of coffee, I promise I'll give you a good beating."

"And funny." Kit smiled as he swiveled in his chair. "My list just keeps growing."

Taly once again ignored Kato's attempt at flattery. "You're getting cute again. Besides, I never said I forgive you. I just acknowledge that everybody lies—even honest men."

"And practical."

Rolling her eyes, Taly stood and walked to the end of the bookcase to retrieve the ladder. "Why does my forgiveness even matter? Aren't you just using me to mess with Skye at this point?"

"It matters because I like you," Kato replied simply, watching Taly climb the ladder a little too closely. "You're fun, and you don't seem the type to take shit from anybody, regardless of rank. I might not be the heir anymore, but I'm still a son of the reigning Duchess of Ghislain. All of the sycophants and their incessant groveling gets boring after a while. It's a nice change to have someone talk back for once."

Taly reached for a book stacked on top of the bookshelf. "Again—I'm not sure I believe that. I get the distinct impression that you *like* having a captive audience."

Kato shrugged, catching the books as Taly dropped them into his waiting hands. "Let's just say that ruffling Skye's feathers would be an added bonus to getting to know you. Besides, if I really wanted to piss him off, I'd tell you about Ava. He really doesn't want you to know about Ava."

Taly bristled when she heard a trace of that veiled animosity she'd seen earlier resurface. "I already know about Ava and everything that happened last summer," she said evenly. "And to be clear, don't think that I can't tell the difference between friendly sibling rivalry and a deliberate attempt to undermine your brother's relationship with me. If you want to play your games, I can't stop you, but I will not be used as a pawn."

"Fiery," Kato said after a pause. "No wonder my brother's so taken with you."

Taly blushed, licking her lips to see if she could still taste Skye there. He was taken with her? Sure, he had basically said as much, but to hear it from someone else… "Go to bed, Kato. You look exhausted."

"Would you come tuck me in?" he asked mischievously. She didn't need to look down to know that he was leering at her.

Taly chuckled. Although she had never worked up the courage to go to bed with a man, she had spent more than enough time in bars. She knew how to handle Kato's type. He was all talk. "So, let me get this straight—you think you walk in on your brother and I doing something *untoward*, and your first instinct is to try to get me into your bed instead?"

"Well, I don't *think* I walked in on something. I *know* I did." She could hear the challenge in his voice. *Ask me. You know you want to.*

And Taly took the bait. "Oh really? And how is that?" She regretted the words as soon as they left her mouth. She had grown up around shadow mages. She already knew how.

"Well," Kato drawled, and Taly's cheeks were already flushing. "Aside from the racket you two were making, his scent is all over you. You must have had him really worked up, because believe me when I say that you're drenched in it. I can barely smell any iron at all."

Taly slid down the ladder, landing hard. She smiled when Kato jumped back slightly. "Didn't your mother ever teach you it's not polite to go around scenting people?" Pushing past him, she started to walk back towards the desk, her boots clicking across the marble floor. Her scent was one of the few things that she had always been self-conscious about, a factor of her humanity that she couldn't compensate for by studying or training harder than everyone else around her. As one shadow mage in Ryme had told her once, humans *reeked* of iron—especially the females when they bled. It was so unpleasant that some shadow mages just made it a point to avoid mortals altogether.

Seeing that he had upset her, Kato reached out to grab her arm. "Hey, I didn't mean—"

"Ow!" Taly flinched away. A sharp, crackling pain radiated up and down her arm as soon as his fingers closed around her bicep.

"Shards! I'm sorry," Kit exclaimed, shamefaced. "I really must be tired. My magic hasn't sparked like that in over a century. Here"

—he reached out and grabbed her wrist, tightening his grip when she tried to pull away—"let me make sure I didn't burn you."

"No, that's not..." But he had already pushed her sleeve up, the oddly shaped bruises easily visible against the pale backdrop of her skin in the dim light of the library.

"What the hell?" Kato ran a finger along one of the angry red welts.

"It's nothing." Taly jerked away, quickly pulling down her sleeve down and rebuttoning the cuff. "I got grabbed by some of those things yesterday. They weren't gentle."

"And you got away?" Kato's eyebrows rose, almost disappearing behind the mop of auburn hair sweeping across his forehead. His eyes flicked back to her arm, prompting Taly to hide it behind her back self-consciously. "How? You're human."

"I got lucky," she replied quietly. It wasn't a lie. Not exactly.

His narrowed eyes seemed to study her, noting the way she shifted under the weight of his scrutiny.

"Sarina might have tried to turn me into a proper lady, but Ivain always believed that even proper ladies need to know how to hold their own in hand-to-hand," Taly offered, fumbling for an explanation. "I've been sparring with Skye for as long as I can remember. That wouldn't be the first time it's come in handy."

Taly forced herself to move her arm to her side, to straighten her shoulders. Shadow mages were trained to read people—to tease out information from physiological responses. She couldn't let him see her fear. She swallowed back a sigh of relief when she saw the tension in his eyes release, remorse taking the place of suspicion.

Kato stuffed his hands into his pockets. "I really am sorry about the..." His voice trailed off. "Maybe you were right. It's been a *very* long day… night? Maybe I should go put myself to bed." He scuffed at the floor with the toe of his boot. "Before I leave, can I just add one more item to my list of things I've learned about Taly Caro?"

When Taly just raised a brow in response, he ducked his head, that guileless mask effortlessly slipping back into place. "She's a puzzle I look forward to solving."

There was heat in his gaze, but it had little effect, and Taly rolled her eyes in response. "Oh, *please*. Were you actually expecting that line to work?"

Kato laughed, shrugging in good-natured defeat. "Well, it was worth a try." With a wink and a wave, he turned to leave, disappearing around one of the towering shelves and leaving her alone at last.

When she could no longer hear the measured clicking of his footsteps echoing down the stairs, she pulled back the cuff of her sleeve. She hadn't noticed it the day before. Or maybe the edges hadn't been as distinct. But now, after a morning spent poring over texts written in an arcane language she had learned as a child, she recognized the bruises for what they were.

Faera. Lines upon lines of overlapping Faera script.

Which meant… spells. The bruises, the flashing runes—they were spells.

And the scar on her palm… it had turned a deeper shade of plum, almost amethyst. If she pressed at the surface, it felt hard, and her finger grazed a sharp, faceted edge just beneath her skin. Or what looked like her skin. When she raked her nail across the spot, it made the pad of her finger itch. Just like her face would start to itch beneath a cosmetic glamour.

"No, no, no," she whispered, flinching when she felt another sharp stab of pain ripple up and down her arm. The air around her fingers began to glimmer, and something in her knew that she wouldn't be the only one able to see the golden apparition spiraling around her arm. This wasn't like the visions. This was something new.

"Well… fuck."

What the hell was she supposed to do now?

CHAPTER 22

-An excerpt from the imperial scrivener's collection of unclaimed letters from the Shade Rebellion, housed at the Arylaan Archive

Dearest sister,

If you can spare your son, I have need of a healer. To my great surprise and most ardent joy, Abel returned from the front last month. However, I have noticed a change in him. At first, I believed that, given time, he would be able to move past the horrors of the front, but now, I fear it may be something else. From the smell, I suspect a lingering infection.

All our village's earth mages have been called to the front line, and our menders aren't able to diagnose him. They have prescribed a draught to help him sleep, but it hasn't helped. He never sleeps, he barely eats, and he has begun to lapse into fits of delirium. Occasionally, he'll come back to himself and speak a few words. In those brief moments of clarity, I've been able to make him eat a few bites of food, perhaps lie down to rest, but these instances are becoming more and more rare.

I pray this letter reaches you. I don't know how much more of this I can take. I love my husband, but sometimes when I catch him looking at me, I start to wonder if something else came back in his place.

All my love,

Abigail

Taly lay on her back watching the slow creep of sunrise brighten the dome of the library with a smoky glow. It was still raining outside, and behind the film of streaked raindrops painting the glass overhead, she could just spy the faint blush of dawn peeking through the clouds. Petal pinks, inky blues, the warm glow of tangerine—a palette of soft hues painted against a backdrop of gray.

Having grown tired of poring through the endless stacks of books, Taly had retreated to an old couch she'd found tucked away in a forgotten corner. The aged and cracked leather creaked every time she shifted, the only other sound besides the patter of raindrops and the crash of thunder to penetrate the silence of the library. Her fingers nervously toyed with the pendant at her neck, and she'd pressed her feet between the cushions to keep from fidgeting. She took deep, calming breaths, but her heart continued to beat a sharp, staccato rhythm in her chest: *what now, what now, what now...*

Kato. When he grabbed her, she had felt a stabbing swell of pain rush through her—like a whip cracking against the skin of her arm. He'd thought his own magical discharge had caused her to flinch away, but he'd been wrong. Something inside her, possibly one of those strange spells inscribed on her arm, had snapped.

What now, what now, what now...

This thing inside her was becoming impatient, straining against an invisible wall. Taly could *feel* that wall now. She could see it in her mind's eye, a vast expanse of black marble streaked with violet veins of glittering energy. It was crumbling—brick by brick, stone by stone—and there were large, gaping holes all up and down the barricade, places where she had forcibly broken through in a desperate attempt to tap into that hidden well of power.

She could even sense a bit of Skye along the magical barricade—faint wisps of his aether still clung to the edges of one of the smallest gaps. He had unintentionally removed the first brick that day in the sparring ring nearly a year ago. She was sure of it.

What now, what now, what now...

Taly closed her eyes against the relentless doubt clouding her mind. Her magic seemed to be sensitive to strong emotions, so she needed to remain calm. Two more of those strange spells had severed before she'd figured out how to shove the flood of power back behind the wall, stoppering up the gaps with will alone.

Without Aiden here, she had no one to talk to,

no way to figure out just what was happening to her, and no allies. That left her with only one option. She needed to tell Skye.

He was going to be angry (well, furious), hurt, confused... He may even decide that this lie she had repeatedly told him over the past year, that she was nothing more than human, was unforgivable. That being a time mage was unforgivable. But he would know what to do. Even if he hated her, he would still help her get back to Ryme and Aiden and safety. He would never betray her.

"There you are."

Although Taly didn't jump, her heart started beating faster as she heard footsteps approaching. *Skye*—would it make her a terrible person if she let him kiss her one more time before telling him that she was a time mage? Would he be disgusted when she told him? What if he was already disgusted? What if it really had been an accident, a fluke, and he was repulsed by the very idea of having kissed a human?

Opening one eye, she saw Skye staring down at her as he leaned over the back of the couch. The sincere, open affection in his expression left her slightly breathless.

"Oh look, *you're* back." She turned onto her side when she felt her cheeks start to warm. "I already sent your brother to bed."

"Ah... so you figured that out?" Skye asked somewhat sheepishly. She didn't need to look up to know that he was raking a nervous hand through his hair.

"When were you planning on telling me?"

Skye sighed heavily. "I'm sorry. Kato caught me off guard yesterday in the courtyard. I had no idea he was on the island, much less a part of the Gate Watchers, and I didn't want to say anything until I got a chance to talk to him—figure out just what he's up to. I meant to tell you last night, but..."

She heard him shift his weight, heard the low tap of his boot on the marble tile.

"Let's just say I got *distracted*." A pause and then, "You see, there was this beautiful woman. We were interrupted before I could get a chance to properly kiss her, but then when she practically threw herself into my bed, well—"

"You know, I'm starting to see the family resemblance." Taly still refused to look at him. If her face got any redder, she might actually combust.

"My brother and I look nothing alike."

"Says you." Sitting up, Taly mustered her best glare. Skye had been just as much of an eager participant in that kiss as she had. Why should she be embarrassed? "You're both shameless flirts, for one."

Skye shrugged, a wide, toothy grin splitting his face when her eyes found his. "I like to think I'm a little more discerning than my brother," he said as he pulled a hand out from behind the couch and presented her with a fresh cup of coffee.

With a mumbled "thanks," Taly accepted the mug, relishing the warmth of the white ceramic against her chilled skin.

There wasn't a shred of uncertainty or doubt in his countenance as Skye casually strode around the couch and sat down beside her. But when he didn't move to place his arm around her, just like he had done a thousand times over the years, she recognized the gesture for what it was—a question. *Is this okay?*

She hadn't given him an answer before—when he had practically laid his heart at her feet. If she moved away, they would forget what happened that morning and move on. That conversation he had confidently declared *on hold* would be closed—forgotten—and that invisible boundary between them would be fortified, never to be crossed again. They really would be *just* friends, from here until the day she died.

Something about that made her feel hollow inside. This was *Skye*—the one constant in her life. The boy who'd found her in a pile of cindered rubble. The man that had proven time and time again that he would do anything to stay by her side. They'd never been *just* anything, and she'd be a fool if she tried to convince herself otherwise.

When Skye shifted, putting a little more distance between them, something inside her cracked.

Could she really do this? After trying to push him away so many times, was she really capable of doing it again? Yes, he might very well reject her when she told him her secret. And yes, she was still going to have to figure out a way to articulate her very confusing feelings when they inevitably picked up their conversation from earlier—even confess that she had been planning to leave him again. And of course, if they made it through all of that, *then* they could start to consider the logistics of what a relationship between a human and a fey noble would actually look like. So many questions to answer. So many hurdles to overcome.

Defeat began to creep into Skye's expression, just around the edges, and Taly felt that crack inside her widen into a gaping breach when he looked away, his shoulders slumping forward almost imperceptibly.

The questions and confessions could wait. For now…

“And second,” Taly said, wriggling awkwardly as she tried to lean into him. As soon as she began to close the now conspicuous distance, Skye blew out a sharp breath, and his arm immediately encircled her waist, pulling her across the couch and tucking her into his side.

“Second?” Skye prompted a little unsteadily when Taly lapsed into silence, her hand resting on his chest. She’d gotten distracted by the rapid pounding of his heart that she could feel just beneath her fingertips. “My brother and I are both shameless flirts, and?”

“Um… oh, right. Second,” she stammered, finally relaxing in his arms as she sipped at her coffee, “you and Kato both do the same little eyebrow waggle when you think you’re being cute. It’s a little eerie.”

“Wait,” Skye said, one eyebrow shooting up, “you think I’m cute?”

“See, you just did it.” Taly poked at the offensive brow, her finger tracing the inhuman arch. Everything about his face was too carved, too sculpted, too *fey* to be human.

Catching her wrist, Skye placed a tender kiss on the palm of her hand. That soft brush of his lips sent a visible shudder down her spine. “I take it since you’re over here, that means you gave up on digging through thousands of years of shadow magic regulations?”

“Um…” Taly’s mind went blank when she felt his tongue dart out, his fingers already pulling at the cuff of her sleeve as he continued to place soft butterfly kisses on the skin of her palm. At the very least, she could safely say he wasn't disgusted by the idea of kissing a human. For a moment, she let herself get lost in the cascade of unfamiliar feelings that washed over her, allowing Skye to pull her close enough that she had to hook one of her legs over his.

She jerked her hand away when her scar began to peek out from underneath her cuff. "Stop that," she said sternly. Skye looked unrepentant as he leaned back into the couch. "I stopped looking because I found the answer." Reaching over him, she dug a hand between the cushions of the couch, retrieving the book she had stashed there earlier and waving it in his face.

"Why'd you put it down there?" he asked, taking the book and opening it to the page she had dog-eared.

"Out of sight, out of mind," Taly replied with a shrug.

Skye leaned forward as he started reading the entries she'd marked, releasing Taly as he frantically turned the page. "No," he whispered. "That's not possible."

"It fits," Taly said softly. She stared into the mug, watching the swirling eddies of cream blend with the light sprinkle of cinnamon clinging to the surface. Where Skye had managed to find cinnamon, she didn't know. Even when they weren't in the middle of the end of the world, the human spice was always hard to come by this close to the Aion Gate connection.

"I suspected…" Skye hung his head. "Shit, I should've seen this sooner."

"I wouldn't take it personally. It's been over 10 millennia…" Taly paused, sinking further into the couch as she thought over what she'd found earlier that morning. "Ivain's the only one on the island old enough to remember it first-hand."

Skye threw the book off to the side. "Of all the million and one awful things we could be dealing with, why did it have to be shades?"

Taly shuddered. She had only heard Ivain talk about the Shade Rebellion—the civil war that had nearly destroyed the Fey Imperium—a handful of times. When the Myridan rebels started losing the war, they had taken their fallen and found a way to piece them back together—harnessed the power of the dead's own souls, their anima, to put them back on their feet.

"No," Skye said, still refusing to believe it. "In every account that I've read of the Shade Rebellion, the shades were almost indistinguishable from the living. Those things we fought yesterday looked very, *very* dead. I also don't remember there being anything about them eating flesh."

"I think I have an explanation for that." Taly reached between the cushions and produced another book. Handing it to Skye, she said, "That's one of House Myridan's lab journals from the Rebellion. Although both the Time Guild and the Infinity Queen sided with House Ghislain during the war, there were a few dissenters."

Skye opened the book, reading over the bookmarked entry. "They were using a time magic enchantment built into their armor to slow the decay rate." The book slammed shut, and Skye hung his head. "Of course. With no time magic, the corpse is still going to decay unless it can feed on aether—which would explain why those things seemed so... hungry."

"But even feeding on aether doesn't completely stop the decay. Not like time magic," Taly whispered, the mug in her hands forgotten. "The things in the square looked old, but some of the shades that attacked me were… fresher, I think. Granted, I can't be sure since his face was all messed up, but I think I recognized one of them, Skye."

"What?" he breathed, his eyes wide.

Taly stared up at the brightening sky outside the dome of the library. "I didn't know him well. I just saw him at Dimas' table a few times buying scouting notes. His name was Femy. From what I heard, he never checked in after his last job a few months ago."

"The people that have gone missing… all those mortals?" Skye went still as he came to the same conclusion that Taly had reached earlier. Not only had there been someone on the island abducting people and turning them into undead foot soldiers, but they might also end up fighting their own people before this was over. "Shit."

"No one really thinks twice if a mortal goes missing," Taly supplied. "And since people already tend to vanish prior to the Aion Gate connection, it made the sheer number of disappearances easy to justify. Whoever is behind this chose their moment well."

"Maybe…" Skye hesitated, then shook his head. "No—this is bigger than that. Just look at the number of shades that attacked us yesterday. There were so many. This goes beyond just a few disappearances. The man, woman, *thing* that created those shades has been planning their attack for a very long time." Pushing himself off the broken-down couch, Skye began pacing anxiously. "And that still doesn't explain where that abomination fits into all of this. I don't remember anything about shades being able to *remake* themselves—change their forms."

"I think that's a side effect of not having time magic to stabilize them," Taly explained. "From what I can piece together, the more they decay, the harder they are to control. If they got out from underneath their creator's thrall… well, I couldn't find anything about what would happen to an unleashed shade. House Myridan's shadow mages theorized but—"

"Their time mages would just patch up the ones that started to get out-of-hand, reverse the decay, restore their anima. A complete reset. Which means that, without time magic, we're dealing with something completely new. Something untested," Skye finished quietly. He stood there, his hands clasped behind his back, staring at the gray sky overhead as he attempted to collect his thoughts. "I suppose," he said after a long pause, "at the very least, we should be thankful that we can tell the living from the dead—that we know just who it is we're supposed to fight. If they had time mages on their side, I don't know what we'd do. The entirety of the Fey Imperium came together to try to fight House Myridan and their army of shades, and they just barely managed to win that fight before our entire civilization collapsed."

"There's one more thing, Em," Taly whispered, her hand grasping at the pendant around her neck. "One more thing that might change the calculus."

Her—the human time mage. The *freak*. She was a problem.

Skye sank back down beside her. "Shards, there's more?"

"That passage about the time magic enchantment..." Taly paused, thinking better of what she was about to say. "No, not here." There were too many shadow mages in the compound, too many listening ears. "It's too public."

"There's no one else in the library." Skye's head tilted to the side, and his nostrils flared. "Or outside. No one that can hear us, at least."

"I take it you got your magic back?"

"Yes," he said, rubbing at his eyes tiredly. "I swung by to see the healer on my way back from talking to Eula. That's why it took so long. So out with it. What's the big secret?"

"Um..." Taly's mouth suddenly felt dry. "Well, it has to do with why I left last year."

She felt Skye's body go rigid beside her.

"Go on," he said carefully.

Taly took a deep breath, then downed the rest of her coffee in a few gulps, wishing it was whiskey. She could do this. Aiden had been telling her she needed to fess up ever since she came back to the manor. And now it had finally reached a point where it was more dangerous for Skye *not* to know what she was. "That day in the training yard, when you discharged the dagger in my hand, that was when I figured out... well, not figured out. That's not the right word. That's when... that's when it started."

Skye's face fell, and he held up a finger to her lips, shushing her. "I just can't catch a break today," he muttered. "Eula's on the first floor looking for me."

"Why?" Taly mumbled, her lips still pressed against his finger.

Skye cocked his head, listening. "She says 'tell Taly hi' and that she managed to track down the rest of the leadership and convinced them to meet early.

"Eula." He paused, snorting in reply to something only he could hear. "Can you give me a minute? Keep the library clear? Thank you." Looking back at Taly, he gave her an encouraging nod. "You were saying?"

Taly opened her mouth, but no sound came out.

"C'mon, Tink. Don't freeze up on me now." There was a hint of desperation in his voice as he tangled his hands in her hair, pulling her eyes back to his. "If you're not ready to tell me that's okay, but… *please*."

Shaking her head, Taly said, "Not here. It's just not a good idea. I'll tell you tonight in the room. It's warded against those pesky shadow senses."

Skye gave her a reluctant smile as he pressed his forehead to hers. "That's not what that spell is called, but fair enough. After this meeting, I'm probably not going to get a moment alone. If you can believe it, finding out we're dealing with shades is only the second-worst news I've received this morning." His hands moved down to cradle her neck. "I only have one request if you're going to keep me in suspense all day long."

"What's that?" The movement of her lips drew his eyes down.

"Let me kiss you again?"

That voice, breathy and low, set Taly's heart racing. His lips twitched at the corners—he could hear it. Now that he could use his magic, he knew exactly the kind of effect he was having on her. But he didn't move. He waited.

Her choice. She set the pace.

Taking a shaky breath, she jerked her head. *Yes*.

Although she braced herself, he didn't kiss her immediately. Not like she expected. First, he placed a gentle kiss on her brow, then both cheeks, even the tip of her nose before ghosting his lips across hers, teasing. All she needed to do was lean forward, but she didn't. She let him play his game.

A low, muttered curse was the only warning he gave before he abruptly tipped her back and pressed his mouth against hers in a kiss that, though brief, would be forever burned into her memory. It was bruising, branding. It dared her to try to continue to see him as only a friend, to try to paint this as an accident or a fluke.

When he broke away, she was trembling, still pinned in place by the intensity of that vibrant emerald gaze, by the fathomless depth of affection shining from deep within. It made her head spin, her already ragged breathing quicken, and when he slid off the couch and yanked her to her feet, her knees buckled as soon as her feet hit the floor.

Skye caught her, one arm wrapping around her waist as he pulled her body up against his. "C'mon," he said, grinning happily as he traced a finger over one of her rapidly reddening cheeks. "We have a meeting to get to."

"We?" Taly winced at how breathy her voice sounded. At least her knees were working again, and she took a few steps back as soon as she regained her feet, trying to get some distance. Skye just gave her that stupid smirk, and she did her best to pretend that she couldn't feel the tips of her ears starting to warm.

"Yes. I want you there," he said as he stooped to pick up the discarded books.

"Are you sure that's a good idea?" Taly's mind flashed to that hidden wall and the churning sea of power she could feel just on the other side. She had no desire to be in a room full of shadow mages with that pool of forbidden magic simmering just beneath the surface. "I mean," she stammered when Skye gave her a questioning glance, "why is anyone there going to want to listen to a human?"

Skye rolled his eyes. "Human or not, you were the only one smart enough to notice that there were shadow crystals embedded in these things. And then, as if that wasn't enough, you figured out in a few hours what 15 Ensigns couldn't in an entire day. I think you could add some useful input, and if anyone in that room has a problem with that, they can take it up with me."

Taly sighed, once again prodding at the barrier buried deep in her mind. It seemed stable enough for now, and if Skye thought she could help, then maybe she did need to go.

"Okay," she finally acquiesced. Shrugging on her coat, a supple brown leather duster that tapered at the waist, she turned to follow Skye.

He gave her an encouraging smile as he ushered her towards the stairs. "We should hurry. Eula was in fine form this morning and" —he closed his eyes as he listened more closely— "apparently Kato managed to insert himself into this meeting as well."

"This sounds like it's going to be so much fun," Taly said dryly. She had to practically jog to keep up with his long-legged strides.

"That's not the word I would've chosen, but *sure*." Ever the gentleman, Skye waited for her at the wide circular staircase, placing a hand on the small of her back as they began to descend. In a low voice, he said, "I shouldn't have to say it, but I will. The leadership is gone, so most of the people in this meeting are going to be Marshals or Lt-Marshals. All of them are relatively new, and they're all from the mainland. That means they're power-hungry and stupid. They'll think they're better than you by virtue of their birth, but in reality, they're all a bunch of weak-willed assholes. Don't for one second be afraid to put them back in their place if need be. I can guarantee that you probably know more about the gates... hell, probably more about shadow magic than all of them put together."

Taly snorted. "Way to make me *not* regret this decision. You know, now that I think about it, that couch up there is starting to look really nice. And I *did* have an early morning."

The hand at her waist tightened. "The couch was a little small. And old. If you'd like, I can tell Eula to push the meeting back, and then I can take you back to bed and—"

Taly gave Skye a hard shove before he could finish that sentence. "Shards, you have a dirty mind."

"Oh, you have no idea," he said with a devilish laugh. Coming to an abrupt halt a few steps below her, he pressed his mouth to hers—soft and gentle but demanding. There was a faint whisper of that same fire from earlier, but he held it in check. Now wasn't the time. *Later,* he seemed to say. He would make it up to her later.

"You didn't ask permission that time," she gasped when he pulled away. At some point, she had wrapped her arms around his neck, and her fingers had made a mess of his hair.

"Do I have to ask every time?" Skye sounded just as out-of-breath as she felt.

Taly pretended to think on the matter. "Yes," she said, smiling when he gave her a good-natured pout. "That sounds like it could be fun for me."

"You're an evil woman." Chuckling softly, Skye reached down and clasped her hand, giving her a tug as they proceeded down the stairs. "And the only thing keeping me going at this point. Never change."

That soft, heartfelt confession had Taly stepping closer, lacing her fingers with his as they continued to descend.

As they stepped off the final stair and started crossing the public section of the first-floor library, Taly could just make out a group of people gathering outside the beveled glass doors on the other side of the wide vestibule. There was Eula and Kato, but also several fey that she hadn't been expecting.

"Here we go," Skye whispered, giving her a wink as he schooled his features into a mask that she was all too familiar with. For once, though, Taly didn't find herself rolling her eyes at the sudden appearance of *Lord Emrys,* future Duke of Ghislain. No—for once, she couldn't help but think that the authority suited him.

She didn't know quite what to make of that.

CHAPTER 23

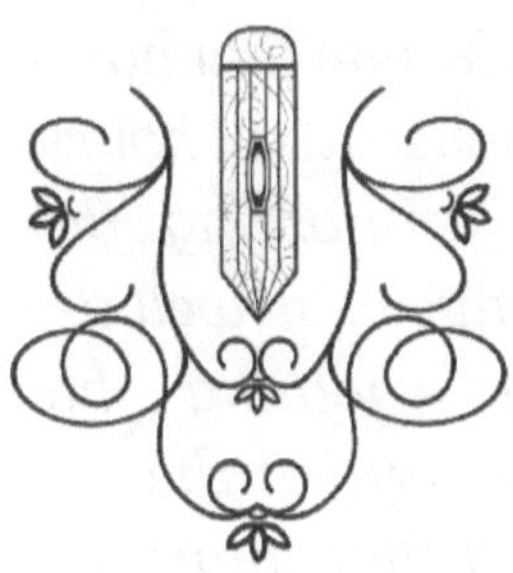

-From the personal notes of Ivain Castaro, Marquess of Tempris

The 26th day of the month Luna, during the 247th year of the Empty Throne

They're doing it again—right in front of me. Eleven years and Skye and Taly still don't think that anyone has caught on to their little game.

For the life of me, I cannot figure out why they felt the need to invent their own language. It was primitive in its beginning stages, but now, I dare say, the lexicon has become quite sophisticated. Every time they start this nonsense up again, I always find myself asking the same question: why tapping? They're both intelligent individuals—surely, they could've come up with something less obvious.

Thankfully, their use of this alternative method of communication has tapered off over the years. When they were younger, it was literally a never-ending percussive racket echoing back and forth across the hall. Sarina has always thought this little quirk of theirs to be "cute," but, as I've told her before, she's not the one that has to hear it vibrating the walls of the house at all hours of the night. Over time, I've tried reinforcing the wards on their rooms, playing music, as well as a myriad of other stratagems, but nothing has succeeded at completely drowning out the noise. I believe there was a mortal poet that summed up my plight quite succinctly: "It increased my fury, as the beating of a drum stimulates the soldier into courage."

I don't know why I find myself so particularly vexed this afternoon. Perhaps it's because ever since my two young wards sat down to take their exam for applied interdimensional mathematics, the dull, rhythmic thud of tapping quill tips has pervaded my thoughts, dashing whatever hopes I had of accomplishing any of my own work this hour.

At first, I thought they had devised a way to cheat. But, no. I wish they were cheating. I wish with everything that I am, everything that I own, that they were cheating. That would be less aggravating than what I'm currently having to witness.

Allow me to summarize the situation. Skye has done something to irritate Taly—certainly not surprising considering he goes out of his way to pester the poor girl. If my translation is accurate, he's unhappy that Sarina is allowing Taly to venture into the village unattended this evening to meet with a young suitor. Skye is insisting that Taly bring him along even though she has now told him to "shove it" no less than 22 times.

I think tomorrow I shall begin a small experiment—purely for my own research. By now, I'm quite fluent in the language of tapping, and I think that I will start embedding hidden messages into my lesson plans and including them in their tests. I'm curious to see how long it will take them to catch on. If they can stop making moon eyes at each other from across the room, I'm guessing maybe six months.

Skye had been right about one thing. The group that now comprised the highest-ranking members of the Gate Watchers were a bunch of ineffectual, self-important dipshits. After almost an hour of pointless jabber, they still had yet to accomplish anything useful.

Taly tapped her quill on the polished oak of the conference table, doing her best not to roll her eyes as Lord-something-or-other once again reminded the room that his family would execute swift and merciless retribution on the perpetrators of this attack. The lordling's empty promises would be far more comforting if his family and militias weren't currently on the other side of the Seren Gate.

The delegation had decided to hold the meeting in the assembly room at the top of the main tower, a soaring, circular structure that jutted up from the center of the compound. Floor-to-ceiling windows surrounded them on all sides, offering panoramic views of the churning bank of storm clouds that now seemed to hang at eye-level. Every so often, a flash of light would illuminate the shadowy mountains of fog and smoke, but the crash of thunder never came. The air wards that had been so artfully etched into the glass to resemble coiling vines dotted with moonflowers kept the sounds of the outside world at bay.

Taly let her eyes drift over the various Lords and Ladies seated at the table. Skye was to her left. Although she had tried to hang back and take a seat by the door with the assistants, he had insisted she sit next to him. That had raised a few eyebrows, but one look from Eula, who sat to the other side of Skye, had silenced any objections.

Kato sat to Taly's right, that mask of boyish charm firmly in place. The smile on his lips never wavered, but his eyes were cold and his responses, though somewhat crude and artless, were leading.

As for everyone else, Taly had met them all at one point or another over the years. There was Lady Lissa Riette—a lovely creature with fiery hair and a permanent sneer. Lady Reya Riette sat next to her. Taly couldn't remember how the two were related. Cousins perhaps, but something in her said they were probably sisters. Although the second woman had dark hair and almost violet eyes, she had the same square jaw and pert, upturned nose as her companion. They also wore matching amulets around their necks—a single shadow crystal surrounded by what appeared to be hyaline carved into the shape of a serpentine dragon eating its own tail. Seated next to each other, the two women looked like the living embodiments of day and night.

Continuing around the table, there was *Mr. Swift and Merciless Retribution,* Lord Rask Ridic, whose sallow skin already looked flushed from all that pontificating. Beside him sat a man Taly recognized as having visited Harbor Manor just last year—a merchant's son. A lowborn by birth, Lord Timo Paysan's family had managed to buy a title when several highborn families migrated to the mortal realm during the Hunt. If he had managed to pass the entrance exams to the Gate Watchers, that meant he probably had a fair amount of magic lurking beneath that skinny, almost child-like exterior.

And then rounding out the group was a man that Taly knew very well—Kane Harin. A fire mage, the man had very little magic, but he was clever and managed his aether well enough to make do. Taly had met him on her first trip to the compound when she was only seven. She remembered being terrified of the swirling scars decorating his hands and face, and she still laughed every time she recalled the look of pained embarrassment on Ivain's face when she had asked why the gruff lowborn wore a patch over his right eye. But even after almost 14 years of visiting the compound on and off, she hadn't really gotten to know Kane until she'd befriended his son—another salvager. There had been several nights over the past year when she didn't have enough coin for both food and a bunk, and his family had been kind enough to offer her a warm bed and a hot meal in exchange for mucking their stable.

Lissa caught Taly's eye, and her sneer turned into a scowl.

"Don't mind her," Kato whispered, winking at

the hateful woman, who promptly turned away with a soft huff. "Lissa hates everyone."

Taly covered her smile with a hand, letting her reply die on her lips. Except for Kane, every person in the room was a shadow mage, and she was sure that each one was channeling their aether, honing those enhanced fey senses to root out the things that weren't being said.

"Shades, Skylen?" Lissa's shrill voice rang out, interrupting Kane mid-sentence. "You truly expect us to believe that those creatures were shades? And based on what? Something a *human* found in the Vetiri? Truthfully, I didn't know humans had the mental capacity to learn to read the common tongue, much less Faera."

"Lissa, that is enough," Eula barked, her red lips set into a stern line. Beside her, Skye stiffened, and Taly could just hear that faint inhuman, fey growl—a warning.

One that Lissa did not heed. "I'm just saying—"

"No," Taly whispered, placing a hand on Skye's arm as he leaned forward, intent on reprimanding the vile woman. Taly didn't mind in the slightest if these people hated her. She was used to it. But Skye needed to keep them on his side.

Taly tapped out a seemingly random rhythm against Skye's wrist before pulling away. When she saw his lips twitch, she knew he'd deciphered her message as he relaxed and let Lissa keep talking.

Their old code. Originally devised as a way to communicate after bedtime, it had evolved over the years, enough that they had figured out ways to hold entire conversations without ever saying a word. Unfortunately, they'd had to stop using it when Ivain caught on and started pranking them during their lessons.

Actually, now that you mention it, I don't think I've ever seen that woman smile, came Skye's silent reply. *Odd. The rest of her family is quite lovely.*

Crossing her arms, Taly tapped out, *Well, if I had a stick that far up my ass, I probably wouldn't be too happy about it either.*

Skye coughed, his shoulders shaking, and Taly noted that they had now drawn Kato's attention. The other man eyed them with a mixture of amusement and irritation, giving Taly a playful pout when she raised a questioning brow. It seemed the older shadow mage didn't like being left out of the loop.

"That's all well and good, Lissa," Skye finally said, interrupting the noblewoman's tirade. She growled in reply but bit her tongue. "However, regardless of whether you want to believe it or not, that's what the research says."

"Again, based on the word of a *human*. Have you at least had it verified, Skylen?" Lissa argued stubbornly.

Growing tired of the woman's snide comments, Taly picked up one of the books she and Skye had brought with them from the library and skidded it across the table. "If you don't believe me, then verify it yourself."

Lissa snatched up the book, her expression stoic as she flipped through the pages.

"You *can* read it, can't you?" Taly prodded, smiling when she saw the fiery redhead's face falter. "Faera? Or should I translate? I think you'll find my accent is quite good."

The book slammed shut, and for a moment it looked like Lissa was going to make a reply, but her strange blood-red eyes flicked to her sister, who shook her head. "Continue," she said, anger simmering just beneath the surface of that strained tone and porcelain facade.

Skye's eyes found Taly's, and the proud smile he gave her made something in her chest tighten. "If that's settled," he said evenly, "can we move on? We need a plan. We can't just hole up in the compound and pray that we don't get attacked again."

"Why not?" Timo, the merchant's son—his voice was soft and reedy, like he wasn't used to speaking up. "Time on Tempris and the mainland will be synced up for at least two more days. We could try to pry open the gate and retreat to the Port of Marin."

Eula sighed, her brow furrowed. "Skylen and I discussed that possibility last night, but the gate's time crystals were stolen early this morning. It's completely inoperable."

"What?" Kato leaned forward. "Stolen? How is that possible? Why weren't there guards stationed?"

"There were," Skye replied gravely. "But they were found tied up and unconscious. Both men remember a woman bringing them wine shortly after the first bell rung, but neither can remember any details about her—her name, her face, nothing. We think they may have been drugged with bloodbane, but we're still waiting on the earth mages to confirm."

Taly felt cold. Bloodbane was hard to come by, even with the right black-market connections.

Kane's gravelly voice was the first to break

the silence. "That means that whoever is doing this has someone in the compound."

"I think that's a safe assumption at this point," Skye replied, his fingers steepled in front of him. "The explosion that tore a hole in the back wall during the attack yesterday... it came from inside." There was a round of hushed murmurs, but Skye held up a hand, shushing them. "That coupled with the sudden disappearance of the leadership—Commander Enix, his Precept, and his Lieutenant—I would say we're dealing with more than one person. Possibly a team that has now managed to create an army of monsters, infiltrate the compound, destroy our chain-of-command, and weaken our defenses."

"How do we find them?" Kato snarled, all signs of mirth gone. There was nothing but cold, unyielding anger left in its wake.

Skye caught his brother's eye, passing on some unspoken message that had the older man reluctantly backing down. Turning back to the table, Skye said, "I've already assigned a team of Ensigns to take a census of everyone in the keep, and we're still questioning everyone that may have seen something last night, but beyond that—"

"We have no way to weed out the traitors without turning this into a witch hunt," Eula concluded grimly. She rolled up her sleeves, revealing three violet lines that had been tattooed on her forearm.

"What do they want?" Reya's cold, listless voice lilted across the table. "If we could figure out what they want, maybe they would leave the rest of us be."

"For the time being, I'm not sure that matters," Skye answered. "They've made no effort to contact us with a list of demands. What we do know is that these things fight to kill and that we can't stay here. We need to move to Ryme."

Kane ran a scarred hand over his shorn head. "I disagree. We'll be too vulnerable out on the road. At least here, we have the walls. We have some measure of defense."

"Last I checked, there was a hole in the wall," Kato interjected. "If one of the fire mages sneezes in the wrong direction, that patch the earth mages managed to slap together isn't going to be anything more than ash. The compound is breached."

Skye crossed his arms, looking at Kane pointedly. "Kato's right. Just because we've had a moment to catch our breath doesn't mean we should get complacent. We're not safe here. The scouting parties we sent out this morning have confirmed that there are still shades moving around the city. They know our weak spots, they have a spy inside the compound—we should expect another attack. Soon."

Eula flipped through a stack of ledgers. "I agree with Skylen. Even if the compound were defensible, food and supplies would eventually become a problem. Although Kato's team wasn't able to retrieve Lord Brenin, they did confirm that the supply stores on the edge of the city were burned during the first attack. By my estimate, we only have enough food to last us until the end of the month. Ryme is the most fortified town on the island. They've been preparing for the Aion Gate connection for the better part of a year, and they have enough land, enough people, and enough resources to be self-sustaining if need be."

"It's too risky," Kane argued. "Without the

scrying relays, we don't know if there's still a Ryme to retreat to."

"Have we looked into fixing the relay?" Rask spoke up. He had quieted down after his initial overtures, most likely cowed by the bleakness of the situation.

"Yes," Eula replied. There was a tightness around her eyes, and she placed both hands flat on the table. "At first, we thought it was nothing more than a glitch, and maybe it was at the beginning. But, under the circumstances, we now suspect sabotage."

A hushed silence fell over the room, the floor underfoot trembling as a particularly violent peal of soundless thunder shook the tower. The runes etched on the glass flashed as the magic strained against what was most likely a deafening crash.

"What about the other scrying relays?" Taly asked, her eyes scanning the room. "Della's was still intact as of yesterday morning. And Plum, even Vale—both are less than a day's ride. We could send scouts."

"We'd likely be sending them to their deaths," Eula countered quietly.

"Eula's right," Skye agreed. "Anyone actually capable of making the journey—we need them here. The men and women we could spare... it would be suicide."

"I vote we go to Ryme," Rask said. "If I'm going to be stuck behind a wall, I'd like it to be intact."

Kane pounded a fist on the table. "If we have nothing but bad options, then I say we stay."

"I'm with Kane," Timo declared, his voice timid.

The two women of dawn and dusk nodded their agreement.

Interesting, Taly thought. It seemed the remaining leadership was starting to split, half for Skye, half for Kane. Crossing her arms, she let her fingers drum out a rhythm against her arm. *If you get Kane, you'll get the others.*

Skye's eyes flicked over to her, his thumb tapping the arm of his chair. *I think so too, but Kane hates me. He'll disagree with me just on principle.*

Taly raised a brow. *Nonsense. You're just not using the right bait.*

Another drum of Skye's fingers, this time against the side of his leg as he pretended to shift in his seat. *Well, don't keep me in suspense.* Although he kept his eyes trained ahead, he tilted his head, listening for her reply.

They had attracted Kato's attention again, so Taly leaned forward in her seat, making a note of something on the stack of papers in front of her. When she saw Kato's eyes slide away, she covertly slipped her hand into Skye's beneath the table and lightly tapped out her message against his palm. *Last I heard, Kane's son was in Ryme.*

The exchange couldn't have lasted more than a minute, maybe two, but Taly could already see a plan formulating in Skye's mind. Sitting up a little straighter, he said, "Kane. I understand the need to exercise caution, but in light of everything that's happened, I think we have to take the risk. If anything, think about how many people downstairs have family that's gone missing. Family that may very well be on their way to Ryme right now. If we're dead either way, don't we owe it to them to try to make the journey?"

The shift in Kane's attitude was immediate. His shoulders slumped, and his eyes became shuttered as he looked to Taly. A question.

"Avi was headed to Ryme night before last," she said quietly. "I saw him in Della with my own eyes."

Shaking his head, Kane stared out into the churning sea of gray rippling past the windows. "It's a risk."

"One we can mitigate," Skye replied calmly. "We can repurpose the debris outside the compound to fortify our caravan, keep the lowborn civilians in the center, train the mages so they can respond more quickly as a unit. If we go, we stand a chance. If we stay, we'll starve—assuming the shades don't get to us first."

Kane hesitated for a long moment, wavering. "Alright," he said slowly, tiredly. "I'll go."

"And me," Timo chimed almost immediately, just as Taly had predicted.

"Are you out of your minds?!" Lissa hissed as she shot to her feet. "This is ridiculous. I will not leave this compound until I know Ryme is safe."

"That is my feeling as well," Reya said far more calmly, pushing herself to stand. "If it is the wish of this delegation to leave, then my sister and I will not be a part of it."

"I can't fault you for that," Skye said with a sigh. "Anyone that wishes to stay with you, I won't interfere. So long as you grant us the same courtesy."

The two sisters departed shortly after their outburst, but it was of little consequence. The meeting was already winding down as Eula and Skye doled out orders. Taly idly wandered over to one of the windows, only half-listening as she stared out into the fog. With her human eyes, she couldn't see anything through the somber, gray haze. Even the flat crystal planes of the Seren Gate that she knew to be standing no more than 100 feet away were invisible.

When the last of the delegation had left, Skye came up behind her, wrapping his arms around her shoulders and tucking her underneath his chin. They stood there for several minutes, just staring out into the storm.

Taly was the first to break the silence. “Why would they take the time crystals? Of all the ways to shut down a gate, why did they remove the time crystals?”

She felt Skye shrug behind her. “I’m not sure. A part of me thinks that whoever is behind this might be trying to recreate the enchanted armor, but that’s not possible.”

“Why not?”

“No time mages,” Skye replied simply. “No Time Shard either. Even if the crystals didn’t go dark as soon as the preservation enchantment was removed, you’d still need a time mage to inscribe the crystal with the proper spell.”

That’s right. Taly had forgotten about that small detail. The Gate Watchers had enchanted each gate before the time crystals went dark, completely losing their ability to channel and convert aether. Without the Time Shard, they were little more than useless. But what had Aiden said? Taly’s very existence was evidence that the Time Shard had been revived. Which meant that maybe re-creating that armor wasn’t so impossible. Not anymore at least.

And then there was her. What would their unknown attacker do if he (or she or they) found out that there might be a living time mage? A human one, but still… Taly shuddered at the idea.

"It's okay, Tink," Skye said, most likely having heard the sharp spike in her heart rate. His arms tightened around her. "We'll figure something out. All we've got to do is stick together, you and me, and we'll be fine."

"What are you not saying?" Taly whispered, noting the slight edge in his voice.

"Am I that obvious?"

Taly shook her head, smiling softly. "Only to me."

Skye sighed. "I'm worried about Ryme and how we're going to get all of these people there. Kane's concerns are valid. Even if we fortify the caravans, we *will* lose people if we get attacked out in the open. I'd feel a lot better if I knew we had backup coming."

A sharp stab of guilt lanced Taly's chest. She stepped away, moving back over to the table to start gathering up the scattered books, notes, and journals. She needed to keep her hands busy.

Reya's dull, lifeless words filtered back through her mind: *What do they want?* Or maybe more precisely, *who* did they want? She didn't have any evidence, but Taly was starting to suspect she knew the answer to that question. And it made her stomach churn.

"There's no one you can send?" Taly asked shakily, glancing at him over her shoulder. A gnawing sense of guilt took root deep inside her, and she took a deep breath, forcefully suppressing the urge to gasp for air. How could she fix this? If this really was her fault, if they were after her, how could she fix this? "What about... woah." A prickling sting rippled up and down her arm, and then the world tilted sideways. She stumbled, grabbing at the table for balance.

A spectral golden hand gripped her arm moments before she felt Skye come up behind her.

Damn it! She'd dropped her guard—allowed her attention to slip. She prodded at the mental wall, frantically searching. The patches she'd put in place were still holding but... *There!* A tiny, almost insignificant trickle of power seeping out from between the stones. Shoving every bit of willpower she had at the leak, the glimmering, golden haze creeping in around the edges of her vision slowly abated.

"Taly?" Skye's voice was soft yet urgent as the world around her came back into focus. "C'mon, Tink, talk to me."

Taly blinked up at him, confused. How had he gotten up there? For that matter, how had she come to be sprawled on the floor with Skye crouching over her?

"I'm fine. What happened?" She tried to sit up, but her head swam as soon as she shifted.

"Easy," Skye said, gently lifting her and leaning her body against his. "You were talking, and then you just went down. I caught you before you could hit your head, but I still think we should take you to see the healer."

"No!" Taly exclaimed. She couldn't have that healer looking at her arm again. Skye's brow furrowed, and he opened his mouth to protest. Before he could say anything to the contrary, she added, "I think this is just a case of too much coffee and not enough food. Sleep would probably also help."

"I guess we have had a pretty rough go of it lately," Skye conceded, his eyes tight with worry. "Still, I'd feel better if you saw the healer. Especially since you were just getting back on your feet again after the harpy."

Taly shook her head. "No, Skye. Let the healer tend to people that actually need healing. I'm fine."

"Hey?" a new voice inquired. "What happened?"

Taly groaned, but Skye cut her off before she could protest. "Taly needs the healer."

"No, I don't," she reiterated.

"What?" Rounding the table, there was genuine concern in Kato's expression as he crouched down beside them. "Is she sick?"

"No." Taly shook off Skye's hold and shot to her feet, wobbling slightly. "I don't need a healer. I need a snack. That's all."

Skye stood. "Taly, please—"

"I said *no*." Taly slapped his hand away when he reached for her, wincing when she saw a flash of hurt in his eyes. "You know that medicine Aiden has me on has my metabolism all messed up. I just need to eat something."

Turning to Skye, Kato asked, "Weren't you supposed to be meeting with Kane right now? I can take her to the commissary."

"I don't need babysitting," Taly muttered. Nor did she want to get stuck spending any time alone with Kato—not with how unstable those spells on her arm were becoming.

"Maybe *you* don't," Kato replied with a grin, "but I do. I'm known for finding trouble—just ask my brother."

Skye chuckled, his eyes zeroing in on Taly when he saw her lean against the table for support. "It's true. All I hear from Mother when I visit is how she always thought Kato would finally grow up once he passed the turn of his second century. But alas…"

"Better a troublemaker than a celibate country hermit," Kato retorted sharply.

"Is that what she says about me?" Skye asked, completely unfazed. "Could be worse, I suppose."

"Okay, boys." Taly held up her hands when she saw something mean creep into Kato's expression. She was starting to get the impression that it irritated the older mage to no end when his barbs didn't find their mark. "That's enough. I'll go with Kato if it means the two of you will shut up and leave me the hell alone."

"You know what, I don't like it, but I'll take it," Skye said abruptly. Lightning streaked the cloudy sky behind him as he turned to Kato, who looked just as shocked as she felt. "But if she collapses again, take her to the healer. No arguments. That's an order, *Marshal*."

Taly opened her mouth to protest, but Skye shushed her by pressing a chaste kiss to her brow. "Yes," he said, ducking down to glare at her affectionately. "Eat. Get some rest. But if you're still unwell after that, go see the healer. We all need to be at our best."

"Fine," Taly conceded grumpily. "But be prepared to eat your words later on because I'm not going to need a healer." Even if she did, once they had a chance to talk that evening, he would see why that wasn't a possibility.

"Thank you," Skye said, pressing another kiss to her brow. His eyes dipped to her mouth, but instead of closing the distance, he just smiled and shook his head before quickly exiting the room. Apparently, he had learned by now to take whatever meager offering of peace she gave him and not ask questions.

"Well!" Kato exclaimed once Skye had left the

room. "I must say I'm impressed at my brother's efficiency."

"I'm sorry, what?" Taly just stared at the arm that Kato offered.

He gave her a disarming grin as he reached for her hand and tucked it into the crook of his arm. "My dear baby brother just managed to back you into a corner of your own making—a feat that I'm starting to suspect isn't easy."

"Your flattery is wasted, Kato," Taly countered, a shiver slithering down her spine. His fingers caressed the back of her hand, and she could just make out a faint tremor of aether prickling her skin. Most humans probably wouldn't have even noticed the almost imperceptible swell of magic, would play it off as some sort of static charge, but she had grown up around shadow mages. Stress and fatigue tended to make their magic slightly unstable, creating tiny ripples in the surrounding aether.

As Kato pulled her along, down the hallway and towards the aether lift that would take them down the 25 floors it would take to reach the courtyard, she tried to play off the weakness in her limbs as hunger, assured him that she was just tired every time she stumbled. But that tickle at the base of her skull, the feeling of his magic ghosting across her skin, was unnerving, almost predatory. It awoke some long-forgotten primal instinct, the need to survive, the need to run. When they crossed the threshold of the aether lift, she pulled her hand back and stepped away, leaning against the wall of the lift and pretending to nurse a headache as she rubbed at her temples.

The rain was coming down in earnest as they stepped through the doors of the main building.

Water had started to collect in the courtyard, and they had to carefully navigate the rapidly forming puddles. As they approached the line for the commissary, Kato offered her his coat, a plain, standard-issue Gate Watcher's cloak made from waterproof canvas. The queue trailed out the door of the kitchens, through the mud and trampled down hay, and Taly accepted the garment gratefully, pulling the hood over her hair as the wind picked up.

"Lovely weather we're having," she said, trying to break the heavy silence.

Kato's lips twitched. "Yes. Funny that the weather should take such a nasty turn as soon as you arrived. In fact, a lot of things seemed to have taken a turn as soon as you arrived. Why do you think that is?"

"Bad luck." Taly took a deep breath, trying to slow her racing heartbeat and praying that the dull patter of the rain would confuse Kato's enhanced senses. "Some might even say I'm cursed."

That's certainly not a lie, she thought, prodding carefully at the mental barrier.

"Very bad luck," he countered blithely. The smile on his lips fell, seemingly washed away by the rain. "You know I'm not sure what I'm angrier about—that someone's creating shades or that there are those inside our walls selling out their own people. I've been thinking about it, and if I had to guess, I would say that our traitor most likely infiltrated the compound as a refugee during all of the confusion. I would also guess that she's looking for something."

"She?" Taly pulled at the coat, trying to pass off the trembling in her hands as a shiver.

Kato nodded, unaffected by the wet and the cold. Fey tended to run a few degrees warmer than humans. "Yes. That's what the guards said when they were questioned—a woman brought them wine just before the time crystals in the gate went missing."

Taly's throat bobbed, the only reaction she would allow herself as she continued to stare straight ahead. Why did everything always circle back around to time magic?

"You know what I find myself wondering?" Kato mused. Although his face was the picture of concerned confusion as he scuffed at the edge of a puddle with his boot, his eyes were cold. "Now that our traitor has the time crystals from the Seren Gate, what do you think she'll go for next? What is she after?"

"I don't know," Taly replied stoically.

"Are you sure?" Kato pressed. "Come on, you're a smart girl. You don't have any ideas?" Taly shook her head, unnerved by the ruthlessness she could see lurking just beneath the surface of that boyish façade. "That's too bad," he said with a convincing sigh. "Because if I knew what she wanted, I'd be tempted to just give it to her. Anyone would. Especially if it would save the lives of all these *innocent* people." He held out his arms, gesturing toward the hundreds of displaced refugees milling about the courtyard. "How many more people have to die, Taly?"

Because of you, her subconscious hissed at her. *Time mage. Freak.*

Taly took a step back, her appetite having grown cold. "You know, on second thought, I'm not feeling very hungry. I think I'm just going to go to bed." Shrugging out of his coat, she tossed it to him as she turned to walk away.

His hand grabbed her wrist, and as he whirled her around to face him, a crest of pain, the sharpest one yet, tore through her, almost bringing her to her knees. She managed to bite back her cry, but when she looked up, what she saw in Kato's eyes had her backing away. Suspicion. Betrayal. *Anger*. There was so much anger behind that deceptive smile. "Now, now… I promised my brother I'd take care of you," he said with just the right amount of concern. "You're starting to look a bit piqued. Stay in line. Let's get something to eat."

"I'll get something later. Promise," Taly replied hastily, stumbling over her feet in her attempt to get away. This time he let her retreat, and it was all she could do not to run as she forced herself to slow her pace, edge around the courtyard as she pretended to shy away from the rain.

He knew. Kato knew what she was. Maybe the first pulse of magic in the library really was an accident, and each spell that had subsequently snapped had been nothing more than a link in a chain reaction that had already been set in motion. But when Kato grabbed her arm just now, when he took her hand in the tower and looped her arm with his—she had felt it. The subtle, *deliberate* bite of shadow magic. Searching. Seeking. Its claws strummed the fraying cords of the enchantments woven across her skin, scraping across the barrier that was just barely holding back her magic. He hadn't been sure before, but now… he had everything he needed. And he must have come to the same conclusion she had. Whoever was doing this was after her. Innocent people had died because of her.

As soon as she passed through the doors of the main building, Taly started sprinting, choosing to take the servants' stairs. The darkened stairwell was deserted, and she finally allowed herself to sag against the wall, panting. Another whip-like snap of pain jolted her body, and her lip bled as she desperately attempted to shove the released power back behind the wall. Gasping for breath, she started taking the stairs at a far more sedate pace.

She couldn't stay here, not anymore. She couldn't knowingly endanger more innocent lives just so that she could stay hidden. And no matter how much she may have wanted to, she couldn't tell Skye. Because if she did, he might not make the right decision. He might not send her away. She couldn't take that chance.

You're the only thing keeping me going. That's what he had said to Taly just hours earlier. Bursting into their room, she hesitated. This was going to kill him. He would never forgive her. If she ran out on him a second time, that was it. He might still care about her, but he would be well within his rights to wash his hands of her. For good.

But maybe it was better that way. Maybe she had been right the first time. He really was better off without her. Everyone was.

Peeling off her now-sopping wet coat and sweater, Taly paused as three tiny, bell-shaped blooms fluttered to the floor. She had found them growing in the courtyard and stopped to pluck them as she and Skye made their way to the tower to meet with the other members of the leadership.

Snowdrops. The same as the twining mass of flowers that Skye had so lovingly etched onto the crystal frame of her pistols.

Picking up one of the wilting buds, Taly twirled the stem between her forefinger and thumb, gently prodding at the wall and teasing out a small trickle of magic from between the stones. As she watched the golden mist snake its way between her fingers, she couldn't help but think it felt familiar in a way, this power—like an old friend. The golden threads wove themselves around the bloom, pulling and tightening until the petals were once again smooth and supple and new.

She had to leave. About that, she was sure. But this time, she wouldn't just disappear into the night with no explanation.

This time, she would say goodbye.

CHAPTER 24

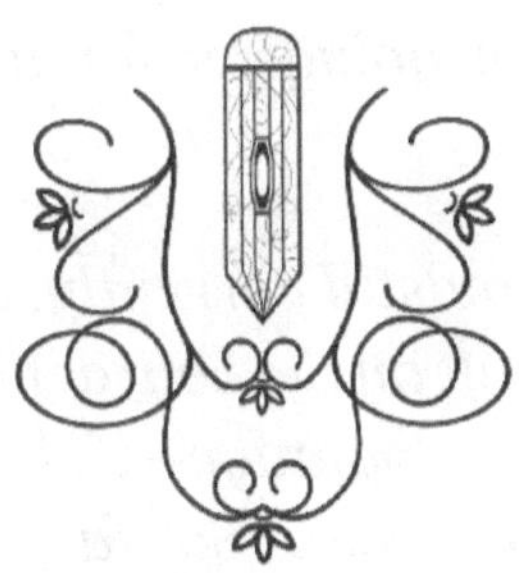

-From the personal notes of Ivain Castaro

The 25th day of the month Ares, during the 246th year of the Empty Throne

As I approach my elderhood, evenings like this are what I live for. Late summer on Tempris has always been my favorite—the sunsets are so vibrant, so heartbreakingly beautiful, that even the most hard-hearted of souls couldn't help but stop and linger.

As I write this, we are all out on the third-floor balcony—Sarina, myself, and the children—enjoying the last of the summer air. Sarina is currently sitting to my left, thoroughly engrossed in her latest hobby. Something with glass and paint that I don't really care to understand. And of course, the children, if I can really still call them that, are doing what they do best—bickering.

In her attempt to educate the younglings on mortal culture, Sarina recently taught them how to play a human game called chess. It has been an entertaining experiment, to say the least, especially considering how antagonistically competitive those two have always been. The game they started this evening has been going on for nearly two hours now.

They are at a standstill currently, and though Skye has more pieces left on the board, I believe Taly may actually have the advantage—if she can keep it. Her strategy is quite bold. So far, she has risked everything, even going so far as to sacrifice her queen two turns back. Skye, however, has chosen a different approach. I daresay he is at times as daring as Taly in his tactics, but only to a point. For he has now retreated and protects his queen at all costs. He has already had several opportunities to take the lead, but he refuses to give up that one piece.

And now I see that she has him backed into a corner. He has nowhere else to retreat and no choice but to play his queen or throw the game. Taly is already quite confident in her impending victory, but Skye seems to be wavering now in the face of defeat. I know for a fact that there is nothing the boy hates more than losing to Taly, but after such dogged dedication to this strategy of his, I can't help but wonder which option he'll choose.

"No," Skye said tersely as he handed off yet another stack of paperwork to a young fire mage.

The petite woman almost had to run to keep up with him as he strode into the main building. "Tell Carlin that the mortals stay inside the keep. The other fey can complain all they want, but the fact of the matter is they're better equipped to deal with the cold. Mortals get sick far more easily, and we barely have enough earth mages to go around as it is. If more fights break out, open up the dungeons downstairs and throw the dissidents down there to cool off. Also, inform Geran that I won't be able to meet with him until later this evening."

"Yes, sire," the girl replied, sounding almost as harried as Skye felt. "And Lord Emrys? Er… the other Lord Emrys? What shall I tell him?"

Skye stopped at the entrance to the servants' stairwell, shaking his head. Kato had been clamoring for his attention all morning, but he just hadn't found the time to meet with him yet. He barely had time for his current errand. "Tell my brother that unless it's urgent, he's going to have to wait. I've got 20 different people bending my ear right now, and they all want something different."

"Yes, sire." The girl bobbed her head before turning and disappearing into the crowd milling about the great hall.

It was just after midday, and Skye breathed a sigh of relief as he started taking the stairs two at a time. This was the first moment of peace he'd had all morning. Between organizing the teams responsible for scrounging the surrounding area for supplies and trying to devise a training regimen to teach the civilian mages basic combat formations, he was starting to regret stumbling out of bed before the fifth bell had struck just to tag along with Taly to do a little pre-dawn research.

There's a lie, he thought, grinning like a fool as he ascended the final stair to the top floor of the living quarters. The worn carpet muffled the sound of his footsteps as he made his way to the end of the hallway, to the suite he and Taly had shared. Yes, he was tired. Well, exhausted. But he didn't regret a single moment of that morning. From waking up with Taly in his arms to that life-altering kiss they had shared in the library—he wouldn't change a thing. Except for the part where Kato had interrupted them. That he would change.

Skye came to a stop in front of the door to their room, and his hands were shaking as he combed his fingers through his hair. *Why am I so nervous?* he wondered, attempting to straighten his wrinkled shirt. It was just Taly. Not much had changed since that morning. Except for everything. Only everything had changed.

What if she says no? That thought had occurred to him at least once or twice since they had parted ways. He had asked her what she wanted, and she had never given him a clear answer. Yes, she had let him kiss her again—seemed open to his advances—but she could still change her mind. She could still decide that she just wanted to be friends.

Before he could second-guess himself, Skye pushed open the door and then quietly closed it behind him as he stepped into the antechamber. He could see Taly just beyond the doorway, her back hunched as she leaned over a writing desk that had been shoved into a corner. Her hair had been swept to the side and braided, and she had changed into a plain white linen shirt with long tapered sleeves that were pulled down and buttoned at her wrists. The toe of her boot tapping out an absentminded rhythm was the only sound breaking the silence as she studied whatever was on the desk in front of her with rapt interest.

"Hey, Tink?"

Taly whirled around, her hand clutching her chest. "Shards!" she yelped, her gray eyes wide. "Wear a bell or something!"

Skye chuckled, his hands in his pockets as he came closer. To his great surprise and delight, she hadn't buttoned her shirt yet, and he could clearly see the lace of her undergarments peeking out from underneath the sheer fabric of her camisole. The long lines of toned muscle, the sharp curve of her waist, the generous swell of her breasts—all were on full display to his eager eyes. Beautiful. *Strong*. A far cry from the half-starved waif he'd had to coax and cajole into talking to him as he walked her back to the manor only a few short weeks ago.

Noticing his intense scrutiny, Taly tensed, her fingers twitching. But she didn't tug at the edges of her shirt, not even when he let his eyes drift down and linger—tracing and retracing the feminine contours of her body.

"What are you staring at?" she muttered, her back stiff as she turned back to the desk.

Closing the remaining distance between them in a few long strides, Skye wrapped his arms around her, pulling up the fabric of her camisole and letting his hands rest on the smooth skin of her stomach. "You," he murmured, delighting in the slight flush that reached even the tips of her ears. Pressing his nose into the crook of her neck, he finally allowed himself to fully take in her scent. Even after he had been cleared to use his magic, he had abstained back in the library, afraid that the extra layer of stimulation might break his already tenuous restraint.

“You know I don’t like it when you do that,” she said with a soft sigh, one hand coming up to tangle in his hair.

“Do what?” he asked, slightly dazed. Shards, she smelled good—like mint and sage, with just a hint of jasmine. There was a faint tickle of iron, just around the edges—distinct but easily ignored.

“I don’t like being scented. You know that. Besides, you’re a shadow mage, not a dog. I know it’s hard to tell the difference sometimes but—"

Skye pinched her sides, just where he knew she was ticklish. “I could be a dog,” he said, his own laughter mixing with hers. “If you feed me, I’ll just keep coming back.”

She turned in his arms, placing a hand on his chest. It was just enough to make him pull back. Yes, he wanted to push her, but, first and foremost, he wanted her to want to be pushed.

“Spoilsport,” Skye muttered, pressing his lips to her brow. “I’m sorry, but that shadow mage in Ryme didn’t know what the hell he was talking about, and you should never have given him a second thought. Humans do not *reek* of iron. That was a gross exaggeration.”

“Says you,” she quipped. Her hands twisted in his collar, pushing the fabric aside. Skye shivered when he felt her fingertips ghost across his skin. “But then again—"

Unable to resist the urge any longer, Skye pressed his mouth to hers, a low moan escaping him when her hands found their way into his hair, teasing and tugging as she eagerly returned his kiss.

She was the first to pull away, and he followed her, placing one last gentle kiss just at the edge of her mouth. “I’ve been wanting to do that all morning,” he murmured against her lips, not ready for the moment to be over just yet. “You were saying?”

“What are you doing back so early?” she asked breathily, turning back to the cluttered tabletop. “I wasn’t expecting you until tonight.”

“I’m between meetings, so I thought I’d come check on you.” Looking over her shoulder at the faded map spread out on the desktop, he added, “See if I needed to put you to bed.” That earned him a sharp elbow to the ribs, and then another when he just laughed shamelessly. “Seriously, though, how are you feeling? You had me worried.”

“Fine.” Taly’s head snapped up. “I’m fine,” she repeated, turning back to the map. “Tell me, have you talked to Kato yet?”

“Nope.” Skye dropped down into the desk chair that had been pushed off to the side. “He’s been trying to track me down, but I’ve been tied up with Kane all morning. Why?”

“No reason,” she replied a little too quickly.

“What did he do?” Skye asked, bristling. If his brother was trying to mess with Taly just to get to him… and when they were dealing with shades on top of everything else…

“Please.” Taly glanced at him from the corner of her eye, giving him a sly wink that made his heart stutter. “I think I know how to deal with you Emrys boys by now.”

“And I like to think I still have a few tricks you haven’t seen,” Skye drawled. Although, he would be more than happy to divulge every trick he knew if it would convince her to crawl into his bed and never leave.

Standing up straight, Taly began buttoning her shirt, rolling her eyes when he pouted. "I have something to tell you, and I don't think you're going to like it," she said, suddenly serious. "I'm going to Plum. I'm going to try to make it to their scrying relay."

"Are you kidding? That's a terrible idea," Skye said, his eyes narrowing. For the first time since he'd walked in, he noticed that her pack rested at her feet, and panic coiled deep in his belly.

Taly began pacing in a nervous circle as she tucked in her shirt tail. "Skye, we have no way of knowing if the other villages have been hit yet. Sure, this might be a one-off thing, but it might not be. Send me to Plum. There's another relay there—one that might still work. If not, then I can move on to Vale, even Bago if I need to. If I can find a relay that's still operational, I might be able to get a message out before this happens again. Or, at the very least, contact Ryme and get you the backup that you need."

Grabbing her by the arm as she passed, Skye said, "No. Were you not there this morning when we all unanimously decided that going to Plum would be suicide?"

"For a fey, maybe," Taly said, pushing him away. "But I'm not fey. I'm human—that means no aether. If I'm careful, I won't attract beasts or shades. And if something does go wrong, I know how to defend myself."

Skye shook his head. "Taly, this is not the time to go off and play hero. If you want to help, then stay. You can contribute more right here than off in the woods somewhere."

"That's not true," she argued stubbornly.

"While I might be good for digging through a pile of old books and repairing a rusty tower gun, I'm just going to be another liability on the road. I've already looked at the preliminary census data, and anything I could contribute would just be redundant. I have no value here. But out there..." She looked at him pointedly. "I need to do this, Skye. I can't just stay here and do nothing."

Skye was silent for a long moment, his eyes taking in her wide stance and crossed arms. She wasn't going down without a fight. "I'm sorry, Taly. I can't let you go off alone."

"You don't get to make that choice," she replied simply. "I know the way, and I can handle myself. I'm going."

Standing, Skye took her in his arms, pressing his nose to her hair and noting the way her arms came up to circle his waist—despite the look of defiance he'd seen in her eyes only moments before. "No." When she tried to push him away, he held on. "Just think about this for a minute. I know you can handle yourself, but you were lucky to get away from those things the first time. We're *both* lucky to be standing here right now."

"I'm going, Em," she said more forcefully. She pushed against him, stumbling slightly when he let her go. That rebellious flame had been rekindled and shone brighter than he'd ever seen it. "We both have a part to play right now. Let me play mine."

No, no, no! his mind screamed at him. It was madness. Had she hit her head yesterday? That was the only reasonable explanation he could come up with to describe this insanity. His fists clenched at his sides as he suppressed the urge to sling her over his shoulder and force her to see the healer.

He had dealt with Taly's stubbornness before. He just needed to remain calm and reason her out of this corner she had somehow backed her way into.

"Look, I can't make you do anything you don't want to do," Skye said. "I can't make you stay. But here's what I will do. I'll make you a deal. It's going to take us a few days until we're ready to move, and we're not giving up on fixing the scrying relay here. Let's see if we can bring it back online. If we can't, then come with us to Della. It's not far, and there's a relay there. If that one's down too, then we'll regroup—reopen the discussion about going to Plum or Vale. If we get a foothold in Della, then that becomes a far more reasonable distance to travel—a few hours there and back. We could even spare a team. That sound fair?"

"That's a great plan, Em, but it's going to take too long. The other villages on the island might not have a few days. I'm going. You can't stop me."

"Fine!" Skye snapped, rounding on her. She refused to give up any ground, her chin raised high as she stared up at him defiantly. "If you want to go get yourself killed, you have to see the healer first." He couldn't help but laugh when her eyes widened. It had been a gamble, but it paid off. While he had no idea why she seemed so reticent to let the earth mages examine her, if he could use that to his advantage, he would.

"I don't need to see the damned healer," Taly ground out, a low inhuman, nearly *fey* growl emanating from deep within her chest.

Skye started at the sound but quickly shook off his surprise. Before she could argue any further, he said, "Prove to me that you're of sound body and mind, and I'll send you on your way. After all, I'm certainly in no position to turn down volunteers at this point."

"Em—"

"Oh, don't 'Em' me," Skye shot back. "If you won't see the healer, then I'm not going to get behind this. I'll tell you the same thing I told Eula—I'm not going to send our men and women to their deaths. You collapsed on me not two hours ago, but now you're saying that you're fit to trek halfway across the island? And fight shades on top of that? I don't buy it."

"Shards, stop being so overprotective. You're as bad as Sarina."

"Really? That's your go-to argument right now?" he asked dubiously, reaching for her wrist and pushing up her sleeve so he could study the web of discoloration. When she struggled against him, he let her go. "You were supposed to go see the healer this morning for those bruises, but you notice I didn't say anything about that."

"Because I don't need a healer. This" —Taly held up her wrist after checking to make sure that the cuff was securely buttoned— "looks worse than it actually is." When Skye looked at her, a single eyebrow arched skeptically, she stuttered, "I-it doesn't hurt—much. I don't know why it looks so bad. I think I'm just getting clumsier."

Skye snorted a laugh. "You always did have a knack for running into anything with a sharp edge." Reaching over, he tucked a finger under her chin, pulling her eyes back to his. "Look, we've both had a rough few days, and I think we're both feeling it. You've already done enough for today. Get some sleep, and then we'll talk again tonight."

When it looked like she was about to protest again, he wrapped his arms around her. "Please, Taly. Just work with me here. In the past month,

I've watched you almost die twice, and that's not including the time I spent yesterday thinking I might not get to see you again. I'm pretty sure I saw a gray hair in the mirror last night, and that's something that shouldn't happen until I'm well past the age of being an elder. So please, for the sake of my sanity *and* my hair, just give me some time to work through all of this. We'll come up with something. And you have my word that if I see a way you can help, I'll use you."

Taly was silent, her lips pressed together in a frown as she fidgeted with one of the buttons on his shirt. She had that look on her face that Skye knew all too well. The look that said she was just getting started.

Shards, he hated that look.

He braced himself, getting ready for the next argument, the next wave of stubborn anger. But it never came. Her eyes briefly flicked to her pack before finding his. Something had just been decided, even if he wasn't quite sure what that was. Then, in a surprising turn of events, her face relaxed, and she gave him a gentle smile.

Skye felt breathless as she reached up and ran a hand through his hair—as though that simple touch had sucked the aether from his veins. Her fingertips lightly grazed his scalp, and a visible shudder shook his frame when he felt the whisper of her touch against the pointed tip of his ear. Still smiling, she said, "Well, I think you're lying about the gray."

Did she just… yes. Yes, she did.

Skye barely managed to bite back a moan as she let her fingers boldly trail along the shell of his ear, bringing her hand down to rest on his chest. Whether she realized it or not, she had just done something very *intimate*, at least as far as the fey were concerned. Something he desperately wanted her to do again.

A large yawn suddenly overtook her, and she buried her face in his shoulder. "Maybe you're right. Maybe I do need a nap."

"I think that's a wise decision," Skye murmured. He released a sharp breath when he felt her lips press against the side of his neck. "But first, I need to hear you say it."

"Say what?" she asked, her tongue darting out to taste his skin.

Oh Shards, she was trying to kill him. He was sure of it now.

"You know what." Skye had to force himself to pull back as that sweet little mouth continued to assault his neck. "*Miss I didn't lie, I just didn't correct you when you made certain assumptions*? I'm not taking any chances. Say it—out loud."

Taly glared at him before finally rolling her eyes. "Fine. I'll get some rest, and we can talk about Plum later. Happy?"

"Thank you," Skye said, squeezing his eyes shut and trying his best to redirect some of the blood flow back into his brain. "Now… I need to go. I was supposed to be downstairs ten minutes ago to meet with Eula, and then I can't even remember what I'm supposed to do after that. Apparently, I'm also supposed to find time to meet with Kato as well."

As soon as he mentioned his brother's name, Taly's eyes became shuttered and her body tensed. Although he was tempted to ask what had happened, Skye didn't push her. Kato had clearly done something to upset her, and when she was ready to tell him, he would listen. Then, he would go pound Kato into the ground. At the very least, he had that to look forward to.

Skye moved to release her, but her fingers coiled in his shirt.

"Wait," she said, peeking up at him through a veil of dark lashes. "Just... not yet."

He knew she could feel the rapid beat of his heart as her hands snaked their way up his chest, and there was no way she hadn't heard his sharp intake of breath when she pressed her body more firmly against his. His arms tightened around her, and the feline smile she gave him when he pulled her even closer would no doubt be playing a leading role in his dreams for many nights to come.

He let her take the lead—trying to be patient as her fingers traced his jaw, then his lips, her eyes trailing every movement as though she wanted to memorize him. And when she finally—*finally*—pulled his head down and pressed her mouth to his, he realized for not the first time that this woman was going to get him into trouble. Because even though she was still shy and tentative and just a little clumsy, that simple, chaste kiss sparked a wave of desire so vicious, it made him dizzy. It made his blood sizzle, sent icy shivers down his spine. It left him starving and yet somehow sated.

She pulled away far too quickly for Skye's liking, her cheeks flushed. "Sorry," she said, a hint of melancholy coloring her words. "You can tell Eula it's my fault you're late. I just really wanted to do that one more time."

If Skye had been thinking clearly as he slowly backed away, reluctantly making his way back towards the door, he might have noticed the way she gripped the edge of the desk a little too tightly.

If he had been able to tear his thoughts away from the fact that he could still taste her on his lips, he might have seen that the smile she gave him didn't quite reach her eyes.

And maybe something inside him did. But during that moment, he pushed that little voice to the back of his mind as his attention was once again pulled back to the never-ending list of tasks still waiting for him. They would talk later that night when he'd finally managed to satisfy the horde of people chasing after him, each one needing something different.

"Hey," Taly called out to him just as he was about to turn the knob.

"Yeah?" Skye asked, turning slightly.

She was still leaning against the desk, still smiling that heartbreakingly beautiful smile. "Bye, Em."

Giving her what he hoped was only a somewhat lovestruck grin, Skye turned the knob, opening the door before he was tempted to blow off Eula in favor of crawling into bed with Taly for some much-needed rest.

"Bye, Tink," he said as he closed the door behind him.

"Where the hell have you been?" Kato exploded as soon as Skye walked through the door of Commander Enix's office. "You were supposed to be here almost half an hour ago."

Skye eyed his brother in irritation as he strode across the long expanse of the tower office. Floor-to-ceiling rows of books lined the walls of the airy space, and the peaked ceiling had been foiled with artfully embossed tiles—something Enix had seen in the mortal realm and then insisted on installing in every suite and office in the compound.

With an irritated sigh, Skye flung the stack of books and ledgers some Ensign had thrust into his hands on top of the cluttered desk—a great massive thing that had been forged from a single living tree coaxed into growing into something vaguely desk-shaped. Spiraling wooden tendrils coiled up the legs and sides, and tiny white blooms dotted each vine, their petals glimmering like pearls. Shrugging out of his coat, he stared out the circular window that dominated most of the back wall. The rain was finally starting to let up, and he could just see the dome of the library peeking through the clouds across the skyway.

That library held some *very* good memories for him now.

"I got held up," Skye finally said when Kato started tapping his toe impatiently. "Now what was it that was so important I had to push back my meeting with Sorin?"

Stiff-backed and tense, Kato checked the door, his hands pressing into the gnarled wood as he activated the wards that protected the room from other *shadow senses*, as Taly liked to call them. "I thought it was only right to tell you first, before... well." Kato sighed as he trudged back across the room, coming to a stop in front of the desk where he shifted restlessly. "It's about Taly."

"What did you do?" Skye growled, his voice low as he recalled the troubled look in Taly's eyes. He *knew* Kato had done something to upset her.

"What?" Kato exclaimed. "I didn't do anything." He held up a hand before Skye could reply. "Just listen. This isn't easy for me either. I… I know I always gave you shit about her because she was a mortal, but I can see now why you like her so much. She's easy to like. But… damn it, there's no easy way to say this. She's part of it, Skye. Taly's a part of this—the attacks, the crystals in the gate. She's not who you think she is. She's a traitor."

Placing both hands on the desk, Skye glared at Kato through narrowed eyes, just barely suppressing the urge to bare his teeth. "Kato, you are on very dangerous ground right now."

"Think about it!" Kato pounded his fists on the desktop. "None of this started happening until she got here."

"If that's your only proof, then I'm just as culpable," Skye countered, crossing his arms as he turned to look out the window. "And so are half the people down in that courtyard."

"It's not," Kato whispered sadly. "I wish it was. Believe me, I do. But it's not. There's magic on her—layer upon layer of enchantments."

Skye forcibly pushed down the bile that burned his throat. It was a trick. If there were magic on her, he would've noticed. "And how exactly would you know that?" was all he said in reply.

Kato ducked his head, a sweep of auburn hair falling across his eyes. "This morning in the library, my magic sparked when I touched her. I thought I was just tired at the time, but something didn't feel right. So when I took her downstairs after the meeting, I did a little more prodding and… I've never seen anything like it. Just on the surface, she's *drenched* in water magic. The subtlety, the grace, the detail... I've never seen a water glamour like that, Skye. I almost gave up, thinking that I was wrong, but then I found a tear in the spell. I was able to weave my way through the overlay."

Skye swallowed convulsively. *No*, he thought, shaking his head. Kato was lying. He had to be.

"And underneath?" Kato continued, either unaware or uncaring of Skye's inner turmoil. "Shadow magic—a… a web of shadow magic. I didn't have much time, so I wasn't able to get a good look at it all. I saw a few aether suppression spells, memory alteration…" Kato's voice trailed off. "I'm sorry, brother," he said with genuine sympathy, "but I think it's safe to say that she was involved with the incident at the Seren Gate."

"Even if what you said was true," Skye choked out, "I was with her all last night. There's no way she could have had anything to do with the crystals going missing from the Seren Gate."

"You never went to sleep?" Kato pressed. "Never left her alone, even for a few moments?"

Skye pretended to study something off in the distance. They had parted ways, he realized, dread snaking its way around his heart. He and Taly. After the attack, after she had found him in the courtyard—he had sent her upstairs to clean up while he saw to his duties. And then later that night, after they had fallen asleep, he hadn't woken up to her soft crying until well after the guards reported being knocked out.

No! his mind howled. It was impossible. This

attack had taken an inordinate amount of planning and coordination. There would've been some sign, some clue before today that Taly had been working with them. As it was, she had been with someone almost every moment of every day since the harpy. If not him, then Sarina or Ivain or Aiden. Even Aimee had come up and played a few hands of cards when everyone else had been busy. And the few rare moments that she had been alone—when Sarina had been out of the house, and he had been chained to his desk—he had heard her at the piano, practicing scales, playing her favorite pieces, or just picking out a tune that she had been humming to herself since she was a child. There wasn't a single second in the days leading up to the attacks that he couldn't account for.

Except for that night in Della. Skye's stomach sank. They had parted ways on the eve of the first attack when he'd so stupidly thought that sleeping with Adalet would somehow slake his growing thirst for the girl he'd known since he was ten—his friend. His match. Taly would've had more than enough time to send a message on the scrying relay while he had been sitting at the bar, desperately trying to figure out how to weasel his way back into her good graces.

And if Kato had sensed magic clinging to her… "Say nothing of this to anyone until I have a chance to talk to her," Skye finally said, a dark, gaping hole opening up in his chest.

Kato raked his fingers through his hair. "I'm not sure that's a good idea. I may have overplayed my hand earlier—tipped her off. I think we need to move on this as—"

"No!" Skye snarled. Kato gaped at him,

stunned. Taking a deep breath, swallowing back his anger and fear, his voice was remarkably steady when he said, "I will not allow you to start a witch hunt until I can verify your claims. There are perhaps… other elements at work here." Like memory alteration, compulsion, or any of a hundred other ways someone could've forced their will on her. "Factors that we haven't considered. Let me speak to her."

Kato looked like he wanted to argue, but thinking better of it, he stepped to the side in reluctant surrender. "I'll wait here."

Skye nodded shakily, ignoring the pitying look he could feel boring into his back as he quickly exited the office. He counted his breaths as he marched across the courtyard. The rain had tapered off to a fine drizzle, but he was oblivious to the mist that clung to his skin and the mud that sloshed beneath his boots.

Too soon, he found himself standing in front of the door to their shared room. For the second time that day, he stared at the carved surface, and his heart pounded out a deafening rhythm in his ears. This time, however, the pulsating beat threatening to tear a hole in his chest was for an entirely different reason. Dread—thick and oily and all-consuming—clawed its way into his body, constricting his throat and making his stomach churn.

Please, he pleaded with whoever might be listening, *not her. Let it be a lie. Let this be just one more of Kato's tricks.* Like the time his brother had dumped him out at the northern edge of their family's territory during the dead of winter, luring him out there with the promise of teaching him how to hunt. Only five years old, and Skye had almost lost a toe to frostbite.

Before he could empty the contents of his stomach across the carpet, Skye forcefully shoved open the door, the thick slab of wood creaking on its hinges as it slammed against the wall.

One step, then another, through the antechamber and then Skye stood in the middle of the main room. Alone. Taly's pack was gone. Her weapons, which had been strewn across the entryway table the last time he entered, were gone. Her maps, the clothes she had hung to dry in the closet, her journal that he had previously spied on the foot of the bed—all gone.

She was gone.

"No," he whispered.

In a flurry of movement, Skye tore through the room, searching for any sign that his eyes might be lying to him. He ripped the blankets off the bed, his panicked mind thinking that she could be hiding there, and the door to the washroom groaned as he flung it open. His eyes took in the white marble walls and gilded furnishings, but it was empty. Her side of the sink had been wiped clean.

Nowhere. Nothing. Gone.

"No," he mumbled, his hands tearing at his hair. Although her scent still lingered in the air, there was no trace of her to be seen. She had even put out the fire. "No, no, please… Shards, no…"

Stumbling over to the desk where she had been standing not even an hour ago, Skye's eyes landed on the single snowdrop that had been laid to rest on a folded slip of paper. With shaking hands, he unfolded the note, that rift in his chest cleaving open even further when he saw her neat, loopy handwriting.

I'm sorry, Em, but I have to make this right. Don't come looking for me.
-Tink

Skye's shoulders started to shake, and it took him a moment to realize that there were tears welling in his eyes as he sunk to the floor. The note slipped from his fingers, and her words from that morning replayed in his head.

There's one more thing, Em. One more thing that might change the calculus.
It has to do with why I left last year.
That's when it started.

Shards, she had tried to tell him. When they were in the library, she had tried to tell him. But he hadn't been listening. He hadn't taken her seriously when she said that her reasons for leaving were important, a small part of him still thinking that her departure was the result of some childish tantrum. But what if it wasn't? Would Taly still be here if he'd given her the priority that morning—pushed the meeting back so he could hear what she had to say? Would he have been able to head this off if he had read the signs better?

Skye felt numb, his body moving of its own accord as he raced down the stairs and back through the massive archway of the main building. He could just detect her scent clinging to the carpets, and he followed it, thinking that maybe, just maybe, he might still be able to catch her. She had taken the servants' stairs, but, just as he feared, the trail ended in the courtyard, the rain having already washed it away. He questioned the guards at the main gate, but neither could recall having seen her leaving the keep. As it was, she could have easily slipped past with one of the teams that had been sent out to salvage scrap.

Skye skipped the aether lift, choosing instead to take the stairs back to the commander's tower office—to Kato, who was still waiting.

"Well?" Kato asked before Skye had even managed to close the door and rearm the wards.

Skye stood there for a long moment, taking in his brother's slightly flushed appearance, the tense set of his shoulders. Kato knew he was right. Although Skye beat him in terms of sheer amount of power, Kato was by no means weak. If there was magic clinging to Taly, he was more than capable of sniffing it out.

The words were out of Skye's mouth before he'd even managed to process the response. "It's nothing. You were wrong."

"What?" A sharp retort. Kato's eyes widened, shock distorting his features.

"You were wrong," Skye repeated, louder this time. More confident. "About Taly. She's not a part of this."

"But I felt magic," Kato burst out. "Shadow and water and—"

"I'm aware." Skye strode across the room, pretending to study something on the desktop. Breathing deeply, he made a conscious attempt to slow his heart, to school his features into dismissive boredom. "But I already knew about the spells."

Kato followed him, refusing to back down. "Why would she have had spells cast on her?"

Clasping his hands behind his back, Skye

turned to meet Kato's questioning stare, hoping that his brother couldn't see the desperation in his eyes as he searched for a plausible excuse. "Taly had a run-in with a harpy several weeks ago. She lost a lot of blood, which exacerbated what the healer said was an allergic reaction to the harpy venom. In the three weeks leading up to today, she's had countless healing spells cast on her. That's most likely what you felt."

"I felt shadow magic, Skylen. And water. Not earth," Kato snapped, a dangerous edge to his voice.

Skye nodded. "The beasts on the island get a little out-of-hand this close to the Aion Gate connection. It can make traveling with active enchantments a little tricky, but Taly was getting so stir-crazy, I told her I'd figure something out."

"Really?" Kato asked dubiously. "And this solution of yours involved both a high-level water glamour *and* aether suppression spells? All to mask the scent of a few healing spells?"

Skye shrugged. "As you well know, earth magic is much more pungent than any other school of magic, so we had to get creative. I cast a few aether suppression spells, but that didn't fully mask the scent. Not naturally. So, I enlisted the help of Ivain's niece. She's a water mage and very talented when it comes to glamours, so that's probably why you had such a difficult time getting beneath the overlaying enchantment to see the spell matrix underneath."

"And the memory alteration spells?" Kato made no effort to mask the suspicion behind his words.

"Nightmares," Skye replied automatically, the story coming to him much more easily than he expected. "Taly was having nightmares about the harpy attack, and she would wake up thrashing. Her wounds kept reopening, so Ivain cast a memory alteration enchantment to help her sleep at night."

A neat, airtight explanation—everything in its place.

Kato looked at him pointedly, his lips curling into a sneer. "And you didn't mention this before because..."

"Because we can't be too careful." Skye turned to look out the window. As he channeled just a little more aether, the shapes of the people milling about below came into focus. Even though he knew she wouldn't be down there, he still searched for Taly among the nameless faces in the crowd. "Someone in this compound is working against us. If it was Taly, then we needed to know, my personal feelings aside. But it's not. I sat down with her, examined the spells—there's nothing out of place."

Finally, a flicker of doubt, perhaps even relief, flashed in Kato's eyes. "Where is she now? I'd like to speak to her."

"That's not possible."

Kato raised a single brow, his face becoming impassive. Unreadable. "And why is that?"

"Because she's gone," Skye replied, allowing just a small amount of his own worry to surface. Kato would no doubt hear the spike in his heart rate, the slight elevation in his breathing. "She volunteered to go to the relay in Plum."

Taking careful, slow steps, Kato rounded the desk, coming to stand next to Skye. "That's suicide. You said it yourself."

"And that's what I told her," Skye replied with

a sigh. At least that part was true. True enough that he hoped Kato wouldn't see the lie behind what he said next. "But her reasoning was valid. She's quick, she knows the way, and since she's coated in several layers of concealment magic, she doesn't smell like aether. She won't attract beasts or shades. All in all, she's the perfect candidate."

Kato was quiet as he stared through the hazy fog just outside the window. "Do you actually expect me to believe that you sent that girl to her death? Taly? *Your* Taly? Don't play me for a fool, Skye. A blind man could see what she means to you."

"We are all having to make sacrifices right now," Skye interjected quietly, letting every ounce of anguish he currently felt leach into his voice. "And this is not one that I made lightly."

A pause, barely half a beat, and then, "Of course, I..." Kato shifted his weight, sensing the genuine heartbreak behind his brother's words. "I'm sorry." It looked as though he might say something else. His mouth opened, and his eyes took on a faraway look. Then, thinking better of it, he gave a half-hearted jerk of his head as he turned to go.

Only when the door clicked closed did Skye finally allow himself to breathe again.

What the hell had he just done? How much would that lie cost him? Sure, he had covered for Taly before... but this? This was a betrayal to his honor, a renouncement of his duty. She had turned against them. She had somehow become a part of something that had taken thousands of lives. Why else would she have just disappeared after Kato questioned her?

Pulling her note from his pocket, Skye ran his

finger along the few lines of script.

I have to make this right.

No. There had to be something that he wasn't seeing. He refused to believe that Taly was willingly complicit in this nightmare. After all, this was the same girl that hadn't been able to kill a rabbit. There's no way she'd be able to take an innocent life. And if Kato had been right about the memory alteration spells, who knew what else could have been done to her. She might not have a choice. She might not even know the full extent of what she was doing.

That day in the training yard, when you discharged the dagger in my hand, that was when I figured out that... that's when it started. That's what she had told him earlier that morning in the library.

What if someone had gotten to her? She had started going into town more often on her own last year, so it was possible. If that was the case, then maybe he hadn't really hurt her when he discharged the dagger. Maybe he just destabilized the enchantments that had been placed upon her—just enough that she had become partially aware that something had been done to her. Enough to try to run. To spare them—Skye, Ivain, and Sarina—from something she didn't understand. *That* sounded more like the girl he knew.

With a heavy sigh, Skye sunk down into the high-backed desk chair that had been rolled off to the side. The leather creaked, and the casters groaned as he leaned back. It was pure speculation. Without examining her himself, he had no way to prove Taly's innocence. Nevertheless, he clung to it. He needed whatever small sliver of hope he could find. Taly was his friend. His *best* friend. But this risk that he was taking went far beyond that. Beyond friendship, beyond a few stolen kisses or some fledgling infatuation.

Infatuation. That word gave him pause.

Shards, he thought, his hand coming to rest on his chest, rubbing at the strange aching void that now seemed to linger there. *I'm an idiot.* How could he have not seen this? How could he have gone this long without figuring it out? This was Taly, and he'd have to be stupid to think that his feelings for her could ever be anything as insignificant and shallow as *infatuation*.

Something clicked into place. Something he'd known for a while now but had refused to admit to himself. The lie he had just told made it impossible to continue to overlook this glaringly obvious truth.

"Holy shit," Skye muttered as he continued to stare out the window with unseeing eyes. "I'm in love with her." He had been for a long time.

He still clutched her note in his hand.

Don't come looking for me.

Her final request. One that he would not honor. Because he was going to find her. And he was going to help her. Then, when he figured out who had dared to lay a hand on what was his to protect, he was going to kill them. With their last dying breath, he would make sure they understood the gravity of the mistake they had made when they had come to his island and brought harm to his Taly.

CHAPTER 25

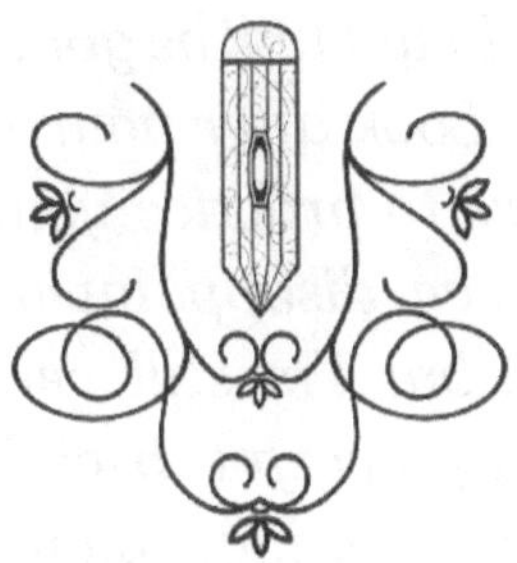

-A letter from Sir Bryer, Knight of the Crystal Guard, to his son, Aiden Bryer

The 32nd day of the month Yule, during the 235th year of the Empty Throne

Son,

I'm afraid I've been called away on a mission of the utmost importance and will be unable to return home as planned. We believe someone connected to the Genesis Shards may be in grave danger, and I've been chosen to oversee the escort and protection detail.

I know this news couldn't have come at a worse time. I too am feeling the loss of your aunt and baby cousin, and I'm sorry that I'm not able to be there to comfort you. Given how close you and Aimee were with little Rin, I'm sure this must be devastating.

However, as you well know, members of the Crystal Guard carry a heavy burden. It is our sole duty to serve and protect the Genesis Lords, and I am honor-bound to uphold my oath. I hope that one day, you'll understand.

I cannot say how long I will be gone this time. A year at the very least. Look after your mother and your sister and be sure to practice your magic. I know you've always been disappointed that you didn't attune to water, but I'm still very proud of you. Earth magic is a powerful discipline, and I know that with time and training, you will excel.

For what it's worth, I still take Aki with me everywhere I go. Although it's been many years since you gave me your beloved teddy bear, he's kept me company on many a long night. I imagine he'll have more than a few stories to tell when I return. Stories that I hope you are willing to hear.

Always know that wherever I go, I carry you, your mother, and your sister in my heart. There is not a day, not a single hour, that goes by that you are not in my thoughts.

With all my love, always until the end,

Your father

Night had finally fallen, and with it came the screams.

Although he tried, Aiden couldn't completely stop the trembling in his hands as he stood atop the walls of Ryme. The sea of rustling treetops stretched out for as far as his eyes could see, kissing the inky blackness of the horizon in a haze of starlight, and the silvery light of the first rising moon bathed the land below in a soft glow. On any other night, the view would have been intensely beautiful, even serene. But tonight, the descending blanket of darkness only carried with it the promise of fear.

"Help me!" came another cry. A woman this time. "Somebody! Please! They've taken my child!"

It's not real, Aiden thought. A muscle in his jaw began to feather. *They're just shades, not people.*

His hand tightened on the hilt of the sword strapped to his waist. The design for the blade was simple, almost austere. A single shadow crystal had been set into the base of the pommel, and three luminous water crystals, each inscribed with a different spell, had been embedded in the hilt. Originally a part of his father's collection, the crystals had been a gift from his mother before his household had given her, as well as all of his father's possessions, to the man that would become his stepfather—Lord Thorn.

Now there was someone that Aiden would love nothing more than to throw off the side of the wall to the creatures that prowled down below. Lord Thorn was constantly belittling Aiden's father, a Knight of the Crystal Guard that had selflessly given up his life in the line of duty. After all, as his stepfather liked to point out, how could a man that had absconded with his Feseraa only to, of all things, *marry* her, have honor? How could a man that had tried to teach his children to be kind even to those below their station have integrity? How could a man that had loved and sacrificed for his family be worthy of remembrance or celebration? No, in the eyes of fey society, the scandal of marrying a human was the only thing that mattered now that Sir Bryer, one of the greatest water mages of his time, was only a memory.

Aiden held on to that spark of anger. Anger was better than fear. Anger would keep him from breaking.

"Help!" A child—his wailing sobs echoed out over the treetops. "Mommy!" Terror, pure and primal, laced the desperate cry.

"No." Ivain placed a hand on Aiden's shoulder when he unknowingly started to move down the ramparts. "Remember, it's just a trick. They're trying to lure us out from behind the wall."

The older shadow mage looked beaten down as he leaned against the parapet, his practical-yet-stately leather armor streaked with pieces of ooze and viscera. His white-blonde hair was slicked back with sweat, and his hands had been bathed in blackened blood. A rapier that looked to have been forged from starlight itself was strapped to his waist, and the grip peeking out of the worn leather scabbard bore such an intricately carved relief of two foxes playing in a glen that the shadows and moonlight almost seemed to breathe life into the motionless creatures.

Aiden clenched his jaw, doing his best to tune out the babel of desperate pleas coming from down below. He had been at the clinic when the first explosion hit. Thinking that there had been an accident, he and several of the menders had rushed toward the sound, ready to tend to the wounded, only to find that a veritable nightmare was unfolding. Undead monsters, *shades* as Ivain had later clarified, were streaming through the gates, ruthlessly cutting down anyone in their way.

It was pure chaos for a while. As he tried to recall the specifics of those first few moments now from the relative safety of the wall, Aiden's mind kept going back to how the ground had felt slick beneath his boots as bright rivers of crimson had begun to flow. He kept thinking about how the smoke from the explosions had looked like steam in the chill spring air. Such insignificant details, but ones that he couldn't seem to make himself forget.

Aiden jumped when he felt the hand on his shoulder give an encouraging squeeze. "You did well today," Ivain said quietly, staring out over the darkened forest. "Your father would've been proud."

"I failed," Aiden replied, equally quiet. Although he had tried to fight back, assemble those around him, their response was too delayed and disorganized to do anything more than slow down the enemy's advance. With no one manning the gates, he had managed to partially block off the entrance to the city with earth magic, but the city's defenses had already been breached before he'd gotten to the main fight. They had already lost.

Ivain patted him on the back before placing both hands back on the wall. "You did what you could with an impossible situation."

Aiden ran a hand over his shorn head, remembering how his mother had teared up when he'd had to cut his hair for his initiation into the Crystal Guard. All that night, when he caught her staring, she had just kept saying that he looked like his father. Without the scars and the beard, of course. "I appreciate what you're trying to do, uncle, but we would've lost the city if you and Sarina hadn't shown up when you did."

Aiden eyed the deceptively lanky man standing next to him. He had heard stories of his uncle's prowess on the battlefield, but he had never seen him use the full extent of his power. A veritable blur, Ivain had effortlessly zigzagged through the throng of creatures, ripping out the crystals in their chests with alarming precision. Sarina had walked behind her brother at a far more sedate pace, her form awash in white-hot flames. Seemingly bored, she had bathed the battlefield with fire as she ignited the bodies falling to the ground. The battle ended very quickly following their arrival. The two siblings worked together with the kind of efficiency and expertise that could only come with years of training together side-by-side.

"Help!" The familiar cry pierced the night air. What Aiden knew to be the soft, lilting voice of one of the gentlest souls he had ever encountered was now edged with abject terror.

"That's one of the menders." Aiden turned for the stairs, but Ivain caught his arm.

There was pity in his uncle's eyes when he said, "It's not her anymore. They've already had more than enough time to convert the captives into shades."

Aiden shook his head, refusing to believe it. "Then how can she still speak? The ones that attacked us today couldn't speak."

"Because she's fresh," Ivain replied. "When the bodies have not yet had time to decay, they can still speak. Without the proper enchantments, though, their vocal cords will rot out over time. The ones we saw today were old—several centuries, I'd say. Nothing more than shock troops."

"So everyone that they took today...?" Aiden asked, dreading the answer. "No," he spat angrily. "You don't know that. You *can't* know that."

"I can, and I do." Ivain sighed. He was silent for a long moment. When he finally spoke, his eyes looked far away. "I was conscripted to fight in the Shade Rebellion only a few days after I turned 200. This was when we thought we were still fighting over some stupid piece of land on the other side of the Odyssea Gate. I had only been at the war camp in Amaranthe for a week when we found out that House Myridan had allied with the giants. These creatures were monstrous, or so we thought at the time. Almost 20 feet tall, a single eye. Their warriors had ripped out their teeth and replaced them with spears of sharpened steel. It was the stuff of nightmares.

"Even though my unit prevailed, we were unprepared for that first battle with House Myridan and the giants. We lost a lot of people—people that we left on the battlefield while we tended to our wounded. Imagine our surprise when our dead walked back into the camp the next morning—a little pale but seemingly whole and alive, if a little confused." Ivain stopped here, his lips set in a stern line. The muscles in his neck flexed as he swallowed convulsively.

"We let them in," he continued, his voice strained, "thinking that maybe the Shards had granted us a blessing. But our joy was short-lived. House Myridan attacked us again that night. Not from across the battlefield. From within our own camp. *Our* soldiers. They had turned our own people against us.

"We tried to fight back, but you can't kill something that's not alive. We slashed and hacked at those that we had welcomed back that morning, but they just got back up, reattaching limbs regardless of whether it had been theirs to begin with. My entire unit was slaughtered that night. The only reason I survived was because I ran. I ran despite the screams at my back. I ran despite the stench of my comrades' own blood that filled my nose. I and the few others that managed to survive—we're alive because we ran. We were able to warn the Genesis Council and their commanders because we ran. The war would've been lost if not for our cowardice."

Aiden felt rooted to the spot. He had never heard his uncle speak more than a few words at a time regarding his involvement in the Shade Rebellion. The flickering light from a nearby lamp cast a long shadow over the older man's haggard face as he continued his story. "This is not an enemy that you can fight with honor, boy. Anyone that has stooped so low as to create shades, to raise the dead and brutalize their bodies for personal gain, has abandoned integrity. We will do what we can to help those that we lost, but you need to accept right now that we won't be able to save them all. As much as it pains me to say it, sometimes, it will be better to run. Sometimes, the greater good will require the abandonment of the fallen. And as you will come to learn, sometimes, it will be kinder to kill. For those that have already been captured, a swift death would be a mercy."

Not for the first time that day, Aiden's

stomach sank. Straightening his shoulders, he looked out over the crowd of people that stood along the wall. A few shadow mages stalked up and down the walkway behind him, trying to repair the wards that had been damaged in the initial blast. Thankfully, the protective spells woven between the very stones of the towering city walls had absorbed the brunt of the explosion, sparing the main gates. Lazy wisps of smoke still rippled through the air, blotting out the starlit sky, but Ryme's defenses were intact.

"Anything?" a new voice asked wearily. "Were you able to find them?"

Turning, Aiden saw Sarina trudging down the walkway. Her clothes had been singed and her skirts ripped, but she was otherwise unharmed.

Closing his eyes, Aiden mentally prodded at the two locator spells he currently had active. After having spent most of the afternoon tending to the wounded, his magic was spent, and he barely had enough aether left to pluck at the strings of the enchantments. Thankfully, he'd had the foresight to cast the spells several days ago, just after he returned to the manor only to find that Taly had decided to tag along with Skye.

"I found them," he replied, the ardent look of hope that lit up Sarina's face making his stomach churn. "Skye is in Ebondrift, but Taly's not with him. I don't have enough aether left to get an exact location, but I think she's somewhere just outside of Vale."

Sarina smoothed back her auburn hair and wiped at a few stray tears that had streaked her soot-stained cheeks. "I should be angry," she whispered. "Shards, I should be angry at that girl. And you, for letting her leave," she said, turning to

Aiden, who hung his head.

Even though Sarina couldn't know the full extent of his guilt, the reprimand struck at him, wedging open something that had already cracked. He had failed his duty as a Crystal Guardsman. The first link to the Time Shard to surface in over two centuries, and he had lost her. "I'm sorry, Sarina," he said, looking away. "If I'd known that Taly would immediately up and leave to follow Skye to Ebondrift, I never would've cleared her. I would've told her she needed to stay in bed."

Sarina sighed as she came to stand next to Ivain. "I'm sorry, I shouldn't have snapped at you," she amended when she saw the stricken look on Aiden's face. "It's not your fault. Even on her best behavior, Taly is difficult and headstrong. And honestly, I can't help but think that everything worked out for the best. If she had stayed, she very well might've been all alone at the manor when those things attacked, and we wouldn't have been able to get to her. Thank the Shards that Aimee just happened to come into town with you today and that the fighting never reached the clinic."

"I told you Skye would end up taking Taly with him," Ivain said a little smugly. "You know that boy has never been able to tell her *no*. He'd cut his own arm off if she asked him to."

"Yes, yes." Sarina waved a dismissive hand. "You were right, and I was wrong. Apparently hoping that those two would learn to exercise a little common sense was too much to ask."

"That's not the only thing I was right about, little sister," Ivain replied pointedly.

Sarina did not seem pleased, and the glare she leveled at her brother had Aiden shrinking back. Ivain wasn't even fazed, apparently used to weathering his sister's ire. "Fine, you were also right about the combat training," she conceded with a huff. "Both for myself and probably for Taly as well. Happy?"

Ivain clasped his hands behind his back as he stared into the darkened forest, his breath puffing in the brisk night air. "Not really. I had hoped that neither one of you would ever have need of those skills. But if there's one thing the war taught me, it's that you hope for the best but plan for the worst."

Sarina placed a hand on his shoulder. "Has there been any news on the scrying relay?"

Ivain shook his head. "Not yet."

Aiden grimaced. It was luck and luck alone that had allowed them to save the town's main scrying relay. Two air mages hiding in the relay tower just happened to stumble upon the device that had been rigged to go off, and they were able to use their magic to contain the explosion.

They all looked up when someone came jogging down the walkway.

"Sire," the young fey girl stammered as she skidded to a stop in front of Ivain, sketching out a stiff bow. She was small, smaller than even Taly, and her inky hair had escaped from the knotted twist at the base of her neck. "It's the relay. There's a message coming in from Vale."

"I stand corrected," Ivain muttered.

"Go," Sarina said to her brother. "We'll catch up."

With a nod, Ivain pushed past the girl and headed for the stairs at a pace that only a shadow mage could sustain. Aiden and Sarina followed him, taking the stairs two at a time even though they had no hope of keeping up.

Aiden prodded at the locator spell. A little pinprick of light sputtered to life in his mind's eye, faint but still there. Taly. She was alive and in Vale.

As Aiden followed Ivain and Sarina across town to the relay center, hope began to blossom. Maybe, just maybe, he hadn't failed in his duty to the Shards. The last time mage—maybe it was still possible to bring her home.

CHAPTER 26

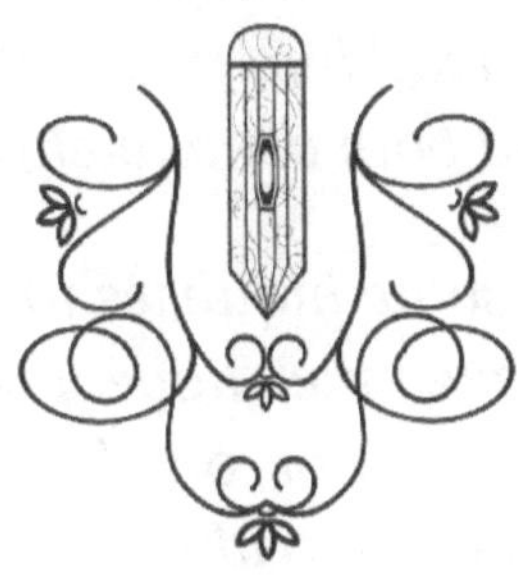

-From the personal notes of Ivain Castaro, Marquess of Tempris

The 22nd day of the month Meridian, during the 236th year of the Empty Throne

It's days like this that make me question whether we truly deserve to endure as a species. Last night, Vale, Plum, and Bago were burned to the ground. I had heard there was a rumor that someone saw a time crystal near the old palace, but I never thought that a mere rumor would warrant this level of destruction. After almost five decades without a death that could be attributed to the Hunt, I had hoped that the Sanctorum had finally managed to curb their bloodlust. It seems I was wrong—so horribly wrong.

Vale was hit the hardest, and I accompanied Sarina and young Skye to inspect the burn site this morning. I had almost given up hope that we would find anyone alive, but Skye somehow managed to find a small mortal girl—Talya. Her home was burned, but, by some miracle, the child's basement bedroom was nearly untouched. For as long as I live, I don't think I shall ever forget the sight of those two younglings walking down that ashen lane, hand-in-hand and both completely covered in soot.

I'll need to make some inquiries to find her next-of-kin, but I don't have much hope. I've never heard of the Caro family, here or on the mainland. If the worst happens and she truly is alone in this world, I'm considering taking her in as my ward. Human or otherwise, both Sarina and Skye are already quite taken with the little one, and I know the boy could benefit from having a playmate.

For now, I'm going to put the child in the eastern wing, just across the hall from Skye. I haven't opened that room in centuries, but it was originally designed with a little girl in mind. I do hope that Taly likes blue. It was my late wife's favorite color, and I daresay the woman practiced very little restraint when she was decorating what we hoped would be our daughter's bedroom.

Taly groaned, repositioning her legs and grasping the gnarled trunk at her back as the tree branch swayed beneath her. A muted whimper fell from her lips when she chanced a glance down, her eyes following the spiraling trails of leaves that had shaken loose and were now fluttering to the forest floor over a dozen feet below.

Since departing Ebondrift, she had made good time, but any hope she may have had that the Plum relay was still serviceable had been quickly dashed as soon as she had come upon the still smoldering remains of the little village. It had been burned to the ground. So, not wanting to waste a single moment of daylight, she had immediately moved on to the next township.

After finding a secure branch, Taly ventured a tentative glance at the nearby town of Vale. She could just make out the outline of the old village to the west. When the villagers had rebuilt after the fire that had stolen away her childhood, they had left the remains of the original town undisturbed, expecting the forest to reclaim the land. So far, that had not been the case. The original roads were still somehow covered in ash, and the fragmented skeletons of what used to be charming little stone cottages cast long shadows across the strange, treeless space. In the span of a single evening, this tiny town had become the gravesite of over 300 innocent people, and it was as if even the forest was afraid of disturbing the ashen tomb, lest it anger the horde of lost souls that was said to roam the area.

Taly suppressed a shiver and pulled at the collar of her tattered leather jacket. Even under the best circumstances, she hated coming to Vale. The other salvagers and guides delighted in telling ghost stories, each swearing on their honor that they'd personally seen the distinct blue glow of fairy fire during their travels through the village that she used to call home. None of them seemed to have a problem with the old town, but Taly had started avoiding it when she could.

Peering through the shadowy forest canopy, she could clearly see men and women sluggishly ambling about the neatly paved roads of the new town square. On the surface, nothing seemed out of place as the villagers went about their evening routine. And if Taly hadn't seen firsthand what happened in Ebondrift, she probably wouldn't have had a second thought about trotting her horse right through the middle of town and straight up to the relay.

But she *had* witnessed the horrifying events at Ebondrift, and she quickly recognized the jerky, uncoordinated movements and listless shambling of the citizenry for what they were. What they signified.

Vale had been taken.

She had a decision to make—either try to get a closer look or move on. While Della was the nearest town, just an hour away by horseback, she couldn't risk it. Although she could make it there by nightfall, she would then be stuck in Della until morning. And since Kato had almost certainly told Skye about her magic and how it was connected to the attacks, there was a possibility they had already sent someone to retrieve her. That meant Della was out.

There was still Bago to the north, but she'd never make it there before sundown. Vale was the only option if she wanted to try to get out a message today.

"Damn it all," Taly muttered. The town was crawling with shades, and the scrying relay tower was on the far side. Even if she was able to get inside the building, there was no guarantee the relay would still be intact. Nevertheless, if there was even a slight chance that she might be able to warn Ryme before it was attacked, the risk was worth it.

Looking down, she grimaced. It had been easy getting up the tree but getting back down was going to be the real problem.

“Shards. Well, come on, Caro. Let’s get this over with.”

Sliding off the branch and catching herself with both hands, Taly let herself dangle as her toes groped for the tree branch she knew to be somewhere down below. It was times like this that she wished she had longer legs. While being small sometimes had its advantages, Skye had always had a much easier time where tree climbing was concerned.

When Taly finally planted her feet on solid ground, she leaned heavily against the trunk, waiting for the dizziness to pass. Ever since the ordeal with the harpy, she had found that she didn’t really fancy being too far off the ground. Her head started to swim as she recalled that aerial view of the canopy, and she could still feel the phantom slice of the harpy’s claws on her back. Her stomach convulsed, and her breaths came in short gasps as the memory of being stuck inside that tiny crevice flashed through her mind.

Jerking suddenly, Taly brought her hand up and slapped herself across the cheek. Again. And then again. The pain—*real* pain—helped her focus.

You don’t have time for this. Get going.

She pushed herself up and started forward cautiously. The scrying relay was on the western edge of the village. If she skirted around the perimeter of the old town, she should be able to get a better look. With a little luck, maybe the situation wouldn't be as bad as it had appeared from the tree.

"Hey Byron," Taly whispered as the little gelding pushed his nose into her palm. Thankfully, the public stables in Ebondrift had been left relatively untouched, and the horses, though slightly antsy and in need of fresh food and water, were in good health. She had heard the guards at the compound making plans to retrieve the horses for the caravan, and so, rather than letting the animals loose, she had taken the time to water and feed the remaining horses when she had gone to retrieve her own mount.

"Okay, boy," Taly said, untying the reins and leading the little gelding through the underbrush, "we have to be quiet."

Byron nickered softly, thrashing his head up and down as if he understood her. Who knows, maybe he did. If the Elvethan, the ancient line of horses that Ivain favored, were as smart as the older fey noble claimed, then it was certainly possible.

As she circled around the older village remains, Taly's eyes were drawn to a burned-out cottage situated near the forest's edge. There wasn't anything left except a few stones that may have once been a part of a garden wall and a hole in the ground that most likely led to a basement.

A dull pain throbbed behind Taly's temples, and she was hit with a sudden flash of... she wasn't sure what. Snowdrops in the spring, then lilies in the summer. The smell of baked bread and burned stew wafting from a tiny kitchen. A stern reprimand when she had been caught drawing stick figures on the closet floor, and a man with kind eyes and hair the color of dawn that helped her catch butterflies in the woods.

Taly started when the ghostly figure of a small child darted past her. A golden fog began rolling in around her feet, and she frantically prodded at that mental wall, only to find the barrier holding strong. Although she could distinctly feel the prickle of magic against her skin, it wasn't her own. Something else was reforming the landscape, building up the stones of the destroyed cottage one-by-one, breathing life back into the scene in front of her and undoing the ravages of fire and time.

Taly's body tensed as panic set in, but a wave of calm immediately rushed in behind it. Whatever magical entity she had inadvertently stumbled upon quickly smoothed away the sharp edges of her rising fear until it felt as though she was walking through a dream, one that felt warm and familiar. If she looked behind her, she could still see the shadows of twilight chasing away the last golden rays of the evening sun, but the cottage itself was bathed in the warm glow of morning. Her fingers gripped the reins and Byron nudged her shoulder, his eyes following hers. He could see it too.

"Cori! It's time to come inside and start your lessons!" a man's voice called out as the blue cottage door opened. Although she couldn't place his name, Taly knew she had seen this man somewhere before. He was so familiar, everything from the neatly trimmed beard to the scar that ran down his cheek. If she were to look closer, she somehow knew that he would have another scar in the shape of a hook on the back of his left hand.

His eyes scanned the garden, but he looked startled when he finally spotted Taly standing just behind the gate. "Breena?" He squinted, trying to get a better look. "What are you doing out there? I told you we can finish the spells later. Come inside and rest."

"What are you talking about, Esmund?" A woman this time. She was wiping her hands on a threadbare rag as she came up beside him. "I'm right..." Her lilting voice trailed off, and her shockingly gray highborn eyes widened when they met Taly's decidedly duller human ones.

A single tear, followed by another and then another, streamed down Taly's cheeks as an intense longing welled up inside of her. She knew this woman. Even if she couldn't conjure a name, she had seen that face in her dreams ever since she was a child.

Both the man and woman stared at Taly for a long moment. The tiniest sliver of fear finally broke through the strange blanket of calm muddling her senses, and Taly took a tentative step back. The woman immediately held up her hands. "No," she called gently, running towards the gate. "Please, wait! Cori, wait!"

Taly shook her head as she retreated another step. "I'm sorry. I don't know who..." The scene vanished, and suddenly Taly found herself standing in front of that same burned-out cottage, the fragrance of summer flowers still filling her nose. "...that is," she finished, her voice barely above a whisper.

Taly looked around incredulously, turning in a full circle as her heart thumped in her chest. Byron stood beside her, seemingly unaffected by whatever had just happened. In fact, if horses could shrug, she was pretty sure that was what he would've done.

What was that? What the hell had just happened? Those were the people from her nightmare, but she had seen them plain as day—both alive and unharmed. How? Restless spirits, maybe? Or perhaps that strange vision was all the work of an overactive imagination coupled with what was becoming a distinctly uncomfortable sense of hunger. Yeah… that made sense. Sort of.

"Shit!" Taly whispered as she tugged on Byron's reins and continued on, her eyes darting around more frantically than before. "I hate Vale!" All she needed now was to hallucinate a few orbs of fairy fire and her day would be complete.

The relay center, a circular structure that backed up to the edge of the forest, was in view now, and she shook herself. She needed to focus, strange visions aside.

Tying off Byron farther behind the tree line, Taly crept forward, teasing out a small trickle of power as she crouched behind the cindered trunk of a burned-out tree. When she blinked, the visions sputtered to life. She could see the golden forms of a few shades shambling down the road just in front of where she hid, but they were faint and indistinct, blurring even further as they moved away. That wasn't good enough. She needed to be able to see if anything was moving near the relay.

Feeling curious and just a little daring, she began pulling out more magic, wedging open the crack between the stones of that mental wall until the trickle became a steady stream. With that flood of power rushing her system, her field of vision exploded, allowing her to see farther than she had ever been able to see before. A golden fog drifted across the landscape in front of her, and even though she could only make out the faint outlines of their physical bodies in the dim light, the shambling group of ghostly afterimages lumbering about the new town square all the way at the end of the main road were blinding against the darkening evening sky.

Damn, Taly thought, a wide grin splitting her face. While she would've given up almost anything to be rid of this curse, she couldn't deny that having time magic could be sort of useful—putting aside for the moment that she had no idea what she was doing.

A low groan and the sound of twigs snapping had Taly shrinking back against the trunk. One of the shades had strayed beyond the main road and was trudging around the back of the nearby relay building. As it lumbered closer, she had to forcibly suppress a shudder when she saw its face, or what was left of it. A large portion of the creature's cheek looked like it had been crudely excised with the edge of a dull blade, and the telltale yellow and black of decaying teeth were visible through the rot. The veins around the wound had turned black beneath its sallow skin and crept across the side of its face like a spiderweb, up over and around its single bloodshot eye.

Its golden aura walked two steps ahead, and as the creature drew nearer, the smell of decomposing flesh assaulted her senses. She clamped a hand over her mouth, but that didn't completely silence the involuntary gagging noise she made as she tried to swallow back the bile that burned her throat.

The shade stopped, its body swaying uncertainly from side-to-side. The bones in its neck snapped dully as its head swiveled in her direction.

No, no, no. Go the other way!

Taly held her breath as the shade took a slow, deliberate step towards her. And then another, its dead eye searching. Reaching out a trembling hand, she picked up a nearby rock. This simple action seemed to trigger something, some divergence, because the creature's aura split. One of the ghostly apparitions continued to move towards her, but the other turned and shambled off in the opposite direction.

Tossing the rock off into the distance, Taly listened for the low thump and rustle of leaves, not daring to even blink when the shade stopped its approach. The gilded image moving toward her began to stutter as the creature swayed listlessly from side-to-side, apparently uncertain which way to turn. The vision flickered in and out of focus, the edges of its spectral form turning to smoke before it abruptly caved in on itself and vanished completely.

The shade twitched, a full-body convulsion, as if the loss of its psychic shadow somehow made it lose its balance. Then with a grunt and a gravelly roll of its bony shoulders, it turned, stumbling slightly, and plodded around the building as it followed the path laid out by the second phantom.

The danger had passed.

Taly let out a hissing sigh as she sagged against the tree. She didn't think she would ever get used to seeing those creatures.

Get going. She had already wasted too much daylight.

From where she hid, she could see two sentries standing motionless in front of the relay's entrance. Their golden forms looked a little hazy from so far away, but they were still distinct enough that she could see their scraggly hair blowing in the gentle evening breeze.

Taly knew she wasn't strong enough to fight them off on her own, and although she still had her pistols, guns were loud. If she fired off a shot, she'd attract every shade in town. She needed to find another way in.

I wonder if... maybe? Yeah, that could work.

Ducking into the shadows, she edged along the tree line until she came to the back of the relay building, praying it would still be there. The Shards must have been listening, because just as she remembered, a rickety ladder leaned against the side of a wooden boardwalk that ringed the building's second floor, two half-empty paint buckets sitting nearby. Almost a month ago now, the mayor of Vale had made the mistake of hiring Caleb to repaint the public buildings. While the old salvager was a nice enough guy, he was lazy and absentminded. Taly had lost count of the number of times he had lost his painting supplies, and she was sure there were probably more than a few old ladders leaning forgotten against the sides of buildings all across town.

If Taly ever saw Caleb again, she was going to buy that beautiful bastard a drink.

Each rung of the ladder gave off a deafening creak as she gingerly made her way up, and Taly's heart nearly stopped every time a twig snapped in the forest behind her. When she finally hauled herself up and over the balcony railing, her hands were trembling. She crouched next to a small open window, avoiding the soft beam of light that spilled out onto the planked walkway.

The hallway beyond the splintered sill looked empty, so before she had a chance to second-guess herself, Taly hopped up and shimmied through the casement, taking small, tentative steps just in case the floorboards decided to creak beneath her feet. She pressed herself against the wall as she slunk down the short expanse of corridor. Doors to what appeared to be offices lined the opposite side. The hinges had been ripped from the doorframes, the wood fractured, and several of the thresholds were streaked with trails of dried blood.

As she tried to step over the shredded remains of what used to be a throw rug, Taly's toe caught on an uneven floorboard, and she barely managed to catch herself on the doorframe of the main relay room before she went sprawling face-first.

She held her breath, only letting it out when she saw that the relay room, a cavernous chamber flanked by a spiraling promenade, was empty.

A pyramidal obelisk carved from a single slab of hyaline crystal dominated most of the room, its tip stretching at least 20 feet into the air. Alternating bands of shadow and water crystals encircled the structure, and Faera runes were etched onto every available surface.

Today, those runes gave off a blazing magenta radiance, scattering the light that shone through the center of the pillar into countless shards of rainbow-colored splendor. The twinkling flashes of light were almost blinding, and Taly had to avert her gaze until her eyes adjusted to the glow. Still, even if she had to squint, and even if the tickle of magic that swept across her skin set her teeth on edge, it was the most beautiful thing she had seen in a long time.

The scrying relay was online.

Taly resisted the urge to sprint down the stairs, taking her time and avoiding the steps that threatened to creak underfoot. Usually, a special technician oversaw the tuning of the larger relays, but she had gone with Skye to the main relay in Ryme dozens of times. It looked easy enough. Plus, she had once snuck a book about hyaline tuning principles out of Ivain's private collection when she was 13. She had been grounded for a week when he found out, but it had been an interesting read nonetheless.

And very useful to her now, almost eight years later.

Taly ran her hand over the carved script embedded in the control panel, smiling when she felt the aether tickle her fingers. Whoever had used the relay last hadn't bothered to cut the connection to the spire in Strio, and she could hear hushed voices filtering in through the speaker. Switching off the glamour interface, she listened.

"When will he be here?" a young boy quavered.

"I don't know," a woman snapped. "He's been delayed. However, he was able to send the list of recruits that we need to track down and convert before his arrival."

"I'm not sure we're going to be able to get to all of these," the first voice replied. Taly couldn't be sure, but the boy sounded oddly familiar. "Especially this one. Our contact in Ebondrift says that they've really tightened up security since this morning. Even if we could subdue him, we'd never be able to get him out of the compound."

"We'll just have to figure something out. Hey!" There was shuffling on the other end of the connection. "Shards, who left this on?" The connection abruptly disconnected, plunging the room into silence.

"Damn it," Taly muttered as her hands raced over the control panel. So, there really was a traitor in Ebondrift, and it sounded like she wasn't the only one these people were trying to "recruit."

The hyaline pillar gave a soft pulse as it attempted to contact the relay in Ryme. Other than Strio, that was the only relay that was still connected to the grid. Taly's heart thundered in her ears as she anxiously waited for the relay technician's voice on the other end.

Please be there. Please be there, she mentally chanted, trying to summon him by will alone.

"This is Relay 12-001—Ryme. Identify yourself."

Taly felt liked she'd been punched in the gut and tears pricked her eyes when she heard the familiar sound. "Ivain?"

"Shards! Taly?! Aiden, Sarina—hurry!" Ivain's voice sounded tinny and far off. "Taly, are you okay? Why can't I see you? Why are you in Vale? Where's Skye?"

"No time for that," Taly said, interrupting his rush of questions. "Ebondrift was attacked by shades, and Vale's been taken."

"Are you safe?" a new voice demanded.

"Hi Sarina," Taly replied, wincing. "You know, safe is really a *relative* term."

"I'll take that as a *no* then," came the frustrated reply.

Taly pressed herself against the relay when something creaked overhead. "Look, there is a very real chance that these things could attack Ryme. You need to secure the village."

"Too late," Ivain sighed. "They attacked this morning. We were able to hold them off, but we lost a lot of people in the process."

"Fuck," Taly cursed. She could hear Sarina mutter something under her breath on the other end, but the reprimand never came. "Well then for what this is worth, Skye is still in Ebondrift. Both the relay and the Seren Gate have been sabotaged, the leadership is missing, the walls are breached, and they think that there's someone inside the Gate Watchers' compound that's working against them. They're going to be transferring the survivors to Ryme by way of Della in a few days' time, and they need backup. I don't know what you've encountered so far, but these things are different from what you saw in the Shade Rebellion, Ivain."

"Taly—" Ivain tried to interject, but Taly continued to talk over him. There was something moving upstairs now.

"I don't know how, but they can use aether to remake themselves—completely change their forms. We had something attack us in Ebondrift. Everyone was calling it an abomination. It… it devoured one of the shadow mages and then used the aether to make itself stronger. Skye nearly got himself killed trying to take this thing out."

"Taly, slow down—" Aiden this time.

"No," Taly interjected, her eyes flitting to the walkway high overhead. She thought she heard the low groan of a door opening on rusty hinges. "I don't know how much time I have. Um… Plum was burned, Vale is overrun, and someone here was talking to Strio. They said something about what sounded like a leader of some sort and they have a list of people that they're trying to recruit. That's all I was able to overhear before they cut the connection."

Heavy footsteps were echoing down the

upstairs hallway. "Uh-oh. I need to go. Just to be safe, I wouldn't trust any more transmissions from this relay or Strio."

"Taly, wait—" Sarina called frantically.

Taly cut the connection and fell to the floor in a defensive crouch. Peering around the edge of the base, she unsheathed the new air dagger Skye had gifted her—Snowdrop as she had decided to call it—and waited as the footsteps came closer. Whoever it was sounded big.

Damn it, Caro, she thought desperately. *This may not have been your best idea.*

Taly shook herself and took a deep breath. She had gotten the warning out. If that saved even one life, if it got Skye the backup he needed, then the risk would have been worth it.

Plan, plan, I need a plan. Wait! She had almost felt bad about it at the time, but she had stolen Skye's aether concealment charm before she left. So far, she had been using it to hide the scent of her magic from the beasts in the forest, but if she drained all the charm's aether in one go, she might be able to hide her presence well enough to sneak past this guy.

Swiveling the silver bracelet around, the crystal set into the center glowed a bright cerulean as she ran a finger over the faceted surface.

The toe of a boot, un-scuffed and newly polished, stepped out of the shadows of the third floor, followed by measured footsteps down the spiraling stairwell.

Taly's hands were surprisingly steady as she pressed a finger to the tiny blue crystal. The tickle of water magic crawled across her skin, making her shiver, and the glow of the water crystal dulled as the aether stored in the shadow crystal set on the inside of the band was consumed.

"My, my, my," came a cultivated voice. "What is that delightful bouquet?"

The man finally descended the last stair and stepped into the light. He wasn't a shade. No, he was very much alive. Although the bearded man was short for a fey, his arms were thick and striated with muscle underneath the navy silk of his rolled-up shirtsleeves. His burly fingers toyed with an amulet that dangled from his neck—a single shadow crystal surrounded by a serpentine dragon carved from hyaline.

He circled the base of the relay, stopping just on the opposite side from where she hid.

"Tell me, little mage—what kind of magic do you practice?" He paused to languidly sniff the air. "Even underneath that glamour and that fabricated human scent, I smell aether. But what kind? The iron makes it so hard to tell."

Shit, Taly thought, a faint tremble shaking her body. *A shadow mage*.

He came closer, forcing Taly to shrink back against the relay base. As a mortal, she wouldn't even have a chance in a hand-to-hand fight. He would be too strong. Instinctively, she placed a hand on the butt of her pistol as she began prodding at the wall erected in her mind, teasing out a little more magic. She saw the man's auric specter walking a few steps ahead of him as he prowled around the base, and as he came nearer, she desperately tried to remember what it had felt like when she had frozen that group of shades.

Nothing happened, though. Nothing at all.

"Oh, that won't work, little mage." The man sounded amused. "Although, I haven't felt *that* spell in a long time. How interesting."

The air around her started to feel thin, and she clasped a hand to her throat, trying to muffle the sound of her desperate wheezing.

"What's wrong? Does that hurt? Don't worry. It's a nasty trick, but it won't kill you."

Taly struggled to stay upright as her legs started to give way. She tried pulling more magic out from behind that wall in her mind, and though that helped to alleviate some of the pain, it wasn't nearly enough. He was almost upon her now, but her entire body felt like dead weight as she feebly slumped to the floor.

Still, even if her legs refused to respond, she wasn't going out without a fight. With her remaining strength, she tightened her grip on her dagger and pulled a pistol with her free hand.

Eventually, she felt the glamour around her break, the magic popping against her skin as the enchantment shattered, and a rough hand grabbed her, seizing her up by the arm and slamming her against the nearest wall. Her head whipped back, striking the wall with a dull thud, and for a moment it felt like her ears were stuffed with cotton as everything went quiet and then crashed back into focus. Something warm and wet dripped onto her neck as her toes left the ground.

"You're not supposed to exist," the man moaned. She could feel his breath on her skin as he sniffed her, starting at her neck and then, almost gently, nuzzling her hair. "Oh," he whimpered, "but you are special." He punctuated this sentence by bringing a hand up and pinching her breast painfully. "And so pretty. I don't think my master will mind if you and I have a little fun before I take you to see him."

Finally snapping out of her daze, an enraged

scream tore from Taly's throat. She writhed and kicked at him, but that just made his grip on her wrist tighten as he shoved a leg between her thighs.

NO! No, no... oh, Shards! Please, no. Not like this. His fingers continued to caress her breast, cupping and weighing it as he pressed her against the wall. When he pulled her hips higher, rubbing himself against her and hitching one of her legs up around his waist, she had no doubts about what he intended to do.

"Don't worry," he cooed. "I know you're scared now, but very soon, you won't remember this. You see, we're going to strip away everything inside that pretty little head of yours and replace it with something new. Now then" —one hand came up to firmly grasp her chin, and those strange yellow eyes studied her intently— "let's get this nasty glamour out of the way, shall we? Then we can get a good look at you."

Taly's back arched as a wave of magic crashed into her, searing her from the inside out. It felt like her skin was being burned away from her body, layer by layer, and though the pain was fleeting, it left her breathless and trembling. Sweat beaded on her brow, making her skin prickle as the chill air wafted against her.

"That's better," the man purred, dragging his tongue up the length of her neck and catching a trickle of sweat. "Now I can really see you. *Taste* you." He pulled back slightly, ripping out the tie that held her braid and untangling the weave. When his hand grazed her ear, it sent an uncomfortable shiver down her spine. "Lovely. Not perfect, mind you. I always hated how desecration spells dull the eyes." Here, he paused to prod at the skin around her eyes. "But at least the scent is right—no more iron. My, my... I have a feeling you're really going to be something once we get to the bottom of all that spell work."

Taly's free hand still clutched at her pistol, wedged between her body and the wall. She couldn't kill this guy. That she knew. But even if he was fey and a shadow mage, she could still make him hurt.

"Now then, my dear," he said as he began to fumble with the buttons on his pants. "Don't be afraid to scream. I like a little bit of struggle."

"Sorry," she bit out as she raised her pistol and thrust it beneath his chin. His eyes widened at the feel of the cool barrel pressed against delicate flesh. "But you're just not my type."

Smiling maniacally, she pulled the trigger.

She fell to the floor, her finger still squeezing the trigger as she fired off round after round. The man stumbled back, dazed, and a grim smile curled Taly's lips when his body burst into flames. She'd decided to give those incendiary rounds another *shot*, so to speak. The immolation rate still wasn't where she'd like it to be, but Ivain had shown her some tricks to increase the burn temperature. As it turned out, the old man had also experimented with different types of ammo.

The shadow mage flailed about as he desperately tried to snuff out the flames, and his legs gave out beneath him when his back hit the relay. His body writhed, flopping a bit like a fish out of water and smearing the mosaic of blood, bone, and hair that had been splattered across the crystal surface.

Taly forced her legs to move. They resisted at first, but she didn't give up, and eventually she managed to claw her way up the wall until she was standing.

There was a loud bang and a crash behind her—the sentries were trying to come through the door, but it was locked from the inside. The doorknob rattled feebly, holding firm, but it was only a matter of time before they succeeded in knocking it down.

Move!

Some of the heaviness from the man's strange spell started to lift, and Taly lurched forward. She needed to get back to the window and down the ladder and back to the woods where Byron was still tethered.

"You bitch!" A hand clamped down on her ankle, pulling her off her feet. The man groped at her legs, his hands and arms nothing but smoldering magma clinging to bone. The skin on his face had all but melted away, and tendrils of smoke rolled out from between mangled sinew and bone. His curses were punctuated with pained moans and gurgles.

Taly gripped Snowdrop, but before she could thrust it deep into his chest, he grabbed at the dagger. The blade bit into the skin of his palm, releasing a flood of crimson that welled up between the cracked and charred pieces of mangled flesh, but he didn't seem to care as he ripped the dagger from her hand and threw it off into a corner.

"How dare you," he snarled. The skin on his face was already starting to reform, the peach veneer slowly creeping across the burned flesh. As he spoke, wisps of smoke wafted out from between his scorched lips, and Taly gagged as the smell of overcooked meat filled her nose. "If you knew who

I was, who it is that I serve, you would be on your knees *begging* for my favor."

"Good luck with that," Taly choked out, still struggling feebly against his iron grip. She couldn't reach Zephyr or her second pistol, but she still had one trick left. Her breaths coming in ragged gasps, she started tearing at the wall in her mind, ripping out the stones and clawing at the power buried deep inside her.

Gold dust filled the room, and the man's bloodshot eyes surveyed the scene with irritation. Taly felt a force push back against her, and with a growl, she brought her knee up and kicked him right between the legs. The man barked in pain, wrenching back and slapping her across the face, but the force dissipated. Not completely, but just enough.

With a furious, primal howl, Taly summoned every ounce of will, every scrap of pain, and threw it against that wall. She pushed, she thrashed, she flung herself at the mental barrier until she finally felt something inside her break. Her body began to burn as sharp, whip-like cracks of pain snapped at her skin, and the weight on top of her was blown away as the world exploded in a blinding eruption of light.

The power was flowing out of her, bursting through the dam, carrying the stones of that mental barrier far away. She kept pushing, even when she felt the magic start to wane. Even when she felt a tug at something that felt… important.

Throwing away caution, throwing away sanity, she dove into that hidden well of power and immediately hit another wall—although this one felt different, almost like it was coming from outside of her. The world tilted, and it felt like she was slipping. Her raging heartbeat stumbled and then… quiet.

Darkness and then…

Taly found herself back at… *the townhouse?*

She looked around in confusion. The Castaros had always kept a townhouse inside the walls of Ryme—a formal set of rooms and hallways that had always felt too new, too polished and unused to ever really be a home.

She recognized the room instantly, even if she didn't know how she had gotten here. Ivory columns graced the center of the circular space, and the walls were adorned with what she assumed were great masterpieces. Sarina had once told her that the room "celebrated the theme of the soul bond," and since she had never really had an eye for art (not in the way that Skye could look at light and shadow and color and see such beautiful stories hidden within), she had no choice except to believe her.

Taly's eyes scanned the room, finally alighting on a small, wood block calendar resting on the corner of a dark wooden desk.

But… She shook her head, blinking in confusion. *That's the wrong month.* It was still Meridian. The moons hadn't moved into the Janus cycle. Not yet.

"Skylen!"

Taly started. She had never heard Ivain's voice sound so *stern.* Looking around, she finally noticed the older fey noble standing on the far side of the room. Skye stood opposite Ivain, his arms crossed defiantly, and Sarina, Aiden, even Kato all milled about the room, ignoring the scattering of green velvet furniture.

"Enough of this!" Ivain barked. "We all want

her back, but you have to accept the truth. She's gone."

"She's not!" Skye insisted. His clothes looked unusually rumpled and stained, and his hair was too short. Everyone else was dressed in black.

"I've seen her," Skye insisted, his hands raking through his hair. "I see her every night. She's not gone!"

"Skye." Sarina's voice was full of pity. "I know how hard it is to accept the loss of a—"

"She's not gone!" Skye bit out. His eyes were wide as he looked to his brother, who was the only one to meet his gaze.

A moment later, Kato hung his head in resignation.

"She's not gone," Skye repeated, this time more feebly.

"Surely you know what this looks like," Ivain said, his tone a little gentler. "We're worried about you."

"What's wrong?" Even to her own ears, Taly's voice sounded garbled, almost like she was underwater.

Five heads whipped around at the sound of her voice, and Taly felt her cheeks warm when five disbelieving sets of eyes found hers. Barely a second had ticked by before Skye was rushing forward, grabbing for her as he fell to his knees. His hands passed right through her body. The vision was already starting to blur as the sound of rushing wind filled her ears.

"Stabilize her!" Ivain's voice sounded far away. "It has to be you, boy!"

Taly's eyes drooped shut, and she felt something pulling her back to the relay room—a gentle tug, almost like there was a string attached to one of her ribs.

A rush of magic washed over her, abruptly jolting her awake, and then someone was shaking her. Opening her eyes, she discovered that she was still in the townhouse. Skye gripped her shoulders, and she felt the distinct tingle of shadow magic anchoring her in place.

"Taly?" Skye's voice was laced with panic. "Taly, where are you?"

Taly reached up to grasp at his wrist, but it was like trying to hold on to smoke. Something warm trickled down her cheek, and she wiped at it, expecting dirt or sweat, maybe even tears. Her eyes widened when she pulled her hand away only to see that her fingers were stained red. She blinked, and more blood began leaking from her eyes, then her nose, even her ears.

Something was tugging at her again. More forcefully this time. Urging her to return to the relay room.

"What's happening to her?" someone snapped. Sarina? Maybe?

"Hold on to her!" But again, the voice was distant, jumbled.

Another spark of shadow magic and Skye was tapping her cheek. His hands remained clean even as they wiped at the streaks of red staining her skin. "C'mon. Stay with me. Just a little longer. Where are you? Are you still on Tempris? Are you at the palace?"

"Oh, my little one," Sarina sobbed. She tried reaching for her, grasping at Taly's shoulder, but it was like trying to touch a ghost. "What have they done to you?"

Taly stared at the blood dripping down her fingers until Skye gently wrapped a hand around her wrist. When she looked up, he was watching her, a mixture of terror and despair distorting his features. "I don't know what's happening to me," she murmured.

"Where are you?" Skye's voice was gentle and sad. "Please. I know you're hurt; I know you're tired. But I need you to tell me where you are. Tell me where you are, and I'll come get you."

Taly shook her head, not sure how to answer that question. She didn't know where she was anymore, if she was anywhere at all. So, she said, instead, "I found the relay. I talked to Ivain."

Skye jerked his head. "Taly, I know, but—"

The world abruptly dissolved into a haze of light and sound and color. Voices whirled around her. She was being pulled in too many directions at once, but Skye—he dragged her back somehow.

"Taly, please." Skye grabbed her chin, forcing her to look back at him. There were tears in his eyes now, and the room still blurred around the edges, snapping in and out of focus. She felt his magic pulling at her, willing her to stay in place, but he was losing his grip. "Please, Tink. Come back to me. Just stay alive."

As the vision continued to fade, Taly did her best to smile. "I'm glad I got to see you one last time, Em." She looked around the room, taking in the faces of everyone she held dear—Ivain, Sarina, Aiden. And Kato—well, she still felt a bit lukewarm about him, but he looked so stricken she couldn't help but feel a pang of reluctant affection. "All of you."

"Taly!"

A sharper tug this time and then she was falling.

The next time she opened her eyes, motes of

dust and ash hung suspended in the air, intertwined with sparkling pinpricks of golden light. Taly winced, shrinking back. Everything was too bright, the colors too vivid. Even the shadows seemed to come alive, and the quiet stillness was a raging tempest of sound to her overly sensitive ears.

Don't do that again, a feminine voice whispered in her ear. The command was stern yet kind, and it stirred something inside her, some distant, forgotten memory. *Now get up!*

Taly pushed herself to her feet, ignoring the burning pain in her lungs. She forced herself to focus on her surroundings, despite the dull ache that had settled behind her eyes. She was back in the relay room, but there was light pouring in *through* the walls. It took her a moment to realize why. It looked like a bomb had gone off in the room, turning the platform into a ruined hulk. The relay had cracked and shattered, and the wooden frame that made up the walls of the building had been splintered—erupting outward in a spray of fragmented pieces.

But the scene stood frozen in front of her—a moment of devastation suspended in time. Shards of crystal and wood hung in the air, and she turned, looking for her attacker, only to see that the shadow mage's body had been flung to the side. His face was constricted in a distorted howl of rage as he reached for her, but his body was still, his limbs contorted in a motionless struggle.

Go! the voice screamed. It was clearer now, almost musical. *Stop dawdling, you stupid child!*

The ground was uneven beneath Taly's boots, and the crunch of shattered wood echoed in the stillness as she staggered forward. The sentries that had been banging at the door as well as the shades that had been drawn by the gunfire had been thrown back by the blast and were lying motionless on the ground outside the relay building.

Not quite believing her eyes, Taly pushed her hair off her face, coming up short when she felt a sharpened point where her ear should be. "What the..." she mumbled, running a finger over the foreign shape.

In a daze, she stumbled through the main entrance, stepping over the door that had been flung off its hinges before setting off at a full sprint toward the forest and where she had tethered Byron.

A myriad of questions boiled and frothed in her mind. What the hell had just happened? Was that real? Had she really talked to Skye or was it just some sort of hallucination?

No, she thought, looking down at her hands. Hands that didn't quite look like her own. Her fingers were too long, her skin too pale, and her wrists looked thinner, more delicate. There was fresh blood staining her fingers, and she could still feel a telltale wetness dripping from her ears. Definitely not a hallucination. If she were to look in a mirror, she was sure that her face would be streaked with drying trails of blood.

She searched for that wall in her mind, but it was gone now. Damaged beyond repair. There were still a few runes inscribed on her arm, but not many. The flesh there looked cleaner than it had in weeks. The remaining lines of Faera were faded and unevenly spaced, and although she didn't recognize all of the characters, she did notice one marking that she was sure hadn't been there before. The symbol for arho—a spiral of evenly spaced dots—had been inscribed on the top of her right hand, and the flesh around the impossibly neat strokes of shadow magic was still red and healing.

All will be explained in due time, child, the voice whispered soothingly. *For now, run. Go to the palace. I will meet you there when I am able.*

Taly shuddered but kept running. Byron reared back when she approached but settled quickly when he heard the sound of her voice. He still seemed uneasy as she swung herself into the saddle but apparently grasped the urgency of the situation as he set off at a gallop through the trees, easily responding to the faintest press of her leg against his flank.

The sound of time restarting followed them—a thunderous explosion interlaced with screams of pain and rage cascading through the dense underbrush of the forest. The distant clamor bounced off the trees but sounded far enough away that Taly could be confident in her escape.

She had no idea what had just happened. Everything was a blur of confusion as she ducked out of the way of the leaves and branches that tore at her skin and clothing. The only thing she knew for certain was that, for better or worse, whatever was inside her had been set free, and she had been transformed—changed. But into what and to what end, she wasn't quite sure.

CHAPTER 27

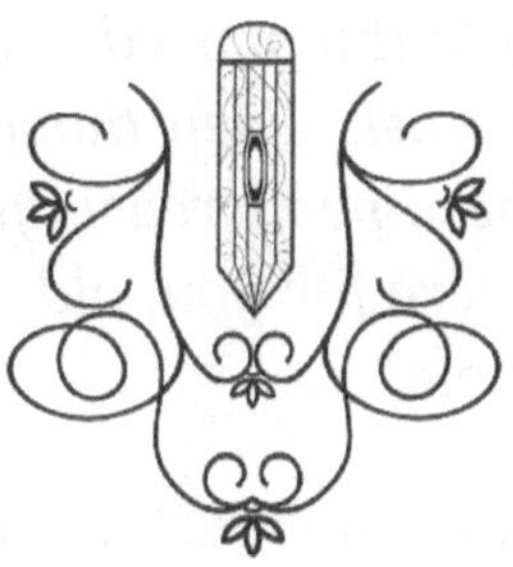

-A letter from Nissa Caeli of House Tira, High Lady of Air, to Atlas Venwraith of House Arendryl, High Lord of Water.

A note from the imperial scrivener: *As per Her Imperial Majesty, the High Lady of Air's request, this letter has been stricken from the official record.*

The 8th day of the month Anon, during the 236th year of the Empty Throne

Atlas,

I hope this letter finds you in good health. Given our long-abiding friendship, Matriarch Bryer has asked me to deliver some most troubling news. It is with the utmost regret that I must inform you that both Breena and her daughter passed away last year. There was an accident during the child's Attunement Ceremony, and she did not survive. I'm told Breena took her own life shortly afterward.

I know that we have not always seen eye-to-eye, especially as of late, but you have my deepest condolences. The others do not know what it is like to lose a Guardian—not in the way that we do. If there is anything that you need in the coming days, do not hesitate to ask. Even though our ability to correspond has become increasingly limited, please know that I am here for you, old friend, whenever you have need of me.

With my deepest sympathies and everlasting friendship,

Nissa

The chill of nightfall was just starting to set in, and it made Taly's teeth chatter. Infinity's Edge, the Time Queen's abandoned seat of power, peeked through the thinning tree cover. The outline of the rusted iron gates was nothing but a shadow set against the bright backdrop of the second rising moon just visible over the next ridge.

Can't stop yet, Taly thought, shaking off the lethargy that had seeped into her very bones. It took everything she had just to stay astride Byron, but thankfully, they were almost at the river now.

So far, she and Byron had encountered neither beast nor shade in their flight from Vale. Their progress had slowed as the underbrush of the forest thickened, but it was that same underbrush that had probably kept the shadow mage from pursuing them. She could smell the water now. The Arda, the river that bisected the island of Tempris, was close by. If they could just make it out of the forest, they could follow the river back to Infinity's Edge. Mysterious voices aside, the palace's old defense system could at least offer some measure of protection if Taly could figure out a way to jump-start it.

When they finally emerged from the tree line, Taly slid out of the saddle, her boots slipping on the smooth stones as she stumbled to the river's edge. The dank smell of moss assaulted her senses as she eased herself to the ground and took several long frantic gulps of the sweetest water she had ever tasted. They had made it. Byron pawed at the water, sending sprays of icy droplets washing over her as he too took a much-needed respite.

When she finally pulled back, she splashed her face, scrubbing at the trails of dried, flaking blood until the liquid streaming through her fingers finally ran clear. She sat there for a moment, staring into the water and doing her best to ignore how each breath felt like fire inside her lungs.

Aether depletion, she thought, placing a hand on her chest. The shortness of breath, the unexplained fatigue—it was textbook aether depletion. Truthfully, Taly wasn't sure why that particular revelation surprised her at this point.

The ripples of river water distorted her reflection, but as the image began to resolve itself, she couldn't help but gape at the girl that stared back at her. Surely, it was a trick of the moonlight. Maybe some spell cast by that horrible mage?

Her eyes looked... *strange* in the river's reflection. Too bright—almost silver. And had her cheeks hollowed out? Or was it perhaps the exaggerated arch of her eyebrows that made the sweep of her cheekbones seem so much more... pronounced?

"What happened?" she asked, pulling at the skin of her face—no longer tanned from the sun. As she patted down her body, she noted that her limbs felt thinner. No, not thinner exactly. Although her arms looked willowy, almost delicate, there was a strength that hadn't been there before. She could feel it.

Were her eyes playing tricks on her? Well, not *her* eyes, but those strange, highborn eyes that could now see farther and with more clarity than seemed natural? It was as though all her features had somehow been enhanced, transforming her into something too smooth, too *fey* to be considered completely human.

Shards, she... she was supposed to be human!

But... *no.* Taly swept back her hair to reveal the pointed arch of her ear. Not human. Not anymore at least. A deep pit opened up in her stomach as the realization slowly began to sink in.

Maybe she hadn't ever really been human.

Her breaths came in ragged gasps as she tried to grapple with these revelations—hell, with *everything* that had just happened. She started when Byron nudged his nose against her cheek.

Not the time, he seemed to say.

Stupid horse. He was right. This wasn't the time to give in to panic. She was beside a river in the middle of the night with an incensed shadow mage most likely pursuing her. No, what she needed to do was go meet this mystery voice whispering in her ear in the ruined remains of a long-abandoned palace. Because that seemed reasonable. That was what a perfectly sane person would do, right?

Stumbling to her feet, Taly pulled herself back into the saddle. Then, urging her horse forward, they continued upstream. Their progress along the bank of the river was slow and arduous. They were both tired, and Byron's hooves kept slipping along the riverbank. She slumped in the saddle, her arms clinging to his neck when she was no longer strong enough to give commands.

Still, Byron continued forward—hearing her silent plea to keep moving. Even when he was a foal, he had always known exactly what she was trying to tell him. And why wouldn't he? Hers had been the first face he'd seen. His birth had not been easy, and after everyone else had given up on him, even his mother, Taly had stayed beside him, night after night in that humid stable, refusing to let him cross over to the beryl-green fields of Moriah alone. He was hers, and she was his, and he kept moving forward, despite the foam that accumulated around his mouth and even after he had thrown a shoe.

"Good boy," Taly murmured. She tried to reach a hand out to pet his flank, but she couldn't muster the energy. She was so tired, and every breath she took just reignited that aching blaze inside her body. It was like continuing to drown even after being pulled to shore. She tried one more time to scratch at Byron's mane, but her hand just fell away, bouncing limply against his neck as he plodded forward. Byron's head cocked to the side, acknowledging the gesture. If she didn't know any better, she could've sworn she saw both affection and worry reflected in his glassy, equine eyes.

The next time she looked up, she saw the

rusted wrought-iron fence that surrounded Infinity's Edge to her left. They had made it. The tumbling rapids that ran underneath the citadel roared in the distance, and she could feel the hum of the four massive hyaline relays that flanked the royal residence vibrating the very air around her.

For as long as she could remember, Taly had always been fascinated by the abandoned palace. She was seven years old the first time she saw it. She and Sarina had been going to Ebondrift to buy fabric, and they had made a detour so they could ride by the front gates. Sarina had lived on the island for a very long time, several centuries at least, and she could remember what the old palace had looked like when the Time Queen was still in residence. She always used to say that the glamographs couldn't do it justice, couldn't come close to capturing the breathtaking beauty of those towering, swirling spires when they were lit up with great blazes of magical fire.

Infinity's Edge had been left to decay after the Schism—a monument to a massacred tribe. The cobbled drive in front of the palace gates was overgrown and strewn with scrap and what appeared to be discarded pieces of old Mechanica armor. Fragments of what Taly could only guess used to be brilliant shades of blue, red, green, and even chrome were just barely visible beneath the corrosion, and if she dared to look closer, she knew she'd see shards of bone beneath that old armor that had yet to decompose. The final resting place of the Time Queen's Crystal Guard—exposed to aether, a corpse could take several centuries to completely turn to dust.

Still, even ravaged by war and neglect and surrounded by the bodies of the fallen, the ruined palace was a thing of beauty. A great dome flanked by columns of white marble crested in gold reached up towards the heavens, and even from this distance, Taly could see the glint of moonlight reflected off the carved, twining roses that stretched up and over the exterior walls of the main palace. She couldn't remember ever being able to see that far, especially at night, but these new highborn eyes could easily detect details that previously would've been lost to the shadows.

They were almost there now, and even the air started to smell sweeter as they approached the gated entrance. The heavenly draft soothed the burning in Taly's lungs and made the dull, throbbing pain that had taken root deep inside her just a little easier to bear.

As they passed by one of the colossal, darkened relays, it unexpectedly flashed, lighting up the night sky. For a brief moment, night turned into day, and she recoiled as the blinding glare hit her overly sensitive eyes.

Byron reared, and though Taly grasped at his mane, she couldn't stop herself from sliding off his back. Her breath got knocked out of her as she hit the ground, and instinct had her quickly rolling to the side to avoid getting trampled. Another flash from the relay sent Byron galloping off into the woods.

"What the…" she panted, her eyes darting from side-to-side.

"Ah! There you are, little mage," a low voice boomed. The malicious, masculine drawl came from everywhere and nowhere, all at once.

Taly clambered to her feet, ignoring the twinge of pain in her knee as her hands groped for the pistol holstered at her waist. She would recognize that voice anywhere. It would no doubt be haunting her dreams from now on. The shadow mage from the relay room had finally found her.

Her hands were steady as she scanned the tree line nearby, but she didn't see anything out of place. Just the bright flashing of the hyaline monolith to the west—a part of the communication system for the palace that had been disabled shortly after the Schism.

He's somehow managed to tap into the scrying relay, Taly thought, raising the barrel of her pistol. If that was truly the case, that meant he was close by.

"That was a very impressive display back there, little mage. You caught me off-guard. Believe me when I say, it won't happen again."

"Who are you?!" Taly screamed into the empty air. She began edging along the fence, towards the gates, but something must have happened to her leg when she'd been thrown. When she went to take a step, she stumbled over a stray piece of scrap. She twisted, trying to regain her balance, but her knee immediately buckled. With a pained groan, she hit the ground, and something in her leg gave a sickening crunch.

The disembodied voice of the man was almost gleeful when he suddenly exclaimed, "Wait! I recognize you. Now that you've managed to burn through the rest of that desecration spell... Shards, I thought you looked familiar. Those eyes—those *gray* eyes." He paused to laugh good-naturedly. "My my, look at how much you've grown, Corinna! I must say, you look *just* like your mother now. It's a little uncanny."

Taly tried to get back on her feet, but her leg wasn't capable of supporting her weight anymore, and she just fell back to her knees.

"Now, now, stop struggling. I know you're scared right now, but I can take that away. Just be patient. If you stay where you are, I'll be there soon. And I promise I'll be gentle with you this time. I spoke with my master, and he has decided to honor you. He is going to raise you up, give you a special place in the great war that is to come. I promise you—all this pain, all this uncertainty... soon it will be gone."

The bushes started to snap and rustle in the distance.

Taly tried one more time to push herself to her feet, but when that didn't work, she started crawling. She needed to get past the gates of the palace. Some forgotten instinct told her it was safe beyond the gates. The grit and pebbles bit into her cheek as she pulled herself across the old gravel drive.

Her lungs were starting to burn again. She was too tired to move, too tired to fight, and something in her already knew that whatever magical ability she might have wouldn't work right now.

A shadow stepped out of the forest just beyond the first hyaline pillar—the man from the relay room. But instead of the hunched and limping figure she expected to see given the extent of his injuries, he stood tall. His fine clothes had been singed, and his skin was still a little flushed from the heat of the flames, but otherwise, he was unharmed. He stalked closer, and the yellow of his eyes seemed to glow as he studied her. He took careful steps as he skirted around the edge of the large, circular patch of gravel, his hands clasped behind him. Snowdrop was sheathed at his waist.

"Before the Schism," he drawled as he drew closer, "there were more like you."

Taly raised her pistol and fired off a shot. She smiled when the bullet embedded itself in the man's shoulder, but her heart sank soon after when he just laughed and dug the bullet out, wiping his hands on his trousers as the flesh instantly knitted itself back together.

"Not very many, mind you," he continued casually—as if they were just two friends catching up. He chuckled when Taly renewed her efforts to put more distance between them. She gripped at the iron railing, trying to pull herself along, but it was no use. Although his pace was halfhearted and mocking, he was still gaining on her. "Even at the height of their power, time mages were considered quite rare, which made the birth of a time mage something to be celebrated, even envied. Oh, how the noble houses used to clamor, trying to arrange marriages, even soul bonds, all so they could introduce a few precious drops of that coveted time mage blood into their family line."

He stopped, pretending to ponder something as he ran a finger along his chin. His beard was gone now, burned away, and the skin that had grown to take its place was smooth and pale. "Of course, that's certainly not the case anymore. These days, breeding contracts are arranged to try to *prevent* the births of new time mages. Not all successfully, obviously." He waved a hand in Taly's direction as he continued to circle. "Granted, your parents were matched long before the Schism. In hindsight, they really should've been more careful—or at the very least kept you in Faro. Shards, what did your poor mother think when she saw that golden glow at your Attunement

Ceremony? She must have been crushed."

Taly wasn't going to make it to the main gates. She could see that now. Eventually, the shadow mage would grow tired of toying with her, and whatever this man and his master planned to do to her, she had no desire to find out. But even if she couldn't escape him, she did have one other option.

She already had her pistol in hand.

She could still control the way this ended.

Her hand trembled as she slowly raised the gun and placed the barrel to her temple. The metal felt cool against her skin, and her heart thundered in her chest as she considered what she was about to do. Would this even work anymore? The memory of those startling highborn eyes staring back at her from the river's edge flashed through her mind.

Yes—it would work. She could see it in the way the shadow mage's eyes widened, in the way his shoulders tensed. He needed her alive. And even if she weren't human anymore, if she didn't have any aether left, her body wouldn't be able to recover from a gunshot wound to the head before her heart stopped.

"Now, now, little mage," he cooed gently, stopping his pursuit. He held up his hands in supplication. "Let's not do anything hasty."

The edges of the carved snowdrops etched into the side of the gun bit into her skin—her last gift from Skye. She still wasn't sure if that vision in the relay room was real, but she hoped so. Because if it was real, that meant he would eventually make it back to Ryme. He would be safe. If she had managed to play even a small part in making that happen, then every risk she had taken had been worth it.

She slowly squeezed the trigger, her thoughts lingering on Skye—on that final image of her family together at the townhouse.

Before she could fully depress the trigger, four distinct claps of deafening thunder shook the ground. The towering, hyaline pillar closest to her shattered, throwing shards of crystal in every direction. Taly flinched, but the shards never seemed to reach her, sloughing off some invisible barrier that encircled the palace.

The shadow mage was not so lucky. Flung off his feet by the blast towards the tree line, he moaned feebly as he was impaled by a large spike of translucent crystal. At almost a foot in diameter and four times as long, it tore a gaping hole in his torso.

Taly's grip on the pistol still pressed to her head faltered. Was he dead? No—he was still moving, already recovering in fact. And Shards, what had caused that explosion? A possible ally or something else? Should she try to fight? Could she make it to the gates? And what protection could the palace actually afford her at this point? When this man regained his feet, he would eventually tear through whatever was left of the palace's defense system. Perhaps her fate had already been set.

With that thought, she slowly raised the gun back to her head…

"Darling, no," a gentle voice said—a woman's voice. The same voice from the relay room that had told her to run. A hand clasped hers, and as the gun was pulled away, Taly found herself staring at a very familiar face—one that looked strangely like her own.

The woman from her dreams crouched in front of her. Although her body looked almost transparent in the dim light, a soft sheen of shadow magic engulfed her, keeping her from completely fading into the night. Her golden hair was pulled back and piled upon her head in a braided coronet, and she wore armor forged from shadows and embedded with glittering waves of shadow crystals. The familiar symbol of the Water Shard's personal guard—a kraken impaled by a trident—was set into the breastplate.

"Don't be afraid," she said soothingly, her hands moving to cup Taly's face. "My baby. My darling girl. How I've longed to see you again."

Something, some long-forgotten memory, finally clicked into place. "Mom?"

The woman smiled. "That's right. I'm Breena. I'm your mother." She paused to wipe at her eyes. "Shards, and here I was afraid that you wouldn't remember me."

Taly shook her head, her overworked mind not quite able to process just what was happening. "How…?"

Arching a single brow, Breena grabbed Taly's wrist, and her finger grazed the shadow crystal that was embedded there. "A little planning and a lot of luck. I knew they would come for you eventually—to Vale. Ever since the day a human girl with my eyes stumbled up to my cottage, I knew the Sanctorum would come looking for us. Thankfully, you were able to warn us long before they set the fire, and my brother and I were able to make the necessary preparations."

Taly simply stared at the woman blankly, her mind reeling. An image of that burned-out cottage she'd passed back in Vale flashed through her mind, and her eyes widened. That moment, however brief it had been—when an invisible power had brushed past her and reshaped the landscape right before her eyes… that had been real. That man as well as the woman she now recognized as being her long-dead mother—they had been *real*.

"I… I don't understand," Taly stuttered. "What do you mean, *before* the fire? The fire was 15 years ago. I just saw you back in Vale a few hours ago."

Breena's other hand came up to graze the pendant that hung from Taly's neck. A glimmer of recognition and relief flitted through the older woman's eyes. "Your magic allows you to view time differently than the rest of us. What happened only moments ago for you can be but a distant memory for others. That is your gift. And in this case, it was your salvation."

Breena sighed, as though considering a long list of painful memories. "I could tell just by that brief glimpse that you had inherited your father's recklessness. You had that same look in your eyes." Turning Taly's wrist over, Breena gave the younger woman a stern look that had her shrinking back instinctively. "Apparently, I was right. You almost burned up your anima when you tore through the last of the spells suppressing your magic." She tapped the still-healing rune on the back of Taly's hand. "I'm not sure where you went or how, but I had to bind your soul just to get you back into your body."

"So that tugging…?" Taly's voice trailed off as she recalled the strange encounter when she had somehow slipped out of her body. "When I was talking to Skye, that was real too?"

Breena's brows shot up. "Skye? You mean that boy Ivain took in as his student? How interesting," she murmured. "I never would've guessed that the two of you would've already… How unexpected."

"You bitch!" the shadow mage howled, finally recovering from his wounds and pulling the crystal from his body with a sickening squelch. Both women's heads turned just in time to see him rising to his feet. He now wielded the bloodied shard of crystal like a mace. "*Breena.* I thought you were dead."

Breena's lips curled into a sneer as she rose, her hand reaching for the sword sheathed at her side. "Close, but not quite, Vaughn."

The man, Vaughn, raked a disdainful eye across the shattered hyaline pillar. "Not bad for a dead woman. I daresay, when I awoke this morning, I never would have imagined *two* members of House Arendryl walking into my web. My master will be very pleased, indeed."

"Your master?" Breena's silvery gray eyes narrowed as they flicked down to the amulet that hung around Vaughn's neck. "So, the rumors were true? He's awake?" Vaughn gave her a smug sneer, and she huffed out a laugh in response. "Well then, that's just going to make this even more satisfying." A violet ripple of energy snaked around her hand, and then the ground erupted beneath Vaughn's feet, throwing him back.

"Aether destabilization?" Taly stuttered as Breena pulled her to her feet. She had to lean against the fence just to keep from falling, her leg still unable to carry her weight. "I've only ever heard of Ivain being able to use that spell!"

"Well, who do you think taught me, dear?"

Breena replied. A snap of her fingers was all it took to set off another explosion, and more shards of hyaline rained down from the nearby pillar. Vaughn moaned pitifully as he struggled against the crystal spikes that pinned him to the ground. The shadow crystal around his neck flashed, and a roiling cloud of magic curled around his body as he channeled his aether. He renewed his efforts, throwing off sprays of blood as he thrashed about. The crystals began to splinter and groan beneath the onslaught.

Breena started pulling Taly along the fence line, toward the gates of the palace, but Taly stumbled when her knee once more gave out beneath her. Breena moved with the kind of agility and grace that only a shadow mage could manage, quickly catching her and slinging an arm underneath her shoulders. Her mother's body felt remarkably solid considering Taly could see right through her.

"Now then, my dear," Breena said, "I wish we had more time, but you need to go." When Taly pulled against the woman in protest, Breena just hoisted her up to her toes and started dragging her along without missing a beat. "If I were still alive, I'd have a chance at killing him, but as it stands, I only have enough power left to distract him while you get to the palace."

"If you were still alive?" Taly asked incredulously. "So you're dead then? I don't understand. How can you be here if you're dead?"

Breena glanced at Taly from the corner of her eye. "When the Sanctorum came to Vale, we had very little warning. When the fires started, I didn't have enough aether left to completely bind your magic, so I gave you my anima. My body died, but my soul was woven into the enchantments that allowed you to stay hidden. When you broke through the last of the spells suppressing your magic back at the relay, you released me. Or rather, what's left of me."

Taly's chest felt uncomfortably tight. Her mother had died for her—sacrificed herself for a child that hadn't even remembered her name.

Before Taly could even begin to respond, Breena growled, and her magic flared around them. "Stay down, Vaughn!"

Looking behind them, Taly saw Vaughn dodge the blast of rapidly expanding aether. His body was streaked with blood, but his wounds had already healed. He dodged again, rolling off to the side. There was an arrogant smile on his face that made Taly's stomach turn.

"Come now, Breena!" he called, a low chuckle shaking his shoulders. "It's been such a long time since we sparred. I think I'm owed a rematch!"

He hadn't even finished the sentence before he charged. He moved too fast for Taly's eyes to follow, his trek across the wide expanse that separated them nothing but a blur. She tensed, but her mother seemed unperturbed. A few moments later, she realized why.

A crack of static followed by a yelp of pain and Vaughn was suddenly stumbling backward. He had run into a wall of electricity. Streaks of blue lightning rippled up and over their heads, creeping across an invisible barrier that shot up into the night sky.

"By the way," Breena said, her voice cocky as she met Vaughn's enraged, silent stare, "I reactivated the palace's defense systems."

Vaughn said nothing as he stepped cautiously

along the barrier, matching their pace. The crystal shard was still clutched tightly in one hand and snaking tendrils of shadow magic coiled between his fingers as he raked his other hand along the barrier.

After a few steps, he seemed to grow tired of this game. With a savage roar, he abruptly slammed the shard into the barrier. Taly felt a tremor as the invisible wall of energy shuddered.

A chilling smile distorted his features as he raised his makeshift mace once more and began attacking the wall in earnest. Growls and snarls punctuated each strike, and when the crystal in his hands cracked, he began beating against the shield with his bare hands. Burns and cuts marred his fists, but the flesh was mending itself too fast to allow even the barest trickle of blood.

The gates of the palace were just up ahead now, but Vaughn was already starting to break through the wall, the barrier flashing more feebly with each strike. "A little help here!" Breena yelled into the night sky as she increased their pace.

As if on cue, a flickering blue orb drifted down from above. Its soft glow felt warm on Taly's face as it danced in front of her, as though inspecting her features. "F-fairy fire?" Taly stuttered. Shards, she had been right! All those years ago, she really had seen fairy fire outside her window! If she ever saw Skye again, she was going to make him eat his words. "Fairy fire is real?"

"Yes!" the orb chimed, its voice delicate, almost bell-like. "We here now! We help!"

More blue orbs began to materialize in the air around them as Breena continued to half-drag Taly towards the palace. Their forms were hazy and indistinct, little more than translucent shimmers of mist that zipped through the air as they chased each other in a game that didn't seem to have any rules. Their laughter sounded like wind chimes, and a tinkling cheer rang out when Breena held up a hand to release more violet energy that she waved toward Vaughn. Bright flares of shadow magic rippled in her wake as a series of concussive blasts sounded from behind them. Each detonation was followed by an enraged howl from the shadow mage, but it was just a distraction—a ploy to buy time. Because even though the explosions slowed down his assault on the barrier, he was dodging Breena's attacks easily now.

Breena swatted at a wisp that flew too close. "Blasted pests. Make yourselves useful!" she commanded forcefully. "Cover our escape! Attack him! For Shards' sake, do what you stayed here to do! Take your revenge!"

"Aye!" they all chimed in unison. "We help! We *kill*..."

The group of wisps scattered, their shimmering forms dissipating into mist as they sunk into the ground. Metal clanged against metal, and Taly tripped as the half-buried scrap at her feet began to tremble. Pieces of ancient, long-discarded armor ripped from the ground in a shower of dirt, shuddering as the threads of blue energy tugged at them, reassembling the rusted shells.

The metal suits looked like great hulking beasts—far bulkier than the sleeker, streamlined models that Skye had shown her in the rare glamograph he had bothered to bring back from his trips to the mainland. The joints and crystal settings whirred as the wisps somehow revived the rusted wiring, and fragments of bone dropped to the ground as the metal soldiers shook themselves off and pulled themselves together. Staring at the towering, haphazard, multicolored amalgamations of suits, Taly couldn't help but think that 200 years ago, when they were still new and whole and polished, they would have been dazzling.

The fragmented suits of armor were striated with streaks of blue energy as the wisps attempted to mimic the living, their movements jerky and uncoordinated. They had managed to restore a couple dozen suits, and as they took giant lumbering steps towards the shadow mage who was now almost through the barrier, he finally backed away, the slightest glimmer of fear flaring to life in those yellow eyes.

The wall yielded to the reanimated soldiers, its electrified tendrils slipping past the corroded metal surfaces like water. There was a sense of recognition there—Taly could feel it, even if she couldn't quite understand it.

The revived Mechanica surrounded Vaughn, and the cannons built into their mismatched greaves began to hum. Rows of air, water, and fire crystals winked and glittered in the dim light as the startup sequences completed.

A pause, barely a breath of silence, and then…

Explosions lit up the night sky as bursts of magical energy rocketed through the air. Each blast sent up a plume of rock and smoke where it collided with the ground, but Vaughn was too fast to get caught in the salvo. He zigzagged across the field, easily dodging each discharge and tearing apart the rusted soldiers with his bare hands. He was bleeding now, the skin taking slightly longer to mend itself as he redirected his aether, but Taly could already see that the diversion wouldn't last long. His blows were too accurate, too fierce, and he'd already managed to take out two of the suits. The dislodged wisps buzzed around him, but he paid them no mind.

"Here we are," Breena finally announced as they came to a stop in front of the main gates, dozens of the blue fairies still dancing around them. The wrought-iron structure looked sturdy despite the delicate filigreed designs woven throughout, and a heavy padlock hung from a thick, coiled chain. Grasping at the lock with her free hand, Taly's mother didn't even flinch when a sharp crack of defensive magic lashed out at her.

"It tickles a bit," she said in response to Taly's wide-eyed stare. "But defensive wards don't work very well on those with no physical body." She gave the lock a sharp tug, and the links of the heavy chain snapped and warped like they were made of clay.

"It's time for you to go with the fairies. They can take you to where you need to be." Breena wiped at a stray tear as she placed both hands on Taly's shoulders, waiting for her to find her footing before she completely let go.

"What? No!" Taly protested. "First of all, I'm not going anywhere with a bunch of homicidal spirits. And second, I'm not leaving you."

Another crackle of energy split open the starlit sky, and... *Shit!?* What to do, what to do?! She could already see that Vaughn had nearly wiped out the group of animated Mechanica suits.

"You must, dear," Breena replied, pushing a stray lock of hair out of Taly's eyes. "Even if we worked together, we wouldn't stand a chance against him. You have no aether left, and me? I still have a few tricks, but I'm just a shadow of what I was when I was still alive. I can't kill him, but I can make sure that you stay safe. That is my duty—both as your mother and as a Crystal Guardian."

"No, I..." Taly fumbled for the right words. This couldn't be the end. Not yet. There were so many questions she wanted to ask Breena. So many things she wanted to tell her. But now, with Vaughn raging in the background and the wisps already tugging at her clothing, she felt paralyzed. "Will I see you again?" was all she managed to ask. The orbs were pulling at her more insistently now, but she resisted.

Breena shook her head sadly. "No. Now that the spells have been broken, there's nothing left to bind me here. I'm already starting to fade." She held up a hand. Faint wisps of smoke were starting to mix with the violet glow of her magic.

"Then come with me," Taly insisted, waving away one of the fairies. "If you want me to go along with these things peacefully, come with me. I won't go without you."

"Still bargaining, I see," Breena murmured with a small smile. "It's nice to see that not everything has changed." Bringing both hands up to cup Taly's face, her mother whispered, "I'm sorry, dear. Where you're going, I can't follow. So, since this is the last time..." Her voice broke slightly, but she kept talking through the tears that were now streaming freely from her eyes. "I love you, my darling daughter. I have always loved you, and I will continue to love you even after I finally pass through the gates of Moriah. Never doubt that. And no matter what, always be proud of what you are—what you can do. I was, and your father will be too. I'm sure of it. Now go!" With that, Breena gave Taly a gentle shove.

Thrown off-balance, Taly stumbled. She grabbed for the swinging metal gates as her knee once again buckled beneath her weight, but the wisps pulled her off her feet before she could find her equilibrium. The spirits cushioned her fall even as they began dragging her past the fence line.

The next time Taly found her mother's eyes, the sadness had melted away, softness replaced with steel as she prepared to face Vaughn. A warrior—her mother had been a warrior. "Farewell, child. When you see your father, tell him I'm sorry I never got the chance to say goodbye."

Vaughn was almost through the line of Mechanica. There was only one remaining soldier, but the shadow mage had already brought the hulking metal warrior to its knees. "You can't keep her from me!" he howled as he crushed its helm beneath his boot. "You can't keep her from my master! He will find her!"

Breena turned away from Taly and assumed a defensive stance, her sword at the ready. Taly tried to push herself to her feet, but the orbs of fairy fire had started to coalesce around her—the cloud thickening and expanding with each passing moment. She struggled to remain upright as a torrent of unfamiliar magic slammed into her. "No!" she screamed desperately. "Mom! Please, not again!"

The wisps had formed themselves into a swirling vortex. They obscured her vision and filled her ears with the rush of wind. Taly reached out a hand, desperately clawing her way back towards the gate. "Please!" No one else could die because of her. Even if her mother could never come back, even if she was already dead, that shadow mage could still hurt her. Fey souls were made of aether, after all.

A wave of shadow magic engulfed Breena's form, and the ground around her erupted in a spray of gravel. Vaughn ducked to one knee, raising a single arm as he bore the brunt of the blast head-on. He was bruised and bleeding now, and his shirt was little more than a few tatters of silk that hung from his burly shoulders. His lips moved as he stepped through the shattered barrier that used to surround the palace, and he eyed Breena in irritation. She widened her stance, ready to face him, but instead of turning to fight, he attempted to sidestep her and run for the gates. For Taly. As he passed, Breena lunged, bringing down the edge of her spectral blade across the back of his knees and forcing him to the ground.

Her bloodied sword still in hand, Breena turned to Taly one final time. She was almost gone now. Her body was already beginning to break apart and disintegrate even as she sent out blast after blast of shadow magic at Vaughn, who was attempting to regain his feet. The older woman's mouth moved as she tried to say something, and although Taly could no longer hear her mother's words over the deafening roar of the magical vortex that threatened to consume her, there was pride mixed with another, unmistakable emotion in the woman's eyes.

That was enough to convey her final parting message.

Her mother loved her.

The ground was trembling now. A great rumbling, almost like an extended peal of thunder, sounded from deep beneath the surface, and the gates squealed as they chaotically swayed on their hinges. Cracks and fissures, small at first but then large and gaping, wedged open, spiraling out from her body in a chaotic web and shining with a golden light that illuminated the night sky.

"No!" Taly was still reaching, struggling to see through the vortex of swirling magic that was starting to pull her down. Not yet. After all these years, it couldn't end like this.

"Mom!" she screamed, praying her mother could still hear her. "I love you too! This is not goodbye! You have my word—this is not goodbye!"

The ground finally gave way just as Vaughn managed a step past the gates, but Taly had already disappeared, the world growing black around her and finally fading entirely from view.

EPILOGUE

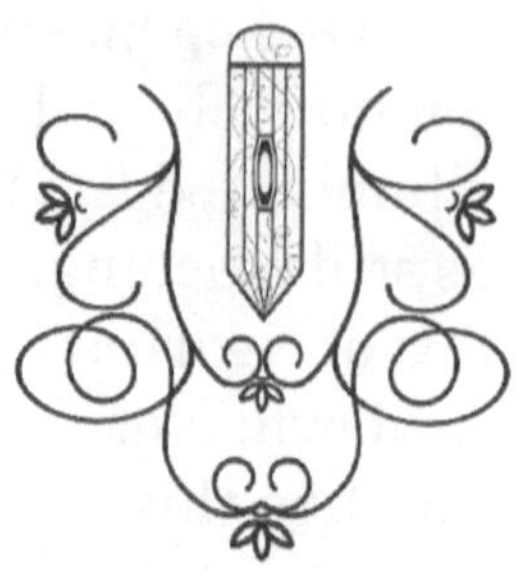

Taly could feel an uncomfortable crick forming in her neck, and even in her languid state, she could tell that she was resting against something hard. None of that mattered, though. She was having the loveliest dream, and she wasn't nearly ready to return to the waking world.

She was back at the cottage in Vale, but for the first time in her life, there was no fire. She barely would've recognized the place had it not been for that strange vision in the woods. The sun felt warm on her face as she lay on the ground, staring up at the sky through the leaves of an old oak tree. If she strained her ears, she could just make out the sounds of birds chirping in the woods outside the garden wall. It was the kind of summer day that poets might've described as idyllic.

A woman sat next to her. The same woman she had seen night after night in her dreams ever since she was a child—her mother. The older woman's clothes were plain but well made, and her golden hair spilled down her back in long waves.

She leaned against the trunk of the tree, humming to herself as she wiped down the blade of a black rapier. The sweepings of the hilt, crafted to look like the tentacles of a kraken, gleamed so brightly in the afternoon light that Taly couldn't help but reach out and run a finger along the lustrous metal.

"Your father gave me this," the woman said, smiling as she ran a hand through Taly's hair. Taly leaned into her touch, clinging to that feeling even as the dream started to fade around her. "On the day I passed the rites to become his Guardian. I told him it was too expensive, but the man never would listen to reason."

"When will I meet him? Father?" Taly asked. Her voice sounded childlike and far away.

The woman shook her head. "Not for a while yet, I'm afraid. Not until the Aion Gate opens."

Taly fiddled with a stray leaf, holding it up so she could see the light shining through, illuminating the intricate pattern of veins. "Do you think he'll like me?"

"Of course, my darling girl," the woman replied simply. "In fact, I have it on very good authority that he's going to love you. Now then," she said, standing and shaking the grass and dust off her trousers. "I should go check on the stew before I burn it." She grimaced slightly as she turned to walk away. "*Again.*"

As Taly watched the woman disappear behind the blue door of the little cottage, she felt a twinge of sadness. The dream was ending. She was about to wake up. But even with the landscape crumbling around her, she couldn't help but smile. For as long as she could remember, she'd always felt an inexplicable sense of loss for a woman whose name she couldn't recall. It had plagued her, more easily dismissed as she made the transition from child to adult, but never completely gone.

As she tipped over that edge that would plunge her into wakefulness, she knew that a part of that wound had somehow mended itself. Something inside her, something that she hadn't even realized was empty, had finally been filled.

Because now, no matter what, she would always know, would never again forget, that her mother had loved her—and that her name had been Breena.

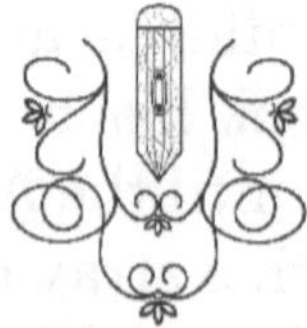

Taly felt a little disoriented as she cracked open her eyes. The storm of magic surrounding her had dissipated, and only a few wisps still lazily drifted above her. Their soft blue glow almost blended into the cloudless sky.

What the hell had just happened? She had been falling and then... nothing. Her mother—she had met her mother, or, the ghost of her mother. *Shards.* What had happened to her, to Breena? She had been facing off with Vaughn before the wisps had completed their spell, but Taly had no idea what had happened after the ground gave out beneath her.

Pushing herself into a sitting position, Taly took stock of her surroundings. Instead of the worn, unkempt path she remembered, she found herself sitting on a perfectly manicured gravel road in front of a securely locked gate. The filigreed wrought-iron had been scrubbed and polished till it shone in the bright afternoon sun, and on either side of her, artfully clipped bowers of wisteria in full-bloom arched up and overhead, covering her in a fragrant veil of dappled shade.

Behind her, Infinity's Edge glowed in the soft light of a late summer day. The structure was no longer crumbling, no longer wasting and withering. It was resplendent, and even from this distance, Taly could see that the crystal roses that decorated the façade were lit from within.

"They're time crystals," she murmured softly. But these looked nothing like the dark, lusterless stones Ivain had shown her once. No, these crystals were shining, brought to life by the roiling eddies of time magic swirling beneath the faceted surfaces of the carved flowers. It almost made the coiling vines that crept across the giant edifice look alive.

"Taly?" came a soft, lilting voice.

Taly whipped her head around only to be confronted with one of the loveliest creatures she had ever encountered. The woman was tall, perhaps as tall as Ivain, with hair as black as the night sky. The inky blue of her dress perfectly complemented her milky skin, and the fluttering chiffon of her bustle floated out behind her like a dark cloud. Her lips were painted the perfect shade of petal pink, and right now they formed a tiny "oh" shape as she stared at Taly with wide, unblinking golden eyes.

"Oh, Taly!" she sang as she rushed forward. Her skirts billowed on an invisible wind, and she threw her lace parasol off to the side. "I was starting to wonder when I was going to see you again! Where's Skye?"

"S-Skye?" was all Taly managed as she painfully pushed herself to her feet, her gun held at her side. Her knee protested, but it held her weight—barely. Her aether must have finally begun healing the injury.

"Yes!" the woman exclaimed, oblivious to the pistol that Taly jerked around, the barrel aimed at the ground and ready to fire off a warning shot. "That boy hardly ever lets you out of his sight. Now, where is he? Shards, he and Kato better not be trying to trick me again. I swear, those two—"

Taly's back hit the gates. "Stay where you are!" she snapped.

The woman stopped—those perfect features the portrait of confusion. "What?" she asked delicately, one gloved hand coming to rest against her breast. "Why… oh, my." Her eyes widened as she finally took in the blood that still streaked Taly's skin, and a small smile tugged at her lips when she saw the gun. "Oh, darling. That won't work on me." Her steps were measured as she approached Taly and placed a single hand on the gun, pushing it off to the side. Taly felt pinned in place, unable to move. Something about this woman made the air around her feel… *heavy*.

"My, my," the woman mused, "look at how *young* you are. I don't think I've ever seen you this young. Shards…" The woman almost looked sad as she demurely clasped her hands in front of her. "You don't know me, do you?"

"Know you?" A hysterical laugh bubbled up from Taly's chest. She didn't know why, but something about this entire scenario seemed exceedingly funny. Had she finally cracked? Had the events of what had quickly become the longest, most arduous day of her life finally caught up to her? "I've never seen you before. How would I know you?"

The woman cleared her throat, sniffing delicately and wiping at the tears on her cheeks. "Shards, look at me—causing a scene. And even after you warned me, I… Shards, I thought I was ready. You said yourself that having a friend not… I'm so sorry, my dear. Please, excuse me."

The woman turned slightly, pulling a lace handkerchief from her sleeve and dabbing at her eyes. "Well, needless to say, I was not expecting you so soon, but since you're already here, we may as well get started. Although," she said, her eyes flicking down to Taly's injured knee, "I suppose we'll have to do something about that first."

A golden cloud snaked through the woman's gloved fingers, and she waved a hand in Taly's direction. Taly yelped when she felt something in her knee shift. She stumbled, but her legs didn't give out beneath her like she expected. The startling burst of pain had been sharp but fleeting. She gave an experimental hop, her eyes widening when she realized that the stinging ache in her knee had completely evaporated.

"Good!" the woman chirped. "Now, let's go." Her toe began to tap, and her hands came to rest on her hips. "We have a lot to do, and not much time to do it in, which, coming from a time mage, I realize is a bit of a contradiction. Still, there's no time like the present." A soft giggle fell from the strange woman's lips at what Taly could only assume was some sort of inside joke.

"I'm sorry," Taly said, leaning heavily against

the gate. This was all becoming just a little too much for her to handle. "But I'm confused. Really, *really* confused. About a lot of things. So, first question—what are we starting exactly?"

The woman's brow furrowed. "Well, your training, of course. You're the last time mage, after all. Who else did you think would be training you?"

Taly pointed a tentative finger at the woman, nausea coiling in her belly when the strange fey nodded in affirmation. "Okay. Um… so, I guess, *next* question. Who are you? Do you have a name or…?"

The woman's eyes widened for a moment, and she let out a shrill, high-pitched laugh. "Oh!" she exclaimed, embarrassment coloring her cheeks. "Look at me! Where is my head? I'm terribly sorry, my dear. Yes, of course. *Introductions*—very important things. Or at least, they used to be before... or was it after…? Anyway, I digress. Let's see, I already know you—Lady Talya Caro. So, I guess that leaves me." Here, she dipped down into a deep curtsey. "I am the Lady Azura Raine of House Thanos. I am so pleased to finally make your acquaintance."

Taly's grip on her gun faltered as her arms fell to hang limply at her sides. "Azura Raine?" She started shaking her head. The edges of the iron filigree on the gate behind her caught on her jacket as she attempted to back away. "That's not possible."

"Oh, I assure you, dear. It is *quite* possible."

"No," Taly whispered. "It's not. Azura Raine is dead."

The woman shrugged indifferently. "I'm afraid you were misinformed."

Taly's mouth gaped. "But… that would

mean..." She shook her head, her heart thundering in her ears as the realization of who this woman was, *what* she was, finally began to sink in. "If you're Azura Raine, and you're alive—that would make you..."

The woman nodded her head, her shoulders straightening. "Yes. That's right, dear. I'm the Time Queen. And *you*... well, I've been waiting a very, *very* long time to meet you."

The End
(for now)

Thank You for Reading!

Well, we finally reached the end, and I hope you enjoyed the story. As for what comes next—I'm a glutton for punishment, and I ultimately plan to make this into a four-part series. Book 2 is already well underway, and I'd love to have you along for the ride.

Please Leave a Review on Amazon!

These reviews are so important, especially for new authors like me. Even though it might not seem like it, I read every single comment, and I'd love to hear your thoughts—good, bad, or anything in between.

For more news on the island of Tempris, you can find me on Facebook and Patreon. Also, feel free to email me directly at **sfisherbooks@gmail.com** if you have any questions, comments, or suggestions.

Facebook: https://www.facebook.com/sfisherbooks/

Patreon: www.patreon.com/stephaniefisher/

Made in United States
Troutdale, OR
10/15/2023